An excerpt from *Rags to Riches Reunion* by Yvonne Lindsay

Cin felt Drum's gaze on her as she settled behind the computer.

Even after all these years, he still had the power to draw her in. She clearly remembered her six-year-old self telling her momma, after Drum's first playdate with Tanner, that she was going to marry that man one day. Her momma had just laughed and done her best to distract her wildly determined little girl away from her brother and his new best friend. But even though her mom had succeeded that day, it had never quenched the longing Cin felt every time Drum was in her vicinity. A longing that even marriage to another man could never quite erase.

A sharp pang of guilt sliced at her.

Suck it up, buttercup, she told herself. *Remember, this was the guy you asked—no, begged—to accompany you to your prom and who categorically turned you down for the dance and everything else you were offering him.* Even now, Cin felt humiliation stain her cheeks at the memory.

He hadn't wanted her and had made it abundantly clear.

So, with persistence, she applied herself to learn whatever it took to be the best darn employee for him she could be.

An excerpt from *The Lost Heir* by Rachel Bailey

"What do you need?"

One side of his mouth hitched up in a rueful smile. "I'm not sure there's anything that can make me forget I'm Joseph Rutherford II."

A flush of heat rippled across her skin as she threw caution to the wind. "There's something that might clear your head of everything else, but I'm not sure whether it's something friends do."

He was silent for several beats and she started to think he wasn't going to reply. Then he turned his head and the look he gave her almost scorched her skin. The pulse at the base of his throat beat hard and she felt herself melting. Even the air around them seemed to be vibrating.

"I can be flexible on the boundaries around our friendship."

USA TODAY BESTSELLING AUTHORS

YVONNE LINDSAY
&
RACHEL BAILEY

———

RAGS TO RICHES REUNION
&
THE LOST HEIR

Recycling programs
for this product may
not exist in your area.

ISBN-13: 978-1-335-45760-8

Rags to Riches Reunion & The Lost Heir

Copyright © 2023 by by Harlequin Enterprises ULC

Rags to Riches Reunion
Copyright © 2023 by Dolce Vita Trust

The Lost Heir
Copyright © 2023 by Rachel Robinson

For questions and comments about the quality of this book,
please contact us at CustomerService@Harlequin.com.

Harlequin Enterprises ULC
22 Adelaide St. West, 41st Floor
Toronto, Ontario M5H 4E3, Canada
www.Harlequin.com

Printed in U.S.A.

CONTENTS

Award-winning author **Yvonne Lindsay** is a *USA TODAY* bestselling author of more than forty-five titles with over five million copies sold worldwide. Always having preferred the stories in her head to the real world, Yvonne balances her days crafting the stories of her heart or planting her nose firmly in someone else's book. You can reach Yvonne through her website, yvonnelindsay.com.

Books by Yvonne Lindsay

Harlequin Desire

Rags to Riches Reunion

Clashing Birthrights

Seducing the Lost Heir
Scandalizing the CEO
What Happens at Christmas...
One Night Consequence

Visit the Author Profile page
at Harlequin.com for more titles.

You can find Yvonne Lindsay on Facebook,
along with other Harlequin Desire authors,
at Facebook.com/HarlequinDesireAuthors!

Dear Reader,

I always love a rags-to-riches story and combined with a reunion, well, for me that ticks a lot of boxes. As a writer, I love getting to play with ideas and figuring out how certain character types tick. Everyone reacts differently to situations, right? So, it was satisfying to play with my poor heroine having to return home to work for the guy she's had a crush on for most of her life.

Drummond Keyes is one of the most honorable heroes I think I've ever written. Now the richest man in the country, he pours his heart into his community, and when Hyacinth Sanderton comes home, he is quick to find her a position in his company—although he finds himself battling the pact he made with his best friend, Cin's brother, never to touch each other's sister. Cin has returned with a failed business and a failed marriage behind her and she's determined to rebuild herself from the ground up. The last thing she needs is a new relationship.

I hope you enjoy Cin and Drum's journey to happy-ever-after.

Happy reading!

Yvonne Lindsay

RAGS TO RICHES REUNION

Yvonne Lindsay

Soraya, this one is for you.
Thank you for your constant nudging,
cheerleading, support, advice and,
most of all, friendship.

One

A favor. That's all it was. Drummond Keyes mentally rolled his eyes and forced himself to unclench his jaw. He thought Tanner had been kidding when he called Drum up and asked him to find a job for his sister, Hyacinth Sanderton. But if the designer-suited, Louboutin-shod blonde standing in front of him was any indication, Tanner had been serious.

Drum looked at her and fought to quell the insidious spark of lust that pinged a line straight to his groin. This was Tanner's baby sister, for heaven's sake! He wasn't supposed to react like this to her—ever! He and Tanner had made a pact; sure, they'd only been fifteen when they'd made it, but honor demanded that you never, *never* hit on your best friend's sister.

He valued his friendship with Tanner deeply. They'd supported one another from the day they'd met at elementary school. Drum had been the new kid when Tanner had sidled up to him and asked if he wanted to be friends. He hadn't realized it then, but Tanner's family's wealth had set him apart from most of the other kids, and he'd been as hungry for friendship as Drum was to fit in at this new school.

They'd promised to have one another's back, always. They'd even planned to join the army together, with Drum applying to the JAG Corps, until Drum's father's heart attack had forced him to stay home. It was also their special bond that had seen him turn down Cin's plea to be her first lover, as challenging as that was. Drum hadn't wanted to do anything to jeopardize their friendship then, and he certainly didn't now. Not that she was throwing herself at him. Tanner's little sister had grown from a precociously pretty teenager into a mesmerizingly beautiful woman. However tempting she looked, it made no difference. He wasn't going there.

"You actually want a job here, with Keyes Tires?" he asked, fighting to keep the disbelief from his voice.

"Yes, I do, and thank you for seeing me personally, Drum. I know you're incredibly busy."

Even her voice was captivating, and the sound of

it sent little prickles of awareness firing along his nerve endings. He clenched his jaw again. Tight.

"I'm not sure we're the right fit for someone with your—" he hesitated before continuing "—talents."

A spark of something, anger maybe, flared to life in her perfectly made-up blue eyes, but it was gone as quickly as he saw it. In fact, if he'd been anyone other than someone who'd watched her grow up from an irritating six-year-old to an eighteen-year-old who had the world at her feet, he might not even have noticed.

He continued before she could speak. "Look, I know that you're a marketing whiz and you're used to a much faster pace than we offer here in Blossom Springs. Are you sure this is what you want?"

"Drum," she said in a voice pitched low and level, as if she was struggling to hold on to her temper, "I need this job. Please."

It was then that he realized—it wasn't temper she was holding back, it was tears. Icy shock drenched his entire body as it sank in that she was, in fact, begging for a job from him. Any job. And suddenly the call from Tanner made sense. Despite the perfect hair and nails, despite the outfit that cost more than most people here in Blossom Springs earned in a month, she really was at rock bottom—and now it was up to him to give her a ladder to help her climb back up.

"Okay," he said on a long breath out. "Let's go down to the tire bay, and I'll introduce you to the guys."

At least if she was downstairs there'd be less

chance of frequently bumping into her and being driven crazy by everything about her, from the scent of her fragrance to the way her gentle curves filled her clothing.

"The tire bay?" she said, her blue eyes sparking with interest.

"Yeah, we need a new coordinator downstairs. Our last one went on maternity leave a month ago, and it's been a shambles ever since. We're losing productive hours in training temps to run the software, and then they leave, and we're back to square one again."

He'd never had employment issues before, but since the worst of the pandemic it seemed that most people preferred to continue working from home. Now, the idea of working in an environment that was hot in summer and could be uncomfortably cold in winter with the tire bay doors open wide from start to finish each day, not to mention the noisy environment, wasn't something a lot of people wanted to consider. Try as he might, Drum couldn't envisage Princess Perfect, as he'd always teasingly called her, working there.

She said nothing as they went down the stairs from the head-office area of the building to the ground floor. Drum looked around the area with pride as he opened the swinging door into the workshop. He'd taken what had been his father's one-man band and, over the past twelve years, had transformed it into a statewide tire business with branches and franchises in over a hundred and fifty towns and cities. And he'd converted the family's fortunes along with it. From barely making ends meet, they could now pick and choose whatever they wanted or needed.

Sometimes he still found it a little hard to reconcile their situation when he'd left high school to join his dad in business to where they were now. But knowing his parents were happy and secure in the retirement complex they'd moved to a couple of years ago and that his sister was now in her dream career made all the hard graft and personal sacrifice worthwhile. So what if he hadn't been able to pursue the law degree he'd craved from childhood? What he did here mattered. He provided employment and gave security to a huge staff and his family.

And because of his commitment to family, he knew that Tanner had had good reason to ask him to help Cin out. The Sandertons had been a founding family of Blossom Springs, and due to their wealth and success had become the district's very own version of royalty. Until Cin's father had made some seriously bad investment decisions just after she had gone to college. Decisions that had seen their family fortunes tank rapidly and drove her dad to cut corners in the orange groves and orchards that fed their fresh-juice business. A blight took out the orange trees, and the apples and pears were soon to follow, and the combined knock-on effect led to the close of the family business. The Sanderton orange groves had been sold to developers for housing, and the extensive factory complex where their popular pure-juice range had been produced had been abandoned and eventually razed—a strip mall and parking lot now taking its place. A severe stroke had taken Ralph Sanderton's life soon after, and his wife, Penelope, had died in her sleep only a few years later.

Tanner had joined the army straight out of high school and was moving through the ranks. And Cin? She'd stayed steady on her course of study, supplementing her income with part-time jobs until she landed the job of her dreams and the heart of her boss at the same time. Tanner said the divorce had knocked her hard, but looking at her now, you wouldn't have guessed it. Except for that fiercely restrained emotion he'd glimpsed in her upstairs.

"Are all Keyes Tires branches set out this way?" she asked as they walked toward the small open-office area adjacent to the workshop.

"Pretty much. We've had years of trial and error to work out the best layout for flow-through."

She nodded and looked around. "And that's the waiting area?"

He looked at the utilitarian plastic seats arranged around an old coffee table scattered with out-of-date car magazines.

"Yes, we find most people prefer not to hang around while their tires are being rotated or replaced or a puncture repaired."

"Hmm, I can see why," she said softly.

Drum introduced her to the guy currently man-ning the phone in the office. She vaguely recognized him from school—he was a year or two younger than her, if she recalled correctly.

"Gil, this is Cin. She's starting today. Show her the ropes with the phones and the computer, would you?"

"Gladly," Gil replied with a quick grin. "I'd rather be getting my hands dirty on that old pickup over there than pretending I know what I'm doing in here."

"Gil's selling himself short," Drum said to Cin. "He was the one who came up with the idea for booking software when the old system wasn't good enough."

"Well, it's not as if I wrote the code or anything," Gil said sheepishly. "I'd still rather be fitting and balancing tires than poking around on this computer."

"His hands-on experience in the workshop enabled Gil to work with the software designers to create a system that is uniquely ours. I'm sure you'll pick it up quickly," Drum told Cin.

"Well, I hope so," she answered smoothly. "I'd hate to be responsible for upsetting such a smooth-running operation."

Drum watched as Gil fell under Cin's spell. She didn't even have to try; it was as if just being around her made people want to please her. Did he fall into that category, too? It had been easier when she was just Tanner's annoying little sister who'd followed them around like a shadow all the time. But the woman she was now was a great deal harder to ignore. And, yes, if he was totally honest with himself, he did want to see the shadows chased from her eyes, and if giving her this job did that, then that's what he'd do.

"Okay, I'll leave you in Gil's hands. See how you feel about the role, and if you think you're comfortable with it, we can sort the admin side of things out with HR."

"Again, thank you," she said in reply before giving her full attention to Gil.

He watched for a moment before leaving them. What had driven her home, to a town where she was no longer the golden girl? She could have stayed in Los Angeles. Could have worked for another marketing company or changed careers. She'd always had the drive. Instead, she'd returned here. The one place, after her parents died, she'd categorically said she'd never return to. Which made him wonder, was she really back for good, or was this just a stepping stone on the Cin Sanderton train to success?

Cin felt Drum's gaze on her as she settled behind the computer at Gil's suggestion. Even after all these years, he still had the power to draw her in. She clearly remembered her six-year-old self telling her momma, after Drum's first playdate with Tanner, that she was going to marry that boy one day. Her momma had just laughed and done her best to distract her wildly determined little girl away from her brother and his new best friend. But even though her mom had succeeded that day, it had never quenched the longing Cin felt every time Drum was in her vicinity. A longing that even marriage to another man could never quite erase.

A sharp pang of guilt sliced at her. *Suck it up, buttercup. Remember, this was the guy you asked—no, begged—to accompany you to your prom and who adamantly turned you down for the dance and everything else you were offering him.* Even now, Cin felt humiliation stain her cheeks at the memory. He hadn't wanted her and had made it abundantly clear.

So, with the persistence that got her through college, while everything at home was in turmoil, and into the role of managing director of one of LA's finest marketing companies, she applied herself to learn whatever it took to be the best darn tire-shop receptionist she could be.

Gil was patient as she took calls and booked in jobs. Especially as, once word swiftly got out that she was back in town and working at Keyes Tires, there was a sudden uptick in people needing their wheels rotated or an alignment check. It seemed the gossip mill in Blossom Springs worked even more efficiently than they had when she was growing up.

"Have to say, you being here is good for business," Gil said with a wry grin when she hung up from yet another call.

Cin snorted. "I don't think you were doing badly before," she said gesturing to the color-coded booking system on the screen in front of her.

"Yeah, but there's usually a bit of downtime here and there. All those nosy old neighbors of yours are filling in the gaps nicely."

She shifted uncomfortably. "I'm not a freak show," she said quietly.

"Nope, not even close," Gil said with another grin. "You were ahead of me in school, but I remember how people always used to flutter around you. Looks like that hasn't changed."

"Well, hopefully the novelty will wear off soon." She tapped a few keys to finish off the last booking she'd taken. "And this will send a text reminder to them the day before their appointment?" she asked, desperate to change the subject back to the job in hand.

"Sure will. Our cancellations and no-shows have dropped by eighty percent since we started doing it. I know Drum hemmed and hawed about the expense when the bean counters upstairs vetoed the idea, but it's more than paid for itself."

Cin smiled at the thought of Drum hemming and hawing. Would he wear a straw hat and chew on a stem of grass while he did it? Even the image of him doing that was as sexy as Drum in a bespoke business suit. She gave herself a mental shake. The man who'd given her this opportunity wasn't someone to be made fun of. He hadn't needed to pander to Tanner's request to find her a job. After all, it wasn't as if he owed her any favors. And while she'd expected an office role, a job was a job, and this would do just fine as she got back on her feet.

"Are you trying to work our newest employee into the ground, Gil?"

Cin looked up in surprise at the sound of Drum'sI voice. She dropped her eyes to her wrist to check the time, but only saw the bare skin reminder that her diamond-encrusted Piaget watch had been one of the many items taken by bailiffs to offset her husband's debts. She glanced instead at the clock on the workshop wall which confirmed it was lunchtime and she'd been at this for three hours already. Her eyes returned to Drum. Seeing him right there in front of her sent a physical shock of awareness sizzling through her. Knowing she was going to see him this morning had given her time to shore up her defenses, but having him just appear, like this, set everything aflutter. This intense reaction had always been there, but now she was older and more mature. So were the feelings that came from his nearness. Feelings she both had no right to and couldn't afford to indulge in, she reminded herself sternly.

"She's a bright one, boss," Gil said. "Got the hang of things in no time."

"Good to hear." Drum turned his attention to Cin. "Can I drag you away for a break?"

"I feel like I only just got here."

"I know, but let's grab a coffee and something to eat, and then I'll introduce you to Jennifer in HR. She'll complete your employment details and give you your contract. That's if you want the job."

Cin thanked Gil for his help and followed Drum outside onto the street.

"Do you do this with all your new employees?" she asked as she fell into step beside him on the sidewalk.

"What? Coffee and something to eat?"

"Yes, that and hand-delivering me to HR."

"Well, no. But you're a special case." He had the grace to look discomforted by his statement the moment it left his mouth. "Look, I'm sorry. But Tanner asked me to look out for you, so that's what I'm doing."

"Thank you," Cin said, fighting to keep her tone friendly. "But it's unnecessary. I've been living as an adult for a long time now. I don't really need my big brother, or his best friend, hovering over me anymore. And if I'm going to be working for you, I'd rather you treated me like everyone else."

"Fair call. For now, let's just call it two old friends catching up over a coffee."

But they weren't friends. Had never been. She'd been the girl filled with unrequited love for a guy who never looked at her with anything other than mild irritation.

"Friends. So it's nepotism?" she said with a persistently acerbic hint to her voice.

She knew she shouldn't be poking the tiger, but it helped to control that burn of attraction that smoldered just under the surface of her skin with him so close.

"Hardly," Drum said, his tone sharpening. "Look, do you want coffee or not?"

"Wow, with that charming invitation, how could I refuse? Lead me to the coffee shop, boss," she said, her voice dripping with honey.

Drum shoved a hand through his hair and growled out an epithet under his breath. "Cin, I'm sorry. Yes, I am treating you differently, but I promise, after this, you'll be just another one of my employees, okay?"

"Thank you," she answered with a calm she was far from feeling. Her stomach rumbled. "You did say something to eat, too?"

Drum burst out laughing. "Yes, definitely. Come on. Sally's is still the best joint in town for lunch. Let's go."

As they walked down the street to the hot-pink shopfront of the diner that was Sally's, Cin worked hard to dull her awareness of Drum walking right alongside her. So close that it would take barely any effort for their hands to brush. So close that every now and then she caught a gentle waft of his cologne. Woody and lightly spiced, it did crazy things to her equilibrium.

To distract herself she looked around, noting what had changed in town and what had remained intrinsically the same. Everyone they passed had a greeting for Drum, and there was more than one glance of recognition her way, too. It's what living in a small town was about. People who knew each other and who were more than just strangers passing by.

This was her old home and her chance to rebuild all that she'd lost. Her marriage, her business, her career and, most important of all, her self-esteem. It had only made sense to go back to the beginning and start again, but now she was here she was beginning to wonder if she'd made the right choice. It was too late now, she told herself. You couldn't change your past, but you could make a new future, and that's what she was going to do. One way or another.

Two

"You know we have a dress code for various staff roles here, don't you?" Jennifer Green, the HR manager said sourly as she eyed Cin up and down. "And what you're wearing is not it."

Cin remembered Jenny from school. She'd been a catty piece of trouble then, but she hadn't moved in the same circle as Cin. Jenny's carrot-orange straight hair had toned down a little with age and had been tamed into a neat bun, and her freckles were hidden by artfully applied makeup. Added to which, the sharp look in her eyes was softened by the tasteful frames of her glasses. Certainly better than the thick black rims she'd been forced to wear as a child. But the sentiment behind her words was still there, no matter how well she'd groomed herself.

Jenny had always silently loathed Cin from afar. Cin had been too popular to worry about it then, but bearing the brunt of Jenny's unpleasantness now was no fun, either. The old Cin might have given in to the temptation to snipe back, but she prided herself on being better than that.

"Thank you," Cin answered with a smile that she was certain would at least look heartfelt. "I'm sure you'll guide me in the right direction. Oh, Jenny, are those your children in the photos? They're adorable!"

They were not. In fact, they resembled their mother closely, right down to the lemon-lipped expression on their wee faces, both of them.

Jennifer was forced to redirect her attention and Cin was treated to a genuine look of adoration on the other woman's face. Wow, she thought, she actually has a heart, then pulled herself up for her uncharitable thoughts.

"I go by Jennifer now. Please remember that. And, yes, those are my children. Do you have any of your own?"

"No, I wasn't as lucky as you in that regard," Cin answered softly. She'd always wanted children, but the reality of having a family with her ex had proven to be something she'd actively avoided, and it had been one of his several bones of contention against her.

Jennifer sniffed, her pointy nose wrinkling across

the bridge as she did so. "Well, as to your clothing, I'll get one of the juniors to take you to the uniform locker. For the tire bay, you need to wear either a company polo shirt or regular button-down shirt, and in winter you can add a sweatshirt and jacket if required. The Keyes Tires cap is optional. Pants are also provided, and safety rules and regulations require you to wear protective closed-toe shoes at all times. We have some sizes here, but if there's nothing that fits you, I'll get the rep to call in tomorrow to discuss the correct sizing."

"Great," Cin replied, keeping that smile painted firmly on her face.

"Oh, and you don't need to bother with so much makeup. You're not here to impress anyone. And I'd advise you to clip your nails as well. You may have to help with tires from time to time, and I'd hate to have to complete an injury report if you tore one off."

And there it was, the cattiness she'd been renowned for. There had to be better ways to have couched those directions, but Cin had to hand it to Jenny—*Jennifer*, Cin internally corrected—with a few pointed sentences, she'd managed to live up to every childhood memory Cin had ever had of her.

"I'll do whatever is necessary. Now, did you have some forms for me to complete? I'd hate to waste any more of your precious time."

Jennifer stared back at her, as if gauging whether Cin was poking fun at her, but eventually gave a little huff of a sigh and reached for a folder on the end of her desk.

"You'll find everything in here. Make sure you return it to me by the end of the day." She paused a moment then continued. "This is a bit of a come-down for you, isn't it? Everyone who knew you always boasted about your success. Didn't you have some high-flying executive position in LA?"

"Yes, I did. But now I'm home. Thank you for your help today. I'll be sure to get this returned to you as soon as I can. Now, if you could point me to the person who is to assist me with my uniform, I'd be so grateful."

More smiles, more honey. If she kept this up her teeth would rot, but Cin was determined not to revert to her old self. The girl who'd left town twelve years ago wouldn't have stood for the not-so-subtle put-downs, but she hadn't spent that time learning how to keep people from getting under her skin for nothing. The trick was never to let them know that their barbs might have struck home, and there was no way she'd give the other woman the satisfaction.

Jennifer marched her down the corridor to an open-plan office area flanked by sliding cupboard doors.

"We keep everything here," she said waving a hand toward the cupboards. "Carey, here, will help you. Once you've got your sizes, please change in the women's restroom before returning to the tire bay."

Without waiting for Cin to respond, Jennifer stalked back down the corridor.

"Goodness," Cin said out loud, "did I say something to offend?"

Carey uttered a choked laugh. "Your existence offends her. Oh, heck, I'm sorry, I shouldn't have said that, but it's true. You're everything she's not. My sister remembers her from school and said she was always..." The younger woman realized she shouldn't say the words that were hanging on the end of her tongue.

"A bitch?" Cin supplied without reservation.

Carey laughed again. "That, and a few other things. Come on, let's get you geared up before she comes and checks on me."

The Day-Glo orange and royal blue of the uniforms she'd seen the guys wearing downstairs looked even more garish here in the soft toned decor of the office. There was no way she wouldn't be wearing makeup with these strong colors, Cin resolved privately. With her blond hair and fair skin, she'd positively disappear otherwise. Besides, it was part of her armor against the world, and she needed it now more than ever before. She took the items on one arm and went to try them on. An interesting combination in her high heels, she decided as she did a turn in front of the mirror before scooping up her suit and heading back to where Carey had rummaged through the shoeboxes in the cupboard.

"I think these might be the right size, but they

look as though they'll be on the wide side," she said doubtfully.

Cin checked the number on the box and nodded. "They'll be fine. I'll wear them with thick socks. We're heading into winter anyway, right?"

"If you say so. To be honest, I'm surprised they stuck you in the tire bay. We have other roles you could fulfill here on the admin floor."

Cin arched a brow but didn't say anything. Maybe they'd offered her the tire bay role because Drum really didn't want her to stick around, or at least didn't expect her to. Carey continued talking.

"By the way, do you remember my sister? She was known as Belinda Styles back then."

"Of course I remember Belinda. How is she?"

"She's doing great. Has three kids now."

Cin racked her memory. "Is she still with Emerson Darby?"

"Yeah, they got married straight out of high school, and they still live here in town."

"Please pass on my regards to her, would you?"

While Cin had never formed the kind of close friendships with other girls the way most people did, Belinda had been one of the few in their circle that Cin had really liked. She hadn't been the type to suck up or try hard to be something she wasn't, and Cin had always admired that about her.

"Here, I'll give you her number. I know she wouldn't mind. You can pass on those regards yourself."

Cin took the slip of paper and shoved it in the pocket of the ill-fitting uniform pants she would now be wearing every workday. "I'll do that as soon as I'm settled. Thank you so much for your help today. I appreciate it, Carey."

"No problem. Although, I have to say I'm sorry we won't be seeing you in clothing like that." She mentioned the designer's name. "I've always wanted one of her suits."

Without hesitation Cin thrust it in the girl's direction. "Here, you have it. We're of a size, and it's not like I'll need it anymore, right?"

"No, seriously?" Carey's eyes grew huge.

"Seriously. And thanks again."

Cin tucked the box of work shoes under her arm and headed toward to the stairs that would lead her back down to the workshop.

Drum came thundering up the stairwell the way he always did. Aside from his regular workouts, he avoided using the elevator as much as possible. He didn't want the legacy of his father's heart condition, which had been brought on by unhealthy choices for most of his adult life, despite Drum's mom's nagging to the contrary. So with his head down, he didn't see Cin as she began to step down into the stairwell, and they collided with a fair bit of force.

Instinctively his arms wrapped around her. The impression of her, willow-slim but soft in all the right places, sent an acute jolt of sheer lust through him, and he rapidly set her back on her feet a step above his. Drum forced himself to let her go and, realizing that his face was now in deliciously close but highly inappropriate proximity to her breasts, he took a step to the side on the stairs, but not before he'd noticed the sinfully alluring purple lace trim on her bra. He averted his gaze.

She was dressed in the tire-bay uniform, her slenderness all but obscured by the boxy men's shirt she wore in the company colors and the ill-fitting trousers that hung on her hips. Surely they could have done better with her uniform, he thought, but then remembered they hadn't specially bought women's sizes and styles in the uniform range purely because no one had ever asked for them. He'd have to rectify that. *What, so you can enjoy the sight of her in something more fitting?* a snaky voice from the back of his mind prompted him. Maybe there was a bit of that, and maybe that was exactly why he shouldn't do anything about it. It had never occurred to him before, so why was it different with Cin?

To be honest, *everything* felt different with her. He'd never struggled to subdue his physical awareness of her in the past, but right now he felt like his personal radar had pinged off the scale. If she'd been anyone else other than Tanner's sister, hell, he'd have made a date with her by now. Maybe giving her a job hadn't been the best of ideas, but he was going to have to shore up his defenses and get through it. He owed it to Tanner, who'd always been there for him with advice and encouragement during the early days of the Keyes Tires expansion, and he owed it to Cin to help her out without complications. And, let's face it, giving in to physical temptation with her was a complication that transcended everything.

Cin started to bend to pick up the box of safety shoes she'd dropped when he'd barreled into her, and he saw the faint tremor in her hands.

"Here, I'll get that for you," he insisted and swiftly grabbed the box before offering it to her.

In their close confines, a drift of her sultry fragrance wafted his way and his body tightened again on that note of desire, his awareness of her intense. She looked flustered, and no wonder, since he'd just about sent her flying. But the heightened color in her cheeks and the brightness in her eyes weren't that of someone who was upset—or had he judged her completely wrong again? Did she feel that awareness that he was certain hummed between them like some invisible line of energy?

"Are you okay?" he asked. "I'm really sorry. Wasn't looking where I was going."

"No problem," Cin said, still a little breathless.

"I haven't hurt you, have I?"

"Not at all," she said, her voice now back to its usual calm and level pitch, which was at odds with the sudden flush on her cheeks. "You make quite an impact, Drum. Although, you always did, didn't you?"

With a smile, she carried on down the stairs leaving him pondering her parting remark. He had no doubt she wasn't referring to the physical impact he'd made when he'd nearly taken her out. Or was she? He shook his head. Women. He'd never fully understand them.

He watched her on the stairwell until she exited through the workshop door and it closed behind her. Even in the staff uniform, with her crazy heels, she had an elegance about her that made him want to watch her all day long.

"Except that's not the way to run a business," he reminded himself sternly.

She was his employee, nothing more. And, as Tanner's sister, could never be anything more. For a brief moment he wondered about the statute of limitations on a buddy pact, then shook his head and carried on to his office. Pacts were lifelong unless mutually agreed. Otherwise, what was the point? For the rest of the afternoon, however, he found it incredibly difficult to settle into his work. His mind kept flicking back to Cin. To how she'd looked, standing here in his office telling him with her eyes how much she needed the job. When he'd known she was coming, he'd spoken with Jennifer about what roles were open and explained that Cin was returning to town, and his HR manager had assured him that the only position open at this, their head-office branch, was in the tire bay. In fact, she'd been emphatic. Never in a million years had he expected Cin to take the role. Mind you, he hadn't expected her to move back to Blossom Springs, either.

Where was she staying? he wondered. *None of your business* came the answer just as swiftly. Would she be staying at the old Sanderton house? It was a huge house all the way on the edge of town, set in a couple of acres of land that had become overgrown in recent years. He made a mental note to check with Cin after work, see if she needed a ride home, wherever that was. All part of his promise to Tanner to keep an eye on her, of course. And absolutely nothing more than that.

Three

Cin had been so caught up in making notes about everything she'd learned about the booking software and answering the phone that she flinched as the big roller doors to the entrance of the tire bay came down with a clatter. She picked up the brochures of tire information, determined to understand them at some point in the next week so she'd be better prepared the next time someone asked her how much for a full set for their SUV. Having to pull Gil or one of the other boys away from their work all the time had been less than ideal, and while they'd been nothing but courtesy itself every time she'd had to do it, she knew she needed to upskill, and fast.

During her afternoon break, she'd gone across the

road to a dollar store and grabbed a pack of socks so she could wear the safety shoes she'd been issued. Two pairs had done the trick, and the shoes didn't rub too much. Just as well, she thought, as the walk home this evening was not one she wanted to undertake in her heels. Yes, she could call a cab, but she was mindful that it would be a while before she'd be paid and the remainder of her money tied up in LA wouldn't be released until every last one of her exhusband's creditors had been paid, so she had limited cash to see her through for now.

A flare of anger ignited deep in her belly, but she forced herself to ignore it. She would get back on her feet, financially and in every other way, and once she'd done that she would never rely on anyone else for anything ever again. It had been both naive and stupid to let Mark take control of all their personal finances. He'd been older than her and, in her eyes, more experienced. When he'd offered her a full-time role at Donnelly Marketing after she'd completed her internship, she'd been over the moon. She'd loved interning there, and it hadn't taken long to develop an attraction to the charismatic man who ran it. When that attraction had led to marriage she'd happily seen themselves as *the* power couple in the industry. But with the arrival of the pandemic and the loss of several key accounts due to a major downturn in business, cracks had begun to form—both in the office and at home.

She still held herself responsible for being oblivious to the online gambling that Mark had become obsessed by. In the end, she'd been made painfully aware of it when their company accountant had asked her about several major withdrawals from the company's accounts which had left them unable to pay wages, let alone rent on their office space.

She'd confronted Mark, and he'd convinced her it was all her fault. He accused her of being aloof their entire marriage, never truly fully committing to him the way he needed her to. She'd been shocked to hear his painful accusations, but in retrospect she could see he'd been correct. There'd only ever been one man she'd truly loved, and he'd been out of bounds her whole life.

For as long as she could remember she'd attempted to attract Drum's attention right up until she graduated high school and left for college. His setdown when she'd asked him to take her to her prom had stung sharply. But the abject horror on his face when she'd plastered herself to him, telling him she wanted him to be The One for her first time with a man, had left its scars.

She'd married Mark knowing she wasn't in love with him the way she should be, and it was a mistake she should never have made. No, it was more than a mistake. At its basest level it was cruel, and she'd tried her entire life to never be cruel. Whether things could have been different if she'd loved him the way he'd said he loved her, she'd never know. All she did know was that by not reciprocating his feelings, she'd driven him to find happiness else-where, and unfortunately that had come with a high financial and emotional cost. Once she'd been made aware of their financial position, Cin had made it her business to ensure that every payroll was met out of her own private funds. Right up until the moment everything she and Mark had owned or saved had been frozen by their creditors.

Which was exactly why she was walking to her old family home, on the edge of town, after a hard day learning a job that she'd never dreamed she'd be doing, while wearing ill-fitting shoes that, despite two layers of socks, were starting to give her blisters. She let the wave of helplessness wash over her. This wasn't where she expected her life to be right now. She was thirty years old with nothing to show for herself. A few yards along the way she came to a sudden stop.

"This is ridiculous," she told herself out loud. "Stop that pity party right now. You have a job, therefore you will have an income. You're going to be able to eat. You have a roof over your head, and you have a future. Make it one to be proud of."

Satisfied she'd given herself a decent-enough pep talk, Cin hitched her designer tote—the one that had been out of the house, thankfully having the zipper repaired, when their possessions were taken by the bailiffs—on her shoulder and carried on along her journey. She hadn't gone much farther when a car pulled up alongside her.

"Cin, let me give you a ride."

She stopped in her tracks and looked at Drum who reached across and opened the passenger door of his electric SUV. He'd shucked his jacket and tie and his collar was open with a couple more buttons undone. Her eyes were instantly drawn to the *V* that exposed his tanned throat and a teensy bit of his chest that made her hunger to see more of him. Everything in her reacted with a powerful surge of longing, which just rammed it home that, damnably, as far as she was concerned nothing had changed in respect of her feelings for Drummond Keyes. Well, aside from the fact that she now bore an even stronger version of the complex physical attraction to him that came with maturity, alongside the crazy crush of her childhood.

Cin sighed internally. It made for an interesting combination, but there was no way she'd ever let him know it. She wasn't going to make a fool of herself over him again. Besides, he was her boss. She'd married her last boss, and look how that had turned out!

"Do you live out this way?" she asked, hitching her tote higher again.

"No, I don't. But Gil mentioned that he saw you walking in this direction, and I figured you had to be walking home."

"It's okay, Drum. I need the exercise after sitting on my butt most of the day."

"You don't have a car?" he asked.

"Nope."

Her much-loved late-model hybrid had been re-possessed along with everything else that had marked her life's journey to date. But she wasn't about to let that bother her. She had enough to worry about with the state of the house, which she'd only barely looked at last night when she'd finally arrived in Blossom Springs after several bus changes and a long walk. This morning she'd been too worried about making her appointment in time to study what work needed to be done to make the house feel like home again. Returning here had been a step into her new life. The one she was not going to mess up this time.

"Come on, get in. You must be tired after today."

"Seriously, Drum, didn't we talk about this? How many employees do you ferry home each day?"

"Special circumstances, Cin, and this falls under the banner of adhering to my duty to your brother."

"Do you live all of your life under banners?" she asked curiously as she took a step closer to the car.

What the hell, she thought, her foot would be rubbed raw soon if she kept up the walking and even her pride knew when it was time to accept help.

Drum grunted in approval as she slid onto the passenger seat and shut the door. "No, I don't live my life under banners. Cin, I'm just trying to help. Y'know, do what I can to ease you back into Blossom Springs. I know it can't exactly be easy for you after what you've been through."

Just how much of her embarrassingly miserable

state did he know? She painted a smile on her face. "Well, aren't you kind? Thank you, Drum. Please don't go out of your way again. Despite what Tanner might have told you, I'm a big girl now. I can see to myself."

He grunted again in a way that left her unsure if he objected to what she'd said or if he agreed. She chose to believe the latter and attached her seat belt before he put the vehicle in gear, and they traveled smoothly down the road. When he slowed down to turn into her driveway, she put a hand on his forearm.

"You can let me off here, Drum. No need to go right up to the house."

If he came up to the house, manners would force her to invite him in, and she wasn't sure she was ready to cope with that yet. After all, the last time he'd have been there would have been after her momma's funeral, and even she had noticed that nothing looked quite the same anymore. And now, with the dust covers everywhere, there was a sad air of neglect and emptiness about the place.

She knew Tanner had visited from time to time to check the property and that he had a landscaping company taking care of the grounds, although they clearly hadn't been for a while. No doubt everything in the cupboards, if they hadn't been emptied already, would be expired and the carton of long-life milk and packet of cereal that she'd picked up at the store on her way out of town which had been weighing heavily in her tote, was hardly the kind of thing you offered to a visitor. At least the water, power and gas had been turned back on.

"I'll see you to your door." Drum's voice was quietly adamant, and Cin knew better than to push back.

She wouldn't let him inside, though.

Four

Five minutes later Drum was inspecting the kitchen cupboards and the refrigerator.

"Well, it still runs, but it certainly needs cleaning. Do you still keep the cleaning stuff under the sink?"

He began to move across the kitchen to check, but Cin stood right in front of him, bringing him to a halt.

"This is my home, Drum. I'll take care of it."

She looked annoyed, so he tried a different track.

"It's a lot of house for one person. I'll send a cleaning crew over tomorrow. The team your parents used are still in business, I use them myself. Think of it as a welcome-home gift."

"No, thank you," she said with a smile that more resembled gritted teeth than anything else.

"There's no shame in accepting help. No one expects you to do everything on your own. I know Tanner would have been here to help you but—"

"Yes, I know, he said. He's on a special operation, but he'll try get here next time he's on furlough, which is why I'll be leaving his bedroom until last."

He was pleased to see that spark of mischief back in her eyes. It had been sadly missing when they'd stepped inside the house. He'd been glad he came in with her. It looked nothing like it had when she'd still lived here. They hadn't even been upstairs yet, but the whole place had a pathetic air of neglect about it that would take a lot of hard to work to erase.

Drum didn't doubt Cin was capable of hard work, no matter how polished she'd looked when she'd arrived in his office this morning…but making Sanderton House a home again was going to be a major undertaking. One he knew, from Tanner's phone call saying she was coming home, that she couldn't afford.

"Tanner usually stays with me when he's home. You could, too, until you get back on your feet," he offered.

She arched a brow at him.

"Yeah, yeah, I know. How many staff do I have living at my house, blah blah blah." Drum shook his head. "Fine, so you don't want me to pay for cleaners and you won't stay with me until this place is habitable."

"It is habitable, just needs a little TLC," she insisted. "And there's nothing that hot water and soap won't fix."

It was his turn to arch a brow at her.

"Okay," she admitted. "It's going to take some time, but if I start here in the kitchen and do one bathroom and my bedroom, I'll be comfortable. Honest. Then I can tackle one area at a time until it's all done. Drum, you have to believe me." She gestured widely with her arms. "This is my home. Momma and Daddy fought hard to keep it when everything else went pear-shaped. I'd be doing them a disservice if I didn't at least try to bring it back to its former glory."

Drum studied her carefully. She was saying all the right words, but was her heart really in it? She had to still be reeling from the major changes to her life that had happened in the past eighteen months. By the sounds of things, if this house hadn't been protected by a family trust, her husband's creditors would have attacked it, too. At least her parents had had the foresight to ensure that she and Tanner always had somewhere to come back to.

She made it all sound so simple. Most women would have been weakened by losing their business and their marriage, but not Cin. It was as if she had a backbone of pure steel and adversity had just made her even stronger. He couldn't help admiring that.

Of course, that same steel made her a stubborn crea-
ture who wouldn't accept help, but he'd find a way.
He just knew it.

"Okay," he acceded. "But promise me you'll reach
out if you need help. I'm ready, willing and very
able."

She laughed at that last part. The first bit of the
old Hyacinth Sanderton that he'd seen all day. The
unbridled, self-confident, carefree Cin he'd known
most of her life. Something ached deep in his chest.
He missed that girl, to be honest, and he didn't quite
know how to read this new version of her. But he'd
figure that out, too.

"Be careful of what you offer, Drum. I may just
take you up on that," she said with a chuckle. "There
are bound to be a few spiders lurking."

He stifled a shudder. He could deal with just about
anything but spiders, and she knew it. "Nothing a
heavy-duty can of bug spray can't handle," he said
bravely.

She laughed again, and it made his stomach
tighten in a knot of awareness as the sound of pure
joy filtered through him, touching him in places that
shouldn't be reacting this way to her.

"Don't worry, your secret is safe with me. Thank
you for the ride home, I'll see you out."

And just like that he was dismissed. Before he
knew it, he was back in his vehicle and heading down
the driveway. He had to hand it to her, she'd sum-
marily sent him on his way with as much charm

and courtesy as he'd seen her mom exhibit on more than one occasion. And she'd successfully managed to avoid any assistance from him at the same time. Well, he'd see about that. First step was finding out why the landscapers hadn't been doing what they'd been contracted to do.

Before he'd even rolled into his garage he'd completed the call and delivered a stinging reminder about contractual obligations into the bargain. That the contractors promised they'd be out at the house the very next day did little to assuage Drum's irritation. He put in a call to Tanner, expecting to have to leave a message, but was surprised when his best friend picked up.

"Drum, how's it going? Has my sister driven you crazy yet?"

He could hear the smile in Tanner's voice. "You will owe me for this one for a very long time," he said somberly, but then he couldn't help but laugh. Tanner always had that effect on people. "Seriously, though, I'm surprised she stuck with it. She's working in the tire bay taking bookings, and it looks like she's going to settle in okay."

"The tire bay?" The incredulity in Tanner's voice made him laugh again.

"Yep, and in safety shoes and company uniform, no less."

"Are you punishing her for something in the past I don't know about?" Tanner continued teasing.

For a second Drum wondered if Tanner knew

about the night Cin had thrown herself at him, asking him to take her virginity, but then he shoved the unwelcome memory from his thoughts hard and fast. If Tanner had known, he'd definitely have said something.

"Look, I know it wasn't what you were probably expecting, but HR assured me that it was the only role going at present in our branch. To be honest, I didn't think she'd say yes, and I'm not even sure if she'll stick."

"She'll stick. If my sister is anything, she's persistent."

"As I well know."

"Yeah, she sure was a pest when she was little. About that… Is she still…?" Tanner asked.

"Not at all. In fact, she doesn't want to spend any time with me at all. Keeps citing boss–staff conflict."

"I think it's safe to say she's boss-averse," Tanner remarked drily.

"Fair enough. But maybe you could have a word with her about it being okay to accept help from time to time?"

"I'll try, but you know how stubborn she can be."

Their conversation turned to more general matters and before ending the call, Drum caught Tanner up to date with the landscapers. His friend was less than impressed but was happy to leave the issue in Drum's hands, as he was about to go out on a military exercise with his team. By the time they said goodbye, he felt confident that Tanner was happy and that he could manage Cin.

Manage Cin? He shook his head. He'd only be able to manage her inasmuch as he was capable of disguising helping her as something else entirely. Which put him in mind of something he could do to assist without incurring her wrath. As the idea formed and took shape in his mind, a broad smile spread across his face. By the weekend, she wouldn't know what had hit her.

Five

Cin got to the end of her working week with a clear sense of relief. Her contract stated she was employed Monday to Friday from eight a.m. until five p.m. and that she'd only have to work a weekend if the weekend admin staffer was unable to work due to sickness or annual leave. Cin was fine with that. Keyes Tires paid a fair rate for overtime, and the extra money, if the option became available, would be welcome.

Right now, though, she was bone-weary and looking forward to a soak in the old claw-footed tub that adorned her bathroom. As she'd said to Drum at the beginning of the week, she'd tackle one room at a time. So far it had just been the kitchen, her bedroom and her bathroom. Working late into the evening to rid each room of dust, cobwebs and spiders had left her worn out.

A good Napa Valley chardonnay from her parents' cellar and a delicious soak in the bath was just what she needed right now. Oh, and maybe something to eat.

"You gonna join us for Friday-night drinks?" Gil asked as he and the guys started clearing the workshop and he coiled and put away the last of the air hoses. Once done to his satisfaction, he dusted his hands off on his work pants.

"Oh, no, I don't—" Cin began, but Gil just talked right over her.

"You can't say no. It's a Keyes staff tradition. Especially on your first week."

"And no one told me about this because…?"

Gil shrugged. "I dunno. Usually, it's mentioned in your staff appointment letter from Jennifer in HR. But come on over to Curly's. They do great ribs and fries, and the boss always puts on a feed for us."

Cin's stomach grumbled, much as it had most days this week. She had yet to put in a decent grocery shop and had hoped to do an online order for delivery this weekend, but her pay still hadn't shown up in her account when she'd looked at lunchtime. The offer of a free meal was more enticing than Gil could know.

"Okay, ribs and fries and one drink it is," she said. "Am I okay like this?" She gestured to her uniform.

He grimaced. "The girls like to dress up a little," he said carefully.

Cin's tentative joy in going out dropped like a ton of lead. "Oh, I'll just give it a miss, then."

She had a few items back at the house that might be suitable, but the walk or bus trip home and then back into town made the idea of going out redundant, no matter who was paying for dinner.

"Leave it with me," Gil suggested.

"You have a line of women's clothing hiding here somewhere?" Cin asked with a laugh.

"I'll ask Carey to help out. She'll be keen to have you along. Like I said, it's tradition."

He made a quick call, and within minutes Carey was down in the tire bay with a colorful scrap of a dress in one hand and a pair of heels clutched in the other.

"Gil said you haven't got anything to wear to Curly's. You can borrow what I was going to change into. Here, try it on."

She thrust the garment and shoes in Cin's direction.

"I couldn't take your things, Carey," she said in refusal. "It might not even fit me."

"You yourself said we're the same size. Look, it's only a loan, and Cindy in accounts is lending me her spare blouse which I can wear with these pants and be all dressed-up anyway. Besides, I want to help you out to thank you for giving me the suit."

When she put it like that, Cin could hardly refuse, could she? She agreed to go upstairs to the ladies' room with Carey and try it on. She was a little fuller in the bust than Carey, but the dress still fit perfectly. The cheerful colors splashed haphazardly in a wild print on the fabric—the kind of thing that suited her more than the garish colors of her uniform. Carey squealed in excitement when Cin came out the cubicle and did a twirl.

"You look fabulous. Do you have any makeup with you, or would you like to borrow mine? I have a lipstick that's perfect with that dress."

Carey offered her the lipstick, and Cin applied it carefully before studying herself in the mirror. She was surprised at the transformation. The person reflected back at her was a flashback to her old LA self. The confident, carefree woman who wore sexy clothes and looked even sexier in them. She smiled at Carey in the mirror.

"Thank you. I feel great."

"You look great, too. I'm so glad you agreed to try the dress on. I'll see you at Curly's after I've finished my backups."

Carey shot out the door, and Cin took one last happy look at herself in the mirror before returning to the tire bay, where she gave the team a twirl, earning a smatter of applause that did wonders for her ego, then gathered her things and followed Gil and the rest of the boys out onto the sidewalk. There was a lot of good-natured ribbing and camaraderie among the team, some of whom were working the weekend, too. Like her, Gil worked Monday to Friday, but the rest of the team were staggered through the week so that there was always weekend cover.

Curly's was down the main street and one block over. Judging by the parking lot, it was already busy. Cin saw Carey going through the front door with a bunch of the other women from upstairs. Carey turned and, on seeing Cin, waved her over.

"I'm so glad you're here tonight," she said with a grin.

"Free food," Cin said with a twist of her mouth. "Who is going to turn that down?"

Carey laughed. "Are you going to come and sit with us?"

The younger woman had the exuberance of an overexcited puppy, Cin thought and quietly envied Carey her bright and cheerful attitude.

"I'm not sure what the protocol is," Cin said with reservation. "Shouldn't I sit with my team?"

"Oh, don't worry. There's no rule about that sort of thing. Mr. Keyes set this up as a way for everyone to get to know everyone else within the head-office team. He said we all need to remember we're building blocks of the same whole and each equally important, so we need to get to know one another. I like the philosophy."

"It sounds sensible," Cin said.

She looked across the bar and found Drum easily as he talked with a group from work. Someone said something that made him laugh out loud, and Cin felt her entire body clench on a wave of longing at the sight of him. It seemed the Drum she'd known as a boy had grown into a very well-balanced and caring man who was admired and respected by his staff. That was no small feat.

By contrast, her ex-husband had discouraged fraternization among their staff, especially between junior and senior members. Said it created familiarity and a lack of respect. Cin had never fully understood his need to be seen as top dog all the time or his iron grip on everything, until it had all begun to fall apart and she realized he was doing it to hide his own insecurities and growing financial distress.

"We usually take a booth over on the back wall over there." Carey gestured with one hand to where some of the HR staff were already squeezing into the seats. "Go on, take a seat. I'll get a pitcher of margaritas for all of us. Unless you'd rather have something else?"

Cin smiled. "A margarita sounds just fine, thank you."

As Carey elbowed her way up to the bar, Cin began to move through the crowded room toward the back. She'd gotten about halfway when she felt an unnerving prickle at the back of her neck. She stopped and turned to see what had caused it. Not far away stood Jennifer Green with a look of sheer vitriol on her face. Startled by the depth of dislike emanating her way, Cin did what she'd always done when faced with adversity. She forced a smile on her face, gave Jennifer a nod of recognition and held the other woman's gaze until she turned her head away. Only then did Cin turn and continue on her path. She hadn't realized before just how much Jennifer Green didn't like her and made a mental note to be wary of her.

As she walked through the crowd of mostly Keyes Tires employees, she was stopped and introduced to several people she hadn't met before along with a couple more people she'd gone to school with. Two things swiftly became abundantly clear. The first, that they all respected and trusted their boss. To them he was the good guy who'd kept things running from the day he'd finished high school right up through the pandemic. The second was that they all wanted to know what she was doing back in town.

She managed to deflect all but the most persistent questions, and it was only when one person asked her what had happened in LA to bring her back to Blossom Springs that she noticed Jennifer standing on the periphery of their group.

"Yes, we're all curious, Hyacinth. What *are* you doing back here?" Jennifer asked acerbically.

"Please, call me Cin."

"You haven't answered my question," Jennifer persisted. "Enquiring minds want to know."

She made it sound as if they had a right to know Cin's personal business, and for the first time in a very long time, Cin was momentarily speechless. Just then she felt someone move in behind her. A solid warmth at her back.

"I think Cin's personal business is exactly that," Drum said firmly from behind her. "And I also think we should respect her decision not to share it with all of us, unless *she* wants to."

Drum's voice was deep and steady, just like the man himself, Cin acknowledged. And he'd slipped into the role of protector without even a second thought. It made her insides warm to know he had her back, even when she was fighting the near-constant physical awareness she had of him. Even in the darkened bar, Cin could see Jennifer's cheeks flush in annoyance. The woman had never liked her, and now it seemed she had even more reason not to. Cin hadn't come home to create conflict; in fact the opposite had been her aim. She brightened her smile and directed it at Jennifer.

"Oh, I don't mind. We had trouble keeping our business going through the pandemic, and our marriage suffered for it, like so many. Once everything was taken care of, it made sense to me to come back here to start again, and I'm very grateful to be working with you all."

Then, with nothing further to add, she began to move away to where Carey now sat with the others in her group.

"Oh, how the mighty have fallen," came the aside from Jennifer in a low-pitched voice so only Cin would hear it as she walked by.

Cin didn't grace her with a response. Right now, that pitcher of margaritas was looking pretty good.

"Cin, this is everyone. Everyone, this is Cin," Carey said as she poured a drink for her from the frosted pitcher on the table.

"Cin by name, would that be sin by nature, too?" one of the women asked before laughing uproariously at her own joke.

"Only when I want to," Cin replied. It was obvious there was no malice behind the woman's remark, but it still stung a little, especially after the bitter confrontation with Jennifer just now. "For the most part, though, I'm a good girl."

The group laughed at that, and Cin found herself laughing with them. They were an easy bunch to be with, their ages spanning early twenties through to midfifties. Cin began to relax and enjoy their company, sharing a story or two of her life in LA into the bargain. But even though she was with them, she never lost sight of where Drum was in the room as he circulated, and every nerve in her body was attuned to him.

By the time the ribs and fries came round they were all treating her like a long-lost friend, and Carey kept encouraging her to have another drink. But Cin politely refused. She wasn't looking forward to walking home in the dark, so she needed to get going sooner rather than later. Besides, she had a big weekend ahead, cleaning more of the house and clearing out the old garage where she hoped to find Tanner's old bicycle. She could maybe use it to get to work until she could afford another car.

Of course, she'd need to learn to ride first, but how hard could that be?

When Cin judged it time to go, she made her excuses and said she was looking forward to seeing everyone at work again the following Monday. She slipped into the ladies' room and changed back into her work shoes and carefully made her way to the main door and stepped outside.

The air was still warm but there was a hint of the cooler months to come. Cin started walking away from Curly's, but a heavy hand on her shoulder made her stop and whirl around, one steel capped shoe ready to strike at her potential assailant's knee, and her arm already swiping away the hand that touched her.

"Whoa there! It's only me," Drum said as he took a healthy step back. "I saw you leaving, and I know you don't have transport. Let me see you home."

"I thought we'd already had this discussion."

"And I won the last time, didn't I? Can't blame a guy for following through again. Besides, I always make sure my staff get home safe on Friday-drinks night. Curly has instructions to put anyone who has had more than two drinks into a cab home. It goes on my tab."

"Well, I've only had the one drink, so I think I can manage walking."

"But why should you when my chariot awaits?"

Cin closed her eyes and drew in a deep breath through her nose. Bad idea because that meant she could smell that enticing cologne he wore. Just a hint again, but it did crazy things to her insides making her feel warm and tingly inside where she definitely shouldn't be warm and tingly right now.

"Okay, fine, you can drive me home."

"Thank you."

Cin looked askance at him. "You're thanking me?"

"Sure, I have manners, and I'm grateful you're not fighting with me tonight."

"Drum, I accepted a ride, not anything else."

He laughed. "No, I think that's pretty clear. My car is back at work. Let's go."

Before long he was pulling into her driveway. The sensor lights came on as they neared the front door.

"It's still such a beautiful home," he said as they rolled to a halt.

"Yeah," she agreed. "But there's a lot of work to be done to bring it up to scratch. I can see that Daddy let a lot of things slide since Tanner and I left home and, of course, now that they're both gone, everything has begun to deteriorate."

"Are you planning to stay here for good?" Drum asked her.

She stared up at the two-storied home with its large wraparound porch and Grecian-style columns which gave it a timeless elegance that even neglect couldn't fully erase.

"I'd like to, and it's not as if I can afford anywhere else."

"You don't have to do it all on your own, you know."

"Are you volunteering to help?" she said on a laugh. "I meant it. There is a lot of work."

"I've wielded a hammer or two in my time."

"I'm sure you have, but right now I'm still trying to come to terms with what needs to be done and how I'm going to afford it. Oh, and getting the dust covers off everything inside without creating a serious allergy attack." She forced a laugh to lessen the seriousness of her comments, but she knew she'd missed the mark when he spoke.

"More than happy to help you with that, too." He looked at her for a moment, his face serious. "When you're ready."

She looked back at the house to avoid losing herself in his confident gaze. It would be so easy to give in to his offer, but hadn't handing everything off to a man been what had got her in the position she was in right now? When she was ready, he'd said. To be honest, she didn't know if she'd ever truly be ready again. The destruction of her life in LA had left her broke and scarred and afraid to trust anyone but herself. From being someone who'd had it all to where she was now was a heck of a change. But she had to try because if she didn't, what did she have left?

Six

Drum returned to Cin's house early on Saturday morning with the back of his SUV filled with whatever he'd been able to lay his hands on at the local hardware store that might make the cleaning job easier. He also had helpers arriving shortly behind him. After dropping Cin home last night he'd gone back to Curly's and rounded up a few of the team and whispered a word in their ear. Everyone he'd spoken to had been more than happy to put their hand up to help one way or another. He only hoped that Cin would let them in.

She'd been different somehow last night. Aside from looking smoking hot in that dress she was wearing, she'd had a fragile air about her, which was not a state he'd ever associated with Cin Sanderton. He'd put it down to tiredness. First week in a new job and all that, but as he'd tossed and turned in his high-thread-count sheets all night, he'd been unable to shift her from his mind.

He'd already talked to Gil about how she was coping, and the other man had hastened to tell him she was doing great and that she'd even had an idea to make the waiting area more friendly and inviting for their customers, without breaching any of the firm's safety and health regulations or incurring extra expense in the branch. It was good to know she was embracing the role. As far as he could tell, she couldn't put a foot wrong, and those he'd spoken to had been only too happy to volunteer a few hours of their weekend to lend a hand to help her out.

He got out of the SUV and opened the hatch at the back and started to unload.

"What do you think you're doing?"

Cin's voice came from the verandah that wrapped around the front of the house. He'd almost forgotten what she looked like in a pair of old jeans and a tight-fitting T-shirt. Almost, he reminded himself as a totally physical response to her fresh-faced beauty flooded his body. He gripped the stack of buckets in one hand and the container of cleaning fluid in the other, reminding himself she was strictly out of bounds.

"I'm here to help."

"I don't recall accepting your offer."

"I don't recall you refusing it, either."

"Drum—" Her voice cut off as she heard the other cars that were now coming down her driveway. "What's going on?"

"Rome wasn't built in a day. Here are your Romans."

He set down the supplies and began to unload the rest. Trash bags, rolls of cleaning wipes, rubber gloves, disinfectant, polish. Pretty much everything he could think of and then some.

"I will repay you for all this. As soon as I get paid," Cin insisted as she came down the front stairs to join him at the back of his car.

"You haven't been paid?"

"Not yet. I thought my pay cycle was weekly but maybe I got it wrong."

Drum's lips firmed in a straight line. No, she hadn't gotten it wrong. He had always insisted his staff be paid on a weekly basis. Growing up, there'd been weeks, months and sometimes years where his dad's business hadn't been doing so well. He'd watched his mom carefully budget, scrimp, scrape and do without herself so as kids he and his sister never missed out.

He'd always sworn that as soon as he could, he'd do everything in his power to make sure she never wanted for anything again. That was part of the reason he'd hoped to pursue a legal career—aside from the fact that he loved every concept about law. The parameters, the logic, the very backbone of what law was. Giving up that dream to help his dad at the tire shop had not been easy. But his dad's unexpected heart attack had meant he'd needed help, fast and cheap, or he'd have to sell the business. Drum had done what he'd had to, and he was still doing it.

"I'll look into it for you," he said grimly, knowing exactly who had likely put the hold on her pay.

"No, please don't. I can do that. I'm sure it's just a minor glitch somewhere. And I'll manage in the meantime."

Other cars pulled up in the parking circle at the front of the house, and people began to pile out, waving to one another and grabbing the supplies they'd brought. Soon there were enough mops, buckets, dusters, carpet sweepers and all manner of things to bring Sanderton House back to life again.

"Drum, why are all these people here?" Cin asked. She barely even knew most of them, aside from a passing hello at work.

"They're here to help, too."

"But—"

He cut across her objection before she could make it. "Look, we're tight here in this community. We help one another where we can. You remember that, don't you? And these are people you work with, they want to help."

He could see she was floored by the care that was steadily wrapping around her.

"I guess I have to let you all in, then," she said on a wobbly laugh. "I'm sorry, though, I won't be able to feed you."

Carey bounced up beside her. "No problem. Belinda is bringing morning tea and lunch for the gang. Did I tell you she has a catering business?"

"No, you did not," Cin said slowly as she swiveled and leveled a glare at Drum. "And who is paying for all that food?"

"It's a donation," he said firmly. As soon as the words were out of his mouth, he knew he'd made a mistake.

"I am not a charity." Her voice was hard and cold.

Drum cursed himself for an idiot. "What I mean is everyone chipped in to help. We have a fund at Keyes Tires that is especially for our employees to help one another out from time to time."

"That's right," said Carey. "It's great. Sometimes it goes to staff with a new baby, needing a hand. Or someone who's been unwell. Sometimes it is simply to help out with chores around the house when things have gotten out of hand. It's not charity, and no one sees you that way. I promise."

Drum watched as emotion chased across Cin's face. He could see she wanted to refuse the help offered, but it would take her weeks, if not months, to get on top of things if she didn't accept.

"Fine," she said, tightly. "We'll start on the main floor and the windows on the verandah."

Drum let go of the breath he hadn't realized he'd been holding. He knew she was proud and unyielding, and in some ways he admired that about her. That she'd accepted the help was a big step up. Every

Sanderton who'd ever graced Blossom Springs had been the same way. Hesitant to accept help, but always ready to offer it when it was needed. He'd heard of Cin's generous gesture in giving Carey one of her designer suits and felt it perfectly encapsulated her willingness to give, even if she was driving him crazy with her reluctance to receive the same kindness in turn. His own father's prideful refusal to accept help had seen them in a tight spot more than once. He didn't want that for Cin. Ever.

As Cin organized people into teams to work in different areas, he watched her carefully. Once she made up her mind, she was all in. And he could see the admiration in her colleagues' eyes as they clustered around her before heading in the direction of their cleaning detail. Once the last group had been dispatched she looked over at him.

"And you? What would you like to do?" she asked with that raised eyebrow that always indicated cynicism.

He wondered if she even knew she did it, and his face broke into a broad grin. "Your wish is my command, ma'am," he said deferentially, hoping to raise a laugh in response.

"You're lucky the old stables were demolished or I'd be sending you to muck them out," she said with a scowl. "Honestly, Drum. This really is an invasion of my privacy."

"You can trust this lot, I promise. No one will

be poking in cupboards or checking drawers unless you ask them to."

"Hmm," she murmured. "I suppose I should thank you, then.",

"It would be the polite thing to do but I don't expect you to," he countered, enjoying baiting her. He knew she'd been raised to always be a lady and, above all else and in all circumstances, to be polite.

He watched as a smile transformed the scowl on her face. "Why, thank you, Drum. I'm just not sure how little old me would manage without big old you, I'm sure."

She'd sounded just like her mother. Dripping in the kind of charm that could slay a man. He couldn't help it. Mirth bubbled up from deep in his gut and barreled out of him, causing heads to turn from the cleaning crew working on the lower-level windows. Through eyes that were glazing with tears of laughter, he saw Cin's shell of annoyance begin to crack and watched as the fake smile she'd offered him slowly became genuine and made her blue eyes gleam with humor.

"Fine, you win," she said with a gesture of surrender. "You can empty the dinnerware in the dining-room sideboard, hand wash it, dry it and, after wiping down the shelving, put it all back again. And once that's done, you can start on the crystal."

He gave her a nod of acceptance and started inside the house. In daylight he could see the encroaching shabbiness that came with not updating a property regularly. He wondered how Cin would cope out here on her own, how she'd eventually restore the home to its previous glory as she so clearly appeared to want to do. In an era of homes that were increasingly eco-friendly and built to be low on energy use and environmental impact, this was a dinosaur. That didn't mean it wasn't still beautiful. The deep verandahs and high ceilings meant the interior stayed cool in summer, with ceiling fans stirring the air when humidity became high. But that meant it was equally hard to heat in the cooler months, where they were headed right now. He made a mental note to ask Cin to get the central heating checked. He'd organize it himself, but he'd learned his lesson. She didn't want to be managed.

Mindful of his duties, he headed to the dining room and eyed the massive breakfront cabinet that had been custom built to house the family's Meissen dinnerware and Baccarat crystal. Of course she'd give him the task that held the most risk, he thought with a reluctant acknowledgment of her win on this score. Some of these pieces dated back to when Cin's great-grandfather had settled here in Blossom Springs and planted his first orange grove. At least she hadn't asked him to polish the family silver, he told himself. That would take hours.

"Well, are you going to just stand there and look at it?" Cin's voice came from behind him.

"As enticing as that may be, no. I'm considering where to start."

"Let's go with the plates and bowls first. We'll need to work around Carey's crew. But they're in the formal sitting room to begin with. Hopefully we can have these glass-fronted cupboards emptied before they need to come in here to clean and polish the floor and table."

"You're helping me?"

"You really think I'd trust you with family heirlooms on your own?"

She cracked a grin that made him smile back in return. When she genuinely smiled at someone, there was an aura about her that transcended the already-beautiful woman she was. It was like a magnet, drawing the recipient to her on an emotional level that he knew she didn't share with just anyone. It made his gut clench on a rise of sensation that he was determined not to give in to. Darn Tanner for putting Cin in his path like this, he thought vehemently. She was temptation incarnate and totally off limits.

Together he and Cin carefully emptied the shelves of the exquisitely patterned blue, white and gold dinner set with all its matching accoutrements and took them through to the kitchen. The broad pine kitchen table was now stacked with items that hadn't been out of the breakfront for likely ten years or more. The Sandertons had stopped entertaining on the scale for which they'd been renowned when Cin's father's investments went downhill. The elite of Blossom Springs hadn't been above a bit of gossip at the time, and he'd been glad that Cin and Tanner hadn't been around to hear it.

Blossom Springs had always had its share of wealthy residents, and these days the hills that bordered the town had become popular with the rich and famous as well. It ensured the town had maintained a lively economy, and it wasn't unusual to be at a local restaurant seated next to some popular television or film star from time to time. But in Cin's parents' day, people had been quick to turn their backs on those that didn't maintain the fiscal standards they privately used to differentiate between the haves against the have-nots.

He was so lost in thought that he didn't realize that he and Cin had both turned to the kitchen table at the same time. She to grab the next stack of dinner plates to be washed and he to put down the bowl he'd been wiping dry. Their collision made the plates wobble precariously, and they both went to steady them at the same time. Their hands met, and the contact sent a wave of electricity through Drum's body.

They were close, so close. It would be the most natural thing in the world right now to close those final inches between them and kiss her lips. Lips that were bare of any gloss or tint and were plump and full and pink and glistening with the tiniest bit of moisture.

The air between them thickened as their eyes met and time stood still. Cin's pupils flared as if she understood exactly what was going through his mind, and he saw a tinge of color stain her cheeks. Her lips parted. An invitation or to tell him to back the hell off? He didn't stop to think, he closed the gap, heard her swift intake of breath, saw her eyelids flutter closed.

"Break time! Belinda is here!" Carey yelled from the breakfast room just beyond the kitchen.

Cin and Drum both flew apart, their movement making the stack of plates wobble again, driving them both to steady it once more.

"We seem to be making a habit of this," he commented as he stepped back and let Cin do the honors.

"You go through and get something to eat. I'll be out in a minute or two."

She looked flustered. Much like he was feeling too, he had to admit. Would she have let him kiss her, he wondered? What would she have tasted like? How soft were her lips? He slammed the door on those thoughts as hard as he could. This was Cin. And being close to her like this was driving him insane.

"Sure. I'll see you outside."

She nodded and turned away, but not before he'd seen the flush on her cheeks deepen and the movement of her throat as she swallowed. He lifted a hand to reach toward her, to spin her back to face him and to finish what he'd started but just as quickly let his hand drop to his side. This was utter madness. They'd been saved from what would undoubtedly have resulted in a very uncomfortable aftermath. Without another word, he made his way out of the kitchen and down the hallway, putting distance between himself and Cin as though his very sanity depended on it. And maybe it did.

Cin felt it the moment he was gone from the room. It was as if a vacuum had just sucked his presence away, leaving her alone. It's what she wanted, she told herself, but a perverse imp inside wondered what that kiss would have felt like. Drum, the boy, had always attracted her. From the moment she'd first laid eyes on him she'd wanted to kiss him. On the cheek, of course. But as she'd grown older, and as desire had begun to unfold in her developing body, he'd filled her thoughts and dreams with longing.

It was better this way, she told herself. She'd come home to heal. To rebuild. Not to get entangled in another relationship, and certainly not with a man who'd always made it clear he wasn't interested. But he'd been interested just then, she would bet every penny that rattled in the bottom of her tote bag on it.

She wiped her hands dry and brushed them down over her hips, drawing in a deep breath at the same time in an attempt to calm the rapid heartbeat that hammered in her chest at the near kiss they'd had. If he could have this effect on her without touching her, what would it have been like if they'd actually made contact?

Cin shook her head. She wasn't going there, but even as she made her way outside to where everyone was taking a break around folding tables set up beside a mobile catering van, she still couldn't halt the craving that Drum incited in her.

Cin took her time descending the wide front stairs and joining the group. Urns of hot coffee and pitchers of iced tea were set up on one table, and on another an array of sweet treats tempted her. She made her way over and grabbed a mug of coffee first, wrapping her hands around the disposable cup as if it was her lifeline. And maybe it was, she admitted. No fear of accidentally brushing hands with Drum if her hands were fully occupied, right? But also no chance of sampling the delicious tiny tarts and pastries that adorned the plates in front of her, either, she realized.

"Do you still take your coffee heavily sugared and with cream?" a woman coming out of the catering van asked her.

Cin looked up and smiled as she recognized her old high-school friend, Belinda. "No, I actually like the taste of coffee now. I take it black, undoctored."

"Wonders will never cease."

"Why, because I've changed the way I take my coffee?" Cin asked with a small frown.

"No, because you're back. The Cin Sanderton I remember swore she was on a ticket out of Blossom Springs and never planned to live here again." Belinda softened her words with a smile.

"Yeah, I know. Strange how life comes back to bite you when you least expect it. But I'm lucky, I had somewhere to come back to."

"Are you okay?"

"I'm fine."

"Seriously?" Belinda gave Cin a hard look.

"Okay, I'm getting there."

"Still a Danish pastry lover?" Belinda asked.

"Always."

Belinda added a Danish pastry to a plate which she pushed across the table toward Cin.

"Good to know that not everything about you has changed."

Cin looked at Belinda and took a sip of her coffee. The brew was perfect and infinitely better than the cheap jar of instant she'd added to her supplies in the kitchen.

"This is good coffee. Thank you."

"I like to provide quality to my customers," Belinda said in acknowledgment. "When Carey told me you were back, I thought you might call."

Ah, so now she was getting to the point. Hurt feelings because Cin hadn't phoned her yet.

"I'm sorry. I meant to, but…" She waved a hand in the direction of the house. "What with work and getting this habitable again, I've been busy. But I'd really like to catch up properly. Find out what you've been up to since I've been gone."

"Sure, that'd be nice. Would you like to come over for lunch tomorrow? We usually attend church as a family in the morning, but we'll be home by eleven, so come on over any time after that."

She scribbled her address on a paper napkin and passed it over.

"Thank you, Belinda. Can I bring something for the table?"

"No, just yourself. I heard—" Belinda's voice cut off when she realized she was about to say something offensive.

"You heard?" Cin prompted.

Belinda sighed. "I heard you weren't as financially comfortable as you used to be."

Cin nodded slowly. She'd wondered how far the gossip around town had spread and exactly what people had been saying. It was no secret she was working at Keyes Tires, and not in a management role, either. There'd be some who would be glad to see she'd come down a few pegs in life. Cin hoped Belinda wasn't one of them.

"You heard right. But I do still have my standards, and I know it's good manners to offer to contribute," she said stiffly. "I don't want to be an imposition."

"You won't be an imposition. Don't worry. Just bring yourself, and I'll put you to work doing dishes after lunch if it'll make you feel better."

"Much. Thanks."

They laughed, and Belinda excused herself to start clearing plates from the other tables. Cin wandered over to a small gazebo her mother had positioned in what used to be a beautiful rose garden. The shrubs weren't looking their best, but Cin remembered a time when they'd been bursting with color and scent and the lazy buzz of bees gathering pollen would fill the air around her. She sat down and looked around and wondered if she'd ever succeed in getting things right here. And not just with the house and gardens—with the people of Blossom Springs, too. She'd sensed a reserve in Belinda that Cin had no doubt earned by cutting all ties when she'd left town. Somehow, she needed to find a way to rebuild a few relationships.

Cin looked across the gathering and noted that many of the helpers were heading back into the house. The mood was very upbeat and positive, and she could hear laughter everywhere. Why were they so willing to lend her a hand? She'd never done anything for any of them in the past. She'd been the quintessential queen bee of her set. The one who took everything and everyone in her life for granted. Even when she'd interned for Mark Donnelly, she'd known he found her attractive, and she'd used that to further her position in the company and in his life. She hadn't seen anything wrong in it: it was just the way she was wired—until her life began to fall apart around her.

He'd complained that she never revealed how she felt about him and that she never let him into her private thoughts. And it was true. She didn't share herself, with anyone. She'd been schooled by her momma to always hold back. "People will always want to know more," she'd said. "Keep yourself interesting by never letting them know everything." But it had all come back to bite her in the butt when Mark's pursuit of something that made him feel worthwhile had led him to online gambling sites. Deep down she knew she wasn't solely responsible for his choices, but she had certainly contributed to them, and that was her cross to bear. She was only lucky that they had eventually managed to clear their debts, both business and personal, and that their divorce had been completed without complications or protracted legal dealings.

Now, here she was. Back at square one and hugely indebted to these people she barely knew. She wondered what Drum had said to get so many volunteers to help her. Thinking of Drum again reminded her anew of the crockery that awaited her attention in the kitchen and, with it, how close they'd come to kissing. At least she'd thought he'd been about to kiss her. It had certainly felt that way. But then thinking about the way he'd withdrawn straight afterward, maybe it had been her that had made the first move. A move she knew, based on her past behavior with him, wouldn't be welcome.

She was so confused by the situation and how her whole body felt, as though it was on constant alert when Drum was around, it was exhausting. Cin knocked back the last of her coffee and wrapped her Danish in another paper napkin to keep for later. It would do nicely for breakfast tomorrow, she thought.

"You should eat that, you know," Drum said from just outside the gazebo.

"Later," she said as she stood up and brushed off the seat of her jeans.

"I know you've only been home a week, but you already look as though you've lost weight."

"Why, Drum, so sweet of you to care," she said in silky tones, trying to deflect his comment with her usual flair.

Her words found their mark, and he huffed a sigh of frustration.

"Just looking out for you, Cin. Shall we go back in and tackle the rest of that ridiculously expensive dinnerware?"

"You don't have to help me if you'd rather work on something less breakable."

"I haven't broken anything yet, and I'm not about to start. Let's get to it, shall we?"

Without waiting for her to follow him, he turned and stalked back to the house. She watched his retreating back and couldn't help admiring the lines of his body. His shoulders were broad and well-muscled beneath an old T-shirt, and his butt filled the seat of his jeans just right. A ripple of yearning spread through her. She may as well reach for the moon. It did no good to tease herself with unrequited longings for something she'd sworn she wouldn't want again.

Seven

Drum had one of the kitchen sinks filled with hot, sudsy water and the other filled with hot, clean water. He'd begun the next stack of plates without waiting for Cin. The sooner he got this chore out of the way, the sooner he could go on to something else and put a decent distance between them both. Even during the morning break, he hadn't been able to keep his eyes off her.

He'd seen her stop and talk to Belinda and had watched their interaction with interest. Belinda had probably been the closest thing to a best friend Cin had ever had, and yet it appeared the two women were not as close as he'd once thought.

"I thought you were on drying duty," Cin said as she entered the kitchen.

He watched as she put the Danish she'd wrapped into the fridge and turned to pick up a dish towel.

"Figured I may as well get started on this lot. Besides, it's not as if I have to worry about dishpan hands."

"Nor do I. I'm pretty sure a perfect manicure isn't a prerequisite in the tire bay," she said with a self-deprecatory grin.

He'd noticed earlier that she'd removed the color from her nails and had trimmed them to a short, practical length. Her hands were still beautiful, though, with long slender fingers that would feel like strands of silk on his skin. Fingers that were completely unadorned, too, he noted. There was a lighter band of skin on her left ring finger. A remnant of the marriage she'd left behind in Los Angeles. He briefly wondered what her husband had been like. What sort of man he was to capture someone like Cin's interest. Tanner had been no use in the information stakes. He'd only met Cin's husband briefly at the wedding before being deployed overseas, and to the best of Drum's knowledge, his contact with his sister had been confined to their parents' funerals and the occasional phone call since.

They worked together in silence until the last of the dinnerware was dried and stacked on the table.

"I'll go wipe out the breakfront and clean the glass doors so we can start putting this back before we get started on the crystal," Cin said, draping her dish towel on the back of a kitchen chair.

"I'll do the shelves, you do the glass," Drum said.

"Really, Drum. I'm sure you'd rather be doing something else. Don't feel you have to babysit me all the time."

"I'm not babysitting you. Haven't done that in years, thank heavens," he said with a chuckle as he remembered the first time he and Tanner had been left in charge of Cin when the Sandertons had gone to attend a civic dinner in town.

Twelve-year-old Cin had led the two fourteen-year-old boys a merry dance, first refusing to eat her meal then refusing to go to bed at her appointed time. She'd also threatened to tell her parents that they'd been watching horror movies, which Tanner had explicitly been told not to screen, if they didn't let her stay up and watch them, too. It had only been the moment their parents' car headlights had swept the front of the house as they'd arrived home that she'd finally scurried up to her bedroom.

"I've always wondered," he said. "Did you have nightmares that night?"

"So many, and not just that night. But I couldn't tell anyone because I wasn't supposed to have been watching and, contrary to what I said to you two, I didn't want to get you and Tanner into trouble."

Drum looked at her and let her words play through his mind. That just about summed Cin up perfectly. That she'd stoically suffer in silence rather than ask for help or comfort. She'd always been like that, and it was clearly apparent that she hadn't changed.

"Well, just so you know, if you still have nightmares, you can call me, okay?"

For a second she looked startled, but then she laughed. It was a genuine belly laugh that took him completely by surprise. The sound of it filling the kitchen and making his lips tweak in a smile he couldn't help. When she calmed down a bit, he discovered he was more than a little miffed at her laughing at his offer.

"I mean it, Cin. Anything. Strange noises, nightmares, changing a light bulb. Whatever, call me. Okay?"

"Thank you, Drum. I'm sorry I laughed. It's just the thought of me calling you to come over and make me warm milk and sit with me and rub my back while I fall asleep again was ridiculous, y'know?"

Ridiculous? His body tightened on a reflexive need to show her he was serious about his offer, that it wouldn't be warm milk and sitting with her but the warmth of his body making her feel safe and secure. But he knew he couldn't go there. He turned away from her and dried his hands on a towel. Her rejection shouldn't bug him so much, but it did, mightily, and he needed to deal with it. For not the first time this week, he cursed Tanner under his breath for putting him in this position.

It was in his nature to protect and provide. He'd always been the guy everyone could rely on. The sober driver, the wingman, the son who gave up his dreams to join his father in business and drove that one-man business into a multimillion-dollar chain. He'd taken a risk when he'd organized the team of helpers today. The Cin of old would have turned everyone away, saying she didn't need help and insisted on doing it all herself. That she'd accepted the assistance was a sign of where she was right now.

She was a conundrum he wanted to unravel. *Be honest. You want to unravel her—period. Layer by slow, intoxicating layer.* He shook his head slightly as if he could unseat the disturbing thought, but it took hold, making him even more aware of Cin as she moved about, gathering the cleaning products to bring the glass in the cabinet back to sparkling life again. Accepting he wouldn't be discovering any answers regarding Cin today, he grabbed a clean rag and a spray cleaner and tackled the shelves.

He and Cin crossed over, their bodies brushing past one another as if they had done this a thousand times before. But when they touched, it was as if she'd received an electric shock and she'd take pains to stay well clear, until her guard would drop and they'd brush one another again. Did she dislike his touch so much now, he wondered, this woman who'd been like a barnacle at his side as a child and a torment as a teenager? Or was there something else?

Together they completed restacking the shelves and he had to admit they looked mighty fine with the Meissen tableware behind the sparkling-clear glass. Next was the Baccarat. Just thinking about the value of these items highlighted the gulf between their lifestyles growing up. She'd been used to this sort of thing all her life, while his family had made do for years with mismatched dinnerware from the thrift store in town or occasionally from the big-box store the next town over.

Even if he hadn't had the pact with Tanner, there was no way he'd have been able to act on any attraction to Cin. He was the boy from the other side of town whose dad was strictly blue collar. Okay to be a friend to the son and heir, but nowhere near good enough for the golden Princess Perfect. At least, that's how he'd felt growing up.

And now look at them. Their positions completely reversed. He was probably the only person here, other than Cin, who understood just how broke she was. Whereas he was now the richest man in town. Hell, in the entire county. There was nothing he couldn't buy—except, maybe, the woman working industriously alongside him.

When Belinda came through the house to announce lunch was ready, most of the team were done with their chores. The downstairs reception rooms and the breakfast room sparkled. The windows clean, inside and out, the wooden surfaces polished, the dust covers all removed, shaken outside and neatly folded and stacked in the laundry for washing. The place almost looked exactly as it used to. Which only left the bedrooms and bathrooms upstairs.

Next to him, Cin put the last wineglass on the shelf on the matching breakfront on the other side of the dining room.

"Well, that's a relief," she said stepping back to admire their hard work. "It looks great. Although I wonder if I'll ever use any of it."

"You could always sell it," he suggested practically.

"What, and have my momma rise from her grave to tell me off? You have no idea how much all of this meant to her."

And there was that Cin Sanderton conundrum again. That she was so worried about how a dead person had felt about material items that she wouldn't consider selling them, even if doing so might help her financially. The items, while beautiful, belonged to an era where people did things differently. And, while he wouldn't be averse to some vintage Dom Perignon out of one of those crystal flutes he'd so carefully washed, he'd be just as happy with a lesser vintage out of glass that he could shove in the dishwasher and not worry about.

"She certainly loved to do things her way, didn't she?" Drum commented, remembering how much control Cin's mom had always seemed to have over the entire family. All done with the best possible taste, of course, but standards had always been high, even for the little boy visiting from school.

"Well, according to Momma, there was her way, and there was the wrong way," Cin said on a chuckle.

"But don't get me wrong, she loved us all deeply. The fact Momma and Daddy never considered selling any of this, or the house, when things started to go bad says a lot for how much she loved the place and everything in it. She never let her standards slip."

Silence stretched out between them, and Cin realized that she may have offended Drum with her comment. When it came to standards, she knew the Keyes household had been vastly different from her own. They'd lived a far simpler life, with a great deal less. And while Mrs. Keyes hadn't worked, like Cin's momma hadn't, it was because her health wouldn't allow it, not because she didn't have to. Even as a younger child, Cin had been aware of the little care packages her momma would send with Tanner when he went to Drum's to play. The cakes and muffins from the kitchen, the clothing that she'd deemed unsuitable for Tanner to wear but was perfect for another person's child to knock around in. It can't have been easy for Drum, knowing he was wearing his best friend's castoffs. She wondered now if it had ever bothered him.

Unlikely, she thought, stealing a sideways glance at him as they made their way outside to where Belinda had the tables groaning with salads, rolls and cold cuts. Even as a kid he'd been pragmatic about the differences in their families' lifestyles and knew that accepting a helping hand reduced pressure on his parents. And even though he was undoubtedly wealthy now, it hadn't altered his character. Everyone was loading their plates and chattering among themselves. Again, Cin felt the sense of separation she'd felt earlier, and once she'd made up her plate, she started to move away.

"Cin, come and join us," Carey said from where she was seated, indicating the empty chair next to her.

Unable to refuse, Cin settled down next to the younger woman. Before she could lift her fork she felt she needed to say something, though, and she stood back up again and tapped her fork against the side of her plate to attract everyone's attention. When that didn't work, she put her fingers in her mouth and whistled loudly. Heads turned and cutlery dropped in surprise.

"Hey, everyone. I just wanted to take this opportunity to say a huge thank-you to you all for the hard work you've put in today. I'm more grateful than you could realize. You've helped make this house feel like my home again, and I'll never be able to repay your kindness. All of you. Also, an extra special thanks to Belinda for the catering. An army marches on their stomach, and you've made this army a fine-tuned machine with your amazing food. Again, I owe you, big-time."

Across the buffet, Belinda nodded in acknowledgment with a small smile on her face.

"Well, that's all I had to say. Dig in, everyone."

There was a cheer of consensus, and the convivial chatter and the clatter of cutlery on plates resumed.

Later, she wasn't sure if it was her thanks or the great food that Belinda had provided, but the atmosphere certainly became friendlier and warmer. In the beginning, she'd suspected people had come along partly out of kindness but mostly out of curiosity. But by three o'clock in the afternoon, when everyone began getting back into their cars and driving off amid toots and waves, it was clear they'd stayed out of a genuine wish to be of service to her. Many of them had shared stories of things her daddy or momma had done for them or their families back in the day when the orchards and the juice factory were running. Hearing those tales made Cin begin to feel like she really was a part of the community now.

She didn't quite know how she felt about that. She'd always found it easier to keep most people at arms' length. Not even Belinda with her nurturing nature had completely broken through the carapace that Cin had always worn around her. But today, there'd been something about being part of a whole that she'd enjoyed—and not just because all their hard work would make her life so much easier. She wanted to pay it back somehow—and not out of a sense of obligation, either—but right now she had no idea of what to do or how to do it. Her mind flicked back to the large lawn parties her parents used to hold, with a marquee and hanging lights and a dance floor. Something like that would be wonderful, but she would have to save hard to be able to pull it off.

But it gave her something to work on, so she tucked the thought in the back of her mind to pull out and consider another day.

Drum lingered, waving to the last departing car before turning and joining her on the porch.

"Good work done today," he commented before settling his large frame on the porch swing where she'd spent time with each of her past boyfriends, before her father would come out of the front door and shoo them home. Drum patted the faded cushion next to him. "Join me."

She hesitated a moment. She'd spent most of the afternoon trying to avoid physical contact with him. Each time they'd brushed against one another, it had set her heart racing and reminded her of the unfulfilled craving she'd had for this man since she was young. She'd had enough of nonfulfillment, period. But short of taking a seat in one of the chairs at the other end of the verandah, which would definitely make conversation more of a shouting match, there was nowhere else for her to sit.

Dragging in a stoic breath, she settled beside him and picked up her feet as he set the swing to rocking gently. Bit by bit the sounds of nature around them increased as the birds and insects realized the workers had left the property.

"It's a nice spot here," Drum said conversationally.

His arm lay behind her, across the back of the cushion.

"I've always liked it. Thank you for today. For organizing it and for making me accept the help. I appreciate it."

"You're most welcome. None of us are your enemy. All you need to do is ask."

She grimaced before answering honestly. "Asking for help doesn't come naturally to me."

"I know that," he answered before falling back into silence.

The quiet between them, peppered with the chirps of birds and the buzz of cicadas around them should have been relaxing, but Cin felt as though she was wound tighter than a two-dollar watch.

"You don't need to stay," she said, shifting farther over and wishing like heck that she hadn't sat down next to him. The warmth of his body heated her side, and her awareness of his arm behind set her pulse to a fever pitch.

"I know that, too," he replied in a quiet drawl.

Irritated, Cin got up and leaned against the balustrade. She dragged her hands along the paint and felt paint chips fall beneath her touch. A lot of work had been done today, but there was still a lot more to be done. Being able to afford paint would be a long time coming.

"You know a lot," she said sharply. "Really, Drum. Don't you have someone to be going home to right now?"

"Nope."

She blew out a breath in frustration. "What are you doing?"

He looked at her, his eyes meeting with hers and not straying. "Enjoying the view."

Every nerve in her body went on alert. "The view?"

"Yeah, the garden, the house, you."

"Now I know you're just trying to get a rise out of me."

"You're right," he said and slowly rose to his feet. "Did it work?"

"No," she lied.

"Pity." He reached out and ruffled her hair the way he always had when she was little. "Well, since there are no further offers of hospitality coming my way, I shall drag my weary body home."

She rolled her eyes. He knew she had nothing to offer him. The leftovers from lunch had been shared out into take-out containers for all the helpers, and she also knew he'd refused his portion and suggested Belinda pass it on to another person whose family would more appreciate it. For Cin, she'd eaten more today than she had any other day since she'd left LA, and right now the deep claw-footed bath upstairs was calling her name.

"Drive safe," she said, moving aside so he could easily access the stairs without coming near her.

He made a sound, somewhere between a laugh and snort, but when he drew level with where she was standing, he stopped.

"You know, you act all tough and brittle and touch-me-not, but you forget—I know you, Cin Sanderton. From the top of your naturally blond head to the tips of your pink toenails."

She felt a rush of heat through her body as his eyes locked with hers once more. There was something in the depth of his gaze that she'd never seen from him before. He'd always been aloof. The guy that stood his ground and never budged and never buckled under pressure. Drum had always had a strong sense of purpose, and she knew that had only grown more robust as he'd gone from strength to strength in business. She knew, through Tanner, that he'd wanted to pursue a legal career, and she wondered if he ever regretted not doing so. No, knowing Drum, he would have simply changed his direction without a murmur—his dedication to his family absolute.

It was the level of dedication she should have had to her husband, and it was no less than he'd deserved. She'd let Mark down, terribly. And that was something she had to learn to live with.

Drum gave her nod and carried on down the front stairs and over to his SUV. In a few seconds more he was in the vehicle and driving away. She lifted a hand in farewell and stood there watching until she caught the flicker of his taillights as he stopped at the road before turning back toward town.

A part of her wished she could have invited him back inside and shared a bottle of wine and whatever else came next, but she given up on that dream long ago. He'd made his stance clear more than once when she was a teenager, and the way he'd teased her and ruffled her hair—as annoying now as it had been twenty years ago, she might add—just proved that he still didn't see her as a woman. Never would. Which only made her feel all the more lonely as she finally turned and went back inside the house.

Eight

Monday morning rolled around quickly, but Cin had enjoyed her weekend so it was no bother to push herself out of bed and out the door in time to make it to the end of the road where she could catch the bus the rest of the way into town. Except today, the bus didn't come. She waited as long she could before striking out on foot, only to see the bus drive past her a few minutes later. And then it started to rain. Needless to say, her mood was less than stellar when she approached Keyes Tires, and she was still cussing under her breath, madder than a wet hen, when she entered the tire bay and clocked in.

Gil looked up from the Porsche he was fitting new tires to and called out. "HR want to see you upstairs."

"Good morning to you, too," she snapped back before heading for the door to the stairwell. She'd only taken a couple of steps before she turned around and proffered an apology to Gil for her short temper.

"It's all right," he said with a grin. "Water off this duck's back."

"How do you remain so darn happy all the time?" Cin asked with a reluctant smile in return. "Every day you're the same. You have to be the most well-balanced person I know."

"Just comes natural, I guess. It's not like I have anything to complain about."

"Good point," Cin said. "I need a bit more of that."

And with that, she took the stairs two at a time until she was on the administration level. She walked briskly into HR and was immediately accosted by Jennifer Green, who looked pointedly at her watch before acknowledging Cin's presence.

"I'm pretty sure your hours of work are eight a.m. to five thirty p.m., aren't they?"

"That's correct."

"And yet it's eight thirty, now. I requested that you come straight up to me on your arrival so I assume that means we'll be docking your pay half an hour?"

Cin bit her tongue. It wouldn't make one iota of difference to let this woman know of her difficulties in getting in to work on time today. Jennifer Green had it in for her, pure and simple. She'd take whatever the woman had to dish out and smile doing it.

"Yes, that's correct. I'm sorry. It won't happen again."

Cin kept her fingers tightly crossed behind her back. She couldn't guarantee she wouldn't be late again, but she'd do her darnedest to make sure Jennifer Green didn't catch her out.

"Well, it had better not, or you'll earn a written warning."

Wow, that was harsh, Cin thought. She'd always allowed her staff a little wiggle room when it came to start and finish times. It made for happier relations all round, and when the chips were down, she'd always been able to rely on her team to go the extra mile and stay back when necessary. This hard-line approach from Jennifer, whether it was solely directed to Cin or not, was counterproductive and showed no level of care or understanding of staff circumstances. But it wasn't her place to point that out, so she decided to tackle Jennifer's own imperfection while she had the woman's attention.

"I'm glad you called me up here," she said with her most saccharine sweet smile. "Could I ask you when I can expect my first pay?"

"Drum already mentioned to me this morning that you hadn't been paid. I'm not sure why there was a discrepancy in loading your details into the payroll, but I'll see it's corrected in time for this week's pay. I'm sure, with you living in that big old house of your family's, that the delay won't inconvenience you too much."

The smile Jennifer returned her way was at odds with the mean glint in her eyes. Cin fought to keep her smile on her face.

"Thank you. I'm so glad you're onto it." Far be it from her to let Jennifer know she was literally down to her last twenty dollars. She'd just need to be more inventive about making ends meet until payday, she told herself. "Was that all you wanted me for?"

"No. Drum requested that we source different uniforms for our female floor staff. Something more appropriate, he said." Jennifer rolled her eyes. "I'm quite sure I don't know why he bothered—unless you asked him to. This request hasn't come in from any of our other branches or franchises."

Cin shook her head. "No, I never asked Drum for anything."

Jennifer sniffed as if she believed Cin was lying. "Well, he does seem to be making a lot of allowances for you. If you don't want to alienate the staff, you'll see to it that you send your requests through the proper channels in future. Now, if you'll go and see Carey, she'll give you your new uniform. I expect you to return the old one washed and ironed tomorrow morning."

And then Cin was left watching the woman's ramrod-straight back as she marched back to her office. After Jennifer's snarky comments on Friday night, Cin had vowed to herself to stay well clear of her, but it was obvious the woman still had a grudge against her and was prepared to go out of her way to show it. All she could do was keep out of her way and hope she never had any other reason to draw Jennifer's attention.

Carey was far more welcoming and full of chatter over how much fun she'd had at Cin's house on Saturday. She'd been at Belinda's yesterday for lunch, too, and Cin had thoroughly enjoyed being enfolded into their family dynamic, even if she still instinctively held herself a little apart. When Belinda had realized Cin had walked all the way into town to attend, she'd instructed Emerson to drive Cin home after lunch, ignoring Cin's protests. Added to that, she'd given Cin a covered dish to take home for her dinner with far more than one person could eat at a sitting. Cin had deeply appreciated the kindness.

After Carey had given Cin her new uniform, a fitted pair of trousers and a tailored shirt, tagged with the company logo and still in the company's colors, Cin returned to the tire bay.

"Wow, new duds," one of the boys commented. "Looks good on you, Cin."

"Thank you," she said.

"Everything go okay with Jennifer?" Gil asked, coming into her small office cubicle and putting a stack of customer orders on the desk beside her.

"As well as could be expected," Cin said noncommittally.

"You know she always had the hots for Drum, don't you?"

Cin racked her memory and came up blank. "She did?"

"Yeah, she always followed him and your brother around when they were in their last year at high school."

"I never noticed."

"You were too busy with your own crew."

"Did Drum reciprocate her interest?" She couldn't imagine he would have, but then life never failed to bring surprises.

"Hell no. I only ever saw him take a few girls out at school, but nothing serious. Not like a lot of the rest of us."

"She gave me a warning about being late today. Said she'd make it official if it happened again," Cin offered, still stung by Jennifer's inflexibility.

"She's one very unhappy woman, and it serves her to make sure everyone she's in contact with is equally unhappy. I'll cover for you if there's a next time, don't worry."

"Thanks, Gil. I appreciate it. Say, you don't know of any secondhand bikes for sale locally, do you? I thought we had one in the garage at home, but it must have been tossed in a cleanup after my parents died."

"A bicycle? Not off the top of my head, but I'll ask around for you, if you like."

"Anything will do as long as it has two good tires," Cin said with a wink.

"Sure. Leave it with me."

* * *

Drum drove out to Cin's house with a brand-new e-bike in a box in the back of his car. He was furious with himself for not thinking of providing her with transportation, but she'd been so adamant about not accepting his help—with the exception of Saturday's working bee—that he hadn't wanted to push the issue. He'd have preferred to buy her a car, but she would definitely not accept that. And he'd been grateful he'd overheard Gil talking to some of the boys about a secondhand bike and had told them to leave it with him. Gil had given him a knowing look, which he'd studiously ignored, and after work Drum had gone to the bike shop at the other end of town and made his selection.

Cin had always been a sucker for purple, and the iridescent purple of this bike and its matching helmet would suit her right down to the ground. If she accepted it. There were few lights on at the Sanderton house when he pulled up outside, making him wonder if she was even home. *Where else would she be? It's not like she welcomes friendships. In fact, she rarely welcomes anyone for anything.*

Undeterred, Drum got out of the vehicle and opened the hatch before maneuvering the box out and grabbing the helmet out of the back. The salesperson had assured him that there were instructions and a tool kit inside to complete its assembly. If Drum had any sense, he'd have done it all before coming out to see Cin, but he hadn't been able to wait. He'd burned to see her again.

His PA had told him about the new confrontation with Jennifer. Cin wouldn't appreciate him butting in over it, but since in some part it was his fault it happened because he'd been brusque with Jennifer while enquiring why Cin hadn't been added to the payroll... He'd itched all day to give the other woman a piece of his mind. He'd tried to tell himself it wasn't just because it was Cin that was involved. It simply wasn't the Keyes Tires way to treat fellow staff members with contempt. He'd let it ride for now, but if it continued he'd be forced to step in.

Drum lifted the box and carried it up onto the verandah. The lightweight frame of the bike ensured the package wasn't heavy, but it *was* bulky and he made a bit of noise as he got to the front door. Cin was already standing in the doorframe before he could raise a hand to knock. She was wrapped head to foot in a soft robe tied in a sash at her narrow waist. Her feet were encased in a pair of well-used fluffy slippers. Clearly she'd been getting ready for an early night.

"What are you doing?" she asked bluntly.

He set the box down by his feet and looked up at her. "I brought you something."

She sighed. "What?"

"Aw, c'mon Cin. You can do better than that. How about a guess?"

"I can see the picture on the box, Drum. It's a bicycle. Although why you felt it necessary to bring it to my house, I don't know."

"It's not just any bicycle, it's *your* bicycle." He flashed her a grin. Surely she was keen to see inside the box?

"Uh-uh. I don't have a bicycle."

"Well, you do now."

"And why would I want one?"

"I overhead Gil asking around on your behalf, so I'm guessing you want one so you can get to and from work without having to rely on the bus." *Or rides from me*, he added silently.

"That might be a good thing," she mused, "if I wanted one and if I could actually ride. Good night, Drum."

And with that she turned around, went inside and closed the door. Drum stood there for a full minute in surprise. She couldn't ride? Didn't every kid learn before they were ten? He racked his memory trying to think of a single time when he'd seen her on a bike when they were all growing up, but there wasn't one. How had he missed that vital piece of information? He was a man who prided himself on his attention to detail, and yet he'd missed that very important fact. He and Tanner had always ridden around town together, and he'd assumed that Cin had learned to ride, too, breaking his own rule of thumb: never take anything for granted.

He lifted his hand and knocked at the door. She

took her time returning to open it, but eventually he heard her steps on the parquet floor of the entrance.

"What?" she said ungraciously, her arms crossed firmly in front of her slender body.

"Missing a bit of that Sanderton bonhomie there, Cin," he commented. "Look, I was just trying to help. I knew you wouldn't accept a car from me—"

"Absolutely not!"

"And I know you got some stick at work today for being late. I'm sorry about that."

"Not your fault. I was the one who was late," she said.

There was a mutinous set to her expression that he knew did not augur well for her accepting this gift from him.

"Anyway, I thought I'd offer you this bike so you could be a little more independent and not have to rely on the bus timetable to get around."

"I've been managing just fine," she answered with a lift of her chin.

"Look, you can't ride, that's fine. Let me teach you."

"You. Teach me?" She laughed.

"Sure, why not? I've ridden a bike for longer than I can remember. I already know you have great balance. Remember that day your daddy caught you up the top of that tree over there and you walked out as far as you could on the branch?"

"He was so mad at me for that. I was grounded, literally, for a month."

"But you didn't fall." He could see he'd piqued her interest. "It's purple," he said enticingly.

She laughed out loud. "Seriously? You bought it in my favorite color?"

"Not much point buying a color you don't like, right? And I have a helmet to match."

He lifted the helmet from the verandah floor and propped it on her head before securing the straps under her chin. This close to her he could see her pulse beating at the side of her throat. And saw the way she swallowed as his fingers brushed the skin under her chin. She wasn't impervious to him, that much was obvious, and perversely that gave him a sense of satisfaction. Goodness only knew he was in physical torment every time he was near her. It was only fair she should feel the same way. Drum took a long step back.

"Okay, let me get the bike from the box and set up a few things, and we'll have your first lesson on the driveway."

"Now? Drum, I don't know if you've noticed, but it's late and it's dark."

"So? You have edge lighting up the drive. It's enough to see by."

"You might have noticed I'm not exactly dressed for bike riding."

"Go and get changed. C'mon, I dare you to give it a go. Where's that old Cin Sanderton spirit? I bet I can have the bike assembled before you're back."

She stared back at him, and he could have sworn

he saw sparks fly from her eyes before she growled, "Fine!" and retreated back into the house, helmet still perched firmly on her head.

He fought back another grin. She was so cute when she was mad. Always had been, and of course he and Tanner had frequently gone out of their way to tease her. Of course, now he actually had to complete assembly of the bike before she got back, so he turned his attention to extracting the frame, handlebars and wheels from the box. The salesperson at the store had showed him exactly what he had to do, and he was just tightening the last bolt as Cin came back.

She was dressed in a pair of black leggings that clung to her like a second skin, making her legs look long and shapely. A loose T-shirt, one of Tanner's old ones by the looks, was knotted at her waist, and the helmet was securely done up under her chin. A pair of old sneakers and bright pink socks completed the ensemble. He'd have bet good money there had never been a single day in Los Angeles when she'd have dressed like this.

He gave her nod of approval and lifted the bike down the front stairs and onto the driveway.

"I'll take it for a spin around the drive first, to make sure I've put it together properly."

"Sure, you do that."

Cin stood leaning against the house as she watched Drum lift the bike and go down the stairs. He hopped on with a fluid grace that made her breath catch in her throat. He'd been a good-looking kid and a handsome teen, but he was an altogether beautiful man now. Especially in a pair of old jeans and a soft knit sweater. And still as forbidden to her now as he'd ever been, she reminded herself.

He took a few turns around the circle at the top of the driveway and then came to a halt at the bottom of the stairs.

"Your steed awaits, my lady," he said with another of those shit-eating grins of his, and everything inside her turned to mush.

With that one grin he'd turned the clock back to when she was a little girl and when gaining his approval, even his notice, had been the object of every single day in the summer holidays. Determined to make a go of this and not to cause herself any humiliation, Cin joined him at the bike.

"Most important thing," he said, "these are your brakes, front and rear."

He demonstrated and Cin did her best to pay attention, but it was difficult with him standing so close to her and smelling delicious. She'd only have to turn a few inches and her nose would be up against his broad chest, right there at the V-neck of his sweater, and she could inhale his scent even more deeply. *Get a grip*, she told herself sternly. *If he's made it clear once, he's made it clear ten thousand times that he's not interested in you that way. Besides, he's just being kind—trying in his own way to make up for the fact you have nothing anymore. An* imp of mischief in her mind prompted, *He probably just wants you at work on time*. She couldn't help a small smile at the thought.

Eventually Drum told her to sit on the seat and he held the bike steady as she put her feet on the pedals.

"Okay, now," he said encouragingly. "Start pedaling!"

"But what if I fall off?" she said on a thread of panic.

"I've got you," he assured her. "I won't let you get hurt."

Trusting that he meant what he said, she began to pedal very slowly. The bike wobbled, and she immediately took her feet off the pedals and placed them down on the ground.

"I don't think I can do this," she said firmly.

"You can't get out of it that easily, Cin. Just pedal a little faster."

For over an hour he patiently held the back of her seat, running behind her, while she wobbled up and down the drive, gaining more and more confidence each time she did so. She didn't realize he'd let go when she took off down the driveway more quickly than before. She turned her head back to look at him and discovered he was still at the top of the driveway, looking at her with a ridiculous expression of pride on her face.

Of course, turning round to look at him had changed her direction, and when she set her eyes forward again she found she was heading straight for a stand of hydrangeas. Behind her she could hear Drum's feet pounding down the driveway as he ran toward her.

"Turn, Cin. Turn!" he yelled. "Or, y'know, stop!"

But it was too late, and she barreled straight into the shrubs, bike and all. She heard him skid to a halt close behind her and felt his strong hands at her waist, plucking her out of the bushes and setting her back on her feet.

"Are you okay? Have you hurt yourself? Oh, hell, Cin, I'm so sorry I let go. You weren't ready, and I should have held on one more time."

"Drum," Cin started, but her voice had a wobble to it; in fact her entire body was shaking. Mostly from the laughter she was fighting to restrain, but also a little from the shock of what had just happened.

"Your shoulders are shaking. You're crying. You're hurt. Cin, I'm *so* sorry."

She couldn't help it then. She let go of the mirth she'd been holding in and laughed and laughed. Drum didn't let go of her. In fact, his hands tightened on her shoulders, and he looked down into her face, confusion written all over his.

"You're laughing? After that fall? You're actually laughing?" Concern replaced the confusion and drew deep lines between his eyebrows. "You must have hit your head."

"I'm okay, seriously. I forgot all about the brakes. I guess I was so excited I was actually riding on my own that I forgot everything else—like steering or stopping. But I found a way to stop."

"You just about stopped my heart with that stunt. Are you sure you're okay?"

"I'm perfectly fine. Might need to cut back the hydrangea a bit, though. I'm not sure it survived intact."

Drum unclipped her helmet and threw it into the bush next to the bike. His hands cupped her face as he tilted it back up to his.

"You're absolutely certain? No broken bones, no double vision?"

"I'm fine, truly," she answered, a little more breathless this time.

"Thank heavens," Drum said on a heartfelt sigh.

His hands were warm and just a little rough on her cheeks, and she didn't rush to pull away. He, too, was reluctant to break contact. She looked up into his eyes. In this unlit section of driveway, they were darker than their usual blue-green, but there was no doubting the intensity that reflected back at her.

Time stretched, until ever so slowly Drum began to close the distance between them. She felt herself lift slightly to meet him halfway, feeling the warmth of him against her face just before his lips touched hers.

Sensation flooded her body. Heat and need and everything in between. His lips were soft, caressing hers with the same intensity with which he'd been looking at her only seconds ago. She parted her lips on a sigh of wonder, meeting the sweep of his tongue with her own. She slid her hands around the back of his neck, holding him to her. It felt as if she'd waited for this moment all her life—her very first kiss with Drummond Keyes—and it was everything and more than she'd ever expected. And then, all too soon, it was over.

Drum stepped back, shoving a hand through his hair.

"Hell, Cin. I'm sorry. I shouldn't have done that."

"Why not? We're both adults."

"It's not that," he said with a muttered expletive.

"What is it, then? Don't I kiss right?"

"No, you kiss—" He muttered a string of expletives this time and paced a few steps away before coming back to stand in front of her again.

"I kiss…?" she prompted, determined to get to the bottom of this.

"I'm not going into this right now. In fact, ever. I'll push your bike back to the house. I shouldn't have started this."

"Which—the bike, or the kissing?" she demanded, starting to feel very angry.

"Either, dammit. And why are you so angry, anyway?"

"Why am I angry?" she asked incredulously. "First you come to my home, uninvited. Foist that contraption upon me. Make me learn to ride it. Then, when *you* let me go and I fall off, you kiss me in a way that makes me want to strip every thread of clothing off your body and find out if the rest of you tastes as incredibly enticing as your mouth. That's why I'm angry. And if that wasn't enough, you then act like it was all some big mistake. Well, I'm telling you, mister, the only mistake was you thinking it meant nothing, because it meant everything to me. Do you understand? So, yes, I'm angry. Thank you for the bike. I will take it back to the house myself, and you can just go on home at your leisure."

With all the dignity she could muster, she wrenched the bike from the bush, grabbed her helmet and shoved it on her head and, mounting the bike, wobbled her way back along the driveway to the house. He didn't follow her immediately, for which she was grateful. Right now, she was beating herself up for telling him the truth about what his kiss had done to her. She'd just dismounted and was lifting the bike up the stairs when she heard him run up behind her.

"Cin, stop, please."

She carried on up the stairs and set the bike against the front railings. "Why? So you can tell me how awfully I kiss, one more time? I don't think so." She hung the helmet off the handlebar of the bike and went to open the front door and escape inside, but he was there before her. His palm flat against the surface of the door.

"Don't run away from me, Cin."

"Me? I'm not the one running away, Drum. *You* keep coming here. *You* keep getting in my space. You're the one who keeps pulling back. So what if we kissed? It's not as if it meant anything, right?"

Even as she said the words she knew she was lying to her back teeth. That kiss had been the culmination of years of dreaming and wondering what his lips would feel like. How he would taste. And more, what would happen next. Never in her wildest dreams had she imagined their first kiss would lead to this.

"It didn't mean anything to you? Back there you said it meant everything."

She looked at him in uncertainty. There was something in the tone of his voice—a grim determination—that made her insides tighten on a swell of desire so strong it sent ripples of want throughout her body. Even her hands tingled, aching to reach for him, to touch him as she'd always wanted to. She swallowed hard.

"I meant that it obviously didn't mean anything… to you," she managed through lips that felt as if they'd grown stiff and unyielding.

Drum closed his eyes and groaned, muttered something about Tanner never forgiving him for this and how it was a stupid idea, then he reached for her with both hands and pulled her toward him.

"Oh, it meant something, all right," he said grimly.

And then he kissed her again.

Nine

This was utter madness, he thought as he teased and tasted her lips like a man discovering an oasis after a week in the desert. She felt small and delicate in his arms, although he knew she had strength in abundance. But right now, he wanted nothing more than to wrap her up and protect her and keep her safe from all and any problems. *As if she'd let you*, that voice in the back of his mind sneered.

He ignored it and everything else and swept Cin into his arms.

"Get the door," he growled. "We're taking this upstairs."

She slung one arm around his neck and reached for the door handle with the other. She said nothing but the look in her eyes told him all he needed to know. There was no objection, no second-guessing. He bumped the front door closed with his hip, and Cin reached to turn the key in the deadlock and then there were no further excuses to delay proceedings.

Drum made his way up the stairs and turned on the landing, unerringly heading for her bedroom. He stalked over to the bed and set her gently on the covers before reaching for his sweater and yanking it over his head. He heard her indrawn breath as she let her gaze roam over his chest, and he saw the appreciation in her eyes. Next his hands went to the buckle on his jeans and, damn it, they were trembling. Whether it was simply in anticipation of what he knew was coming next or because he was still torn about it and his promise to Tanner, he couldn't be sure. Either way, he shoved both thoughts directly to the back of his mind.

Cin gracefully rose to sit and hung her legs over the side of the bed. "Here, let me. I don't see why you should have all the fun undressing."

Her voice wound around him like a spell, and he dropped his hands to his side, watching, teeth clenched, as she methodically undid his belt then slowly lowered the zipper on his jeans. His erection was already straining at the denim, and the second she shoved his jeans down his legs he knew he wanted her so badly he only hoped he didn't mess this up.

He drew in a sharp breath as Cin danced her fingers along the edge of the waistband of his boxer briefs and even though he wouldn't have thought it humanly possible, he grew even harder. He had never in his life wanted someone the way he wanted her. Or maybe it had always been her and he'd simply suppressed it. It would go a long way to explaining his dissatisfaction with other relationships. The continual sense that while things were okay, they were never totally right, either.

But what Cin was doing to him now was right on every level. She'd slid her fingertips under the waistband of his boxers and gently removed them. His length sprang free and then jerked in response as her slender fingers closed around him, stroking him with a firm grip that made his entire body rigid with the control required to keep from letting go.

"You like that?" she asked huskily.

"Oh yeah."

She bent forward and flicked her tongue across the tip of his cock. A tiny dart of pressure, there, then gone again. Then she blew her warm breath over the swollen flesh, making his whole body jerk this time.

"Cin?"

She looked up at him, devilment in her expression, and it just about undid him completely. "Yes, Drum?"

The innocence in her voice was at total odds with the look on her face, highlighting the enigma that was Cin Sanderton. But he wasn't into solving puzzles right now. He needed to give her a solid dose of the torment she had just delivered to him.

"Take off your clothes for me…please?"

She slipped out of her T-shirt and drew it off over her head, exposing the most exquisite lacy mint-green bra it had ever been his privilege to view. Cin had never been into tanning heavily as so many of her teenage friends had back when she still lived in Blossom Springs, and it seemed that all her years away hadn't changed that habit. Her skin was smooth and unblemished, almost glowing in its perfection. Drum's mouth dried as she reached behind her and unsnapped the garment. A small shrug of her shoulders and the scrap of next-to-nothing fell away from her, exposing the perfection of her breasts. He reached with his hands to cup the compact globes of flesh, let his thumbs graze across the pale pink nipples and felt them tighten and harden into nubs.

"You are so beautiful," he said, his voice thick with desire.

"As are you," she murmured before lying back down onto the bed and gesturing to her leggings. "Can you help me with these?"

"With pleasure," he said with a grin and slipped off her sneakers and socks, then peeled off her leggings, exposing long slender legs.

She wore panties that matched her bra, and he came to a sudden conclusion his new favorite color was definitely mint-green. Drum joined her on the bed. His hands still shook slightly as he touched her. Her skin was smooth as alabaster but warm, so warm, to the touch. He skimmed his fingers over her ribs and back to her breasts again. She pushed herself upward, meeting his touch, silently begging him for more.

"You like this?" he asked, bending closer to one of her tightly furled nipples and rolling it gently between a thumb and forefinger.

"Yes," she said in that same husky voice she'd used earlier.

"And what about this?"

Drum took that nipple in his mouth and flicked it with his tongue then softly grazed it with his teeth.

"Yes. That, too," she said. "Give me more, Drum. I need more."

"I'll give you more. In time," he promised. "But first, I'm going to explore."

"Explore?"

"Yeah, it doesn't pay to rush these things. Trust me."

He continued to play with her nipples with his mouth, his teeth, his tongue until Cin was moaning with pleasure. Her hands fluttered to his shoulders, gripping tight as he alternated from one to the other. With his right hand, he caressed her side, sliding over her ribs, noting her slenderness with a notch of concern that he shoved aside to consider another time.

He caressed her hip, tracing the line of her pelvis to where it disappeared into the lacy green bit of fabric that passed as her underwear. He no longer trembled, but she did. Especially when he hooked one finger into the side of that green lace and tugged it down. She lifted her hips, and he pulled the pants down to her thighs, imprisoning her and preventing him from racing ahead and exploring the darker recesses of her body too quickly.

His fingertips again followed the contour of her pelvis, lower this time, until they met the neatly trimmed thatch of hair at the apex of her thighs. Skimming over it, he felt her draw in a sharp breath and saw her hips push upward off the mattress as she waited for him to touch her there, but he had no intention of giving her what she wanted just yet.

Lower he went, his fingertips stroking her inner thighs, exploring her tender spots and committing them to memory.

"Drum, please, take my panties off. I can't move," she begged him.

"But you can still feel, right?"

"Yes, but I need to move. I don't like to be restrained like that."

There was something in her tone that warned him he was in danger of losing her willing participation if he didn't accede to her request. He lifted himself away from her and quickly slid her panties down, letting them drop on the floor in the pile of their clothing before he lay back down on the bed beside her, propped up on one elbow.

He kissed her neck and said, "Better now?"

"Yes, thank you. Now, where were we? Or more importantly, where were you?"

He chuckled and shifted so he could begin that slow assault on her senses once more, except this time he lingered when he reached those soft curls between her thighs, stroking his fingertips through them, edging ever closer to her sex. She bucked as he brushed over her clit, again pushing her hips up in a silent plea for him to touch her there again, but he had other plans for her right now. He let his hand drift to her inner thighs, stroking first down one and then back up the other until he brushed her clit again.

"Drum, what are you doing to me?"

"Do you need me to spell it out for you?" he said carefully. "I'm happy to narrate."

As he'd expected, she laughed, and he felt some of the tension leave her body. Good, he thought. That meant he could start over again, stoking her fire until her entire body was aflame for him. The next time he touched her clit he circled it, and Cin's moan was more guttural this time. With his thumb circling the hardened bead, he let his fingers play lower, parting the wet folds of heated flesh, and he probed her carefully with one finger.

She was so hot, so ready, her hips pushing against his hand as she reached for completion that he knew wasn't far away. He'd give her this, he decided. His own pleasure was nothing in comparison to his desire to send her soaring. She'd closed her eyes, every part of her focusing on his touch. On the circles he drew with his thumb, on the rhythmic ease of his finger in and out of her. Her thighs shook and her hips moved in time with his hand until he increased the pressure of his thumb on her clit and once again took one of her nipples in his mouth and sucked firmly on the tender flesh.

Cin broke apart, crying out as her orgasm swamped her body, making her shudder against his hand. He slowed his movements, letting her drift back to normality at her own pace. Keeping his touch light and undemanding, pressing small kisses on her shoulder, her neck, her cheek until his lips recaptured hers in a sweet caress that sent a piercing spear of need through his body.

"Okay?" he asked as Cin opened her eyes to meet his.

She nodded and licked her lips. "Oh yes, better than okay."

"Ready to go again?"

"For that? Always," she answered with a sultry smile.

Cin stroked her hands over his body sending currents of electricity firing all over him. He reached down to the floor and snagged his jeans and extracted the condom he kept in his wallet.

"A bit cliché, isn't it?" Cin said to him with humor brightening her clear blue eyes.

"Better a cliché than a mistake, right?"

For a second she looked serious, but then she laughed. "Absolutely."

He slid the condom onto his aching erection and went to settle between Cin's legs, but she shifted position and coaxed him to lie on his back. He certainly wasn't going to argue this one, he thought, as she straddled his hips and positioned herself over him. And then thought fled as the heat of her body slowly encapsulated him. Her inner muscles tightened around his length, and he flexed his hips in response, reveling in the sensations that poured through him. She, too, moaned in reaction, her entire body tensing.

And then she began to move, and he lost himself in the building need for release that clamored inside him. Drum reached between them and found her sweet spot, drawing tiny circles with his thumb, his other hand at her hip. He didn't want this to end, but he knew his body would let go soon, and he wanted to be certain she found her pleasure right along there with him. Her movements gathered in momentum, and she tilted her pelvis so there was no chance of him losing connection with that tight bundle of nerves at her core. He stroked a little harder and felt the moment her climax began in the sudden pull and release of her muscles against his cock. As she threw her head back and gave herself over to pleasure, he let go of the last remnants of his iron control and joined her, letting wave after wave of satisfaction pummel through him.

Cin eventually collapsed against him, and he wrapped his arms around her tight and rolled them onto their sides. He could feel her rapid heartbeat, answered it with his own. Their breathing was ragged, their skin dewed with perspiration, and a sense of rightness filled him in a way he'd never experienced before.

* * *

Cin snuggled into Drum's strength, amazed he still had the ability to hold onto her when she felt as though every part of her body had gone liquid with pleasure. Her entire adult life she'd wondered what sex with him would have been like. Now she knew. Her deepest, darkest fantasies weren't a touch on what it felt like to have him inside her, to feel his fullness stretching her and completing her in a way that made her feel powerful and feminine all at the same time.

She inhaled his scent, a sense of peace and belonging filling her. She'd never felt this way with anyone else. As if her world began and ended with the man holding her like she was the most cherished woman on earth. And, she realized, right now she was that woman, and it was Drum that made her feel that way. No questions, no recriminations, no guilt. She felt as if she'd waited her entire life for this moment, for the perfection of their joining. Slowly the delicious lassitude that had swamped her began to recede, leaving reality in its wake. Reminding her she'd just slept with her boss.

History repeating the same old mistakes again? a sharp voice asked from the back of her mind.

No, this was nothing like her relationship with Mark, and what the hell was she doing thinking about him right now, anyway? It had been bad enough that almost every time they'd had sex, she'd been wondering what it would have been like if it had been Drum instead. She tried to force those moments from her thoughts, but they lingered like the bad memories they were and, with them, her failure to be the kind of wife Mark had needed.

A cold chill shivered across her body.

"You're cold?" Drum asked instantly, her care his obvious concern.

"I'm fine," she said, but she pulled loose from his embrace and got up from the bed to use the bathroom.

When she returned, Drum was sitting up in the bed with the covers drawn over his lower body. His broad shoulders leaned against her padded headboard, and her eyes feasted on his male beauty. The warm tan on his skin, the definition of his muscles, the taut lines of his abs and followed the light dusting of hair that circled his belly button to where it arrowed beneath her sheets. Instantly her body warmed and became aroused again, her nipples growing hard, demand thrumming at her core.

She should be sated, she told herself. She'd never considered herself overly sexual, but right now all she wanted to do was rip the sheets off Drum's body and explore every inch of him before taking him into her body once more and finding that sublime joy they'd achieved together only minutes ago.

"You look pensive. What are you thinking about? No regrets, I hope?" he asked.

"You like to get straight to the point, don't you?" she said evasively as she grabbed her T-shirt from the floor and tugged it down over her to hide herself from view—as if that could assuage the hunger she had for him.

He pulled a face. "No point beating around the bush, Cin. I think we've known each other long enough not to lie to one another." He reached out to grab her arm and drew her to sit down on the bed beside him. His hand reached up to stroke her cheek, and he leaned forward to kiss her. "C'mon Cin. Spill. What's bothering you?"

"I just… I dunno. We shouldn't have done that," she answered flatly.

"Why not? Neither of us are in a relationship with anyone else. We have no other ties. Hell, it's all I've been able to think about since you came into my office last week, and now all I want to do is repeat the experience."

"We can't," she protested.

"Why not?"

"You're my boss."

"You're fired. Happy now?"

"You're not serious, are you?" She looked at him in horror.

"Your job means that much to you?"

In actuality it was the small, but regular income that meant that much to her, but she wasn't about to say that. He knew she was down on her luck, that her financial circumstances were straitened at best, but flat out broke? Her pride did not want to let him, or anyone else, know that fact.

"Yes, it does."

He grimaced. "You're going to throw me over for a job in the tire bay? A job, I might point out, that doesn't stretch you intellectually in any way and doesn't make use of the skill set you've spent every day building since you graduated college. A job where you ought to be simply biding your time until the next great role comes along for you. We both know you couldn't wait to leave Blossom Springs when you were a teenager. You're an adult now with the world at your feet. You won't stay, so why not make the most of this—of us?"

When he put it that way, she began to wonder why she was so fixed on the idea of not having sex with him again. It had been fun and fulfilling, and even now her pulse thrummed, waiting for the opportunity to do it all over. But he was wrong about her using Blossom Springs as a staging post. Or was he?

"You don't understand," she said, shaking her head.

Even she didn't fully understand why she was pushing away this big, beautiful man who was tucked up in her bed. It was her every vivid dream come true, and yet she was rejecting it, rejecting him. What the heck was wrong with her? She wasn't that one-track-minded little girl or that forward teenager anymore. She was a grown woman who craved this man. Wasn't a moment like this everything she'd ever wanted? She deserved happiness, too, didn't she?

His fingers had traveled from her cheek to the indentation behind her ear. A spot that was probably her most sensitive, and his touch sent tiny shocks through her body.

"Help me to understand, Cin. What didn't you like about what we shared?"

"Nothing!"

"Then, why shouldn't we do it again and keep doing it until whatever this is burns out between us?"

Trouble was, she knew it would never burn out.

"I'm not looking for a fling, Drum," she said with all the honesty she could muster. "In fact, I'm not really looking for anything, with anyone."

He stared at her, his eyes boring into her as if he could figure out exactly what she meant if he just looked hard enough.

"You still love your ex-husband, is that it? Do you feel as if you were just unfaithful to him?"

The idea couldn't be further from the truth, but how could she tell him that? She'd messed up her marriage because she'd never been able to put Drum from her mind or her heart. Messed up another man's life completely, broke him, emotionally and financially. Oh sure, she hadn't meant to do it and, yes, no one had forced Mark into the choices he'd made. But because she hadn't been invested in him as her husband, in their marriage and the vows they'd made, it had happened, anyway.

She didn't deserve this, didn't deserve Drum and, most of all, didn't deserve her dream to come true. Because what if she messed it all up again? All her life her momma had told her to hold something back, but with Drum she didn't want to hold anything back anymore. She loved him. Had always loved him. But what if she wasn't enough for him the way Mark had never been enough for her?

What if the whole reason Drum had never shown any interest in her until this night was because he couldn't or wouldn't be as invested in her as she was in him? She couldn't live with that. Wasn't prepared to accept scraps of attention while all the time waiting for him to leave her. Wasn't he already talking about this thing between them burning out? For her it had never burned out. It still flamed now, even brighter and hotter than before.

"It's not as simple as that, Drum. I'm sorry."

His fingers ran through her hair as he cupped the back of her head and leaned forward toward her.

"It can be, if you let it," he said quietly.

And then he kissed her and obliterated all her fears and worries, replacing them with promises of physical delight and sensual bliss. His tongue stroked hers, coaxing her to open fully to his carnal onslaught. His free hand slid under her T-shirt, tracing her ribs and moving ever upward to her breast, to her aching nipple. He took the tender bud between his forefinger and thumb and tugged gently, making her gasp at the jolt that pierced her.

"Tell me to stop if you don't want this, Cin," he murmured against her lips. "If you don't want me."

She could no more deny him than she could stop the sun from rising in the morning. But, she asked herself as she let him pull her T-shirt off and draw her down beside him, what would be the price?

Ten

"You have no food," Drum declared after peering into her refrigerator and inspecting her cupboards in search of breakfast. "I need to stop at home and get changed for work. Why don't you come with me, and we can grab something to eat before going into work together?"

"I have no food because I eat later, and besides, I wasn't expecting company," she answered without telling an outright lie. "You're welcome to head home and get fed and dressed in your own time. I'm heading into work now."

"Now? But it's way too early. You don't start for another hour at least."

"I know, but it takes me that long by bus and walking. Besides, I can't afford to be late, or I'll end up with a written warning."

Drum straightened and closed the fridge door. He looked at her, not quite sure he'd heard her correctly.

"Say what? A *written warning*?"

"Apparently. I was warned when I arrived late and Jennifer had been looking for me to give me one of the new uniforms. She wasn't impressed."

"You don't answer to her," he said with anger rising. "Gil is the floor manager in the tire bay, and if he has a gripe with you, then he takes it to her. We have protocols regarding disciplinary measures."

Cin shrugged as if it didn't matter, but as far as he was concerned it absolutely did. First the nonpayment of Cin's wages, then a censure over something pretty much everyone did at least a couple of times a year for one reason or another. Add to that the mean remark at the Friday-night drinks, and he was seeing a theme between Jennifer Green and Cin. One he did not like the sound of.

Sure, Jennifer was a little prickly at work, but she was good at her job and kept HR running like a well-oiled machine, but the way she was treating Cin was something else. Either way, the behavior was not an accepted part of Keyes work culture.

"You're not taking me to work. It's bad enough I let you stay last night. Maybe I should just ride the bike in, now I have it."

"Don't be silly. One lesson isn't enough."

"Then, I'll walk and bus it, like I always do."

Drum stared at her. Dressed in her Keyes Tires uniform and safety shoes, she was a far cry from the woman he'd made love with through the night. He had yet to work out how he felt about what they'd shared together. Even looking at her now ignited a fire in his blood. He wanted nothing more than to strip off that uniform and take her back upstairs. In her room they'd been in a cocoon of only the two of them. No one and nothing else had intruded. But as soon as they'd woken this morning, he'd sensed her withdrawal, her regrets. He walked over to her and tipped her chin up with his hand before kissing her deeply.

"Cin, about last night," he started when he finally raised his head.

"Last night shouldn't have happened, Drum. I'm not in the market for a relationship. My life is complicated enough as it is."

While she'd kissed him back, she created some distance between them now.

"Let me help you uncomplicate things," he offered. After all, wasn't that what he did for the people he loved? He solved their problems, he made their lives easier, he—

Hang on, wait. What was that? People he *loved*? He turned the idea over in his head. Since when did he include Cin in that small group? But he knew the answer. She'd been a part of his life for a long time before she left for college, and seeing her again had been both familiar and strange at the same time.

The attraction he'd kept firmly in check when she was still a teen and he was embarking on life as his father's right-hand man had morphed into something new and a whole lot more complex when she'd walked back into his life. He couldn't see her without wanting to touch her. Couldn't prevent the concern that filled him as she faced obstacles on her own.

He knew the kind of life she'd had growing up, and while most of his refusal to enter into any kind of relationship with her had been because of the pact he and Tanner had made, he'd always known that there was no way he could give Cin the lifestyle she was used to. He could offer that same level of luxury now. She could have anything she wanted with him, provided she wanted *him*, too.

And there was the question. Did she want him? She'd been aloof with him from the moment she'd set foot in his office. Sure, it had been a comedown for her to ask for a job, but she'd always been the kind of person who bounced back and who never let circumstances get her down, so he was pretty sure it wasn't that he was her employer that had created the wall between them. Hell, she'd married her last boss, hadn't she?

Maybe she was still in love with Mark. She hadn't actually answered him when he'd said as much last night. Was that the real reason behind her reluctance and her continued refusal to accept his help? Something twisted in his gut at the thought. He'd been sure Tanner had told him things were completely over between her and her husband. The divorce had been finalized. Their marriage dissolved. And yet, here he was, standing in her kitchen after the most incredible night of his life, still with absolutely no idea of how she felt about him.

"Uncomplicate things?" Cin said disparagingly. "You know that being seen with you first thing in the morning will just complicate things even more."

"If it comes up, you can simply say you needed a ride. It's not a lie," he countered.

"When you live on the opposite side of town?" she said with her hands on her hips and irritation pulling her brows together.

"Fine, then," he huffed, throwing his hands up in surrender. "You don't want my help. How about we reach a compromise? I'll put your bike in the car and take you most of the way into town, and you can ride the rest of the way in. But you have to promise me you'll be super careful."

"Yes, Dad," she said in a withering tone.

"Uncalled for," he answered. "I care about you, Cin. Whether you want me to or not, I'm looking out for you."

"Oh, and was last night on Tanner's list of what to do for me?"

"You know damn well it wasn't, and don't try making what we shared into something to be ashamed of. We were great together."

All the bluster and standoffishness that had stiffened her posture seemed to seep out of her.

"We were, but we can't continue like that, Drum. Even you must be able to see that."

"I don't see why not. There's nothing in company rules about it. I should know. I'm the boss, remember?" He sent her a grin that he could see hit its target as she smiled back in response.

"Yes, and it was getting involved with the boss that messed up my life last time," she snapped before giving an exasperated sigh. "Fine, I'll accept a ride with you part of the way, but then I'm biking the rest. Deal?"

"Deal," he agreed even though he wasn't pleased with the idea.

"Can we go now?" she asked.

"Sure. I'll load your bike."

Cin sat next to Drum in the car feeling more wound-up than a spinning top and just about as confused. She knew it bugged him that she struggled to accept his help, but she was just as determined to learn to stand on her own two feet. She'd been that spoiled little rich girl for too long. She struggled to hide the snort that almost escaped her at the ill-fitting moniker. Rich girl? She was anything but that these days. *Girl*, or *rich*.

The email she'd read on her phone this morning from her attorney had set out the dying remnants of her financial position. She literally had nothing but the clothes she'd left LA with. She had no savings, no credit, nothing. But she still had a roof over her head which put her streets ahead of others facing tough times. Plus, she had a job. Not great pay, but it meant she could be independent.

Drum pulled over on the side of the road and looked at her.

"You sure you want to ride the rest of the way? Traffic is building up now."

"I'll be fine. I promise not to wobble into the path of oncoming traffic."

His lips drew into a straight line, and she knew he was biting back some comment that she'd only argue against.

"Okay. I'll get your bike. Make sure your helmet fits right."

"Yes, boss," she said.

"Well, at least that's better than calling me Dad."

"You know, I'm quite capable of looking after myself."

"And yet you have no food in the house and no car and aside from a low-paying role with my company you have no other prospects. You call that looking after yourself?"

"Ouch. Why don't you say how you really feel, Drum?"

"I'm sorry. I just know what you're used to and—"

"Life changes. We both know that. I'm managing. Trust me."

"I trust you, Cin, but do you trust me?"

Without waiting for an answer, he got out of the car and opened the back to lift her bike out for her.

He set it on the side of the road and checked the brakes and the pedals and that the seat was secure.

"Happy now?" she asked after standing on the sidewalk waiting for him to complete his inspection.

"Just erring on the side of caution."

"You've always been like that, haven't you? Even with all the stunts you and Tanner pulled as kids, you were always in risk-management mode."

"One of us had to be," he answered with a wry grin. "Your brother always said *Go hard or go home*. I just wanted us to be able to go home in one piece."

"Do you miss him?" she asked, suddenly curious.

"Yeah, but we catch up when he comes home. Like I said before, he usually stays with me. Lately, though, he's been too busy to take a break."

"I haven't heard from him since just before I left LA."

"Don't worry. We both know that sometimes he has to be out of contact."

She shivered, knowing that being out of contact meant he was involved in something that endangered him. Cin loved the fact that Tanner was living his dream in the army, but she hated the varying levels of danger his work brought him. In the past she'd always been able to message him through a secure link, but this time he hadn't provided one.

"I understand that, but even though we don't live in each other's pockets, I miss him when I can't reach out."

Drum cupped the side of her face with one large

warm hand. "I'm here for you, Cin. I'll always look out for you."

She looked into his eyes and saw the sincerity reflected back at her. She pressed her cheek into his palm, relishing the affection in his touch. She knew she shouldn't be doing this: it was a dangerous path to tread. Even though they'd been intimate together, she couldn't allow her old feelings for him to rule her future. And she would not put herself in a position where she could lose everything all over again.

"Thanks, Drum. I'd better get to work."

She slung her leg over the bike and settled on the saddle. Putting one foot on a pedal, she gave him a nod and then pushed off. She wobbled a bit, but then she found her balance and carried on down the street. It was liberating riding the bike, giving back a freedom she'd taken for granted all her life. She'd driven herself from the moment she'd been legal to hold a license. Relying on public transport in their small town and walking had been great for her fitness, but not so great for her mindset.

It was busy in the tire bay that morning, and Cin tried hard to keep her mind on her work, but every now and then snippets from last night would intrude on her thoughts and send tiny pangs of longing through her body and wind her nerves tight. She'd get lost in a reverie of the sensation of Drum's body next to hers, of his strength and heat and power. Even though he could easily have physically dominated her, he never for one moment made her feel like she wasn't in control of everything that they did together. And they'd done a lot. Her body ached with a sense of being well-used and intensely pleasured. And it wanted more.

She slammed the door on those thoughts as she looked up from her computer close to lunchtime and saw Jennifer driving her car into the workshop. She checked her bookings but there was nothing there to say the old sedan had been scheduled. Jennifer got out and strolled up to Cin's window.

"I need my tire pressure checked," she said without even a greeting.

"As you can see, we're kind of busy. Perhaps you could book—"

"I need it done now. You can do it. After all, you're not just a pretty face, are you?"

There was a challenge in the other woman's voice that set Cin's teeth on edge. "Certainly, I can check your tire pressure. Or I could show you how to do it yourself?" she suggested with a smile she had to force to her lips.

"Why would I want to do that?" Jennifer said. "I'll wait over there," she informed her and strutted off to the waiting area that Cin had made over.

Cin set the phone to voice mail and left her small office. She had a quick word with Gil, who was working on a full tire fit-out, balance and alignment for the town's mayoral vehicle, and checked Jennifer's tires before adding a little more air where needed. Getting up, she rolled up the hose and hung it on its hook before dusting her hands on the seat of her pants and walking over to Jennifer.

"You're all set to go," she said, hoping the other woman would do exactly that—go.

Jennifer rose slowly to her feet and pinned her with a glare. "I saw you early this morning getting out of Drum's car."

"That's right," Cin said seeing no point in denying it.

"Are you having an affair with him?" Jennifer asked.

"I don't believe that's any of your business."

"So you are, then. Well, I guess I can expect a directive to find you a more lucrative position upstairs any time now." She sighed expressively.

Rage flooded Cin from the soles of her feet to the top of her head. Her hands curled into fists, and she pushed them deep into the pockets of her pants. Where the hell did Jennifer get off conjecturing about her and Drum?

"I think you had better leave. As you can see, we are very busy, and I don't have time for idle chatter."

She spun on her heel and went back to her office, but it seemed Jennifer hadn't quite finished with her.

"You know, you really should have held out. I mean, why would he buy the cow when he can get the milk for free?"

"I beg your pardon?" Cin bit through clenched teeth after turning back to the other woman.

"Well, his last floozy got promoted all the way

from front-desk reception to head of the marketing department. You should have at least held out for a similar role. You'll never be any better than you are right now. Mind you, that's no surprise."

"I don't know why you have it in for me, but I don't deserve it. I'm here to do my job, that's all."

"And screw the boss, too, it seems. Well, I hope for your sake that doesn't backfire."

Cin was speechless as Jennifer got back into her car. What was it to her, anyway? What Drum did in his own time had nothing to do with her. Gil sauntered over as Jennifer backed out and took her car back to the staff parking lot.

"Everything okay? You look upset."

Cin shook her head. She shouldn't let the woman get under her skin like that. Toxic people needed to be pitied, she reminded herself. But the deliberate power play executed by Jennifer Green had made her blood boil. "It's nothing," she said sharply. "I'm going to clear our messages and get back to work."

"What about your lunch break?"

"I lost my appetite."

Gil kicked at the floor before pinning her with a stare. "I notice you don't go out to buy food and you don't bring lunch. Are you on some diet or something?"

"No, I just—"

"Look, the missus always makes me far too much. Why don't you share what I've brought today? I'd hate to see you pass out and hurt yourself and make me fill out an accident report."

Cin laughed self-consciously. She didn't think anyone had noticed. "Well, when you put it that way, how can I refuse?"

Gil laughed in return and went to his locker to grab his lunch. They went to an outdoor seating area provided for staff, and he opened up his lunch box and took out two separately wrapped packets of sandwiches. Cin gave him a steely look.

"You got your wife to make me lunch, didn't you?"

He had the grace to look shamefaced. "What can I say? I like having you around, and I notice things. We have to look after our team, okay?"

She accepted the wrapped sandwich he passed over to her. "Thank you, Gil. I really appreciate it."

Cin felt better after having lunch with Gil. A couple of the other guys joined them, and there was plenty of laughter and banter between them all. Cin watched without really contributing much to the conversation, the encounter with Jennifer playing over in her mind. She'd never been mean to Jennifer at school—she'd hardly paid her any attention at all, except for noticing that she could be mean to some of the weaker kids from time to time. *I guess, once a bully, always a bully,* she thought to herself as she scrunched up her paper and tossed it in the trash bin.

"C'mon guys, back to work. We have a full schedule today."

There was some good-natured ribbing about her being a hard-ass, but everyone got to their feet and followed her back in, releasing the other half of the team to go on their break. Cin settled back at her computer and checked the phone messages, calling customers back where necessary. She enjoyed the simplicity of her work. There was none of the cut and thrust of her job in LA, none of the tension on deadlines or waiting to see if they'd hit the mark with a new campaign or not. True, there were none of the highs associated with their successes, either, but she enjoyed the ease and repetition of what she did now.

It wasn't long, however, before her thoughts turned back to Drum. He'd been a giving and considerate lover. While she'd been no novice when it came to the bedroom, her experience wasn't wide, either. But she did know that Drum had played her body like some kind of sex virtuoso, taking her to limits she hadn't believed her body capable of experiencing. And she wanted more.

No! She slammed the door on that thought pattern before she could let it unfurl into something else. She wasn't in Blossom Springs to rashly embark on a love affair. She had some serious rebuilding to do before she would be ready for that—if she was ever again. It was scary being alone and responsible for all her decisions herself, but it was past time she learned how. She'd always shared her major decisions first with her parents and, then, after her marriage, with Mark. It was ridiculous for her to get to thirty and to have never really made her own way.

Even when her parents had hit financial difficulties, they'd always been there for her emotion-

ally. Losing them had been tough on her, and she'd
turned to Mark more and more. Letting him take all
responsibility without question. She had never truly
understood who he was or what he needed. Never
actually understood the same about herself, truth be
told. All she'd wanted to do was fly high in her job
and accept the accolades that came with it.

She'd been shallow, she realized. Shallow and
self-centered, and it was past time she grew up and
changed. Her thoughts flicked back to last night. She
hadn't been self-centered then, she remembered with
a small, knowing smile. She'd given Drum pleasure
equally, relishing exploring his body and learning
what he liked and what he loved. He was surpris-
ingly ticklish, too, and vulnerable in the immediate aftermath of their lovemaking. That had come
as a surprise. He was so big and strong and capable.
The big boss man. And yet, when it came to sharing their bodies, he had showed a sensitivity she'd
never expected.

And then she'd shoved it all back in his face this
morning, telling him in no uncertain terms that it
had been a mistake. She had to be crazy. He was
the boy she'd adored in her childhood, yearned for
in her tweens and lusted after when she was a senior
in high school. He was everything she'd ever wanted,
and more. And yet, letting herself as a grown woman
love him terrified her. What she'd felt for her former husband had been insubstantial. The loss she'd
felt after their divorce was driven more by her own

guilt at not being the person he'd needed than by their marriage ending.

Again, self-centered. So, yeah, she had some serious growing up to do before she committed to anything new. With anyone. Even a pet, which would at least be company in the big old house she'd grown up in and taken for granted all her life.

The end of the working day finally arrived, and Cin retrieved her helmet from her locker and made her way outside to where she'd chained her bike to a fence that formed the perimeter of the staff parking lot. Most of the office staff's cars were gone. Aside from Gil's truck at the far end of the row, only Drum's and Jennifer's cars remained. Not really wanting to bump into either of them right now, she unchained her bike and fitted her helmet, but before she could ride away, Jennifer was out of the office building and marching toward her car. She stopped a couple of yards away.

"What on earth!" she exclaimed loudly then wheeled and faced Cin with fury written all over her face. "You did this, didn't you? As payback for me asking you to check my tires."

Eleven

"I beg your pardon?" Cin answered her, thoroughly confused by what could have triggered such vitriol.

It was then that she noticed that Jennifer's tires were all flat. She knew for certain she'd checked them appropriately and pumped them to the right pressure. Whatever had happened had to have been deliberate, but Cin hadn't done it, and she said as much.

Jennifer, however, had other ideas.

"You've been trouble from the day you started," she accused loudly. "First the uniforms, then being tardy and now this. Endangering another staff member is an offense worthy of dismissal. I hope you realize that."

Cin became aware of others now gathering around them. Among them were Drum and Gil, as well as

Carey from the office upstairs. Jennifer wheeled around to Drum.

"She has to go. Look at what she's done to my car."

Drum looked across at Cin. He knew it was the kind of prank she might have played on him or Tanner when she went through her early teens, but she hoped he would understand that she'd never dream of doing something like this now.

"Cin? Have you got anything to add?" he asked in a level tone.

"Of course you'll take her side," Jennifer spat. "Ever since she arrived you've been sniffing around her like she's a bitch in heat. She needs to go."

"Let Cin speak, Jennifer. We both know there are always at least two sides to every story."

Drum spoke calmly, but Cin could see the irritation in his gaze. Cin shifted on her feet, hating being the center of this kind of attention. Drum hadn't taken his gaze off her from the moment he'd arrived in the parking lot.

"I had nothing to do with it. I finished my day, came out here to get my bike and was getting ready to head home when she came out and accused me of letting her air out."

"She must have tampered with the valves when she checked my tires at lunchtime," Jennifer said with malice dripping from every word. "She's never liked me and was probably just waiting for an opportunity to get at me."

Cin blinked in surprise. Never liked her? That

was reaching. She'd never bothered to get to know Jennifer, but that was no crime. Besides, they were talking high-school era, not now as adults working for the same company.

"That's a serious allegation you're making, Jennifer. Cin, did you check her tires at lunchtime?"

"Yes, Jennifer came in and demanded that I do it," Cin said with a glare in Jennifer's direction. "The pressure on her two front tires was a little low, so I pumped them up. The back tires were fine. Then she left."

"And you didn't tamper with them?" he asked.

"Of course I didn't!" Cin was outraged that he felt he needed to ask.

Gil stepped forward. "I can vouch for Cin. I saw her do the pressure check, and we had lunch together straight after that. After lunch she returned to work and didn't leave the tire bay until just now."

"I expected you would support her. You're all a bit in love with her, aren't you? Hyacinth Sanderton. Blossom Springs's answer to everything. Well, I'm saying she risked my life and that of my children by tampering with my car."

"First, let's check those wheels," Drum said, and he bent down next to Jennifer's car.

Sure enough, the valves had been loosened. He called Gil over to confirm his findings, and Gil went back to the tire bay and retrieved a portable compressor and the tools to tighten the valves back up again.

"See! I told you what she did. She ought to be fired on the spot," Jennifer insisted.

"We can't be certain it was Cin," Drum said reasonably.

Cin felt a reluctant admiration that he hadn't automatically sided with her on the situation, which just would have inflamed things further, combined with a surge of relief that he wasn't accepting Jennifer's word at face value, either.

Drum continued. "However, we can review the security footage of the parking lot."

"S-security footage?" Jennifer asked, her voice not quite as strong as before.

"Yes. After a few staff reported thefts from their cars, we installed cameras. We didn't make it public knowledge for a variety of reasons. I'll make a call to our security-monitoring company."

"I'm sure that won't be necessary," Jennifer blustered. "There's only one person here who could be responsible for this vandalism, and she is standing right there!"

She thrust a shaking finger in Cin's direction. Cin had had enough. She'd tried to keep her voice reasonable throughout, but now anger threaded her every word.

"You and I both know that I had nothing to do with this."

"Cin, calm down. I've got this," Drum said firmly.

He gave her a hard look that left her in no doubt that he had her back, too. Just like he had that night at Curly's. He lifted his phone and made a call. "Yes, from midday, focus on any activity around a dark blue sedan in parking slot number six, and email it through to me, please."

The noise of the compressor just added to the strain everyone was obviously feeling as they stood around waiting for Drum to receive the security footage. Jennifer was beginning to look a little ill. Cin would have suggested someone find her a chair before she keeled over, but she reckoned any offer of assistance would be emphatically turned down. Carey sidled over to her.

"She's lost the plot, hasn't she?" Carey said.

Cin just shook her head. "I don't know why she's so mad at me. I didn't do what she's accusing me of."

"She's been unreasonable upstairs, too. Running to Drum over minor issues in the office. Complaining about everyone. So it's not just you."

"Somehow that doesn't exactly make me feel any better," Cin said with a twist of her lips. "Something is definitely upsetting her."

Gil had just finished working on Jennifer's tires when they heard Drum's phone ping to indicate an incoming message. They all looked at him as he held up his phone and studied the footage that had been sent to him. His face grew grim, and he cast Cin a brief look before stepping closer to Jennifer.

"You guys all need to head home," he said to Cin, Gil and Carey.

"But what about—" Jennifer began to protest.

"You and I will go back inside. We need to talk."

He sent another look in Cin's direction and gave her a small nod which she took to be a complete dismissal of the accusations that had been made against her. Without another word she climbed on her bike and wobbled her way out of the parking lot, her movements gaining more balance and surety as she gathered momentum.

She made it home without incident, but her butt certainly knew she'd been astride a bike. She decided to stow the bike in the shed next to the garage at the back of the house and then made her way inside. She'd just changed into a pair of jeans and a sheer long-sleeved blouse when she heard a car coming up the driveway. It was Drum, and he looked none too happy.

Cin felt a shiver of nerves run down her spine as she watched him get out from the car and walk toward the house. There was a sense of purpose in his stride, as if he was about to deliver some bad news and he'd decided the sooner he got it over with, the better. She swung the front door open and gestured for him to come inside.

"Would you like a coffee or something?" she asked as he followed her through to the kitchen.

"Or something," he said grimly.

"Whiskey?"

"Sure."

She went to the dining room and grabbed two Baccarat tumblers and sloshed a good measure of her father's twenty-one-year-old Scotch into each one. Drum had gone into the formal living room to sit down. She passed him his glass and sat opposite him, waiting patiently for him to speak, even though her mind was cluttered with all the questions she wanted to ask.

"Jennifer will be taking an extended leave of absence," he began.

"Is she going to be all right?" Cin asked immediately.

"I hope so. The footage showed her tampering with her own car, which was what I expected, to be honest."

"You knew I didn't do it. Might have been nice for you to have supported me at the time." She couldn't help it. She was a little bitter that he hadn't immediately said there was no way she could have been involved, especially when Gil had backed her up.

"I had to remain neutral. I hope you can respect that. It wasn't my first instinct, though, I can tell you that. For some reason Jennifer has a grudge against you. I noticed it at the staff drinks, and I've sensed it here and there in the office when you've come up in conversation."

Cin stiffened in her seat. "You were talking about me?"

He gave her a hard look. "Cin, you were pretty much a local celebrity when you left Blossom Springs, and now you're back, working for me. Of course people talk about you, but mostly good things.

Jennifer excepted, of course, and that had begun to bother me."

Slightly mollified, Cin took a sip of her whiskey, rolling the single malt around on her tongue before letting it slide down her throat. She realized that Drum was watching her intently, and color rushed to her cheeks.

"She hates you, Cin," he said bluntly.

"I know she dislikes me, but *hate*? That's a very strong word."

"I know, but it's true. Seems she's been harboring perceived injustices since elementary school, and having you join the Keyes team was the straw that broke the camel's back."

"Oh, surely not," Cin protested. "I haven't even lived here for the past twelve years. She can't blame me for her shitty attitude to people."

"No, it's not all down to how she feels about you. Turns out her husband left her last year and took custody of the kids, citing her erratic moods and behaviors at home that were potentially dangerous to their children. She's only allowed supervised visits."

Cin blew out a breath. "Wow, that's a kicker. And she hasn't sought help?"

"No, but I've insisted on it now. There's provision in the staff health plan for her to have a full assessment and treatment plan done. She just needs to want to do it. I can't force her. But I'm also not allowing her to work until she has taken action regarding her conduct and enters therapy. That sounds harsh, I know, especially when her job is about the only thing anchoring her at the moment. But I'm worried she could become dangerous if she becomes more unhinged."

"It's that bad?" Cin asked, shocked at what Drum was sharing with her.

"It sure could be, and I would never forgive myself if you were physically hurt as a result of that. Hopefully she'll take the aid that is offered to her."

"And if she doesn't?"

"I guess I'll have to dismiss her."

She could see he was between a rock and a hard place and that he hated that one of his staff, even if it was Jennifer, was in so much torment. Cin rose from her seat and went to sit next to him on the large sofa where he'd settled. She put a hand on his arm in comfort.

"You're a good man, Drummond Keyes," she said earnestly. "What can I do to help?"

He put his tumbler down on the coffee table in front of them and turned to her.

"I need you, Cin," he said simply.

His arms wrapped around her, and he lowered his face to hers, kissing her with a hunger that sent fire rushing through her veins. All day she'd thought about this very thing with this very man. And she'd told herself that last night had been an aberration. Something she dare not repeat because doing so would undo her on every emotional level she'd ever known. But here she was. About to be undone.

Twelve

Drum's fingers were at the buttons of her blouse, slowing undoing one after the other. She ought to stop him. Hadn't she promised herself this morning that last night would not be repeated? Once had been enough. In fact, it had been too much. It had shown her what she'd been missing all these years.

Drum had finished unbuttoning her blouse and pushed the garment off her shoulders. Now he bent his head to kiss the top of her breast gently—so gently that the touch of his lips was lighter than the caress of a butterfly. It made her skin become even more sensitive, more attuned to the warmth of his lips as he moved to kiss her lower and lower until he slid her bra straps down and pulled down the cup of her bra to expose the taut, aching bud of her nipple.

She moaned as he closed his lips around it, his tongue hot and wet and drawing the tip deeper into his mouth. The action sent a spear of heat and longing direct to her core, and suddenly she didn't want to think of all the reasons they shouldn't be doing this and only of the one reason they should. Need. Right now he needed her, and she would fulfill that demand with everything she had in her and, she realized to her chagrin, whenever and wherever he wanted to.

Cin was putty in his hands. He was her kryptonite and her rock at the same time. The juxtaposition of that truth wasn't lost on her. It had always been that way for her when it came to Drum. She reached behind her back and unsnapped her bra, frustrated by what was left of the barrier between her skin and Drum's extremely talented mouth. She shifted so she was straddling his lap, and she deftly unknotted his tie and slowly slid it free of his collar before unbuttoning his shirt and yanking the fabric from the waistband of his pants.

She ran her hands over his shoulders, loving the sensation of her palms against his heated skin. Her hands drifted lower, her fingers skimming his nipples and felt him shiver as she lightly pinched them between her fingertips. Cin arched her back as he transferred his attention from one breast to the other, her pelvis rocking against his. He was hard for her, and she ached to have him inside her again, but first she wanted to touch and taste him, to remind herself that their exploration of one another last night had been no aberration.

She shifted so that she could begin to unbuckle his belt and release his length from his pants. It meant she had to relinquish the delicious sensation of his mouth on her, but it would only be momentary before they were intimately connected once more. Drum lifted his hips so she could drag down his trousers and briefs. She pulled off his shoes and socks then finished removing his lower clothing. All he had on now was his crisp white business shirt, unbuttoned and spread wide, exposing his chest, his stomach and now his proud erection, too.

Cin knelt before him, her long fingers wrapping around his length. He was steel and silk and heat all in one delectably hard package. She looked up at him, seeing the glaze of desire in his eyes, which were more green than blue right now. Was that what lust did to him? She'd have to make a note of that if they were going to keep doing this going forward. It was his tell.

And then, pushing all thoughts to the back of her mind, she lowered her mouth to the tip of his penis. Her tongue darting out to flick tiny caresses over the smooth, shiny skin. Drum's hands tangled in her hair, holding her back from taking him fully into her mouth.

"Are you sure?" he asked when she looked up at him in again in inquiry.

"Never more so," she answered, her voice husky. "Now, let me get to doing what I've been thinking about all day."

"All day, huh?"

"Well, most of it," she admitted with a grin.

"Far be it from me to hold you back."

And he didn't. She took him in her mouth, the fingers of one hand wrapping around his length and she took her time—licking, sucking, stroking—until his entire body went rigid and his climax shuddered through him, and she knew he was totally and utterly undone. Afterward, she stood and stripped off the rest of her clothes and straddled him again. Pressing kisses against his face, his lips, his neck, his shoulders. Gently stroking his arms, his back—wherever she could reach, until she felt his length come to life again beneath her.

Drum's hands were at her waist, his fingers firm and strong.

"Pass me my pants?" he said in a voice that was thick with desire.

Cin gave him a cheeky smile then literally bent over backward while he held her in place. She grabbed his trousers and pulled herself back up again. Drum's gaze was fixed at the juncture of her thighs, at the tempting sweetness she'd exposed to him when she'd flipped over.

"That was quite a view," he commented as he took

the trousers from her and drew out his wallet and eventually a condom.

"Did you enjoy it?" she asked with another grin.

"Oh yes, but I think we'll both enjoy this more."

He swiftly sheathed himself with the condom and shifted on the couch to position her beneath him. He was hot and heavy as he settled between her thighs and she tilted her pelvis to accept him. She felt his blunt tip nudging at her folds and shifted a little more, just so, until she felt him at the entrance to her body. He slid into her, slow and deep, waiting a few seconds before withdrawing and sliding deep inside once more.

She lost track of any sense of time as he prolonged each stroke and focused only on the spiraling sensation that was building in her from somewhere deep inside. He picked up the tempo, and the spiral grew tighter, driving her closer and closer to orgasm until in a perfect moment she went soaring over the edge, her body locked around his, as wave after intensifying wave of pleasure crashed through her, leaving her trembling and weak beneath him.

Another stroke and he stiffened, cried out and plunged even deeper as his climax hit, and once again she was transported into surprising, blissful oblivion, her entire body pulsing on a level of satisfaction she'd never experienced so strongly before. Cin wrapped her arms around Drum's waist as tight as she could hold him, as if by doing so she wouldn't float away, and the sensation of his skin against hers only made her satisfaction all the sweeter.

* * *

Drum supported himself on his forearms so he wouldn't crush her but allowed his forehead to drop softly against hers. He was shaken by the power of their lovemaking. It had transcended anything he'd ever known before, even last night, their first night together. How had he made it through life this long without knowing what sex could be like with the right person? Sure, it had never been bad, but this... this beat all and then some.

When he could find his voice he asked, "Are you okay? I'm not too heavy am I?"

"*Okay* is an understatement," she said softly before lifting her chin and pressing her lips to his. "How can it keep getting better?"

"I know, right?"

They lay together a few minutes longer, but then he withdrew from her, knowing he had to get rid of the condom before it did something stupid like fall off and land on her mom's hand-knotted Persian rug. He got up and walked naked to one of the downstairs powder rooms. Cin was still sprawled, equally naked, on the couch when he returned. She got up as he drew closer.

"Can you stay tonight?" she asked.

"How about we go out for dinner and then you come back to my place?" he countered. "You could pack an overnight bag."

Her stomach grumbled, and they both burst out laughing.

"Well, something to eat is a definite," Cin said on a laugh. "So yeah, I'd like that. But not in town, if that's okay with you. I don't want everyone to know we're…" She couldn't quite find the right words to describe their relationship.

"*We're together*? Is that what you're looking for? Sure, I'm happy to take you out of town. Go upstairs and put on something gorgeous," he suggested. "I'll be okay in my suit."

"Do you want to come upstairs and take a quick shower?" she offered.

"With you?"

"Well, of course, but you can use one of the other bathrooms if you prefer."

"I think I'd better do that," he replied ruefully. "Otherwise, we might never make it to dinner."

She pouted but could see his point. "Come on, then. You can use the bathroom off Tanner's old bedroom. You know where to find it, right?"

"Sure."

They gathered up their clothing and went upstairs, and Cin gave him a long lingering kiss as they reached the landing before heading toward her bedroom. Drum watched her walk away. She had always had an incredible grace about her movements, and naked it was as if that grace was multiplied a thousandfold. He couldn't take his eyes from her, and a specific part of his anatomy gave him a solid nudge to follow her and see just how inventive they could get in that shower of hers. But Drum resolutely turned and headed to her brother's old bedroom and straight into the shower.

He was waiting downstairs when he caught a movement up on the landing. He looked up and saw Cin begin to descend the stairs. He'd said to put on something gorgeous, but he hadn't been expecting this. She was a vision in a shimmering coral-pink cocktail dress that skimmed her thighs. She'd teamed that with a stunning pair of jeweled high heels that, combined with the high hemline of her dress, made her legs look a mile long. Legs that had not so long ago been wrapped around him as they'd made love, he thought with a breathtaking surge of remembrance. But what really turned him on was the overnight bag she'd obviously packed to bring with her. It meant she was coming to stay at his house, and for some reason that felt like the biggest gift of all.

"Wow," he said with true appreciation as she reached the bottom of the stairs and he reached to take the overnight bag from her.

"Exactly the reaction I was hoping for," she answered with a smile that made her blue eyes sparkle.

She was more than *wow*: she was breathtakingly beautiful, and he was torn between wanting to take her out and show her off and taking her back upstairs to bed and keeping her there until they wearied of one another. Although, he didn't think wearying of her was likely to happen. Not with the way he felt about her. Thing is, he wondered, how did she feel about him? Yes, she had willingly made love with him, but how deep were her feelings for him now? Would they be enough to make her stay? He'd just have to wait and see, he told himself as he offered her his arm and led her out the front door.

They were just about to get into his SUV when they saw a car approaching down the driveway. It was being steered somewhat erratically, and a little fast. Drum automatically stepped in front of Cin as the car drew to a halt in the turning bay.

"Jennifer? What on earth?" Cin said, moving out from behind him as Jennifer got out of her car.

His HR manager looked terrible. Her usually neat hair was falling loose of its bun, and her clothing hung askew from her shoulders. Her feet were bare, and she looked none too steady on them, either.

"Jennifer, what are you doing?" Drum said, firmly. "You were supposed to be at home, resting."

"I came to apologize to Hyacinth," she said, her voice slightly slurred. "But now I see she's busy, I'll just make my way back home again."

"You can still make your apology, if you genuinely mean it," Drum replied.

"Oh, we both know I wouldn't have meant it, anyway. What are you doing here? Giving poor old Cin a shoulder to cry on? Where's my shoulder? Haven't I done enough to warrant your care and attention?" Jennifer's voice rose hysterically. "Or am I just not enough of a whore for you?"

With that question hanging heavily in the air between them, she got back in her car and slammed the door closed.

Drum covered the distance to her car in record time. He tried to pull her door open, but she'd already locked it. He tapped on the window.

"Jennifer, unlock the door, please. You're in no state to drive."

But she didn't. Instead, she put her car in gear and planted her foot on the accelerator. Her car lurched forward. Cin took a few steps back so she'd be behind Drum's SUV and Jennifer's sedan raced past her with inches to spare. The mood the woman was in now it was clear she wouldn't have cared if she'd hit Cin or not, and he was filled with fury at the risk Jennifer had exposed Cin to.

Drum snatched his mobile phone from his pocket and dialed emergency services and gave the details of Jennifer's car and her whereabouts.

"Yes, I'm concerned she's unsafe right now, to herself and to others." He paused while the dispatcher spoke confirming the details he'd given. "Yes, that's right. Thank you."

The call made, he hurried to Cin's side. She was pale, but steady on her feet.

"Are you okay?" he asked, running his hands up and down her bare arms.

Her skin was cold to the touch, and she trembled slightly.

"I'm fine. At least I will be in a minute. Poor Jennifer, she's really lost it, hasn't she? I can't help but feel responsible in some way. I seem to trigger her."

"That is not your fault. Hopefully the police will stop her before she harms someone, and she'll have a night to cool off and get herself in order." He pulled Cin into his arms. "I can't believe she drove right at you."

"I saw she meant to hurt me. She's seriously pissed at me. And Drum, I don't believe for a minute that she came here to apologize. That was just a convenient excuse. I don't know what she expected in coming, but I know that seeing you here with me changed whatever she had planned."

"You're right. Cin, look, I might be overdramatizing things, but I don't think you're safe out here on your own with no immediate neighbors—not with her in that state. I want you to move in with me until things settle down with Jennifer."

"Seriously? You really think that's necessary?"

He looked at her grimly. "Yeah, unfortunately, I do. You might need to pack a bigger bag."

"Not now, Drum, please. Let's leave it for tonight and not let her spoil our evening."

"Are you sure?"

"One hundred percent," she said firmly before kissing him equally firmly on his lips. "Now, weren't you taking me out for dinner?"

Cin watched Drum from across the dinner table. He hadn't just taken her out of town, he'd taken her to the local small airport and had them flown in a charter helicopter to the coast where a car had collected them and driven them to one of the top seafood restaurants in Ventura. She felt as if he was trying to impress her, but surely he knew he didn't need to do that? As much as she was trying to keep him at arms' length, he was invading the nooks and crannies of her heart, nonetheless. She closed her eyes a moment and tried to ignore the twist of pain in her chest at the thought. She couldn't let him back in. Her obsession with him as a child and teenager had been her measure for anyone else. So much so she'd been incapable of truly giving herself to any relationship.

She knew Drum wasn't in love with her. He'd spent most of her life keeping her at a distance while still making sure she didn't get into trouble. Sure, they were lovers right now, but that alone didn't make a commitment. It was just sex—great sex, yes, but not a meaningful connection based on mutual love and respect. Should she take what she could get for now? But what about when Drum eventually turned away in search of the woman he could love forevermore? Could she bear to witness it?

By the time they flew home, she was feeling spent both physically and emotionally. They completed the drive to Drum's home in the hills just outside of town in near silence. Giant gates swung silently open as they entered his driveway, and they continued up the hill to a single-level dwelling that looked, in the dark, as if it was part of the landscape.

"Home sweet home," Drum said as they parked in a multicar garage and exited his SUV.

He grabbed her overnight bag from the trunk and, with a hand at the small of her back, guided her into the house. Everything around them was top specification, from the subdued low lights that lit the slate-tiled hallway from the garage to the master suite he showed her into, which overlooked a softly lit swimming pool surrounded by tropical garden plantings.

"Did you want to see the rest of the house?" he said.

She could see he was eager as a child with a new toy about showing her around, but she was absolutely shattered.

"Do you mind if I take a rain check on that until morning? It's been a heck of a day."

Understanding flooded his eyes. "Tomorrow's soon enough, especially if you'll be staying here awhile."

"About that—" she started to protest, but Drum interrupted firmly.

"Again, something we can leave until tomorrow. Why don't you get ready for bed? The bathroom is right through there."

Cin grabbed her overnight case and extracted a nightgown and her toilet bag and did as he suggested. By the time she returned to the bedroom she was drooping. Drum was dressed in pajama pants that slung low on his waist. She wasn't so tired that she couldn't appreciate how gorgeous he looked in them, but she was far too exhausted now to do anything about it. Drum had turned the lights down low and closed the drapes to the windows that looked out over the pool, making the room feel like a cozy cocoon. She slid under the bedcovers and curled up on her side. She heard Drum leave the bathroom and walk softly over the thickly carpeted floor to the bed and felt the depression of the mattress as he slid in behind her. He hooked an arm around her waist and pulled her firmly against him and pressed a kiss against the back of her neck.

"Good night, Cin. I'm glad you're here with me. Sleep well."

He was asleep within seconds, his breathing deep and steady. Despite her weariness, she found it hard to do the same. Her mind kept turning over the events of the day, and for the life of her she could not figure out why Jennifer Green had targeted her so viciously, unless what Gil had said about her having a crush on Drum was true. But then again, Jennifer had married and had kids and gotten on with her life. *As did you,* the voice inside her head reminded her. *And did you ever stop loving him?*

The emphatic *no* reverberated through her. Maybe it was the same for the distraught woman who'd almost run her down tonight. Drum did have that effect on people. He drew them in, he made them feel important and cared for. But did he love? Cin really didn't know, and she was wary of losing herself in loving him all over again.

Thirteen

"What the hell are you doing sleeping with my sister!"

Drum struggled from sleep and forced his eyes open only to see his utterly furious best friend standing in the doorway to his bedroom. Tanner in fatigues, bristling with anger, was a very dangerous sight. In his arms, Cin stirred and stretched before opening her eyes and half sitting up.

"Tanner? What are you doing here? I thought you were away on an exercise."

"I'm asking you the same thing, although I have a pretty good idea of what exercise you've been doing."

Drum rose from the bed and placed himself between brother and sister.

"Tanner, that was out of line."

"Out of line? You have to be kidding me. We had a pact."

With that, Tanner threw a fist that caught Drum neatly on the edge of his jaw. He took it without stumbling and kept his own hands firmly at his side.

"I'll give you that one, Tanner, but that's it. No more free punches."

"I should beat you to a pulp," Tanner growled.

"I'd like to see you try," Drum returned just as aggressively. He was prepared to accept that one punch from Tanner because he had broken their pact, but that's where it began and ended.

"Hang on a minute. *Pact*? What *pact*? And what business is it of yours who I sleep with, anyway?" Cin slipped from the bed and stood staring from her brother to him and back again. Neither man spoke. That she was getting pissed was really clear when she asked again. "I said, what pact?"

Drum looked at Tanner, but he was staring at his sister with his mouth firmly closed. Which left the explanation to him, dammit.

"We had an agreement from when we were in our early teens," Drum started before stopping again, somewhat lost for words.

"Yes?" Cin said, crossing her arms firmly.

With her shoulder-length blond hair tousled from sleep and no makeup on, she looked so deliciously sexy, and all he really wanted to do was swoop her up in his arms and take her back to bed and this time they wouldn't be sleeping. But that sure wasn't about to happen with her brother in the vicinity. Drum drew in a deep breath and explained.

"It's a guy thing."

"A guy thing?" Cin was really starting to look mad. "Like, something little old *female* me wouldn't understand?"

"No, not that," he protested. Shit, he was really messing this up.

"How about you tell me exactly what, then?" she demanded.

"We had an agreement that we wouldn't…y'know… with each other's sister."

"Wouldn't what? Go out? Kiss? Have sex?" Cin's voice rose with each question.

"Yeah, all of the above."

"And that's why you turned me down when I ask you to be my first lover?"

"Say what?" Tanner interjected. "You did *what*?"

"It's none of your business," Cin snapped. "You don't have any say over my life any more than I do over yours, soldier."

She turned to Drum again, and he found himself choosing his words carefully. He had no desire to destroy a friendship of twenty-four years, but equally he had no interest in shattering the fragile relationship he was creating with Cin, either. That Tanner and Cin were brother and sister just added another whole level of difficulty. He loved them both. Differently, of course, but to lose one or the other or, even worse, both would be shattering.

"There's no simple answer to that question," he said carefully. "I'd already left school, and you were on the verge of going to college. You still had so much to discover in your life. I didn't feel it would be right, even if Tanner and I hadn't made that stupid pact."

"Oh, so our pledge to one another is stupid now?" Tanner asked.

"Stay out of this!" Cin and Drum said simultaneously.

"So you're admitting that you found me attractive back then?" Cin asked with a glint of something he couldn't quite define in her eyes.

"Cin, seriously, anyone with a pulse thought you were attractive. In fact, with few exceptions, I'd say everyone still does."

She shook her head. "You're deliberately avoiding giving me the truth, Drum."

"Fine!" he said in frustration. "Yes, I thought you were attractive. Yes, if you had been anyone else's sister but Tanner's, I probably would have taken you up on your offer, even though I was two years older than you and you were on the verge of leaving town. But it was time for you to go and spread your wings. You didn't need anything to distract you from that.

"If you hadn't left, you'd eventually have become stifled here in Blossom Springs. Let's face it, it's hardly a bustling metropolis like LA. Besides, I knew what it was like to step aside from a dream. I didn't want that for you. From when you were sixteen, all you talked about was going to college, earning your marketing degree and going out and making your mark on the world."

"So you made the decision for me?" she said coldly.

"No, you made your decisions for yourself, un-clouded by any feelings you may have had for me."

"So it wasn't because of your *pact*?"

She said the word as if it tasted foul in her mouth.

"Well, yeah. That, too."

"I can't deal with this," she said in a shaky voice. "I'm out of here. You two deserve each other."

Drum watched as she turned and grabbed her overnight bag and stalked toward the bathroom, coming out a few minutes later dressed in her work uniform with her hair tied back. She marched straight up to Tanner.

"Give me your car keys," she demanded.

"I'll drive you," he said.

"No, you won't. I don't want to be in the same space as either of you."

To Drum's surprise, Tanner meekly handed over his keys. Cin snatched them out of his hand and stepped right up into his face.

"And don't think you can come and stay with me, either. You're not welcome."

A few seconds later she was gone. Drum looked at Tanner, who stared back at him before grimacing.

"For heaven's sake, Drum, go put some clothes on. I'll make coffee."

By the time Drum had showered and dressed for work, Tanner had made a strong brew and was sitting with a morose expression on his face at the breakfast table.

"I'm sorry, Tanner. I tried to resist her."

"You didn't try hard enough," his friend bounced back with a voice about as flat as Drum felt right now.

"I love her," he said simply.

It felt good to finally admit it to someone, even if it wasn't to the woman he loved.

"Yeah, I know."

"What?"

"I think I knew before Cin left for college, but I didn't want to think about you both in those terms. But I know for sure now. I just expected you guys would take a bit more time getting to know one another again before..." he waved a hand uselessly in the air in front of him "...y'know."

"So I have your blessing?"

Tanner snorted. "As if that would make a difference."

"Your friendship was everything to me growing up. I knew I came from the wrong side of town and that some kids looked down on my family because my dad was strictly blue collar. None of that mattered to you. So of course it would make a difference if I didn't have your blessing. You matter to me, Tanner.

You're part of the fabric of my life, but Cin is, too. She's my heart, my breath, my soul."

"You'd give her up if I said no?"

Drum felt his heart clench at the very idea. "I'd be prepared for our friendship to change, but there's no way I'm letting Cin walk away from me now. Not without telling her how I really feel about her."

"Good."

"You're okay with that?"

"Yeah, she deserves someone like you, Drum. Steadfast and prepared to make her the center of his world. Someone who'll love and adore and protect her. But most of all, someone who will let her be who she is. So we're good?"

Tanner offered Drum his hand, and Drum grasped it firmly in reply.

"Yeah, buddy. And I have to say, you're getting soft if that punch was any example."

They laughed, both knowing that Tanner hadn't held back. The ache in Drum's jaw would remind him for some time of how Tanner felt about finding him and Cin in bed together. Clearly the guy was going to have to learn to knock in future. Especially if Drum achieved his aim of getting Cin to agree to him being a permanent part of her life and not just as her brother's best friend, either.

Cin was still fuming when she arrived at work in Tanner's rental. The stick shift he always insisted on had tested her initially, but she wasn't Hyacinth

Sanderton for nothing. Drum had taught her to handle a stick when she was seventeen. He'd been the only person with the patience, she discovered after both her father and Tanner had given up on her. It was a stark reminder of just what a fixture he'd been in her world.

Anger rose anew. And he could have been more, if he hadn't stuck to that stupid pact. Who did that? Who suppressed any chance at happiness with someone purely because they were their best friend's sibling?

By the time she stomped into the tire bay and assumed her seat behind the reception window she had built up quite a head of steam. Gil and the boys took one look at her and focused on the job sheets at hand. When it came time for their morning break, Cin grabbed her coffee from the machine in the waiting area and took it back to her desk.

"Not taking a break today?" Gil said, popping his head into the office area.

"Nope."

"You know that Drum makes it clear all staff should take allocated breaks."

"I. Don't. Care."

"What's he gone and done to get you all riled up?" Gil said, coming into the office and leaning against the side of her desk. "I thought you were old family friends."

She expelled a short, sharp breath before turning her chair to face him.

"Tell me this, Gil. Is it normal for a man to make a promise with his best friend that he will never, under any circumstances, have feelings for—or act on them with—his best friend's sister?"

"Of course. It's a bro-code thing."

"You're kidding me."

"No one wants to imagine their buddy hitting on their sister. That's just wrong."

Cin rolled her eyes. "I can see anything I have to say on this subject is wasted on you."

"Is that what's got your back up today?"

Cin looked at him before allowing herself a swift nod. "But I don't want to talk about it. I'll work through my break and then take a slightly longer lunch, if that's okay with you."

"Sure, and if you change your mind and want to talk some more, I'm happy to be a sounding board."

"You're a good man, Gil. Your wife is lucky to have you," Cin said with genuine feeling as she turned her attention to the ringing phone.

She refused to let herself dwell on it while she was at work, but at lunchtime she decided to go for a walk. It was a beautiful early-fall day, and heaven only knew she needed to blow the cobwebs out of her mind. The whole time she walked, she turned things over in her head. Remembering all the times when she was younger that she'd all but thrown herself at Drum, only to have him gently turn her affection aside. He'd never been cruel: that wasn't his way. But in being the loyal friend he was to her brother, he'd ended up shaping her life in such a way that she hadn't been able to move forward, either.

That was on her; she understood that absolutely, but how different would her life have been if he'd allowed himself to love her? She'd like to think she'd still have gone to college and achieved her degree with honors. She'd always been driven like that. And she could happily have applied what she'd learned back here in Blossom Springs. Yes, she knew she'd said she would never live here in Blossom Springs again, once she'd graduated high school. But part of that had been hurt and a desire to somehow shake Drum's equilibrium. He'd refused what she'd seen as the only thing she could give him—herself—and that had stung.

Pretty much every adult decision she'd made after that had been with him in mind. Showing him she could be mature and complete her degree. Proving she could make it in a city like LA which was as far removed from Blossom Springs as diamonds were from gravel. But in the end, none of it had made any difference. She'd ended up making mistakes—big ones—emotionally and financially and now here she was, back at square one in a far worse position than when she'd left twelve years ago.

She stopped walking a moment, clenched her hands into fists and closed her eyes before letting out a scream that disturbed the birds settled in a nearby tree and earned her several concerned looks from passersby. She forced herself to smile in return—that was something at least that she knew she was good at. Faking it. She'd faked it through her entire marriage to Mark, feigning feelings that she was far from invested in.

Well, she told herself, it was time to put on her big-girl panties and take absolute charge of herself and her life, without Drum. As soon as she could, she'd find another job. Heck, it didn't even have to be in Blossom Springs. She had no ties here, aside from her parents' home, and she had to admit, she'd been dreaming to imagine that she could restore it with no money and no real prospects of earning the kind of cash that would be needed.

Maybe Tanner would agree with her that it was time to wind up the trust that their daddy had set up and let the house go before it became impossible to sell. She made a mental note to discuss that with him after she finished work. If he was staying a while, that was. She'd been so mad at both him and Drum that she hadn't even found out how long he was back for.

She was just about to turn into the driveway at Keyes Tires when she felt a vibration in her pocket. Her cell phone, which had been mostly unused since her return home, announced a call. She didn't recognize the number, and wary that it might be Jennifer calling to offer her more abuse, she declined it. A few seconds later when she got in to work, it rang again. She stood there holding it, trying to decipher who might be calling. This time she recognized the area code as one from LA. Hesitantly, Cin answered the call.

"Hello, this is Cin Sanderton."

"This is Officer Clint Gardner from West Traffic Division. I'm looking for a Hyacinth Donnelly. Would that be you, ma'am?"

The voice at the other end was male, older and had the rough edge of too many cigars and late-night whiskeys behind it.

"Yes, that was my married name," she said cautiously.

"I'm glad to have reached you, but I'm afraid I have some bad news to impart. You were married to Mark Donnelly?" he asked.

"Yes."

"I would normally do this in person, ma'am, but as we've been able to find no other next of kin, I'm required to phone you."

What? Had he said *next of kin*?

"Is Mark okay?" she asked breathlessly.

"I regret to inform you Mr. Donnelly died last week after his car ran off the road in the Hollywood Hills. As I said we've been unable to find any other family to notify. His lawyer gave us your number."

"I see," she managed to say through lips that now felt rubbery and uncooperative. "Was there…was there anything suspicious about the circumstances of his death?"

She had to ask. In the final months before their divorce had been finalized, Mark had become intensely dramatic and tried to use emotional blackmail to get Cin to withdraw from the dissolution. She'd never believed for a minute that he might have followed through.

"No, ma'am. A witness saw him swerve to avoid a loose dog on the road. He lost control and went through the barrier arm. I'm very sorry for your loss."

"Th-thank you. Is there anything I need to do?"

"Now we've located you, his lawyer will no doubt be in touch. I understand there are some matters that need to be finalized, including the release of his remains."

Cin blinked back the sudden sting of tears. Mark had no immediate family to claim him and was completely estranged from his only cousin and uncle. He deserved better than to be given a send off by total strangers. She might have been the wrong wife for him, but she would see to it that he had a respectful and dignified goodbye. She'd borrow money from Tanner if she had to, but right now her priority was to get back to LA and take care of Mark. She owed him at least that.

Drum had waited all day, barely capable of focusing on his work, before checking on Cin downstairs. But when he entered the tire bay, she wasn't at her usual post.

"Is Cin on a break?" he asked one of the tire technicians who was nearby.

"No, she left after lunch. Some family emergency."

Drum felt his brows draw together in a knot. A family emergency? Tanner?

"Thanks," he said abruptly before grabbing his phone and dialing Tanner's number.

"Yeah, buddy. What's up?" Tanner answered.

Drum fought his relief that Tanner sounded fine, but that didn't answer the question as to Cin's whereabouts. "Cin's not here at work. Is she with you?"

"No. I thought you knew. She rang me and said something about going to LA urgently. Something to do with her ex. I loaned her my rental, but I'm not sure how long it'll be before she's back. She sounded upset."

"She was upset when she left us this morning."

"This was different. She was mad at us and, after thinking about it all day, rightly so. I tried to press her for details, but she said she had to go and thanked me for the car. I haven't heard from her since, and with her driving to LA, I didn't want to distract her with another phone call."

"Do you know where she's staying?"

"I don't, although since she referred to her ex, maybe she's staying with him."

Drum felt as if someone had speared him right through the chest. He'd wondered if Cin still had feelings for her ex. If she did, that would stand in the way of the two of them taking their relationship further. This was clearly the answer he *hadn't* been seeking. One phone call had been all it had taken for Cin to hightail it back to the city to be with him.

He felt like a total fool.

"Right," Drum finally answered. "Say, do you want to go to Curly's tonight? I could really do with a drink." Or several, he tacked on silently. They could always get a cab home.

"Sure, except I have no transport. Are you planning to pick me up?"

"If that's what it takes to have my drinking buddy, then, that's what I'll do."

Tanner laughed. "That's so you, Drum. Always there for everyone else. Thanks, buddy."

Drum disconnected the call and tried to ignore the ache that felt like a gaping hole inside him. She'd gone to her ex. She hadn't even told him her plans. Right now, he had no idea if she'd be back or not.

While he'd known that the reception role was way beneath the pay grade Cin was used to, he'd really loved the idea of her being nearby and of being able to see her daily if he wanted to. And he did want to. Daily and nightly, if it came to that. He'd hoped after last night that that was the direction they'd been moving in. But now he had no idea where he stood with her. Sure, he could have blamed Tanner for barging in on them this morning, but all that had done was bring the truth to the forefront. At some stage, Drum would have had to have told Cin about the pact and then told Tanner he'd broken it. And he knew, in his heart of hearts, that while she was furiously angry with both of them this morning, that anger would have burned out eventually. At least, he'd hoped it would.

But with the specter of her ex still hanging in the balance and the fact that with one phone call she'd gone racing back to him, Drum had to face the possibility that he'd been completely off the mark with Cin becoming open to building a future with him. There wasn't a great deal he could do about it now. Yes, he could phone her, but would she welcome a call from him while she was with someone else? No, he would wait for her to return. He wouldn't like it, not for one minute, but short of cavalierly going to LA and trying to track her down—which was pretty much the definition of impossible in a city of that size—he had no other option.

He just hoped she'd stay in touch with Tanner so he'd at least have some idea that she was okay. He was reminded that she'd hardly been able to restrain her excitement at the prospect of leaving Blossom Springs twelve years ago and how, after her parents' deaths, she'd openly admitted she never wanted to return. He'd never presumed to cage the bright and beautiful butterfly she'd been at eighteen. Someone just beginning to unfurl her wings and test them against the world. And he certainly wouldn't now, even if it made the prospect of the future a dark and empty place without her in it.

Fourteen

Cin pulled up outside her parents' old home, exhaustion pulling at every part of her body. She'd been gone only four days, but it felt like four weeks.

Mark's lawyer had arranged cheap accommodation for her while she sorted the last of her ex's affairs. There hadn't been much, but to her surprise she'd received a small windfall through an accidental-death insurance policy he'd taken out which named her as sole beneficiary. She'd had no idea about it and had told the lawyer that the money would be better held and distributed to any further debtors that might yet come out of the woodwork. But the lawyer had explained that Mark had insisted on her remaining his beneficiary even after their divorce, saying he owed it to her. The money was hers to do with what she wanted.

She looked up at the big old house. There was so much she could do with that money here. But did she want to anymore? She'd wondered if going back to LA would feel like returning home, but instead it had been the opposite. The traffic, the noise, the busyness of the city that she'd once thrived in were now little more than irritants. It had become a world unfamiliar to her, and while she might once upon a time have relished conquering that world, now all she craved was the old familiarity and gentle pace of Blossom Springs.

Try as she might, she still couldn't stop questioning whether or not his car wreck was an accident or not. Yes, a witness had reported a dog on the road, but Cin knew Mark had been in a dark place, and she still blamed herself for that. Accepting he was gone now had come with the delivery of his cremated remains and a written wish in his will that they be scattered on the coast north of Malibu, off a point where they used to go and watch the sunsets in the early stages of their relationship. She'd observed his wishes, alone. Not a single soul that they used to work with had been prepared to accompany her nor any of their old so-called friends. So she'd said her goodbyes and scattered his ashes as he'd requested before getting in Tanner's rental and driving back to Blossom Springs.

The drive shouldn't have taken more than two hours, but construction on the interstate and an accident on the road between Ventura and home had caused delays which left her tense and worn out. Right now, all she wanted was a hot shower and then her bed.

She got out of her car, grabbed the small case she'd packed for the trip and started for the front stairs. She jumped as she saw a dark shadow unfold from the porch swing, and her heart hammered in her chest.

"Cin, are you okay?" Drum's voice reached out through the darkening night.

"I'm fine. Tired is all."

He came down the stairs. "Can I carry your bag for you?"

"No, I have it, I can manage. I didn't see your car. You startled me."

"I got Tanner to drop me off when he told me you were coming home today. He wanted to go visit with some old friends so suggested I take his car back to my place."

She forced a strained smile to her face. "Sounds like you two have it all sussed. Just like old times, huh?"

He obviously heard the tension in her voice, and she heard him sigh.

"I wasn't sure you'd be back."

"I wasn't sure I wanted to come back," she admitted. "But I don't belong there anymore. Although I'm not sure I belong here, either." Saying the words out loud was scary and made her feel insecure. "Anyway, I'm tired and I'm going to bed. Alone," she said firmly. "I'll be at work tomorrow."

She held Tanner's keys up, dangling them in front of her. He took them but not without some reluctance, she thought. What had he expected? That she'd welcome him inside with open arms?

"Good night, Drum," she said firmly again and started up the front stairs.

"Cin, about work," he started.

She turned sharply. "What about it. Am I fired?"

"Not exactly."

"What does that mean?"

"When you come in tomorrow, come into my office first. Unless you'd like me to pick you up and take you in?"

"Is this about me leaving without notice? It was an emergency."

"No it's not that, although I do feel that I'm due an explanation."

"Not now, though," she said.

"No, not now."

"And not in your office, either," she stated firmly. There was no way she was having a personal discussion with Drum at work.

"Then, where would you suggest?"

Cin thought for a moment. "Here, tomorrow evening, after work."

"Okay, I can do that."

"And the other thing? Do you still need me to come to your office?"

"Yeah, and the offer of a ride tomorrow still stands."

"No, I'll ride my bike."

He nodded and despite the fact there was nothing more to say between them right now, she could see he was reluctant to leave.

"Good night, Drum," she said again and walked past him and up the stairs.

He didn't reply, and after she'd gone inside and shut the door she waited. It was awhile before she heard his footsteps and then the car door slam before the vehicle drove away.

The next morning she put on her uniform and rode her bike to work, chaining it to the fence as she usually did. Gil was glad to see her when she entered the tire bay.

"Welcome back. I hope we haven't left your desk in too much of a mess," he said apologetically.

"No problem, Gil. I'm sorry I left you guys at such short notice."

She could see he wanted to talk, maybe to ask what it was that had driven her to leave so suddenly the other day, but she wasn't ready for that, with him or anyone else.

"The boss man asked to see me in his office. Will you be okay if I head up there now?"

"Sure, it's quiet this morning. See you when you get back."

Cin gave him a nod and headed up the stairs and along the hall to Drum's office. Carey looked up from the HR department and gave her a cheerful wave and a smile as she went through. She returned it automatically, and the smile was still on her face as she knocked on Drum's open door and went inside. He rose from behind his desk as she entered, and she was immediately struck by how imposing he looked in his suit. It reminded her of how far he'd come from the son of the guy who ran the small tire shop that used to be on these premises—and how far apart they were now.

His hair was impeccable, not a strand out of place. Not like when they'd made love and he'd been deliciously rumpled. It made her want to reach out and mess his hair some, but she couldn't do that, not while she was still mad at him and certainly not with everything that remained unsaid between them. Even so, seeing him now made everything inside her draw tight with anticipation. Her mind and her body were not exactly on the same wavelength. No matter how angry she was at him, her body still lit up with desire when she saw Drum.

"You asked me to come and see you?" she said.

"Yeah, thanks for coming straight in. Take a seat."

He looked aloof, not his usual style, she realized, and she felt a moment's trepidation that she was about to be reprimanded for taking off like she had the other day. But what he said next made her glad she was sitting down, because if she'd been standing she'd likely have plonked down straight on her butt in surprise.

"I want to offer you the head of marketing role for all of Keyes Tires. It would involve a creating a statewide campaign as well as designing individual curated campaigns for the branches in their own areas. You could either work from here or, if that's uncomfortable for you given our relationship, from another office or at home—wherever that might be. It's a large account, and I'm sure you'll find it challenging enough to fully occupy your time. You would report directly to me, and you would have a team of five underneath you, more later if you found you needed them."

He named a salary that made her eyebrows rise. It was far more than the salary she'd drawn from her business in LA.

"I didn't think you had any other roles available here. That the tire-bay receptionist was the only thing available." Anger flicked hot color in her cheeks as another thought occurred to her. "Was that some kind of test?"

"Calm down, Cin. It wasn't a test. It was an abuse of power, pure and simple."

"Whose? Yours?" she demanded, not ready to back down an inch.

"Jennifer's. Since her departure, several oversights have been brought to my attention, and I can only apologize for what happened with you."

"What if I want to stay in the tire bay?" Cin asked, determined not to make this easy for him. What he'd proposed was likely her dream job, but if it had been there all along, how come he hadn't known about it? "And what's going to happen to your current head of marketing? I understood the position was already filled."

"As it transpires, our current head was randomly promoted by Jennifer after the previous incumbent left unexpectedly. She's in over her head and came to me to say so after Jennifer was stood down. She'd be an excellent assistant to you as she already knows our systems and processes, but she lacks your experience and maturity in such a role. I'd really like you to consider it, Cin."

Cin turned the idea over in her mind. She knew Drum wanted an answer now, but she needed to take some time to think about it. She knew heading back to LA wasn't for her, but there was so much baggage here. She was staring at the biggest piece right now. Would they even be able to work together?

"I will consider it," she said carefully. "When do you need to know by?"

"As soon as practical, to be honest. Anna is floundering and needs guidance. I'm doing what I can, but marketing isn't my strength."

No, she thought. His strength was caring and loyalty to others. She knew that to the soles of her feet. He'd made it his life's goal to solve the problems of the people around him. Even Jennifer, whose behavior had been disgraceful toward Cin, was still within his purview of care. Drum had always been a problem-solver, the risk-management king. But it was his sense of honor and loyalty that had created this divide between them now.

The entire time she'd been in LA she'd been wondering how different all their lives could have been if not for that stupid pact. But conjecture over what might have been wouldn't get her through any of this. She still had so much to mentally unpack from her trip to LA and from the legacy that Mark had left her.

"Okay, give me a couple of days."

"And tonight?"

"Yes, we still need to talk. Especially in light of the job offer you've just made."

"What time do you want me over?"

"Seven will be okay."

"Can I bring anything?"

"No. See you tonight."

She had the distinct feeling he was stringing out their time together right now when all she wanted was distance. Cin got up, gave him a nod and walked out of his office. All the way back to her station she couldn't stop thinking about the prospect of taking over the marketing department. Her mind was already beginning to brim with ideas, making her feel as though she'd woken from a deep slumber and was ready to tackle the world.

The problem was, the world still contained the only man she'd ever loved, and aside from the fact that they had great sex together—okay, mind-blowing sex together—there had never been a single moment when Drum had said that she had his heart as well as his concern. Care was all well and good: she'd *cared* about Mark, but she hadn't loved him.

It had ruined them. And she knew, without doubt, that Drum's care, without love, would ruin her, too. She respected herself enough not to accept crumbs of what could be. She'd rather be alone the rest of her life than settle for less. But could she stay here in Blossom Springs, work directly with Drum and maybe have to watch him fall in love with someone else, marry them and start a family?

The thought alone drove a spear of pain deep into her chest. She couldn't do it.

The rest of the day went smoothly, even if she was mildly inattentive at times. Cin was relieved when it was time to pack up and leave for the day. The week stretched ahead but first she had to get through tonight. That meant getting some decent groceries in for dinner. She'd decided on something simple—bacon-wrapped boneless chicken thighs stuffed with herbed butter together with baked potatoes and salad. Even she couldn't mess that up. And she knew Drum would be appreciative even if she served a burned offering, because he was just geared that way. No judgment, no recriminations. It was his strength and his weakness.

If only she could have loved him less, she thought as she pedaled to the grocery store. She made her selections and bought a frozen dessert and whipped cream. If she served it in a fancy dish no one would ever know it was store-bought. As she reached the checkout, she felt a prickle of uneasiness at the back of her neck. As if someone was staring at her. She turned her head, and while she caught a glimpse of movement at the end of one of the aisles nearby, she didn't see anyone looking her way. Cin rubbed the back of her neck to rid herself of the sensation.

By the time she'd completed her purchases, packed them in her backpack and headed outside, she'd all but talked herself into believing she'd imagined it, and she completed her ride home without further incident. She stowed her bike in the shed and took her things through to the kitchen. After washing her hands, she prepped the meat and covered it before racing upstairs to shower quickly and dress for the evening. She fussed about before deciding what to wear. It wasn't a formal occasion, but she didn't think jeans and a T-shirt were appropriate, either. She settled on a midseason dress in an icy blue that matched her eyes. The dress had sleeves which came down to her elbows, and the tulip shape of the garment with its outside pockets at her hips was loose and comfortable. A set of chunky faux pearls at her neck jazzed it up a little. She slipped on a pair of nude ballet slippers and returned down the back stairs.

She had just walked into the kitchen when she became aware of a pungent odor. She checked the oven and stovetop. Not them, but something wasn't right. Cin went from room to room downstairs. The smell grew stronger as she approached the formal living room. Her eyes locked onto a fuel canister sitting open in the middle of her momma's favorite Persian carpet and sitting on the sofa behind it was Jennifer. In front of Jennifer, on the coffee table, sat a cigarette lighter. In horror, Cin realized the woman had doused herself in petrol along with the couch and the carpet. The implicit threat was abundantly and terrifyingly clear.

"Jennifer? How did you get in?"

"You really need to update your security. Although, after tonight, that won't be necessary."

"I beg your pardon?"

"And here I thought you were a clever woman. I said, after tonight, that won't be necessary."

Fear clutched like a fist in her chest, but Cin forced herself to remain steady. "And why would that be, Jennifer?"

"Because we'll be gone."

Jennifer said the words in a singsong voice, and Cin noticed that Jennifer's eyes were slightly glazed, as if she was under the influence of some substance.

"Where are we going?"

Jennifer laughed, but it was an ugly sound. "Well, I'm guessing you'll be going straight to hell where you belong."

Cin caught her breath. "Can we at least talk about this? I know you've been having troubles. Maybe I can help?" Cin asked, keeping her voice as level and friendly as she could.

Jennifer shook her head. "Don't go using all your fake sweet charm on me. I know you're a snake in the grass. I could see it when we were at school, and you're worse now. You just use the people around you. You never let anyone get close. Oh, except for Drum. You let him get close—too close. I saw you last week through the window. Saw you on your knees. Disgusting, perverted whore."

Cin felt the blood drain from her face. The night Jennifer nearly ran her over?

"You watched us?"

"I came to talk to you. I couldn't help but see you through the windows flaunting yourselves. I left, but I knew I had to say something, so I came back."

Cin didn't bother pointing out that no one was flaunting anything. They'd been in a private home on private property and had every right to be doing whatever they wanted without worrying about someone watching them. Instead she went for a calm and measured reply.

"I can see that Drum and I being together upsets you. I'm sorry for that."

"Stop it! I hate you! I've always hated you with your perfect skin, your natural blond hair, your friends, your family money. But that didn't last, did it?" She laughed again. "And I know about your husband. He killed himself, didn't he? Over you. What a waste. You weren't worth it."

"Mark died in an accident." It offended Cin that Jennifer could twist his death this way, even if she, too, had had cause to wonder if he'd chosen to go off the road. Jennifer was instinctively playing on

Cin's own fears, and Cin had to find the strength to fight back.

"Is that what you really believe?" Jennifer said with a cruel smile.

"Yes, it is," Cin answered firmly. More certain now than she had ever been.

She knew Mark hadn't been happy, but to take his own life… That didn't gel with the man she'd known. While she had worried if his unhappiness had been a motivator behind the crash, she realized now, faced with her own mortality, that nothing could be further from the truth. After their divorce, Mark had wanted to live his best life. As she did now. But to do that she needed to get Jennifer to move away from the lighter.

"Jennifer, I'm really sorry for hurting you," she said with sincerity. "It wasn't deliberate, but I can see that I've done you wrong. How can I make it right?"

"Oh, very good. You always did know what to say," Jennifer jeered. "You barely even saw me at school. I didn't exist in your sphere. Well, I exist now. And maybe when you're gone, Drum will realize it should always have been me for him. Not you—never you, you shallow bitch."

Jennifer reached forward and grabbed the lighter.

Fifteen

"No! Jennifer, don't do it!" Cin cried out.

Before she could move, a figure shot across the room from behind her. Jennifer looked up in shock as Drum barreled toward her, and she frantically tried to flick the lighter, but the child-safety switch was on, and she couldn't get it to work.

"Cin, stay back!" Drum yelled as he tackled Jennifer to the floor.

But Drum was in immediate danger. Cin couldn't bear the thought that Jennifer might yet manage to get the lighter to work, and she raced forward and, putting her foot across Jennifer's wrist, bent down and peeled the lighter from the other woman's fingers. Jennifer screamed continuously as Drum pinned her body to the floor. Outside, Cin saw the flashing lights of approaching police and fire-rescue vehicles racing down her driveway.

In seconds the room was full of emergency personnel, and Cin was being led away. She looked back in time to see Jennifer cuffed and dragged to her feet by two police officers.

"Bitch! Whore!" Jennifer yelled in her direction.

"Step outside please, miss. It's not safe here. We need to secure the scene," a firefighter in full gear said to Cin blocking her from getting to Drum.

The scene? This was her house. Her family home. And yet now it was the scene of an attempted arson and worse. She heard the firefighters work their way through the house, opening doors and windows to air out the fumes. Cin began to shake. Someone put a blanket around her shoulders and settled her in the gazebo in the garden, well away from the house, around which a cordon had been created. She sat there, numb with shock, a police officer sitting with her for company.

"Why are they doing that?" Cin asked indicating the firefighter setting up the cordon.

"Gasoline is more volatile than a lot of people realize," the officer said. "They'll be checking the house for flammable vapors with a multimeter, making sure it's safe. Your power and gas will have been turned off, too, to avoid any surprises."

Cin was glad to hear it. She'd had quite enough surprises for one day.

On the other side of the garden, the fire department set up a decontamination shower. A protesting Jennifer was taken through it, before being bundled up in blankets and taken away in a squad car. Drum was next. He'd shed his clothes and stood there only in his briefs as the cold water sluiced his body. A body she had quickly come to know as intimately as her own. A shudder went through her at the memory of what Jennifer had tried to do and how close she'd come to taking Drum with her.

Cin felt as though she was a spectator to some crazy movie. This wasn't her life, surely? How had things degenerated to this? A familiar car drew up at the end of the driveway and her brother got out. Cin rose unsteadily to her feet and watched as Tanner had a quick word with Drum then looked around. Finding her, he ran toward the gazebo and was with her in seconds. As soon as he put his arms around her, she turned in to her big brother's strong chest and began to cry. It was several minutes before she calmed.

"You talked to Drum? Is he okay?" she asked as she pulled free of Tanner's arms.

"He's fine. Just cold and wet. I told him to help himself to clothes from my pack in the trunk of my car. The important thing is how are you?"

"I… I'm okay. A bit shaken, but I'm more worried about Drum. He took her down, Tanner. She'd have killed us, otherwise."

Tanner's arms tightened a moment before he released her again. "I'm so glad it didn't come to that. Do you want me to see where Drum is?"

"Please. I need to know he's okay."

"I'll be right back."

She watched as Tanner's demeanor transformed from caring older brother to full on military man. He marched to the edge of the cordon to find whoever was in charge. Cin settled back in the gazebo, grateful for the warmth of the blanket and wondering when she'd be permitted back inside. She worried, too, for Jennifer. Cin doubted the poor woman had even understood what she'd been on the verge of doing. She hoped that Jennifer would get the help she so desperately needed.

A movement near the emergency vehicles caught her attention. Cin felt her heart begin to race as she recognized Drum's tall figure, dressed in a pair of Tanner's sweatpants and a T-shirt, jogging toward her. He settled on the seat next to her and pulled her into his arms. He still smelled faintly of gasoline, but Cin didn't care. She was just relieved he was here and okay.

"That had to be the scariest moment of my life! I thought she was going to kill you. Are you all right?" He ran his hands over her shoulders and arms and studied her face intently.

Cin could only nod.

"I was asked to give my statement, or I'd have been with you sooner," he said quietly as he pressed a kiss against the top of her head.

"Is Jennifer going to be okay?"

"I hope so. I'm told she'll be assessed at a secure facility this time. Apparently she checked herself out of the last place, which brought us to this. I can't help but feel responsible."

"No, Drum! Don't you dare take this on your shoulders. It was not your fault in any way at all. You saved us all! Are *you* okay? That was quite a tackle you made there," Cin said.

"I might have a few bruises, but I'll be fine."

He sat there holding her for a while longer, clearly not wanting to talk. Cin was happy to oblige. This evening certainly hadn't turned out how she'd expected. After a few minutes, Tanner joined them.

"Drum, I'm sorry to have to leave you with this, but I've been called back to base. I've contacted our insurance, and they're sending an inspector who will no doubt make a recommendation regarding getting an emergency cleaning company, but the earliest they can come will be tomorrow morning. In the meantime, the fire chief tells me the house is still volatile and needs to be aired before it can be decontaminated. They've moved out the gasoline-soaked furnishings, but it could still be a while before you'll be allowed back inside. Power and gas have been disconnected. The insurance company has agreed to organize security to watch the house, but the upshot is that Cin can't stay here. In fact, I don't know when she'll be allowed back."

He looked at Drum who stared right back.

"She'll be staying with me until further notice," he said grimly.

"Oh, hey, guys. Do I get any say in this?"

They both turned and looked at her. "No!" they said in unison.

Cin looked from one to the other. The two men were such a unit. But she was a part of that unit, too. And she had a voice.

"Shouldn't I be the judge of where I stay? Surely insurance will cover the cost of a motel?"

Drum looked at her steadily. She couldn't see what he was thinking from his gaze, but she had the impression she'd hurt him somehow.

"Or," she continued, "I could just stay with you."

Her capitulation met with instant relief on both men's faces.

"But I will need some things. I hope they'll let me inside soon to pack a bag."

"The police want your statement, too, so that'll fill your time until the fire department deems the house safe enough for you to go in and collect what you need," Drum said.

"Fine. Let's get that over with, shall we?"

Cin got up and folded the blanket and left it on the stairs. She and Drum said their goodbyes to Tanner, who drove off, before Drum introduced Cin to the detective who had taken his statement. It took a while to go over everything in detail, and reliving the experience again made her begin to shake all over. Drum was quick to put an arm around her and interrupt the interview.

"Perhaps this would be better completed tomorrow at the station? Ms. Sanderton has been through a lot today," he said firmly.

Cin put a hand on his arm. "No, Drum, it's okay. I'd rather get it over with now, if I can."

After finishing her statement, it was another hour of waiting around before she was permitted back inside the house to gather her things. As she stepped into the main foyer, she was instantly aware of the pungent smell of fuel. Her stomach clenched on a wave of anxiety. She didn't know if she'd ever be able to smell gasoline again without remembering how scared she was this evening.

Using a flashlight provided by one of the firefighters, Cin went to her bedroom and pulled out a suitcase, filling it with clothing for the next several days. She hadn't even unpacked her toiletry bag from her hasty trip to LA yet, or the small case she'd taken, so she added them to the things she needed to bring with her. Drum was waiting for her on the veranda when she was done and took the cases from her.

"Is that everything? I'll put them in my car for you," he said.

"Thanks," she said gratefully.

He had to be exhausted, she thought. She knew she was the moment the adrenaline that had carried her through the incident with Jennifer had ebbed, and yet Drum kept on going. Always there. Always a strong, steady presence. Always dependable.

It was getting late now, and they hadn't eaten, which reminded her that the meal she'd planned was still sitting in the refrigerator.

"I'll be with you soon. I'll just grab our dinner."

"Seriously, Cin? We averted a catastrophic event here tonight, and you're worried about some un-cooked meat?"

When he put it like that, it made her feel a bit ri-diculous, but truth be told she wanted some kind of normality after this evening's chaos.

"Humor me," she said and walked to the back of the house.

In the kitchen she grabbed some grocery bags and unpacked the fridge. The power to the house was al-ready off, and everything would spoil anyway if she didn't take it. An ironic smile quirked her lips. *Every-thing* amounted to the food she'd bought for tonight and a carton of fresh milk. She really needn't have bothered, but she knew she must cling to what was or-dinary and routine if she was going to get through this.

It wasn't long before she was back outside. She spoke briefly with the officer who had kept her com-pany in the immediate aftermath, and with the fire official in charge of the scene, thanking them and the teams around them. Drum was at her side quickly, taking the grocery bags from her hands as if she was too fragile to carry anything.

"Thank you," she said, "but I can manage."

"What was it you said to me a few minutes ago? Ah yes, 'humor me.'" And with that he went and stowed the grocery bags in the back of his car.

She followed him to the vehicle, and they drove to his home in the hills in silence. The longer the silence continued, the heavier it got, and the more Cin was reminded of the seriousness of the talk they'd planned to have tonight. She was determined they'd still have their discussion. She needed something to distract her from the worry about the house and how long it would take to get things back to normal. A shudder ran through her as she realized just how easily it, and they, could all have gone up in smoke.

"You okay?" Drum asked after bringing in her cases.

Cin shook her head. "No, I don't think I am. It's all starting to weigh on me now."

"Would you like to go to bed?"

She shook her head again. "I doubt I'd sleep. If you don't mind, I'd like to cook our meal and maybe have a glass of wine. You know, just do regular, everyday things."

"Yeah, I get it. Come through to the kitchen. I'll show you where everything is."

Drum's kitchen was modern and well laid-out with top-quality appliances. It didn't take Cin long to put the chicken and potatoes in the oven and prepare the salad. The dessert and whipped cream she left in the fridge for another time. She doubted they'd get to it tonight anyway.

"Dinner's nothing special, but I hope you'll like it," she said as she accepted a glass of wine from Drum.

"I will love it. I'm a basic cook at best."

"Oh, there's something in this world you can't do?" she teased.

He laughed. "I can cook, just not well."

Silence fell between them again, leaving Cin feeling awkward. They hadn't discussed where she was to sleep tonight, and she wasn't sure how to bring it up, either. As if he could read her mind, Drum spoke.

"I've put your cases in the guest room that Tanner usually uses. He always leaves it made up with fresh linen, ready for the next visitor, so I know you'll be comfortable there, if that's where you prefer to be."

She didn't know what she preferred, that was the problem. But she didn't want to sleep with Drum and be intimate with him with the gulf that lay between them right now. She still felt as though her biggest life decisions hadn't even been hers: they'd been governed by two teenage boys who'd grown into strong and capable men who'd apparently never stopped to consider she was a woman with a heart and mind of her own and whose feelings were important, too. Yes, they'd always been protective of her, and thankfully so, especially tonight. But where did she have a say in her life? Her choices? Her desires?

That she desired Drum had never changed. But she'd made major life decisions based on his rejection of her when she was younger. Decisions that had impacted other people's lives as well. Yes, they'd been her decisions to make, but if not for that stupid pact, could things have been completely different?

She'd never know, and that ate at her as she sipped her wine. She set the small table in the breakfast nook off the kitchen. While she'd finished the cooking, he'd gone to have a shower—with hot water and soap this time—and changed into his own casual clothing. The jeans he wore were snug in all the right places, and Cin had trouble averting her gaze when he walked back into the room.

"I like having you here," he said as he helped her bring the food to the table.

"You have a great place," she answered neutrally. "And it's not as if I can be at home right now, is it?"

"You know you always have a home with me, Cin." His voice was low and serious.

"Thank you," she acknowledged before beginning to dish up the meal. But inside, her stomach had clenched tight, and she knew there was no way she'd be able to eat the food she'd prepared.

Drum, it seemed, had no such issues, and he complimented her on the chicken after cleaning his plate.

"You're not hungry?" he asked as he reached for the bottle of wine to top up her glass.

"No. I thought I'd be okay, but…"

"I get it. It was a helluva thing, wasn't it?"

She nodded. But it wasn't just the situation with Jennifer. It was Mark and Drum and Tanner and, well, *everything*. Cin didn't even know where to start anymore. She jumped as Drum reached across the table to take her hand.

"Talk to me, Cin. It'll do you no good to keep it all bottled up," he said.

She looked from his hand and then to his eyes and saw nothing but care there. But love? Did he actually love her? Or was she forever destined to be his best friend's little sister? Yes, they'd shared passion. Beautiful, luscious, incredible passion. But relationships took a lot more to knit together than great sex.

Sixteen

Drum watched her from across the table, her hand still held lightly in his. It hurt to see her going through so much turmoil when all he wanted to do was sweep in and make everything better. But how could he do that when they had so much unsaid between them? He cleared his throat and searched for the words to open the conversation between them without causing further harm.

"How about we talk about tonight, first. Then we can attack the rest when you're ready, okay?"

She nodded, but even though she'd agreed, words didn't come easily to her.

"I don't know where to begin," she admitted.

"How about I go first, if you're okay with that?"

he suggested gently, and when she nodded again, he continued. "When I arrived at your house this evening and saw Jennifer's car there, I felt sick to my stomach. After that last time, when she nearly ran you down, I knew that her being at your house wasn't good. I rang the police straight away and decided it was probably best not to announce my arrival immediately to either of you. The dispatcher told me to wait before entering the house, but I caught a glimpse through the window—saw the gas can and told the dispatcher to send the fire department, too. She told me to stay outside and remain on the line, but I couldn't just stand there and wait for what I knew would come next.

"Your back door was unlocked, and I came in through the mudroom. I could hear Jennifer talking and knew that as long as she was engaging, she wasn't hurting you, but I could tell things were escalating."

Cin nodded. "She was so furious at me. She blamed me for everything. I apologized to her, but it did nothing but make her rage even worse."

"She wasn't in a state to be reasoned with. I could see that the second I came farther into the house and could see you both in the living room. When I smelled the gasoline, I knew I had to get you out of there as fast as possible, and I acted instinctively when she picked up the lighter. But it was your quick thinking when I tackled Jennifer that saved all of us, and I haven't thanked you for that yet, so thank you, Cin. I owe you my life."

"I'm pretty sure I owe you mine first," she said with a weak attempt at humor.

"We made a good team, didn't we?"

"Yeah," she answered softly. "We did."

She was agreeing with him, but he couldn't help feeling there was a finality to her words that didn't necessary bode well for their future, and try as he might, he couldn't see a way past that. There was still so much they needed to talk out, but he could see she was drooping with weariness.

"Why don't you head on to bed. You're worn out after today. We can talk more tomorrow."

"The dishes—" she started to protest.

"Are my responsibility. Go on, get some rest."

He watched her rise to her feet and look at him, her eyes filled with a deep sorrow. She nodded once, the barest movement of her head.

"You're right. I am tired. I'll see you in the morning."

"Sleep as long as you need to. I'll make a call and explain why we won't be in tomorrow."

She barely even acknowledged his words and turned and headed out the room and down the hallway toward her bedroom.

Drum watched her with a heavy heart. Every step she took was a step farther from him physically, yes, but emotionally and mentally, too. He felt it like a thread drawing tight between them, a tangible pain.

But what could he do? He couldn't exactly go racing after her and force her into his arms. He gave a wry smile as he collected their dirty dishes. As if he could ever force Princess Perfect to do anything she didn't want to. As much as he and Tanner had tried while they were growing up, Cin only ever did what Cin wanted to do. But if she ever returned to him, he wanted her to do so of her own accord.

After he'd cleaned up, he headed to bed. On the way to the master suite, he passed Cin's bedroom and hesitated a moment outside the door. Everything inside him urged him to knock gently and open the door. To check on her and make sure she was okay. To offer comfort if it was needed. He listened, but it was silent beyond the door.

Drum rested his forehead on the frame and fought back a groan. It had been a nightmare to see Cin at Jennifer's mercy this evening, especially knowing that in the state she was in, Jennifer had no mercy and that she'd had every intention of sending them all to a fiery hell. The thought of a world without Cin in it was an echoing, empty, dark cavern in his soul. Even a Cin that didn't want to be near him was a more bearable thought.

He forced himself down the hall to his room. Despite the late hour, though, sleep eluded him. All he could see was the image of the two women in a frozen tableau loaded with the potential for disaster. He only hoped that the morning might bring with it a more hopeful resolution than how things felt right now, because if Cin walked away for good this time, he didn't know what he would do.

Cin lay in bed staring at the ceiling. A glance at the bedside clock a few moments ago had revealed it was just past two a.m. She felt as though she hadn't slept a wink and despite her weariness still felt wired and restless. She'd heard Drum go to his room hours ago and wondered if he was plagued with the same agitation she felt.

She decided to make herself a cup of tea. Maybe Drum even had something herbal in that flashy kitchen of his that might help her sleep. The hum of the refrigerator was all she could hear as she entered the room and began poking in the cupboards for a mug and teabags. Eventually she found what she needed and silently applauded Drum for his range of teas. Mind you, it was no less than she expected of him. He was the kind of man who covered all the bases all the time in his attempts to look after everyone.

Attempts? That was probably a bit harsh, Cin conceded, as Drum did more than attempt it. He achieved it, as he'd achieved everything he'd set out to do in life. And he was the most open and caring person she knew. So why had it been so hard to open up to him tonight? To tell him of her turmoil and the crossroads she felt she stood at. To tell him she loved him and that she wanted to stay in Blossom Springs but only if he loved her back.

The answer rattled around in her mind. *Because it's my decision to make, not anyone else's.* While she'd been in LA the past few days, she'd had plenty of time to think. She'd been so angry with Tanner and Drum for their pact, had blamed them for where it had sent her with her own life. And, yes, maybe in part that was true. But no one had ever forced her anywhere and certainly not into Mark's arms. That had been all on her, and her late husband's choices were on him, too. She was clear on that now, but she still had no idea of where she stood with Drum.

Yes, he'd saved her life tonight, but he was the kind of man who would have done that for anyone in peril. In fact, he'd saved Jennifer, too, hadn't he? Cin went over to the window, sipped her tea and stared at the darkness outside. A darkness that seemed a fitting metaphor for where she was in her life right now. Yes, she had opportunities here careerwise with Keyes Tires. The job Drum had outlined to her yesterday was a dream for someone with her background and skills in marketing. But could she take that role, see him every day and know that he wouldn't let himself love her the way she wanted to be loved—mind, body and soul—because of some idiotic pact with her brother?

Sure, Drum had embarked on a sexual fling with her, but she knew in her heart that would never be enough for her. She'd gone into her first marriage with her body, not with her heart, and the outcome had been an abject failure—proving to her that love anchored everything. Without love, she knew she had nothing. Drum, too, deserved love—both to receive it and to give it. He was a man who'd sacrificed all his dreams for others. Noble and strong and, without a doubt, the best lover she'd ever had.

Her body twinged on the reminder of his attentiveness to her pleasure, of the satisfaction he'd given her time and again. He'd felt perfect beneath her touch, and even now she burned to touch him again, to give to him, physically at least, a measure of how she felt about him. In fact, how she'd always felt about him. Since childhood there'd only been one person for her, but while he was giving her an easy avenue to stay here in Blossom Springs, it wasn't because he loved her.

She needed to know, and she needed to tell him about her feelings and what she needed going forward. And if he wasn't on board with that? Well, Cin knew she'd need to move on. How else could she repair her wounded heart and scattered soul if she stayed?

"Can't sleep?"

Drum's voice made her spin around, splashing tea on the front of the T-shirt she'd chosen to sleep in.

"That's not hot, is it?" he said with concern, moving instantly to grab a towel for her.

And there it was again. The care he showed. Care, but not necessarily love.

"I'm fine. The tea is fine," she snapped, brushing his hand away at the same time. She drew in a breath. It wasn't his fault he was the person he was, and she was being unfair. "I'm sorry. I shouldn't take it out on you."

Drum shrugged. Standing there in low-slung pajama bottoms with his hair tousled, he looked sexy as hell. Sexy but unattainable at the same time because she wanted more than his body, more than how making love with him made her feel.

"I couldn't sleep, either. Is that chamomile?" he asked, gesturing to her mug.

"Yeah. You want me to make you some?"

For a minute she thought he was going to say yes, but then he shook his head.

"No. Since you're awake, I want you to talk to me. Really talk. I need to know, Cin. Do you still love Mark? Is that why you're so distant right now? I know you went back to LA to see him. Are you moving back there permanently?"

She took a step back, shocked at the raw emotion in his voice. "Drum, I…" She didn't know how to tell him, so she asked him a question instead. "Why do you need to know?"

"Why? Because I don't want you to go. There, I've said it." He turned and gripped the kitchen counter as if that was the only thing holding him on this earth right now.

"Drum, you've said nothing," she said gently.

And he hadn't. There'd been nothing significant of his feelings in his bald statement. Without knowing how he really felt about her, whether they had a future together as a couple, she had no reason to stay here. She crossed the short distance between them and laid a hand on the back of his shoulder. His muscles were tensed as hard as rock, and she heard his indrawn breath as she touched him.

"I told you I don't want you to go. Isn't that enough?" he ground out.

"Would that be enough for you? Because it isn't enough for me, Drum. I need more than that. I need to know how you feel about me."

He spun around. "Isn't it obvious? I love you, Cin. Oh, I tried not to. For years I tried, and I thought I'd succeeded, until you came back and I couldn't lie to myself anymore. Do you honestly think I would have made love to you if I didn't love you?"

"I wondered, but I'm not a mind reader. You never said a thing about wanting me in your life. In fact, the first time we made love, I knew you were going through an emotional battle and that our need for one another won over everything else."

"Well, I've admitted it now. I love you, Hyacinth Sanderton, and I don't want you to leave. I don't want you to go back to your husband, and I don't want you to return to LA. Can I make it any plainer than that?"

A kernel of hope began to glow deep in her chest. She owed it to him to tell him everything now.

"Mark is dead, Drum. I only went back there to scatter his ashes and to meet with his lawyer."

Drum looked as though she'd struck him with

a tire iron. "He's dead? Oh hell, Cin, I'm so sorry. Here I am making demands of you, and you're dealing with grief—"

"I don't love Mark. I never did," she interrupted. "I'm not dealing with the grief of a widow. If anything, I've been dealing with the guilt that I drove Mark to what he did before our marriage ended. Goodness knows he blamed me for his gambling addiction and our bankruptcy together with everything else. And, yes, some of it was my fault because I never loved him, and I did blame myself. I didn't think I was worthy of anyone after that. Going back to LA last week helped me to put things in perspective. Coming home to Blossom Springs was what I wanted. Sure, initially it was because I felt like I had nowhere else to go and I didn't see this as a long-term option. But being here felt right, and even if I wasn't making the most of my abilities, I was *home* where I belonged. But I couldn't stay here when I thought you didn't love me."

"How could you think that? I have done my utmost to make it easier for you to stay here. I would have done more, but you wouldn't let me," Drum remonstrated.

"I needed to stand on my own two feet, Drum, and you helped me to do that. I didn't need another person to make all my decisions for me. I needed someone who'd support me in what I wanted to do. But I also needed more than that. I needed your love. I know I have that now."

"You do. Forever, if you'll let me."

"You have no idea how long I've waited to hear that," she said on a swell of emotion that threatened to make her sob like a child.

"Oh, I think I do. It was me who you followed around every day from when you were six. It's kind of hard to shake that memory. Come here. You're standing too far away."

He met her halfway and drew her into his arms before kissing her as if she was the only thing that mattered to him in his world. His lips teased hers open, and she relished the gentleness of his touch. When he deepened their kiss, pouring all his love and emotion into it, she felt as though her heart would burst with joy. It was only when he let her go that she remembered one particularly important thing.

"So," she said, assuming a serious look on her face, "the pact."

Drum had the grace to look shamefaced. "It was a guy thing. It has well and truly been dissolved now. Back then, neither of us wanted to imagine the other with our sisters. Just, no."

"You broke my heart when I graduated and you wouldn't—"

"I know." He interrupted her with another kiss. "But even if I had felt ready to give you what you wanted from me, there was no way I was in a position to do that. My dad's health was deteriorating. His business was struggling. I'd only spent two years helping him at that point, and I knew there was no way out for me until I could turn the business around and really make something of it and myself. You were the golden child of Blossom Springs—Princess Perfect—with the entire world at your feet. The last thing you needed was a life on the poor side of town with no prospects of improving things for years to come."

"Do you think I'd have cared about that?" she protested.

"Eventually, yes. Cin, you were used to the best of everything."

"You make me sound shallow."

"No, never shallow, but let me rephrase. You deserved the best of everything, and I couldn't offer you that. When I heard you'd married in LA, I was happy for you. You were achieving your potential in every way possible."

Cin snorted inelegantly. "Drum, that was all a sham. I've always loved you. I should have known my marriage was doomed from the start. By the time we added in the pandemic and downturn in business together with Mark's gambling and my inability to keep up the facade of our marriage, there was no way we were ever going to come back from the brink. Bankruptcy forced us to face ourselves, and I think that when we did that, neither of us were happy with the people we'd become. I'd seen Momma and Daddy lose just about everything, but they'd always been a loving unit who remained devoted until death. Mark and I were never that kind of couple. How could we be, when I couldn't let go of how I felt about you?

"Coming back and asking you for a job was humiliating, but I've learned that pride doesn't get us what we want or need. Only love does that, and only when it's reciprocated equally."

"So you'll stay?"

"Of course I'll stay. I never wanted to be anywhere else but here with you."

"And the new marketing role? You'll take it?"

She kissed him again. "Ask me in the morning," she said. "Right now I want to take you bed. After that, maybe we can both get some sleep."

He laughed and swung her up into his arms.

"Princess, your wish is my command."

Cin threw her arms around his neck and let her head rest against his chest—against the heart she knew beat for her. Princess Perfect had finally won her Prince Charming.

* * * * *

LOYAL READER
FREE BOOKS VOUCHER
WELCOME BOX

YES! I Love Reading, please send me a welcome box with up to 4 FREE BOOKS and Free Mystery Gifts from the series I select.

Just write in "YES" on the dotted line below then return this card today and we'll send your welcome box asap!

➡️ YES ⬅️

Which do you prefer?

☐ **Harlequin Desire®**
225/326 HDL GRA4

☐ **Harlequin Presents® Larger-Print**
176/376 HDL GRA4

☐ **BOTH**
225/326 & 176/376
HDL GRCG

FIRST NAME

LAST NAME

ADDRESS

APT.#

CITY

STATE/PROV.

ZIP/POSTAL CODE

EMAIL ☐ Please check this box if you would like to receive newsletters and promotional emails from Harlequin Enterprises ULC and its affiliates. You can unsubscribe anytime.

HD/HP-622-LR_LRV22

Rachel Bailey lives on the Sunshine Coast, Australia, with her partner and three dogs, each of whom are essential to her books: the dogs supervise the writing process (by napping on or under the desk), and her partner supplies the chocolate. She loves to hear from readers, and you can visit her at rachelbailey.com or on Facebook.

Books by Rachel Bailey

Harlequin Desire

The 24-Hour Wife
Return of the Secret Heir
The Nanny Proposition
The Lost Heir

Visit the Author Profile page
at Harlequin.com for more titles.

You can also find Rachel Bailey on Facebook,
along with other Harlequin Desire authors,
at Facebook.com/HarlequinDesireAuthors!

Dear Reader,

I'm excited to share this book with you because it has some of my favorite elements: it's a rags-to-riches story (always my catnip!), and the hero, Heath, is a hot Australian surfer who is about to inherit more money than he'd ever dreamed of. Also, Freya's life has just a small nod to one of my favorite movies, *Sabrina* (either the Audrey Hepburn or the Julia Ormond version—they're both fabulous). And the whole story is set in the gorgeous city of New York, with a cameo of the Australian beach town Noosa. The combination made it so much fun to write!

The Lost Heir is the first of two connected books about brother and sister Heath and Mae as they're caught up in the whirlwind of a large inheritance. As you'd imagine, it's not a smooth transition for either of them! Mae's story will be out very soon, and I can't wait for you to meet her.

Happy reading,

Rachel

THE LOST HEIR

Rachel Bailey

For Javaria Farooqui and Caylee Tierney,
the best thesis support group that ever there was.

Thank you for the cheering,
the late-night laughs, the discussions and,
most importantly, for marching by my side.

Acknowledgments

A supersized thank-you to my editor,
John Jacobson, for believing in me, as well as
believing in this story and making it shine.
And bunches and bunches of thank-yous to the
amazing trio of Barbara DeLeo, Amanda Ashby
and Sharon Archer for the brainstorming,
critiquing and moral support.
I can't imagine writing books without you!

One

Freya Wilson woke with a start. Something was different. Weirdly different. Wrong…

She put a hand to her pounding forehead and glanced around the strange room, filled with early-morning sunlight from its high ceilings, with its mismatched furniture and messy decor. This wasn't her bedroom. Awareness crept in—she'd traveled to the other side of the world, to the Australian beach town of Noosa. Even so, this was no hotel. She swallowed hard, but her throat was dry, and there was a sour taste in her mouth. Clearly she'd had too much to drink last night, but everything in her head was too fuzzy to remember details.

As she sat up, the pale blue cotton sheet fell away

and she realized she was naked. Strange country, strange room, no nightdress. She cast a frantic look at her surroundings. The other side of the bed was empty, but rumpled. She couldn't hear any sounds and could see most of the small apartment, so she was alone. But *where* was she?

She'd landed in Australia on the second stop of this fool's errand of a mission that her godmother Sarah Rutherford had sent her on—searching for the lost heir of the billion-dollar Bellavista fortune. According to this latest batch of research, there were five possible people, scattered across the globe, who could be Joseph Rutherford II, including the fitness trainer in New Zealand she'd already eliminated, and the owner of a bar in Noosa: Heath Dunstan. He had no social media presence, and unlike the fitness trainer's file, she'd been sent no photos or useful information besides the location of his bar.

She remembered the driver picking her up at the Brisbane airport and depositing her at Noosa Heads with a carry-on suitcase. The bustling bar had been easy to spot, and the bartender had welcomed her with a lopsided smile and dark eyes that sparked, so she'd made herself at home on a barstool, peppering him with light questions to get some background on the owner. Unfortunately, he hadn't known much, so she'd used the time to set up her cover story of being a tourist on vacation so she'd be able to come back regularly as she tried to glean information. And… then what?

She found her sage-green sundress on the floor and slipped it over her head as she went to the window. Sparkling blue water, edged by powder-white sand, stretched before her, and even this early in the morning, the beach had attracted an assortment of swimmers and surfers.

She smiled, remembering the bartender telling her that he surfed every morning...

Her stomach dropped. Oh God. Surely she hadn't.

She glanced around the room, looking for an indication of where she was, of whose room she was in.

The hot bartender—Karl? Kelly? Cody?—was the only person she remembered talking to, besides an occasional word with the female bartender who'd been working the other end of the long wooden bar.

Her heart beat an uneven rhythm as her stomach lurched. She was not cut out for this kind of work, and she'd told Sarah as much when her godmother asked her to help with the plan. Freya was a forensic accountant with the FBI, not a special agent, and certainly not someone with any experience at all in investigating actual, real-life people. She liked numbers. Columns and pages of them were her happy place. Tracking down people who were in hiding was most definitely not.

A key turned in the door and she froze. She could grab her handbag and carry-on suitcase—no, she could *find her bag and case*, then grab them—and run out the door when it opened. Or she could play it cool. Or she could use the opportunity to probe a little and gather some information on Heath Dunstan so she could cross him off her list and get out of this town. Or she could—

The door squeaked as it opened and the bartender from last night was pushing through, his chest bare, a beach towel hanging over a shoulder and a surfboard under his arm.

"Morning," he said with that same lopsided smile that had been lurking in her mind. "I wasn't sure if you'd still be here when I got back."

She tried hard to meet his eyes and not stare and the expanse of bronzed, muscled chest on display. "Uh, yes."

He stood the surfboard against the wall, then dragged the towel off his shoulder and rubbed it roughly over his dark blond hair. "The water is magic this morning."

Freya glanced out the window, more to give herself a moment to think than to appreciate the beach view, although the bright sunlight made her wince and her headache ratcheted up a notch. There were memories floating just at the edge of her mind and when she tried to grasp them, they slipped away. Surely, if she'd slept with this Adonis, she'd remember every second. Fate wouldn't be so cruel as to let her have him but not remember it...?

Hot bartender rested his hands low on his hips, covering the black band at the top of his board shorts. "I'll just jump in the shower and then if you're up to it, we could duck downstairs and get breakfast. Or at least a coffee."

"Sure," she said, but heard the word come out like a question.

He frowned. "Are you okay?"

There was no way around this—she had to come clean. She drew in a fortifying breath. "So, here's a funny thing. I don't actually remember last night or..."

She trailed off as a horrified expression settled over his face. "You didn't seem drunk," he said, then covered his jaw with a dark tan hand. "I wasn't... I didn't..."

"I'm not accusing you of anything," she said quickly. "I'm embarrassed."

"Want a drink of water or something?" He reached for a glass with restless hands. "You did mention feeling pretty jet-lagged. Maybe that combined with your drinks?" He filled the glass from the faucet and handed it to her.

Grateful, she took the water and downed it before handing it back to him. "Thanks. Actually, jet lag was likely part of the problem. I feel like I've been flying for days—from New York to LAX, then on to New Zealand. I spent one night there, then a flight to Australia."

"Jet lag and a lack of sleep aren't a great combination." He wrapped a hand around the back of his neck and she watched the play of his biceps as they bunched and contracted. The simple movement sent a delicious shiver racing across her skin, and she remembered watching the same movement last night, being mesmerized by it. Running her fingertips along his arms—she could still almost feel his smooth skin, and her breath hitched. Dragging every available brain cell together, she tried to bring her focus to earlier in the night.

"When I arrived, I asked you what was good."

Thankfully he dropped his arms—and their distracting biceps—and dug his hands in his pockets. "And I made you a mango daiquiri, then you sat on a couple of gin and tonics until closing time. We flirted a bit. Well, a lot."

The mango daiquiri was clear—she'd liked the idea of it being tropical to match her surroundings— and a gin and tonic was her usual drink. That didn't sound like enough alcohol to wipe her out, even with the jet lag, but her friends had called her a lightweight more than once.

"I'm not a huge drinker. Or a regular traveler for that matter. Note to self: do not combine travel and alcohol again." She winced, then shook it off. "So how exactly did the night play out?"

"You said you didn't have a room booked and it's peak tourist season here, which means rooms are scarce. I offered to let you crash on my sofa for the night."

The sofa? She arched an eyebrow. "I woke up in your bed. Naked."

It was his turn to wince. "You hung around after

we closed up for the night, and Tina went home. I brought out the good gin, and we sat at the bar and had a couple of glasses each."

"And one thing led to another?" She wasn't sure if it was because he was describing the situation or more memories were coming back, but she had an impression of sitting at the long wooden bar with him and breaking into song when some classic nineties hits came over the sound system. "Did we do any spontaneous karaoke by any chance?"

"You did," he said with a slow smile spreading across his face. "To be honest, I couldn't keep up with you. You're a devil with a microphone."

The memories were stronger now, and definitely included belting out a couple of ballads. But when she'd been singing, she was standing… "Where was I when I sang?"

He tried to hide his grin as he said, "On the bar."

She sagged back against the wall, slightly mortified. "And then I called you up on the bar with me—"

"You did. And I'm ashamed to say that after five years it was my very first time up on that bar."

The image of grabbing him by the front of his shirt and pulling him close flooded her vision. "I kissed you," she whispered, shocked at herself. At home, she was reliable, consistent. Boring. And last night she'd had an overwhelming urge to do something wild. She was on the other side of the world, where she knew no one—the perfect time to break out and do something that no one at home would expect of her. She'd kissed the hot bartender and then told him to take her to bed. Heat flamed up her neck and filled her face. Part of her was mortified. Another part of her was just a little proud.

"You did kiss me, yes," he said slowly, eyes simmering and one corner of his mouth hitched up. "It was a helluva kiss."

Intensity rolled off him in waves, flowing over her, robbing her of breath. It took two attempts to fill her lungs with enough air to speak.

"And then we…" She gestured awkwardly to the bed.

He nodded. "And then we absolutely did. Twice. You don't remember?"

"Just flashes of images really, though I'm remembering more as we talk about it." He looked so disappointed that she felt obliged to add, "Sorry. I'm certain you were great."

He let out a roar of laughter before collecting himself and murmuring, "My ego thanks you."

She replayed the words in her head and realized they had sounded condescending but his dark eyes were alight with humor, making it a shared joke instead of taking offense, and she chuckled with him. "The worst part is that I don't remember your name."

"Heath," he said, holding out his hand. "Heath Dunstan."

The world tilted and everything swam before her eyes. No, no, no. It *couldn't* be him. The one time she'd let her hair down, and now…

"Heath," she said through a dry throat. "I thought your name was Kyle or Cody or something."

"Ah. Tina the other bartender calls me Kelly, after the surfer Kelly Slater. She says my style is like his."

"But you're really Heath Dunstan," she clarified, hoping she'd somehow heard wrong.

He stilled. "That's me. Why, is it a problem?"

"Yes," she said. "Well, no, I guess. Or maybe." At least he looked nothing like the Rutherfords with their dark hair and narrow faces, so chances were that he wasn't the lost heir—she clung to that hope as the situation spun out of control.

His eyes wary, he said, "And why would that be?"

"I was looking for you. It's why I'm in Australia."

His posture stiffened and his entire demeanor changed. "It's time you left." He reached for her bag on the kitchen counter and thrust it into her hands. "Nice to have met you, but don't come back." He opened the door and with one hand between her shoulder blades, he ushered her out onto an open mezzanine that overlooked the bar with a spiral metal staircase at the end.

Everything was coming in and out of focus as she grasped the size of the mess she'd made. How would she explain this to Sarah? *I'm sorry, I slept with the target before I realized he was actually the target and now he's refusing to even talk to me.* Possibly the least professional thing she'd done in her entire life and, worse, Sarah would be disappointed in her.

As he pushed the door closed behind her, desperation kicked in and Freya shoved her foot in the doorway just in time to stop it from closing. "Heath, I'm sorry I'm not handling this well, but I have maybe the worst hangover of my life and my head feels like it's about to split open and I need to ask you some questions. Please, just a few minutes."

"Not in a million years," he said between clenched teeth. Eyes that only moments before had been alive with heat and then amusement were now cold, accusing.

She had no choice—she had to lay it all on the line before she lost him. "There's a chance you're a billionaire and don't know it." He hesitated, and in that moment, she shoved her foot further in the door and managed to get an arm back in, too. "Give me ten minutes to explain, and then I'll leave. I promise."

As he loomed above her, a deep groove appeared between his eyebrows. The world around her hung in a state of suspended animation as she waited for his reply. Finally he blew out a breath. "Five minutes. You get five minutes, then I never see you again."

"Deal," she said, and hoped she could pull this off.

Heath swore under his breath as he opened the door to the redhead with the tawny brown eyes who'd rocked his world only hours before. If he'd ruined everything—after all his mother's sacrifices and their years of hiding—with a one night stand, he'd never forgive himself.

The rules and precautions his mother had drilled

into him for his entire life meant that he was usually more careful than to invite a stranger into his home, but he'd been desperate for a distraction last night and let his guard slip. On his mother's birthday, he and his sister Mae would usually visit the place in the hinterland where they'd scattered her ashes four years earlier, but this year he'd had a last-minute hiccup in the staffing schedule at the bar. As the owner, the buck stopped with him. Mae had offered to postpone the trip, but he'd insisted she go—at least one of them should be there to honor their mother.

Now that Freya—assuming that was even her real name—had tracked him down, he was glad that Mae was out of town. If they had to move again and change their names, it would be easier if those chasing them continued to be in the dark about Mae's existence.

Freya walked to the tall windows overlooking the view of Noosa's main beach, then slowly turned to face him, fidgeting with the strap of her handbag.

He checked the time on his watch. "You have five minutes. I suggest you talk fast."

"This is fairly delicate. Do we really need the ticking clock?"

"Do I really need this at all? I think five minutes is generous." His stomach dropped as another thought hit. "Was last night part of this—did you deliberately seduce me? All that talk of forgetting, was that part of the game?"

She flinched and the faint freckles across her

cheeks disappeared as her face flushed red. "That is not why I was here. In fact, it's made everything more complicated and it shouldn't have happened."

"On that, at least, we agree." He ran a hand down his face. "How about you tell me why it is that you're here. You have four and a half minutes."

She nodded. "I'm looking for someone and you're on the list of people who could be that person." She shifted her weight from one long leg to the other. "This is rather blunt, and I'm sorry, but your countdown is on. I know your birth certificate says you were born in Mexico. Is there a chance that you were adopted there, or that you were really born in the US to a different father?"

Knowing the contents of his birth certificate was a red flag. Questioning its validity was another. He glared, hard. "Not really sure why I'd disclose a single thing about myself to you. I have no idea who you are."

"My name is Freya Wilson and I'm a forensic accountant with the FBI."

A cold chill passed across his skin. "The FBI is looking for me?"

"No, I'm on leave. This is…" She lifted one shoulder. "A favor for someone I care about."

"Let me get this straight. You're on a personal mission, you have zero authority here, you've slept with the person you're supposed to be tracing, and now you want me to spill my life history. Instead of asking questions, how about you start telling me some details."

There was still a slim chance that this had nothing to do with him, and if so, he wasn't giving her any information that would spark the FBI's interest in him or his sister. He folded his arms and waited.

"Sure, that's fair," she said, smoothing down the side of her green dress. "I've been asked to find a man who was born as Joseph Rutherford II. People have looked for him in the past and come up blank, but this is the first time I've been involved."

Heath put all his effort into not reacting, not giving anything away. "It doesn't sound like this Joseph Rutherford II wants to be found."

"His mother ran away with him when he was just an infant. Perhaps he's not aware of his options."

"You say you're looking for a man. An adult. Surely, by now, he would have looked for lost family if he wanted to."

"There's some information he doesn't know."

"The money."

She nodded. "There's a substantial sum being held in trust for him. He has a right to know that."

"Money doesn't fix everything." His mother had taught him that money actually brought out the worst in people. The bar brought him enough to be comfortable, and it didn't come with strings the way this money would.

"Joseph Rutherford's wife ran from him, and I

have an idea why. There's no blame. But Rutherford is dead. So if this is about fear, then that threat is gone."

He checked his watch. "Your time is up, and you've wasted a trip. I'm not him."

"Heath," she said, and this time there was sympathy in her gaze. "I won't be the last person knocking on your door. If you really are Joseph Rutherford II, others will come. I didn't make this list of potential options, I'm just following them up."

"Tell whoever is looking that I was a dead end."

"I can't do that. Besides, this is about more than money. It's about family."

"You said the old man was dead."

"He had a sister." Freya's face softened and her mouth tilted a little. "Sarah. She never stopped hoping to find her nephew. She's the one who sent me."

Something tugged in his chest. He'd grown up with a mother and sister who meant the world to him, but part of him had always yearned for an extended family. He dismissed the feeling. "I'm still not interested."

"If you're the man I'm looking for, then Sarah is your best option. She only wants the best for her nephew and can help navigate the…complexities." She bit down on her lip, then released it. "Heath, do you think it's you?"

He pushed off the wall and paced to the window. He watched one wave crash to the shore, then another. Water had always brought him peace. This time, peace was too much to ask for, but clarity was forming. Freya had a point—now that they'd been found, he needed to face his past. His birth family. His true self.

But he wouldn't mention Mae. If Freya and her colleagues had done their homework thoroughly, they'd know Mae existed, but his mother had registered her birth a year after she was born—an extra layer of protection, so that even if they were discovered one day, Mae would appear to have a different father from him. His mother's sacrifices wouldn't be wasted.

"Truthfully," he said, his throat feeling like it was coated in gravel, "I have no idea. My mother ran from someone who scared her and changed our names several times. She never told me my birth name, or hers, just in case I accidentally blurted it out when I was a kid. She took her secrets to the grave."

With his mother's death, he and his sister were stuck in Australia with fake identities—if the Australian government found out about them, he and Mae could be thrown out of the country. He would have US citizenship since he was born there, but he'd never known his real name to access his paperwork. And even if he was this Joseph and could live in the States, Mae was in a different situation since she'd been born in Mexico. Being separated from Mae was not an option. They just wanted to keep their heads down, be good citizens in their adopted country and get on with their lives. The redhead with the bewitching eyes was complicating things no end.

"There are two possibilities here." She took a step closer. "The first is that you're not the man we're searching for. If that's the case, you do a DNA test, get eliminated from our inquiries, we compensate you for your time, and you go about your life."

"And if I am this Rutherford guy?"

"Then you come to the US, we sort out your father's estate, and if you really want no part of it, you flush the money down the toilet and come back to your life here. But at least that way, you don't have to be looking over your shoulder for the rest of your life. Plus, you'll have an aunt in your life, one who is desperate to meet you." She took another step closer. "You have nothing to lose. Either way, it's a win."

He closed his eyes. She was right. He'd always worried that this day would come. Even though his mother believed she'd hidden them well enough, he'd always had a voice in the back of his mind whispering that whatever they were running from would eventually catch up to them. The easiest thing to do now was get everything out on the table and deal with it. That way he'd have some element of control, try to stay one step ahead, and could best protect Mae.

"Okay, I'll do it. But I want one thing to be clear." He pushed aside the allure of her, the need to feel her close even now, the way her mouth drew his gaze. Only once his body's responses were completely locked down did he meet her eyes. "Whatever the outcome, you and I are done."

She swallowed hard, then nodded, and Heath could practically see his life fall into pieces and scatter across the floor. He silently apologized to his mother, and then went to make coffee.

Two

A little over two weeks later, Freya spotted Heath at LAX and her breath hitched high in her throat. She waved awkwardly and he gave her a tight smile in return and headed over. She'd seen this man pouring drinks in his own bar, commanding the space with his presence, and she'd seen him in his apartment, hair wet with ocean spray, wearing board shorts as if they'd been invented for the sole purpose of displaying his muscled torso. She'd wondered since if he would affect her quite so much without the sexy backdrops. Now that she saw him, tall and broad, striding through the throng of people in the airport of a strange country, she had to admit that, no, it hadn't been the settings. It was 100 percent Heath

Dunstan. The most inconvenient man she could have an attraction to.

After his firm *whatever the outcome, you and I are done*, she'd let one of Sarah's lawyers deal with the DNA testing and, once that had been a positive match, make the arrangements for his passage to the States. Part of her had hoped he wasn't Joseph Rutherford II so she could put their one-night stand behind her and approach the next possible person on her list with more professionalism.

Another part of her, though, the part that had dreamed of Heath Dunstan in the dark of night, remembering the feel of his fingertips on her skin, his mouth hot on her body…yeah, that part wasn't so sure.

"Freya," he said with a nod when he reached her. His dark eyes didn't quite meet hers and his posture was stiff—possibly from the long flight from Brisbane to Los Angeles, but just as likely from the discomfort of seeing her. She knew how that felt.

"How was your flight?" she asked brightly as she indicated the door to his right.

He rubbed a hand over three-day-old stubble. "After we got through the turbulence it was fine."

She looked up sharply. "We have another flight from here to New York. Are you feeling okay to get going?"

"Sure." He stretched his arms above his head and stifled a yawn. "My stomach settled pretty soon after the turbulence finished so I'm good to go."

"Okay, great." She determinedly looked at the floor and not at those strong surfer's arms.

They walked in silence until Heath casually said, "I was surprised to not see you for the DNA test or the results."

Startled, she glanced up. "I assumed you'd be more comfortable with someone else as liaison after...the way we left things."

She'd flown back home the next day and postponed her leave so she could go back to work early, desperately needing the distraction that only a complex page of numbers could give. The only reason she was here now was that Sarah had thought a familiar face would ease Heath's arrival in New York. Freya hadn't been able to explain that although her face would be familiar, it wouldn't be welcome, and she'd ended up bundled onto the flight.

"You were right." He didn't sound annoyed at her anymore. It was worse—he sounded disconnected, as if nothing at all had passed between them.

The flippant rejection hurt more than she would have expected, and she had to remind herself that taking their personal history out of the interaction was what she'd been hoping for.

Once they'd boarded the private jet and taken their seats across from each other, Heath glanced around at the luxurious interior with its plush white seats, highly polished wood tables and throw pillows that matched the carpet. "I don't need all this. Business class on a public flight was already more than enough. A private jet for this leg of the journey seems wasteful."

She smiled at Andrew, the cabin attendant, who'd been on the flight from New York with her, as he offered drinks and snacks. With a quick word of thanks, she took a water and a packet of salted nuts.

"This is your world now, Heath." She waved a hand to take in all the visible wealth around them. "Your life is about to change. Brace yourself."

His brows drew together. "It's really not. I'm here to sort a few things out and then get back to Australia so I can resume my real life. This—" he stabbed a finger in the air, pointing to the plane's interior "— is not, and never will be, my life."

Freya surveyed him. Did he truly think it would be that easy? The lost heir to the Bellavista fortune had become something of a legend and now that he'd resurfaced, especially in the form of a gorgeous Australian surfer-bartender, he was going to cause a stir. More than that, it was going to suck him into the slot that had been waiting for him—roles, expectations and the temptations of wealth.

But all she said was, "Okay, if that's what you want." It wasn't her job to make him confront his new reality. She was simply here as a favor to her godmother to escort him home. He'd find out the rest soon enough.

The pilot's voice came over the speakers announcing that they were ready for takeoff. Neither of them spoke as the plane taxied down the runway and the engines roared as they lifted the plane into the sky. Once the plane's trajectory evened out, she sneaked a glance at Heath. He was watching the sky through the window, appearing to be lost in his own thoughts.

With his hair neatly combed and his dark blue shirt buttoned to the base of his throat, he already looked more like Joseph than Heath. The man she'd met in Noosa gave easy smiles to customers, not missing a beat as he dealt with unruly patrons, before returning to pouring drinks and charming everyone around him. He'd been all loose-limbed ease in his T-shirt and jeans and his rumpled hair. The man on the plane with her was… contained. His strong jaw was tense, his tall frame unnaturally still. No question, though, that both versions of Heath made her skin prickle with heat, and that even these stolen glances were making her breath come a little faster. What *was* it about him that affected her so much?

"Heath?"

"Mmm?" he said, turning to her.

Her mouth was dry, so she took a sip of her water. One of the reasons she'd agreed to travel this last leg with him was to have a moment alone to address her mistake. "Will you do me a favor?"

"Perhaps." His gaze was steady, his expression unreadable. "Ask and we'll find out."

She picked at the edge of her jacket, then, when she realized what she was doing, folded her hands together on her lap. "Can we keep our night together just between us?"

She'd considered telling Sarah once she'd arrived home but hadn't been able to do it. It wasn't just that her lapse in judgment had got Heath's back up, risking Sarah's chance to know her nephew, but also, something about their time together felt…private. Personal. Something she wasn't prepared to share with everyone else.

"There's no need for anyone else to know," he said, and shrugged. "We're consenting adults. It's between us."

A little of the tension in her shoulders eased. "Thank you." She chewed the end of a thumbnail. "Actually, I have another favor to ask. Can you be gentle with Sarah? She's an amazing woman and she's been desperate to find you since you disappeared. So the feelings you have about your father and this world," *and me*, she silently added, and was pretty sure he heard anyway, "can you maybe not let them taint your interactions with her?"

"Sure." He rubbed a hand through his dark blond hair. "But if we're throwing around favors like they're candy, I want one, too."

She'd been expecting him to ask for something and was pretty sure that most people who had suddenly come into unimaginable wealth would have had a long list of requests already. "Ask and I'll do my best."

"I want the names and addresses of my mother's family."

She winced, mainly because she was shocked that

she hadn't thought to track them down for him. Of course he'd want to meet them. She could ask some friends at the FBI to gather that information fairly quickly. In fact, it was probably already in the files she'd been given. "I'm sure that can be arranged."

Heath nodded, then pulled out a thick book from his backpack and settled in to read.

Following his cue, Freya drew a sheaf of papers from her satchel that she needed to review, but for the rest of the flight, she spent as much time watching Heath over the top of the pages as she did reading them. She told herself it was part of her job to keep an eye on the man she was escorting home, and she very nearly believed it.

As the plane taxied to a stop, Heath tucked the science fiction novel into his bag and stretched his arms. Freya had spent the flight working on a pile of papers and they'd only shared the basics of necessary conversation, which had suited him and his mood.

Unfortunately, he'd been painfully aware of her at every moment. When she'd run her fingers through her long hair, he'd practically felt the silken strands on his own hands. When she'd wriggled in her seat to get more comfortable, he'd remembered the feel of her in his arms as they'd drifted off to sleep in his bed. When she'd tapped a pen against her lips, he'd almost lost himself to the memory of kissing that lush mouth and feeling it move across his body.

He blew out a harsh breath. He *had* to find a way to move past this awareness. Freya Wilson was not on his side. He had no idea what her endgame really was, so allowing himself to get carried away with an attraction only put him at risk of being blindsided.

She stood, gathered her things and turned to him. "Welcome to New York."

The coffee he'd had twenty minutes earlier turned sour in his stomach. A few weeks ago, if someone had offered him an all-expenses-paid holiday he'd have jumped at the chance. But this was no holiday. And even though the lawyers had already covered the financial expenses, he was certain this trip would cost him in other ways.

At least he'd had two weeks to put some plans in place and buy himself an escape hatch in case this all went pear-shaped.

Andrew, who'd served their drinks and meals, opened the door that led to the six metal stairs and the tarmac. "It's chilly outside, but a beautiful night. Mind your step."

"Thank you," Heath said, and smiled. Years in hospitality had taught him to never overlook the staff.

"You're very welcome, Mr. Rutherford," Andrew said. "I hope you enjoyed your flight."

Heath stiffened at the wrong name and opened his mouth to correct him, then closed it again. It wasn't Andrew's fault—he'd been given the Ruth-erford name. Hell, he probably even worked for the

Rutherfords. So all he said was, "It was great. Please say thanks to the pilots, too."

He stepped out onto the narrow metal stairs and was immediately assaulted with air colder than he could have imagined. Apparently, "chilly" to a New Yorker was arctic to someone from subtropical Queensland. Turning up the collar of his jacket, he made his way down as Freya thanked Andrew and passed on her compliments to the pilot.

A shiny black Suburban with tinted windows crept across the tarmac and stopped nearby.

Freya waved at the car and headed over, so he followed in step beside her. The driver—a middle-aged woman with short red hair and a long dark coat— stepped out and opened the rear door. Freya smiled widely and hugged the driver, blocking his view of the passenger as she emerged. The woman who stepped out had to be Sarah, his aunt. She looked like an older version of Mae with the same dark hair and eyes, similar narrow faces with full lips. He'd taken after his mother, but it was clear now that his sister had the Rutherford features. He was glad Mae had been away when Freya had come looking for him. One look at his sister and Freya would have known that their father had two children.

Sarah crossed the few feet to him, brushing at damp cheeks with one hand and holding her thick black coat tight at her neck with the other. "Hello, Heath," she said. "I'm very glad to meet you."

Heath stood for a long moment, paralyzed as the

desire to keep his distance on this trip warred with the unexpected warmth in his chest.

"Hello," he finally said, and opened his arms, offering the hug that she clearly wanted. His aunt stepped straight into his embrace and hugged him tightly.

Something shifted in his chest, as if his heart was stretching to make room for someone new, but he refused to allow it. He had to remember that regardless of how she appeared, this woman was the sister of the man who'd scared his mother enough to risk everything. He'd be wise to keep his guard up.

"I can't believe we've found you," she whispered. Then she stepped back and gave Freya a quick hug. "Thank you for bringing him back. Come on, let's get out of this cold air."

The driver, who was quickly introduced as Lauren, held the door for the three of them to step in. Sarah slid in on the seat beside him and Freya took the bench seat across from them with her back to the driver. Her knees bumped his as they both twisted to find their seat belts, but Heath ignored the sparks the contact created. He needed to focus. No one here was on his side, not even Freya. They all had their own agendas.

The trip back was filled with light chatter, mainly between Sarah and Freya, and an occasional comment thrown in from Lauren in the front. Heath had a feeling they were doing it on purpose to let him adjust, and he appreciated it. He'd been young when they'd moved to Australia, and the majority of the time since then he had been in a small town, so everything about New York at night seemed off-kilter. The air outside was too cold, they were driving on the wrong side of the road, the scenery they were passing was all bright lights and tall buildings. His battered Jeep with sand on the floor and his surfboard on the roof was a world away.

"Where are we headed?" he asked, suddenly realizing he hadn't thought much past the flight and the technicalities of the trip.

"My apartment," Sarah said. "It's on the Upper East Side, so not too much farther now. I have a room made up for you. It's yours for as long as you want it."

He offered a nod and a tight smile. For some reason he'd assumed he'd be staying in a hotel, not invited right into his aunt's home, and he was unsure how to feel about that just yet. "Thank you."

By the time they'd reached the apartment and gotten his bags up the elevator to her penthouse suite, he was beginning to feel tired. Freya had lingered with the chauffeur and he felt her absence now, which was ridiculous, since he barely knew her.

"Do you want something to eat?" Sarah asked. "A drink?"

"No," he said, then his stomach rumbled, and Sarah grinned.

"How about I give you a few minutes to freshen up, then I'll meet you for a nightcap in the living room? I'll have some food made up in case you're in the mood."

"Okay, sounds good."

After she showed him to his room, he closed the door, dug out his cell and called Mae.

"Hey," she said. "That took ages. Did you fly to the other side of the planet or something?"

He chuckled. "Something like that. Feels like I've been in a plane or a car for a week."

"Where are you staying?"

He'd told her he was coming to the States to investigate a possible business opportunity. If what the Rutherfords' lawyer said was true, then Heath wasn't lying—he'd inherited a business, or something. He hadn't paid a lot of attention to the details. Although actually, he and Mae had inherited, despite his being the only name on the paperwork. Once he'd scoped out the situation and ensured it was safe, he'd tell his sister everything. Their mother had trained him too well to do otherwise. They always looked before jumping, never acted rashly or assumed anything was safe. And as the older brother, he'd been told to look after his sister since he could remember. He wasn't going to undo all that planning because someone dangled money in his face. Once he was confident this was safe for her, he'd tell Mae everything and split whatever money their father had left fifty-fifty with her.

"I'm staying at someone's place."

"Is it nice?"

Heath glanced again at the furnishings and then pulled the drapes back to reveal a sweeping view of

Manhattan. "Yeah," he said in the biggest under-statement of the year.

"And what's New York like? Tell me everything."

He paced around the room, stretching leg muscles that had been restrained for too many hours now. "I haven't seen anything yet except through the car window, and that was...bright. Busy."

Mae sighed melodramatically. "I still can't believe you refused to take me. I might never recover from the injustice."

He laughed because he knew she meant to make him laugh, but he had to force it because her comment cut close to the bone. "Well, if you hadn't chosen a career in teaching with its inflexible holiday times then it might have been different. Next time."

"Promise?" she said in a tone that reminded him of five-year-old Mae who wanted an extra scoop of ice cream.

He closed his eyes. "Let's see how this pans out first. Hey, I have to go. People are waiting for me."

"Isn't it late at night there?"

"Yeah, but I slept a bit on the plane and my body thinks it's morning."

"Call me often."

That was one promise he could make with a clear conscience. "I will."

Heath disconnected and shoved the cell in his pocket. He and Mae didn't normally keep secrets from each other—they'd spent all their lives ensuring their own and each other's safety, which meant they'd needed to be open. This trip, the DNA reveal, the money…it was a whopping big secret, and it was heavy on his shoulders. It had been good to hear her voice, though—grounding. Reminding him why he was doing this and to not be seduced by wealth and glamour.

He shucked off his coat and found a hook for it, then splashed some water on his face in the attached en suite. But as he headed out of his bedroom, he found himself lingering, wanting just another couple of minutes to collect himself. One side of the hall was covered in artwork and the other side was open, with only a railing separating him from the floor below. The structure of the apartment was impressive— high ceilings, sweeping views from the many windows and elegant fittings, but the decor was warm and comfortable, making it a home, not a showpiece.

He turned to the framed works on the wall and hesitated. Frowned. They weren't paintings, they were photos. Dozens of photos of a baby who matched the one photo his mother had kept. Some were the baby on its own, others were with a younger version of Sarah. This was a wall of photos of *him*.

In the middle of the display hung a huge painting of the same baby, and the title "Joseph Rutherford II" along the bottom of the frame. And then the clincher—a photo of his mother holding the baby. He swallowed two, then three times to get past the lump in his throat. The expression on her face as she looked at her baby, at him, was unlike anything he'd seen on her face in person. She looked younger, sure, but her features were softer, her expression shining with innocence. And the whole situation came around and hit him square in the chest, knocking the breath from his lungs.

He really was Joseph Rutherford II.

He really had been born to this family, should have grown up in this house or one like it. *Would have*, if his mother hadn't taken him and run as far away as she could get to keep him, and the child she'd been carrying, safe. An act of bravery he could barely comprehend.

He reached up and placed two fingers on the glass over his mother's face. "Thank you," he whispered. "I'll make sure Mae is safe."

Footsteps on the carpet behind him jolted him back into his surroundings. He dug his hands into his pockets, turned and saw Freya. A tentative smile lifted full, pink lips at the edges, softening the delicate curve of her cheek, and, annoyingly, that was all it took for his pulse to pick up speed. He took a deep breath to try to steady himself. Distance from everyone here was crucial to surviving this trip.

Freya glanced from him to the photos. "Ah. I see you already found our Wall of Joseph. This one is my favorite," she said, running a fingertip down the frame holding the photo of Sarah balancing a toddler up high, over her head, both of them laughing and joyful.

Instead of focusing on the photo, Heath turned his gaze to Freya. "For an FBI agent who tracked down a missing person, you seem to be right at home in the missing person's family home."

It seemed like this whole situation was a complex jigsaw puzzle and he only had a few of the pieces.

"As I said in Australia, I'd taken leave. I was working in a private capacity when I found you."

There was more to this story, he could feel it. He crossed his arms over his chest. "So what's your connection to my family?"

"Sarah is my godmother," she said simply, "and I grew up in her household."

His jaw slackened. "Okay, that's not what I was expecting. She raised you?"

Freya shook her head. "My mother is here, too. She works for Sarah."

He remembered their arrival on the tarmac. "Lauren. Sarah's driver."

"That's her." A warm smile crept across her face. "She became Sarah's chauffeur when she was pregnant with me, so I've literally known your aunt all my life."

His stomach clenched. He'd been right to be wary. Freya wasn't an impartial FBI agent doing someone a favor in locating a missing person, she was a part of his father's world.

"Do you still live here?"

"I have a place of my own in Queens, but I keep a few things here in case I want to stay a night."

He glanced back up at the photos of himself, taking in this new piece of the puzzle.

"I'm sorry, Heath," Freya whispered.

He turned and found her closer than he'd expected and had to draw in extra air to get his lungs to work. "For what?"

"For having what you missed out on—living with your aunt when you didn't even know she existed."

He laughed at that. The idea that he'd choose this life over being with his mother and sister was preposterous. "Let's be clear on this—I'm not jealous, Freya. I don't wish that I had any of this growing up." Sarah might seem nice now, but people like his father didn't emerge from a vacuum. Unlikely his father was the only asshole in the family tree. "In fact, I don't think I want it now, either."

Her head tilted, sending her long red hair spilling over a shoulder. "What are you saying?"

He found his mother's face on the wall. "This is the world that almost destroyed my mother. The world she risked her life to shield me from. And I'm not going to be sucked back in after all her sacrifice just because someone offers me money."

"Wouldn't the best type of justice for your mother be to take their money?" Her voice was soft; her scent surrounded him. "I know she left with very little, and it must have been hard, and it's heartbreaking that she's not here to benefit. But you can." She laid a hand on his forearm. "Take it and do whatever you want with it. Whatever she would have wanted you to do with it."

He looked down at Freya's hand on his arm, the

warmth of her skin seeping in through his long-sleeved polo. She must have realized at the same time because she withdrew it and he had to stop himself from reaching for her and bringing her hand back to him. He blinked and stepped back, his gaze again finding his mother's face on the wall.

His mother had loved him fiercely and would have given him the world if she could have, so he couldn't deny that she'd want him to have the funds now that it was possible.

"You're right," he said, straightening. He'd take their money and split it with Mae and they'd do whatever the hell they wanted with it, not what the Rutherfords wanted them to do. And along the way, he'd find his mother's family. "Let's go downstairs and talk to my aunt."

Three

Freya led Heath into his aunt's living room and watched as Sarah and Heath greeted each other awkwardly—Sarah clearly wanting more but remaining tentative, and Heath giving her a fake smile in return.

After a couple of minutes, Freya took pity on them and headed for the discreet bar at the other end of the room. "Nightcap?"

"I'll help," Heath said, and followed her. She showed him the setup and he did a quick scan of the alcohol and mixer options. "How about a sidecar? Or maybe a boulevardier or a reverse Manhattan?"

Freya blinked. Her plan had been to offer scotch or brandy, maybe with one mixer. "Well," she said, "since you're offering, I'll have a boulevardier."

"Make that two," Sarah said as she settled into a blue wingback armchair.

Heath nodded. "Three boulevardiers it is."

He poured with quick, assured movements, the dark tan skin of his hands contrasting with the crystal glassware that sparkled in the overhead lights. Mesmerized, she watched him work, and when he handed her a glass and their fingers brushed, the crackle of magic seemed to pass between them. She glanced up, but Heath appeared unaffected, so she turned away.

Once they had their drinks and were seated around a carved wooden coffee table that had a plate of sandwiches in the middle, Sarah raised her glass. "To family."

"Family," Heath repeated, lifting his glass in the air, then taking a slug.

"I want you to know that I never stopped looking for you," Sarah said quietly. "There were times that other people told me to let it go, but if there was a chance you and your mother were out there, needing help, I couldn't."

Heath and his mother had disappeared around the time Freya was born, so Sarah's search for them had been a constant in Freya's life. Over and over, she'd watched her godmother get her hopes up only to have them dashed again.

"Probably better that you didn't find us," Heath said, gaze on the amber drink in his hand. "In the past couple of weeks, I've done a bit of online research on my father, and he sounds like a piece of work. If you'd found us, you might have led him to our door."

Sarah flinched and wrapped her fingers tighter around her glass. "Discretion was a top priority, but maybe you're right. Either way, I'm glad we've found you now. You can't know just how glad."

Freya's heart swelled to see Sarah so happy, then she caught Heath's troubled gaze and her heart deflated a little.

"Look, Sarah," he said, setting his glass on the table. "I'm happy to have found some extended family. Mae and I didn't grow up with that. But I'm concerned that you want more from me than I can give."

"Sweetheart, I promise I won't ask for anything that makes you uncomfortable."

This was going worse than expected. Freya tried to think of something to change direction. "Speaking of Mae, do you want to bring her over?"

Heath's brows drew together. "She's not part of this."

Freya knew that—Mae had a different father on her birth certificate and had been born long after their mother had left the US—but the sharpness in his expression seemed out of place. "I just meant you might like the moral support. I remember you saying that the two of you are close."

"We are, but she has her own life. This trip is just about me."

Freya exchanged a look with Sarah as the silence

stretched out. Then Sarah sat up and said brightly, "I expect you're keen to know about your inheritance." She reached for a small satchel on the table beside her and handed it to him. "I've kept your portfolio ticking over for you since your father died and there's some legal untangling to be done now, but once you're ready, we can sit down and go through the accounts. In the meantime, here is some cash and credit cards to pretty much do what you want until then."

Heath unzipped the satchel and looked inside. "Thank you, I appreciate all of that. Especially that you kept the portfolio running despite having no assurance of ever finding me."

"You're my only blood family, Heath," she said, her gaze on him steady. "I wasn't giving up until either I found you or I took my last breath."

Heath shifted in his seat.

"This is an excellent cocktail." Freya lifted her glass to the light, examining the way the brightness made the drink glow.

One corner of Heath's mouth tipped up. "A better nightcap than gin and karaoke?"

Freya snorted a laugh then, embarrassed, covered her mouth with a hand. Sarah watched the interaction but when neither of them explained, she glanced away. Freya wondered how much the other woman had read into the teasing.

"I've been thinking," Sarah said. "I'll throw a party to celebrate your return and for you to meet everyone you need to know."

Freya leaned back in her chair, glad to be able to miss that. The people Sarah would think Heath needed to know would be the people Freya didn't want to be around.

Heath waved that away with a sweep of his hand. "No need to go to any trouble on my account."

Freya could see that Heath didn't understand. "Joseph Rutherford's missing heir has become a favorite for gossips and conspiracy theories. Everyone has their own ideas about where you went and whether you'd come back. Your return will send ripples through our world, so may as well lean into that."

Sarah sighed. "Too true. But to start with, I have three tickets for the fundraising gala tomorrow night. I thought we could all go."

Freya's hand paused midair and she had to force it to continue bringing the glass to her mouth and taking a sip as she watched Heath, who clearly wasn't thrilled with the idea.

"Tomorrow night?" she said. "So soon?"

"I realize Heath probably didn't bring anything formal to wear, so I booked my personal shopper for tomorrow. She'll come and take your measurements and ask for your preferences, and be back with an assortment of tuxedos for you to try on. The timing is quick but it's for a great cause—the East River Children's Hospital."

Heath ran a hand across his forehead. "Sarah, I need to let you know that I'm not the prodigal son returning home. I'm not staying. I'll be flying straight back to Australia, to my life, once this is all sorted out."

Sarah's face fell and Freya jumped in. "Everyone understands you have a life in Australia. Maybe after you see the sort of life you could have here—"

"Freya," Heath said, cutting her off. "I'm not the person that you or Sarah want me to be. I'm Heath Dunstan, a bar owner from regional Australia. No matter how well the tuxedo fits tomorrow, I'm not Joseph Rutherford II and I won't be. It's too late for that." He pushed to his feet. "I'm sorry, that came out blunter than I meant. I'm tired from the flights, so it's probably better I head to bed."

"Of course," Sarah said, rising from her chair. "I hope you sleep well."

Heath gave a tight smile before heading for the door, and Freya made to follow him.

"Freya," Sarah said. "Can you stay a minute?"

Sarah was smiling but Freya stilled. Had Sarah guessed? Had the gin and karaoke line—and her own reaction to it—given their one-night and away? She relaxed her stance, determined to play it cool. "Sure."

They waited for a few minutes to give Heath a chance to clear the hall, then Freya jumped in. "Don't feel you need to invite me tomorrow night. Now that he's here, the job is done. I'll step back and leave you time with your nephew."

"Actually, I'm hoping you'll come with us. I'd like you to be around to show him the ropes—not just tomorrow night but for his entire trip here. The smoother this goes, the more likely he is to stick around afterward."

Freya stepped back. This wasn't how things were supposed to go. She was putting distance between them now that she'd escorted him home. "That's your role, though. You're his aunt, and you're much more involved in that world than I am—you know that."

"He's on his guard around me. Still making up his mind. But he seems to trust you."

"I can assure you, he absolutely doesn't." He'd made it plain back in Australia and on the plane tonight that he didn't trust her an inch.

"On the surface, maybe, but I can see there's an ease between you two, a shared understanding of his situation. And friendships have been built on less."

Freya scanned her godmother's face for anything behind that comment—had Sarah guessed after all? "I…"

"Please, Freya? Just be around for him through this transition phase."

She looked into Sarah's eyes and sighed. There were two people in the world she couldn't say no to—her mother and her godmother. And she had a feeling Sarah knew that. "Okay, but only for the transition. I'll see if I can extend my leave. But then you need to let me get on with my life again."

"Promise," Sarah said, and hugged her.

Freya returned the embrace and then walked back up to the bedroom Sarah kept here for her, feeling that she'd somehow just walked deeper into a spider's web. Whether the web was Sarah's or Heath's, she had no idea, but when she climbed into bed and closed her eyes, it was Heath's face that filled her mind.

The next night, Heath sat in the back of Sarah's car, wearing his brand-new tuxedo. The shopper had taken his measurements, found a tux, then made alterations in the afternoon so that the fit was perfect. Beside him, his aunt was in a blush-pink gown, a string of pearls at her neck, with her hair swept up in a complex style.

"I'm so thrilled you agreed to come tonight," she said as the car moved another spot closer to the drop-off point.

"There was an option?" He smiled to show he was joking, but he was half-serious—he'd been engulfed in a whirlwind for the entire day, carried along by the force of Sarah's will as he was fitted for his tuxedo, dress shoes were obtained and a thousand other details seen to. Apparently, the rules around attendance at glamorous fundraising galas were extensive.

Freya had been at her own place today, and Sarah had been buzzing with things to do, so besides the discussions with the shopper about his clothes, he hadn't had a proper conversation with anyone all day. At least he'd be able to call Mae later in the evening, and Freya would be meeting them here at the fundraiser.

"I can't wait to introduce you tonight," Sarah said as they pulled up at the start of the red carpet. Lauren—

Freya's mom—hopped out from the driver's seat and opened their door so they stepped out into the group of other finely dressed people, making their way in.

"Thank you," Heath said, but the other woman's attention had been snagged by something at the entrance. He followed her line of vision and felt the world around him fade away.

Freya wore a long-sleeved ice-blue dress that hugged her curves to her waist, then fell to the floor in soft folds. The whole thing was covered in tiny little silver sparkles that caught the light, making it seem magical. Her long red hair was down, and had been styled with gentle waves. He found himself moving toward her without having to think about it. From the first moment he'd watched her take a barstool the night she'd burst into his life, he'd known she was gorgeous. But tonight, in that dress, surrounded by the ornate marble entrance, she glowed. She was ethereal.

She glanced over and saw him and smiled, and his heart damn near stopped in his chest. Sarah caught up to him and tucked her hand in his elbow, and reached to kiss Freya on the cheek.

"Sweetheart, you look beautiful. Doesn't she, Heath?"

Both women turned to look at him and he could barely get his voice to work. "Beautiful," he finally agreed, even though that was such a plain word for someone who was throwing some kind of spell over him. Again.

Freya smiled. "You look pretty nice yourself. Sarah, your shopper needs a raise."

"I pay her pretty handsomely already. Here, Freya, take Heath's other arm. Heath, Freya is going to be… let's say, orienting you to the people here tonight."

"What does that mean?" he asked suspiciously as they walked together along the red carpet.

Freya patted his biceps. "I'll be your personal briefing file. Telling you who people are, what's going on, etc."

The combination of Freya sliding a hand into the crook of his elbow with one hand, and patting his arm with the other had him instinctively swaying toward her. He managed to stop himself just before doing anything embarrassing, but how would he make it through a whole night when she looked like an angel?

"Sarah!" came an excited voice from across the lobby.

"Hugo," Sarah called back. "Just the person I was looking for." She peeled away, leaving Freya and Heath alone.

"Okay," Heath said. "If you're here to orient me, we can start with what the event is for."

"This is the annual fundraising even for the Rutherford Wing at the East River Children's Hospital."

The Rutherford Wing? He turned to watch Freya's face as he asked, "Are you serious?"

"I'm a forensic accountant, I'm always serious."

Her eyes glimmered with humor, and he couldn't stop the chuckle.

The venue had old New York splendor, with its marble lobby, ornate staircase and chandeliers hanging from vaulted ceilings. Over the top of the clink of glasses and the murmuring crowd, he heard what sounded like a live orchestra playing from the next room.

They spent the first half an hour drinking champagne while Freya pointed people out and gave him brief summaries.

"That's Eleanor Morris over there in the black dress. She owns a string of high-end fashion stores throughout the city. She's nice enough, but don't get her started on her company or you'll never get her to stop."

"What about that one?" Heath asked, inconspicuously pointing at a red-faced man.

"A cousin of the Morningtons. The Boston branch of the family. Two more glasses of champagne and he'll be telling stories to anyone who will listen about having dated a bunch of Broadway stars."

Heath laughed and realized he was enjoying himself. "And that couple? The bald man and the woman in the gold lamé dress?"

For the first time, Freya hesitated, but then she gathered herself and Heath wondered if he'd imagined the small hiccup. "Mr. and Mrs. Leyland."

A woman walked past selling raffle tickets. Heath reached into his pocket for the cash Sarah had pressed on him before they'd left and found a bunch of folded hundred-dollar bills, so he bought ten.

"Come and look at the silent auction tables," Freya said.

He followed her, and once they were perusing the items up for auction, he said, "Not that this hasn't been entertaining, but why did Sarah want me to come tonight?"

"Your aunt wants you to get to know the people from the world you were born into—a place in this society is your birthright."

"But if I'm not staying, does it really matter?"

A man with carefully coiffured dark hair and a smarmy expression stopped in front of them, threw back half a glass of champagne, and dumped the glass on the tray of a passing waiter.

"Freya," the man said in mock surprise as he tugged a blonde into their small circle. "I didn't expect to see you here tonight."

"I'm not sure why not, Dominic," Freya responded coolly. "It's a fundraiser for a hospital wing that literally has my godmother's name on it."

The man—Dominic—barely registered her words, instead pulling the blonde closer. "I'm sure you know Prairie Leyland."

"We went to school together," Freya said in that same cool tone. "Hello, Prairie."

The blonde raised her nose a fraction, looking down at her. "Freya."

Freya didn't seem surprised by the rudeness, simply resigned to it. "And this is Heath Dunstan. Heath, this is Dominic."

Heath followed the exchange, trying to read the undercurrents. He extended his hand. "Good to meet you, Dominic."

Dominic shook his hand, but his gaze was on Freya. "That's how you introduce me? Just a name? I'm wounded."

Heath watched the man, unsure if the display was for his benefit or he was just needling Freya.

"Fine," she said. "Heath, this is my ex-husband Dominic."

Knowing her ex wanted a reaction, Heath stared blankly at the man.

"Better," Dominic said. "Though to be more accurate, we would of course say I'm your second ex-husband. I saw Milo on the other side of the room somewhere. Have you run into him yet tonight?"

"Not yet," Freya said.

"But," Heath smoothly interjected, "I do see someone else we need to say hello to. You two enjoy your night now."

With an arm around Freya's waist, Heath moved them in the opposite direction from Dominic and Prairie, and didn't stop until he spotted a waiter with a tray of champagne flutes as well as martini glasses filled with a blue concoction.

"What's in these?" he asked the waiter.

"This is tonight's signature drink, sir. The Fresh, Flirty Fundraiser."

Heath took one and sipped. "Vodka martini with curaçao and lime?"

The waiter grinned. "You got it."

"We'll take two." Heath took a second glass and handed it to Freya. As the waiter moved off, Heath raised his glass to hers. "To a life free from self-important assholes."

A laugh bubbled up from her throat and the stress lines around her eyes eased. "To a life free from self-important assholes," she repeated, and clinked her glass to his.

Before he could say more, there was a break in the music and the high-pitched sound of someone tapping a wineglass with a spoon. Heath looked around until he saw a large white-haired man on a raised dais, the offending teaspoon in one hand and a microphone in the other. The crowd quieted and he raised the microphone to his mouth.

"Good evening. Don't you all look lovely tonight." He paused and smiled benevolently at his audience. "For those of you who don't know, I'm Hugo Beckett, the chair of the Children's Hospital fundraising committee, and I'd like to welcome you all tonight. While you're here, I hope you enjoy yourselves and spend all your money." A ripple of amusement flowed through the crowd. "And, as I do every year, I'll now hand over to our founder, the incomparable Sarah Rutherford."

Surprised, Heath looked at the edges of the stage until he spotted his aunt, smiling as she acknowledged the round of applause. She hadn't said she was the founder of this organization, just that they were going to a fundraiser. Well, good for her, doing something with all her privilege. He finished his cocktail, caught the attention of another waiter, and passed his and Freya's empty glasses to the man.

Sarah took the microphone, seemingly at home under the spotlight. "Thank you, Hugo. I'm not sure about being incomparable, but I can tell you that just this morning while I was struggling to get my new cell to work, I felt pretty incompetent." Her rueful tone hit the spot for the audience and they rewarded her with a laugh. "I'm here to thank you all for coming out on a cold winter's evening to support our foundation. There are several new pieces of equipment the Children's Hospital needs and state-of-the-art medical equipment doesn't come cheap. However, I'm sure if we pull together, we can raise that money here tonight. Or at least get drunk trying." The audience laughed again and raised their glasses to her, and Sarah raised her own champagne glass back.

Then the amusement faded from her expression, and she pressed a hand over her heart. "And now I hope you'll all indulge me for a moment. I have some news to share, news that is both incredible and thrilling. My nephew, the man you know of as Joseph Rutherford II, or, as some of you call him, the lost heir to the Bellavista fortune, has returned home to us."

Heath's stomach dropped hard as a loud murmur

spread across the crowd in a wave, accompanied by the rustling of fabric as people turned, looking around them as if he would pop up and shout, "Surprise!"

"Did you know she was going to do this?" he whispered to Freya.

"No," she said near his ear. "I promise I had no idea she'd announce it so soon."

Clearly, once they arrived home, he was going to have to establish some boundaries with his aunt.

Up on the stage, Sarah put her glass down and used the hand to shield her eyes from the lights as she looked out. "Heath? Where are you? Will you give us a little wave?"

Lord above, had she really just asked him to take part in his own humiliation? But having no real options in the moment, Heath raised a hand to just above his head, holding a couple of fingers in a little salute.

"Oh, there you are," Sarah said, pointing so everyone else could see him as well. "Welcome home, darling."

He tipped his head in acknowledgment, and for the rest of Sarah's speech, where she thanked individual donors and went into details about the equipment they were hoping to purchase with the funds, Heath was acutely aware of the of being an object of curiosity to everyone in his vicinity.

Finally, Sarah finished and stepped off the stage to a round of applause. The music started up again and Heath was inundated with people wanting to shake his hand and generally crowding him. There wasn't enough air to fill his lungs—all these people sucking it out of the room, pressing down on him. He looked past them, scanning for Sarah, too annoyed to pay attention to strangers who suddenly wanted to know him.

A tall sandy-haired man clapped him hard on the back. "Good to meet you, Joseph. Or can I call you Joe?"

Heath smiled with clenched teeth. "Actually, you can call me Heath."

"No, no," the man said. "There's no reason not to claim your real name. It's one to be proud of."

The sandy-haired man was edged out by a short man with a finely manicured gray beard who looked him up and down. "Claiming to be Rutherford's son, eh? Well, I can't see that you look much like him."

Thankfully, Freya inserted herself between them and distracted the bearded man.

A woman in a dark red dress, with long black hair that fell to her waist, slid into the space Freya had been standing in and held out her hand. "Hi, Joseph," she said, her voice breathy. "I'm Elodie and I'd love to show you around town. I hear you only just arrived and you don't know anyone, which is too, too awful."

Heath grabbed Freya's hand and held it up. "Already have a tour guide, but thanks for the offer."

Elodie leaned close and whispered in his ear,

"Call me when you want to trade up," and tucked a card in his pocket.

Trade up? Heath retrieved the card and handed it back, allowing the ripple of contempt show on his face. He might not have a future with Freya, but he knew her worth.

Heath looked longingly toward the arch that led to the marble lobby, and when he looked back his field of vision was filled by a man with gold-rimmed glasses whose mouth was smiling but eyes were filled with undisguised loathing. By his side was a younger man whose gaze was laser-focused on him.

"The prodigal son," the man practically spat, then turned to Freya. "A little heads-up would have been polite."

"Heath has been in the country less than twenty-four hours," Freya said with a thread of steel in her voice. "This *is* the heads-up." She smiled with no trace of warmth. "Mr. Newport, Sebastian, this is Heath, who was born Joseph Rutherford II. Heath, this is Christopher Newport and his son Sebastian Newport. They own the other fifty percent of Bellavista Holdings, so they are your business partners."

Her tone told him the rest—they were his business partners, but not his friends. Noted.

He stuck out a hand. "Good to meet you."

Christopher stared at his hand a moment too long, then Sebastian stepped forward and shook it. "Good to meet you, too," the younger man said, though Heath didn't believe him for a second. The son might have more manners, but he wasn't happy about Heath's reappearance either.

Christopher sank his hands into his pockets. "So you're alive after all, walking around bold as daylight, drinking champagne, flirting with the pretty women. And all these years we'd assumed Joseph murdered you and your mother and disposed of your bodies." He laughed uproariously and slapped his stomach. Beside him, Sebastian winced.

Heath felt Freya stiffen beside him, but after years of owning a bar and throwing drunks out on the street, he recognized ego and bluster when he heard it.

"I can only apologize for not dying as an infant, Mr. Newport, but it's true what they say—what doesn't kill you makes you stronger." He paused and then sank one hand casually into a trouser pocket. "I understand that our business interests are tied together, so you'll be lucky enough to see the resulting internal fortitude in action."

A couple of people in the gathered crowd chuckled; Christopher Newport opened his mouth then closed it again, clearly trying to think of a comeback. Without waiting for a response, Heath grabbed Freya's hand, turned so he could shoulder his way through the onlookers and didn't stop until he found a spot with enough space around them that he could breathe.

Freya put a hand on his biceps. "I'm sorry about these people, Heath. It should die down once they're used to you and you're not a novelty anymore."

He glanced at his watch. "Back home it's early morning. What I wouldn't give to be on the beach right now." No people, no tuxedos, just the sun, his surfboard and him.

Freya's eyes softened. "I didn't spend that much time in Noosa, but the water was so blue, and it sparkled in the morning light like it was strewn with diamonds."

Heath saw the image in his mind's eye and his shoulders relaxed a fraction. "The water is warm year-round, so it's always a good day at the beach."

Prairie glided past, saw Freya, and backtracked to stop in front of them with an overly dramatic smile. "Oh, I'm glad I caught you, Freya," she said, heavy on the condescension. "I wanted to say well done. You've made a lovely catch there." She tipped her head meaningfully to Heath.

Heath looked from Freya, whose cheeks were reddening, to Prairie, who seemed very pleased with herself, sure that there was something else going on here.

At that moment, Dominic returned and offered Prairie his arm. "Ready, darling?"

"Never been more so." Prairie leaned over between Heath and Freya with a conspiratorial wink and added, "And now that I think about it, you were always good at catching the rich ones, weren't you? Though whether you can hold on to this one, either…" Her voice trailed off as she flashed her teeth in an expression that was nothing like a smile.

Heath wasn't sure what was going on, but he was sure he didn't like it. He turned his back on the other woman and focused on Freya. "Have I told you how beautiful you look tonight?"

A little of the tension left Freya's shoulders. "You did, actually."

"Well, since you are by far the most stunning woman here, I think it should be repeated. You, Freya Wilson, take my breath away."

Behind him, he heard "Humph," and felt a surge of satisfaction.

"They've gone," Freya said after a moment.

"I don't like that woman," Heath said, turning to watch them through the crowd. "Or that man."

Freya laughed humorlessly. "We can agree there." She blew out a long breath, then looked up at him. "Do you want to get out of here?"

"God, yes." Heath could have kissed her for the offer of escape. "Anywhere."

"We have places where you can see the water, but it's far too cold to be outside tonight." She tapped a finger on her lips, thinking. "Actually, I know somewhere you might like."

"I'm already one hundred percent sure I'll like it better than here." He grabbed her hand again and headed in the general direction of the entrance before pausing and looking back. "Do we need to tell Sarah we're leaving?" He might be annoyed with his aunt, but he wouldn't scare her by disappearing.

Freya cast a quick look around the room, then shrugged. "I'll text her from the cab."

Heath slid an arm around Freya's waist to hold her close as they threaded their way through the crush of people. Without conscious thought, his mind flashed back to holding her naked form against him on the night they met, and he almost stumbled with the intensity of the memory. Her curves pressed against him, her arms twining around his neck, the smell of her skin filling his senses. When someone accidentally bumped into them and he reflexively pulled Freya closer still, he told himself that it was necessary. The feel of her lush form finally pressed against his side again, though, that was an indulgence he knew would be hard to give up once they reached the street, so he made the most of the feeling while he could.

Four

Within an hour of leaving the fundraiser, they were seated in a softly lit bar with views of the Hudson River and Freya allowed herself the luxury of relaxing. She always liked leaving the big society events, but leaving to spend some time alone with this man? That was a pretty sweet deal.

She glanced over at his strong profile. "It might not be the beach on a summer's day..."

He tipped his head to the tall windows nearby. "A river view on a cold winter's night has a charm of its own."

As he lifted the beer bottle to his mouth, her attention snagged on his lips and she was momentarily disoriented. Seeing him in a tuxedo when he and Sarah had arrived at the gala had sent a jolt of electricity through her system. Since then, the tux had fallen somewhat into disarray—the bow tie hung loose, draped around his neck, and the top two buttons of the crisp white shirt were undone. A stark memory reappeared of pushing his shirt off his shoulders in a darkened bedroom and suddenly her mouth was so parched and her brain so frazzled that she quickly gulped down half her beer.

"So that was…" he began, then seemed to give up on the thought.

"It truly was."

"Is your whole life like this? Parties and expensive clothes and champagne and one-upmanship?"

"I rarely go to anything like that anymore. My life consists of going to work, visiting Mom and Sarah, coffee dates with friends, and quiet nights in my apartment." Saying it aloud didn't sound that exciting. Maybe she should get a cat?

His gaze was sharp, assessing. "Then why tonight?"

"Honestly?"

"Always my preference."

"Sarah thought you'd find it easier with a friendly face by your side."

"You were babysitting me?" he asked, incredulous.

She snorted a laugh. "More of a wingman."

One side of his mouth hitched up in a lopsided smile and her heart skipped a full beat—he hadn't offered her a genuine smile since the night they'd first met, when she'd planted herself on a barstool and flirted all night with the hot bartender. A night of no complications, no strings. Or so they'd thought. She'd missed that smile more than she would have expected and she savored the sight of it now.

"She was probably right," he admitted on a sigh. "I would have refused if she'd made the offer beforehand, but it was good to have someone to explain what was going on. I saw you run interference for me a couple of times, too."

"You're welcome." She looked out over the water, then reached into her pocket and pulled out a folded slip of paper. "I have something for you. The names and addresses of your mother's family. Along with their cell numbers and email addresses."

He stilled, yet his entire being seemed to vibrate with tension. Her knee accidentally brushed his under the table, and then his knee pressed firmly against hers, as if physically anchoring himself through her. Despite the layers of fabric separating their skin, electric shivers spread from the point of contact, down from her knee to her toes, and a spider's web of sensation across her thigh. It took all her focus not to move, yet he barely seemed to notice—all his attention on her hand. Then he slowly reached out and took the slip of paper, unfolded it and scanned the contents.

"Her parents are both on here," he said without looking up. "They're still alive."

"From what I could tell, none of her immediate family have died. They're pretty much as she left them, just older and with extra kids."

He traced a finger over the page. "I have grand-parents."

"And aunts and uncles and cousins."

He shook his head, as if it was too much to comprehend. "My mother used to tell us stories about her family. Our family. These were the people she was talking about."

There was deep gratification to be gained in providing something so important to another person, and she sat in silence, giving him a beat. His hands rested on the tabletop, still holding the scrap of paper, just inches from hers, close enough to touch if she slid her pinky a little. His hands were square, strong, with blunt-tipped fingers, and she could remember them trailing across her skin, and even now, just the memory sent a prickle of awareness sweeping through her system.

Before she completely lost herself to her own imaginings, she pulled another folded piece of paper from her pocket. "There's something else."

He looked up sharply, his brown eyes sparking. "Which is…?"

She handed the slightly crumpled slip of notepaper to him. "Your mother's name."

His Adam's apple worked up and down in his throat as he opened the paper flat. "Evelyn," he whispered. "Evelyn O'Donohue."

"You had no idea?"

"None." He paused and scrubbed a hand over his angular jaw. "She wouldn't trust names like that to a child in case I accidentally told someone, and then we never revisited the topic. She died suddenly, hit by a car as a pedestrian, so even if she'd been planning to tell me on her deathbed, she didn't have a chance."

"Heath," she started, but didn't really know what else to say. She might not have had healthy relationships with most of her family, but at least she knew who they were. And what her mother's name was.

"Was it hard to find?" he asked, finally looking at her.

She sucked her bottom lip into her mouth, working out the best way to tell him. "The last thing I want to do is ruin your moment, but you have a right to know."

He frowned. "That sounds pretty ominous."

The happy glow she'd had evaporated, and she schooled her features into a neutral expression. "When your father died, you inherited everything. Since you weren't here, his sister—Sarah—as the executor, received all his personal effects. She has boxes and boxes of stuff in storage for you, waiting until you're ready to go through and decide what you want to keep."

"I can't imagine wanting to keep anything of his," he said, scowling. "But it feels like you're heading toward a different point."

"In a locked drawer there was a folder, and inside that folder was a history of private investigator files."

Understanding dawned across his face and her heart squeezed tight at the raw emotion in his features.

"He was having my mother's family watched," he said with disgust.

"He was. All their names, details and contact information were in there, so all I had to do was check it was current."

"Son of a bitch," he said with feeling, and she had to agree.

It was an awful feeling to know your blood relation was an abhorrent human. Worse still to know another family member had suffered at their hands—something she knew from experience.

She laid a hand over his on the table. "Heath, I'm sorry."

"I keep thinking it can't get worse, but it does."

He turned his palm over and interlaced their fingers, and her heart broke a little for him. She was happy to provide that comfort, even if did cost her the price of having to hide her body's reaction to his.

"What are you going to do?"

He watched their entwined hands for a long moment, then casually rubbed his thumb across her palm, once, twice, in a soothing movement that set off fireworks in her veins before withdrawing his hand.

"I don't know yet, but I think the starting point

will be meeting them." He refolded the piece of paper, slipped it in his pocket and took a long swig of his beer. "So, tell me about the husbands. How many, exactly, do you have tucked away?"

Freya sat back. She recognized the tactic of changing the subject and was on board with giving Heath some space to process the news about his family. "Just the two. Dominic, who you met, and Milo, who apparently was also there tonight. He's much like Dominic, but less pleasant."

Heath's eyebrows shot up. "I'm going to need more than that, especially from the woman who knows everything there is to know about my family."

"Fair," she said. "Milo and I were teenage sweethearts. Or so I thought. I was desperately in love with him and ignored my mother, Sarah, and my own better instincts to marry him when I was nineteen. Turns out, Milo was hoping to get closer to my father, and once he realized that marriage to me wasn't going to help—in fact it made my father less likely to acknowledge him in public—Milo walked out." The hurt and humiliation still sat in a hard ball at the base of her stomach whenever she thought about it.

Heath glared daggers at his beer. "Probably better that we didn't meet up tonight."

"That's always my thought when it comes to Milo."

"Then came Dominic?" he prompted, and then asked the waiter to bring two more beers and a large bowl of fries.

Freya sighed. "Then came Dominic. I made it clear to him from the start that I was not a golden ticket to my father, but apparently Dominic wasn't listening. He's a social climber, and on paper I seem well connected, not only to my father but to the Rutherfords as well. He thought he could spin it once we were wed. Once again, I ignored everyone who cared about me and rushed into marriage and had it all blow up in my face."

"He walked when he couldn't get close enough to the money?" Heath asked, eyes narrowed.

"This time I ended it." It had been a tiny salve to her heart and ego, but something at least. "I overheard him plotting with a friend—he still had hopes he could leverage my connections—so I threw him out."

"Good for you."

She raised her beer. "To a life free from self-important assholes." It was her new favorite toast, thanks to Heath.

"Hear, hear." He clinked his bottle to hers and finished his beer.

"At least that time I learned my lesson that marriage is not for me. Twice bitten." She'd never come close to being tempted again, but if she ever did, all she had to do was remember Milo and Dominic and she'd be cured.

"Can I ask you something personal?"

"Sure. As you pointed out, I know a lot of personal stuff about you so this is only turnabout."

"You've given reasons why they wanted to marry you. But why did you marry them?"

She'd asked herself that one a lot over the years. "They both flattered me and convinced me they loved me, and I was pretty naive back then." She picked at the label on the bottle. "To be honest, I was escaping into a fantasy. For a girl who never fit in, that was predictably seductive."

The waiter returned with their beers and fries. Heath thanked him and threw back some fries before asking, "What were you escaping?"

"Wow, you're coming hard with the big questions tonight."

He gave her his slow, lopsided smile. "Hard? Should I remind you of the piece of paper you just handed me and the conversation that ensued?"

She chuckled. "Okay, you asked for it." She ate a handful of fries and considered how to start. Maybe at the beginning. "My mother was a housekeeper at a huge mansion. The man of the house got her pregnant, and when he—and his wife—realized, they threw her out. She had no living family and now she had no job, nowhere to go, and she was pregnant."

"Jesus, I hate your world."

She tilted her head in acknowledgment. "She'd worked for the Rutherfords before and Sarah had always been kind, so she asked her for a job. Mom wasn't optimistic because she was pregnant, but she was running out of options. Thank goodness, Sarah put her on the payroll and gave her a roof over her head. Even making her the chauffeur because Mom hated being a housekeeper anyway. Then Sarah wheedled the full story out of her and went straight to my biological father's place to confront him. She made him cover the costs of Mom's prenatal care as well as ongoing child support."

He let out a low whistle. "I'm liking Sarah more by the minute."

"She's pretty much Mom's hero. Mine, too." Sarah had secured Freya's and her mother's lifelong loyalty that day. "I grew up going to the fancy schools but didn't have the same money the other kids had, plus, my parentage was an open secret and it seemed to endlessly amuse the other kids, so that ensured I was kept on the fringes."

"Well, crap." He reached for her hand again and squeezed it tight.

She looked down at their joined hands, appreciating the support, and also aware that he'd taken her hand a number of times over the night. Something fragile and lovely fluttered in her chest, and she squeezed his hand back.

"I'm guessing from the story about your marriages," Heath said, "that your father didn't come around in the end, wanting to play happy families."

"Not even a little." The very idea was laughable. "In fact, he had two daughters already when I was born, and they were not happy about my existence, so they made an effort to remind me that I wasn't really part of that world whenever we crossed paths."

"Do you cross paths often?" he asked, snaffling more fries with his free hand.

"You saw my father tonight." She knew she was laying herself bare to him, but there was no going back now. Besides, with Heath so close, holding her hand and giving her all his attention, it felt as if nothing else could ever matter enough to hurt her again. "The bald man who was with the woman in the gold lamé dress."

He looked up at the ceiling for a few seconds, face screwed up in thought. "Leyland?"

"That's the one."

She turned their joined hands over, loving the feeling of his touch, loving even more that he wanted to touch her like this after all they'd been through in Australia.

"Hang on, that name... Leyland. There was someone else there with that name."

"My half sister," she said, and grabbed more fries.

"Prairie." His eyes widened. "Prairie is your half sister. And she was hanging off your ex-husband."

"It was possibly on purpose, but if so, I have no idea if it was her plan or his, since they both hate me with a vengeance."

Heath scooted his chair closer and used their joined hands to pull her into a comforting embrace. Except it wasn't comforting—it made her skin heat and her heart start to thump. Surrounded by his scent, she let him hold her, and felt the moment his breathing changed, became faster, uneven.

He eased back a little and she looked up.

"Heath," she whispered, but didn't know what else to say, what she could say, so his name hung in the air between them until he whispered, "Freya," and leaned down to kiss her.

The sounds of the busy bar around them faded away. His mouth was gentle and hot and tasted of beer and there was nothing she wanted more in the world than to be here in his arms. His hand came around the back of her neck, pulling her closer, and Freya melted into him. She sucked his bottom lip into her mouth and gently bit down and he groaned.

"Freya," he said, this time her name sounding like it was being wrenched from him, and rested his forehead on hers. "I was starting to forget we're in a public place."

Slightly dazed, she squeezed her eyes shut, then opened to peek around. No one else seemed to have noticed that she'd left all her senses behind the moment Heath had kissed her—the bar, with its patrons and noise and waitstaff, was exactly as it was a few minutes earlier. She, though…she felt like her world had shifted. She moved her focus to the man beside her, and found he was watching her with a rueful gaze.

Heath was silent for a long minute, a pensive look on his face. "So," he finally said, "how much money is on the credit card in my pocket?"

A ball of laughter burst from deep inside and she slapped a hand over her mouth. As methods to break the tension went, it had been effective. So she grabbed her beer and tilted it to him. "It's black. You can pretty much do what you want."

He grinned. "Enough to buy a motorcycle?"

"An expensive one," she said. "Buy whatever motorbike you want."

He crossed his arms over his broad chest and nodded. "I think I will."

Heath sat in the back of Sarah's car, Sarah beside him briefing him on Bellavista Holdings, Freya across from him briefing him on Christopher and Sebastian Newport, and Freya's mother Lauren frowning at him in the rearview mirror.

Since the fundraising gala, he'd had a couple of days to himself, which had been a relief. Both days, he'd chatted to Mae in the mornings, connected in with Tina, who was running the bar in his absence, then walked around Manhattan, getting his bearings. He'd found a motorcycle dealership and bought a sleek, beautiful bike. Following Freya's advice, he'd bought the one he wanted—the one he'd have bought back home if he'd had that much money to spare— as well as all the accessories he'd need, from Bluetooth helmets to armored jacket and pants and riding gloves. He'd splurged and was surprised at how good it had felt. How fun. Maybe there was something to this wealth thing…

The bike would be delivered, perhaps even today, and he couldn't wait to test it out.

He hadn't seen Freya in those couple of days, either, and he was trying to control the hunger in his gaze whenever he looked at her. Which, come to think of it, might have been the reason that Lauren was still glowering at him in the mirror.

They were on their way to the main office of Bellavista Holdings. Freya and Sarah had been briefing him since breakfast, and it was continuing nonstop. When Lauren dropped them at the building's front door, the briefing didn't stop—they continued to give him last-minute details while they traveled up in the elevator to the forty-second floor. Given that his plan was simply to get in, have a look around, be ready to sell once the estate settled, he wanted to tell them not to bother. He had no need for a business like this, or a New York business at all once he was back in Australia.

"Oh, another thing," Sarah said, "my PR consultant says that she's getting media requests about you."

Heath snapped to attention. "About me?"

"It's a fascinating story," Sarah said. "Australian bar owner turns out to be heir to billions. I've told her that you need some breathing room before having to face media scrutiny, so she's made a few deals to have the story buried for now in exchange for exclusive access later."

"Sure," he said with a shrug. "Later is better than now."

As they stepped in the door, they were met by

Sebastian, who moved forward, hand outstretched. "Joseph, so good to see you again."

Heath bristled at the false charm and the memories of the last time they'd met. "Heath."

"Right. Heath." He turned to the others and shook their hands in turn. "Sarah, Freya."

"Just you today, Sebastian?" Sarah asked mildly.

"I'm afraid so. My father had a meeting he couldn't move." He turned back to Heath. "And while we're on the subject of my father, let me apologize for his behavior the other night. He was out of line."

"Agreed," Heath said. "But it's good of you to mention it." His opinion of Sebastian Newport went up, but only marginally.

"Let me show you around." Sebastian led the way, introducing him to staff, showing him key offices, pointing out maps on the walls, talking big and explaining fast.

Heath nodded in the right places and smiled when he met new people, but he was growing more and more irritated by the minute. He might not know property development, but after years of owning his own bar and working in other people's bars before that, Heath knew about reading people. Sebastian Newport was throwing around every big word and bit of jargon he could think of, clearly hoping to bamboozle Heath. Little did Sebastian know, he didn't have to try so hard. Heath simply didn't care. In fact, he was barely paying attention since he'd be selling the company as soon as the paperwork was ready and he could talk it through with Mae. Sarah was adding in comments here and there, obviously hoping to clarify things, and he wanted to tell her to enjoy the view instead, but Sebastian was getting annoyed at the constant interruptions.

As they reached a large meeting room, Sebastian stopped. "Heath, I wonder if we could have a quick word alone?"

Heath almost smiled. A classic divide-and-conquer maneuver—get the new guy on his own, away from his companions who knew something about the company.

Heath shrugged. "I don't own anything until the estate is settled. Until then, Sarah is still the executor, so you can talk in front of her."

Sebastian hesitated, then nodded. "Look, I have sympathy for your position—this must all be a lot to take in. But what do you really know about property development, especially in the US? It would be like throwing me into running a bar in Australia— I'd flounder. I'm prepared to buy you out."

"You have that much money lying around?" Heath asked, poker-faced.

"I can raise the capital. Then you can do what you want with the money. You won't be tied to a company that means nothing to you."

Selling to Sebastian would be the easiest solution. Heath wanted out, and here was a buyer who knew the company already, but something about this felt wrong. He glanced at the two women beside him and clocked Sarah's face, full of tension.

"You know, a quick chat alone is a good idea, but I'd like it with Freya, thanks."

Sebastian's brows shot up but without missing a beat he said, "You can have this meeting room for as long as you like. Sarah, can I offer you a drink?"

Once they were alone, Heath put his hands low on his hips. "Tell me what I'm missing."

Freya adjusted her bag on her shoulder. "Like what?"

Heath thought back through the office tour. "Let's start with whatever's going on with Sarah."

"Okay, but settle in." She pulled up one of the high-backed chairs on wheels and sank into it. "Two men started this company and made a bunch of money. When they retired to their neighboring houses in the Hamptons to play golf and drink expensive scotch, they handed it down to their sons, Joseph Rutherford and Christopher Newport."

The names clicked into place. "My father and the jerk I met at the fundraiser."

"That's them. They hated each other and spent most of their time either trying to undermine the other or get the other one to sell. Added to that, Sarah and Christopher had a youthful romance and she was head over heels for him, until she realized he was awful. He never forgave her for breaking up with him and it just intensified the hatred between the families."

"Whoa." He sank his hands into his pockets. "Sarah and Christopher?"

Freya screwed up her nose and nodded. "Then your father died, and Sarah has had control of your half of the company, and Christopher has tried all sorts of dirty tricks to get her to walk away."

"That explains the glower she's had all morning."

"He's currently in the process of retiring and handing the reins to his son Sebastian and would love to have complete control of it first. To win before he retires. And now you're back, so you and Sebastian are the third generation of Rutherford and Newport men to own Bellavista Holdings."

"Nicely summarized," he said, and she flashed him a quick smile.

Heath looked out through the glass panels to the bland hall and office cubicles branching off it. All this history, all these machinations going on in this office for years before he'd arrived, and he hadn't wondered or asked questions before this moment.

"So," he said, and rested a hip on the long oval table, "I waltzed into this situation, only thinking of myself and what I wanted, which is to sell and return home. And being self-centered in this, or any, situation is exactly what my father would have done."

Her eyes widened. "Now that you mention it, that does sound like him, but it's too harsh to be about you."

Sweet of her to say, but untrue. "You know what?

I've been thinking I'm my mother's son, but it turns out I'm just as much my father's."

"No," she said fiercely, "you're yourself."

"A person's character is shown through their actions and the choices they make." It was one of his mother's favorite things to tell him. And that meant he needed to make a conscious choice to not do the thing his father would have done. "It's no secret that I want to sell and go home, clearly Newport knows that, too, but I have to act with integrity."

She reached out and took his hand, in the first real contact since their kiss in the bar, and every cell in his body sat up and took notice.

"Choosing based on what you think other people want will lead you to disaster," she said, gaze steady. "You can only choose what's best for yourself."

"I don't want to be like my father, where I walk in and override other people and do whatever I want. I need more information first before making any decisions. I'll wait."

Freya smiled at him, as if she was proud of his decision, and her expression lit up his insides until he smiled back.

"Come on," he said. "Let's tell Sebastian that I'm not making any decisions about selling, then we can get out of this place."

Five

When they arrived back at the apartment building, the doorman met them at the car. Freya had been listening to Heath tell Sarah about his hometown of Noosa. But when the doorman said, "There's been a delivery for Mr. Dunstan," and pointed to a sleek black motorcycle, Heath quickly finished his sentence and practically leaped from the car.

Sarah raised an eyebrow and Freya grinned. "I told him he should buy himself something. Looks like he did."

Sarah smiled indulgently. "Good for him. And well done you."

Freya, her mom and Sarah followed him over to look at the bike. Sarah made appropriately approving comments, said she'd see him later and left. Freya's mom checked that he'd ridden before and had worked out if his Australian license could be used, and then went to talk to the doorman.

Freya, however, leaned back against a heavy column and simply watched him for a few minutes. It was a rare indulgence to see Heath in an unguarded moment, and she wasn't wasting the opportunity. His cheeks, still carrying the kiss of the Australian sun, had an extra glow that she hadn't seen since he'd arrived in the States. He'd rolled the sleeves of his business shirt to the elbows, exposing muscled forearms sprinkled with dark blond hair. She remembered those arms wrapped around her when they'd lain in his bed. A delicious shiver ran down her spine.

But the thing that wormed its way right into her heart and held tight was the pure emotion sparking in his eyes. Since the minute she'd mentioned the Rutherford name all those weeks ago, he'd had a shield up—every word, every expression, was measured. And yet right now, he was simply experiencing the moment, and the effect on her system was electric. She had to force herself not to reach out and touch him, to warm herself against the fire…

He glanced up and caught her watching and she held her breath, worried his shield would snap back into place. Instead a lopsided smile spread across his face.

She pushed off the column and crossed the drop-off area to stand beside him. "You want to take it out right now, don't you?"

"More than you can imagine." He ran a hand over the seat, slowly, luxuriating. "My skin's been itching since this whole thing began."

"You want the freedom."

"I do." He looked up at her, but left one hand draped on the handlebars. "A little independence from having my own vehicle while I'm here is appealing, but yeah, I'm after a little freedom."

The way he spoke of freedom called to her. For as long as she could remember, she'd been doing the expected thing, the right thing. Wanting a little of that freedom—and that fire in his eyes—for herself, she tentatively laid a hand on the soft seat. And then swallowed hard. "Where will you go?"

"You know what? I have no idea." He speared his hand through his hair and glanced at the cars moving along the avenue in front of the building. "The only plan I had was to see where the road took me, but I've seen the streets of this city now, and I'm not convinced that's the best plan for a newcomer traveling alone. So—" he paused and grinned at her "—want to come for a ride?"

Her mouth dried and she couldn't form words. Not that she'd have known what words to use anyway. It was just a simple ride, yet it felt like he was beckoning her to cross a line in the sand. Everything they'd done together since he'd arrived had been to do with the Rutherford inheritance; even the bar on the Hudson had been about debriefing from a Ruth-erford event. This…

This was Heath Dunstan inviting her somewhere for no practical reason. Maybe it was because he enjoyed her company, or that he only knew a handful of people in the country, or he just wanted a navigator and she was there. Whatever the reason, she wanted to go.

Wanted to be the sort of person who impulsively jumped on the back of a hot guy's bike.

Wanted, desperately, to be on Heath's bike with him, heading out for no reason other than they wanted to go.

Her stomach fluttered. "I don't have anything to wear that's appropriate for a bike."

"Not a problem," he said, his eyes dancing. "I know a guy."

She arched a brow. "You know a guy."

"I had them deliver top-of-the-range protective jacket, pants and gloves with the bike. I'm sure he'll be happy to bring another set over in your size. After all, I just dropped a lot of money in their dealership."

"You seem to be taking to this rich-guy thing like a duck to water," she teased, deadpan.

He smothered a smile. "You wound me, but I'm going to look past that comment and order you a set of riding gear anyway."

After she told him her size, he pulled out his cell and walked away to make the call. Still smiling, Freya turned and caught sight of her mother—casually leaning against the black Suburban, watching her, eyes hidden by her mirrored sunglasses but definitely frowning.

Freya wandered over. "Something wrong?"

"So many things," her mother said, taking off the glasses and hooking them at the front of her shirt. "They discontinued that chocolate with the raspberry pieces and shredded coconut. Last night I finished the last book in a mystery series and I don't know whether to reread from the beginning again or find a new series. Since I had my last haircut, one side keeps flicking up no matter how much product I put in it. How many do you want?"

"Mom," she said, exasperated but amused anyway. "Every time you think no one is looking, you frown at Heath. Any reason you don't like him?"

"To be fair, it's not only when I think no one is looking. I've been doing it in front of people, too."

"Mom," Freya said using her best stern voice.

"He seems fine, but he's clearly not sticking around. He's going to break my baby's heart."

"It's not like I'm in love with him." Freya crossed her arms tightly under her breasts. "He won't break my heart. Besides, he's a good guy, he won't do anything horrible."

"That's what you thought about Prairie and Constance when you first met them at school and they pretended to be your friends," she said pointedly.

"Oh, come on. That's not fair—Heath is nothing like them." Even as children, Prairie and Constance had been horrible, but Freya had wanted a sister so badly she hadn't cared. That wore off pretty quickly and she'd been intolerant of mean people ever since.

"It's also what you thought about both Milo and Dominic at first."

"I'm a much better judge of character now." Partly thanks to her ex-husbands teaching her what to avoid.

"Okay, sure," her mother said, and threw up her hands. "But I reserve the right to frown at him, or about him, as much as I want."

"Mom."

"Oh, all right. I'll just narrow my eyes occasionally and throw in daily pursed lips."

Freya laughed and hugged her mother tight. "You're the worst."

Her mom hugged her back. "Just be careful with your heart, sweetie."

"I will, I promise," she said, and went to find Heath.

Just over an hour later, she was on the back of Heath's bike as they headed out of Manhattan. Their helmets had Bluetooth but she only spoke to give him directions, not wanting to distract him from riding a new bike, in an unfamiliar city, and on the opposite side of the road than he was used to. Which meant there was nothing to distract her from the nearness of his body. Perched behind him, with her thighs wrapped around his hips, her chest pressed into his back and her arms gripping his torso, she was acutely aware of him. Worse, her position made her think of their night together in Noosa in excruciating Technicolor, and her body was remembering the same details.

By the time they reached the New Jersey shoreline and Heath brought the bike to a stop, she was ready to burst out of her skin. They dismounted and she removed her helmet, gulping lungfuls of cool, salty air, desperately trying to focus on something that wasn't Heath's body pressing against hers.

They walked a little, chatting about the different color of the Atlantic Ocean to the Pacific, until they found a bench to sit on. Beside her, Heath watched the waves break and roll in, and she was again struck by the unguarded emotion on his face. This time, however, it made her sad. This used to be his life. When she'd been searching for Joseph Rutherford II, she'd been so certain she was about to improve his life—who wouldn't want billions of dollars?—but had she? She had thought she wasn't the right person for the job, but she hadn't doubted the job itself.

"I think I owe you an apology," she said.

He bumped her shoulder with his. "Because you didn't think to bring cookies?"

"No," she said, though that was a definite oversight. "This whole thing hasn't been a picnic for you. This morning at the office, and the way people spoke to you at the fundraiser…"

He shrugged, seemingly unconcerned. "None of that was your fault."

"Maybe. But I'm the one who found you and dragged you into this." He'd asked her to walk away, said money didn't fix everything, but she'd kept her focus on the job at hand.

"If it hadn't been you it would have been someone else," he said, laying a warm hand on her knee and squeezing. "And for what it's worth, I'm glad it was you."

"That's generous of you. And if it had to be someone, I'm glad it was me, too." At least she'd been able to ease his way a little.

He hadn't moved his hand from her knee, and it felt so good there that she wasn't going to draw attention to it and risk him taking it away.

"But you're right that it hasn't always been a picnic." He leaned back and rested an ankle on the opposite knee. "I'm fine, but I'm glad I didn't bring Mae with me—that gala would have crushed her. She didn't grow up with quite as much pressure from our mother as I did."

"What do you mean?" She couldn't wrap her head around living the way Heath's family had—hiding, isolated.

"She trained me young to look for people at the playground who were watching me, or anyone outside our house with a camera, or strangers following us or lurking outside our windows. Mae had some of that but most of it was focused on me, which means that she's a little more…trusting. Optimistic." An affectionate smile flickered across his features. "Bringing her into this world would be like throwing her to the wolves."

He said it all in a matter-of-fact tone, as if it was completely normal. What would a childhood like that do to a kid? To the man that kid would grow into?

"You're still doing that, aren't you?" she said softly. "Checking everything is safe before making a step."

He turned to her, brows drawn together, sliding his hand from her knee to his own. "Of course I am."

"You know that's hypervigilance and it's a trauma response." She might only have a desk job at the FBI, but she'd done some courses and training.

He tipped his head in acknowledgment. "Possibly, but my mother's hypervigilance is what kept us safe. Speaking of mothers," he said, nudging her thigh, "yours doesn't like me much, does she?"

He was changing the subject again, but she couldn't blame him, so she went with it. "She's just worried that you're not going to stick around."

"I mean, she's not wrong… I'm definitely not sticking around."

"It's…" She fiddled with the sleeve of the new riding jacket. "She's just very protective of me and keeps an eye on the people around me."

"Well, with the stellar choices you made in your ex-husbands, I can see why she might feel that way."

Freya punched him lightly on the arm. "I'm perfectly capable of running my own life, thank you very much. She's just worried that I'm falling for you."

His dark eyes were suddenly serious. "Are you falling for me?"

"After two marriages that each pretty much sucked the life out of me, I can assure you that I'm not looking for a third. I promise I'm not falling for you. Or *anyone*." It wasn't lip service. Relationships had never brought her anything but grief and pain and so were off the table for the foreseeable future. Maybe forever. The two men she'd married had both used her for their own agendas—she'd been nothing more than a tool for them, even though she'd thought she was in love. Both damn times. She'd thought they were building something together, but each time she hadn't seen their true selves until the end.

She really did need to look into getting a cat.

"Okay, good." He wrapped a hand around the back of his neck. "Because falling for me would be a bad idea. I'm not very good at commitment, or long-term anything. We moved around too much as kids and had too many secrets to risk making friends. I learned never to get attached, and it's a hard lesson to unlearn. Mae's the same."

"You're a love 'em and leave 'em guy, leaving a trail of broken hearts?"

He huffed a laugh. "There has been no relationship long enough for anyone to get attached to me and have their heart broken."

She found that hard to believe—she could imagine someone falling for Heath Dunstan in one night. "You're so sure?"

"It wasn't safe to share much about myself, so women usually find me aloof and drift away of their own accord. Besides, I had no role models—I've never seen a relationship up close. Mum refused to date for the same reasons, and we had no grandparents, no aunts and uncles. Even if I wanted a relationship, I'd be terrible at it. I've simply never had to learn to be in one."

She wanted to ask more but he shifted his weight and looked away—he'd obviously shared more than he'd intended—so instead she said, "I can be your ally or your friend, though. Help you while you're here."

He nodded, considering. "What do you get out of it?"

"I love Sarah, and she wants you in her life, and the smoother this all goes, the more likely you are to visit her." Which was why she'd agreed to help Sarah find him in the first place. "Plus, you have a cool bike."

"Okay, I'd appreciate that." He stuck out his hand, and when she shook it, her skin tingled at the firm pressure of his grip. "We'll be friends. So, friend, one thing I'd really like help with is an accountant I can trust to go through the papers that Sarah gave me and the others she's threatening to show me. There are really only two things left that I need to do before going home, and that's one of them."

She ignored the way her stomach dropped at this casual mention of going home soon, and said, "I can do that." Going over pages of numbers was always a fun day. "What's the other thing?"

"Contact my mother's family." Lines appeared around his eyes and he didn't sound as keen as she'd expected.

"Have you thought any more about how you'll handle that?"

"I want to meet them but…" He shifted his weight on the bench.

"But…?" she prompted.

"They don't know yet that my mother is dead." He ran a hand down his face, then looked up at the sky. "How do I break the news that their daughter, their sister, is dead? That they didn't get a chance to see her again before she died, and now her ashes are scattered in another country."

She edged closer to him, offering the support of her physical presence, her body heat, another human heartbeat. "I'll go with you if you want. Be your wingman."

"Thanks." He blew out a breath. "Give me another couple of days so I'm in the right headspace. I want this to go really well but my head is currently full of Sebastian Newport and Rutherford stuff."

"Is there anything I can do to help you clear your mind?" Maybe they could head for Sarah's house in the Hamptons for a couple of days, or she could show him some of the sights, perhaps fly to LA so he could surf. "What do you need?"

One side of his mouth hitched up in a rueful smile. "I'm not sure there's anything that can make me forget I'm Joseph Rutherford II."

The torment in his dark eyes called to her heart, and as he turned to look out past the breaking waves, the curve of his jaw, the tense set of his mouth, the memory of his skin called to her on another level. A flush of heat rippled across her skin as she threw caution to the wind. "There's something that might clear your head of everything else, but I'm not sure whether it's something friends do."

He was silent for several beats and she started to think he wasn't going to reply. Then he turned his head and the look he gave her almost scorched her skin. The pulse at the base of his throat beat hard and she felt herself melting. Even the air around them seemed to be vibrating. "I can be flexible on the boundaries around our friendship."

She had to run her tongue over her bottom lip so she could speak and his gaze flickered to her mouth as she did. "Then let me help you forget, even for a few minutes."

"As long as you promise," he said, his voice gravel-rough, "it's just a friend doing another friend a favor and not because you're falling for me."

"I won't fall for you. Cross my heart." She made slow strokes across her chest as she crossed her heart and she watched Heath follow the move, his breaths coming faster.

He leaned over and she met him halfway, and their lips touched, and she had the strange, almost déjà vu sensation of coming home. She dismissed the feeling— it was just that they'd kissed before so he was familiar, nothing more, though this wasn't anything like their kiss in the bar or the ones in his apartment, which had been heated and hungry. This was slow, tender and sweet enough to touch her soul.

His hand came up to hold the side of her face and her skin tingled in the spots his fingers and palm made contact. She could drown in this kiss if she let herself, and the temptation to let herself was strong…

She laid her hands flat on his chest, feeling the strength, remembering the night she'd explored his body, yearning for the freedom to do the same again. He gripped her hips, then suddenly she was in the air, then landing on his lap, and he was so much closer that she trembled with delight and wanting. She could feel his erection pressed against her and she squirmed to make the contact more snug. Heath grunted at the connection so she did it again.

"I always seem to want you," he said against her mouth, then moved to make a trail of kisses across her cheek, down to her jawline.

"It's just a bad idea," she said, but struggled to remember why now that he was scraping his teeth across her earlobe. "For…well, reasons."

"I'm leaving soon." He pressed a kiss to the side of her throat. "And I'm not great at commitment anyway." He gently blew on the skin damp from his kiss. "And the relationships between our families are already entangled." Another kiss, this one to the base of her throat. "Your mother would murder me." His tongue pressed to the soft skin there. "We live in different worlds." He nipped the flesh and held gently before moving back up to her ear. "We'll probably see each other over the years when I came to visit Sarah and we don't want it to be awkward."

And, she forced her mind to recall, after their first time together, things had gone spectacularly badly and they were only just getting back on track now. Not to mention he was clearly still keeping secrets. If they became involved and it went even half as badly, then there could be fallout for Sarah, who'd only just gotten her nephew back.

The thought was enough to pull her back to reality and she eased away, her lungs heaving to drag in enough air.

"We did it again," Heath said with a faint smile.

"It's turning into a habit," she said, trying for a light tone but failing. "Though making out in New Jersey is new."

"I really am heading back to Australia soon and I don't want to start something and leave it hanging." There was regret in his eyes that he didn't try to hide, but his hand on her back was moving, circling, creating shivers wherever it went.

"Me either," she said, but it was more than leaving something hanging for her because the situation was bigger than the two of them. Sarah had asked her to find her nephew and Freya had slept with him. And now Sarah had asked her to show him the ropes of New York society and ease his transition, and if Freya slept with him this time, too, and things became awkward enough that she had to step back before finishing the job, she'd never be able to face her godmother again. But his hands were still moving, and she couldn't make herself crawl off his lap.

"What if…" she began, but wasn't sure how to finish the thought.

His breath caught. "I'm listening."

"What if," she said again, and took a shuddering breath.

"It sounds great so far." He leaned in and pressed a heated kiss to her throat, and she moaned. And she couldn't resist any more.

"What if you come back to my place now, and we indulge our habit. Was it Byron who said the only way to get rid of a temptation is to yield to it?"

"Oscar Wilde," he said, his gaze dark and longing. "What about all the reasons not to? Didn't we just list a bunch of them?"

"They're reasons not to get *involved*." She threaded her fingers through his hair. "I'm not suggesting we start dating."

He nodded, very slowly. "We've already slept together once, so it's not exactly crossing a line."

"And I'd been drinking that first time, so we could think of this as a do-over." She knew she was talking herself into it—they were talking themselves into it—despite intellectually knowing they shouldn't, but feeling his breath feather over her face and his body pressed against hers, she simply couldn't bring herself to care.

He regarded her for a long moment, then slid his hands under her thighs, stood, and let her slide down his body until her feet hit the ground. "In that case, let's get going."

Six

Somehow they made it back to her apartment, their closeness on the bike good but not close enough. After making it up two flights of stairs, Heath behind her, hands on her hips, sliding around her waist as they moved, she fumbled her key as his breath, hot on her ear, distracted her. Then it clicked and she opened her apartment door and they tumbled through, kissing and pulling at each other's clothes.

"This is my apartment," she said, breathless from his kiss.

"It's great," he said without looking around, and kissed her again.

She found his belt buckle and held tight with trembling hands. "Coffee?"

He dipped his gaze to her hands at his belly. "No, you."

"Water?" she asked, knowing it was probably pointless, but needing to offer since it had been ages since they'd left Sarah's place and she had lengthy plans for him now that he was here.

"You," he said, and the tone of his voice sent a shiver down her spine.

This time she couldn't help teasing a little, fluttering her lashes. "Snacks?"

"You." He walked her backward until she reached a wall, hands firm on her hips.

She slid her hands up to run through his hair, the silky strands ticking the soft skin between her fingers. "Music?"

"You." His dark eyes were shining with delicious heat as he leaned into her, pressing her against the solid wall.

"Shower?" she said, voice uneven.

He kissed her hard, then murmured against her lips, "You."

She paused. Now that she'd started thinking about it, a shower wasn't a bad idea. She'd been hot in the riding clothes for hours. "What if the shower has me in it?"

He grinned. "That works."

Another quick kiss, and she tugged him by the hand into the bathroom and ran the water while they stripped out of their remaining clothes. Freya took a moment to watch him behind her in the mirror—

the crisp hair of his chest, the ridges of his abdomen, the bunch and release of his muscles as he moved. After forgetting their first time, the memory had come back, but was still a little blurry in places, so she didn't want to miss a second this time. They'd had no promises, no guarantees, so this might be the last time she would be with him.

He looked up and caught her watching, and with one raised eyebrow, he stepped up behind her, wrapped his arms around her and lifted. And then stepped into the shower.

The press of his naked body against her back was heavenly, but she wanted more. Turning, she squirted body wash over a soft sponge and rubbed it over his back. He let out a low groan, so she pushed her advantage, nudging him forward and positioning his hands above his head on the shower wall so she had full access to wash his skin. He was slick with soap, and as she moved from his arms down the sides of his torso, he shuddered. And then she went lower, and wrapped her hand around his erection, feeling the heat, the thick shape of him, lingering until he turned in the tight space to face her.

"I think I'm pretty clean now," he said, his mouth hitching up, but his eyes blazing. "My turn."

She handed him the sponge and body wash and, starting with her stomach, he rubbed the sponge in luscious strokes over her sensitized skin. When he reached her breasts, he cupped them, one at a time, while his other hand washed and teased, the warm water spray caressing, adding to the sensation.

He bent a knee and pressed it between her legs. Her belly fluttered and the throb between her legs grew. His hand snaked lower, and when it reached the apex of her thighs she almost melted into the shower floor.

Suddenly the water went cold and she squealed and flung the shower door open and they stumbled out. "Sorry," she said between breaths. "It does that sometimes."

He grabbed a towel and wrapped it around her. "It could have been worse—you're still naked and here with me."

"Bed?" she offered.

"No," he said, dark eyes laser-focused on her.

"Sofa?" She dropped the towel.

"Here," he said as he reached for her waist and lifted. He slid her up the wall until she was higher than him and he could only kiss her by tilting his head up. Instinctively, she wrapped her legs around his waist, her hips cradling his, his erection hard against her.

The bathroom was full of steam that wrapped around them like a cocoon, keeping them warm and in their own little world, so she was more than happy to stay. Besides, she was pinned to the wall.

She flashed him a smile. "Here works."

She traced her hands from the side of his face, down his neck to his shoulders, taut with the tension of holding her, then ran her nails lightly down his beautiful surfer's biceps, fully flexed from their task. He shuddered as her nails continued their exploration.

"Condom," he said, voice like rough gravel, and slowly let her slide back down the wall until her feet touched the floor.

"Second drawer." She gestured in the general direction, but he was focused and found a packet and had himself sheathed in what felt like record time — while simultaneously being an eternity away from her as she was delirious with wanting.

He lifted her again, her shoulder blades against the wall, her legs wrapped around Heath's hips, open to him. He arched his neck back and kissed her again, a long, thorough, scorching kiss.

The throb between her legs became an ache. "Now, Heath." She kissed him again. "Now."

Holding her gaze, he pulled his hips back a little, then slowly thrust into her, filling her, and she wiggled a little as she adjusted to him, feeling like everything in the universe was finally *right*. He paused, widened eyes filled with wonder, and he whispered her name.

He moved one hand to her hips, angling them the way he wanted, the other hand roaming her body. His lips and tongue wove a trail of magic along her throat, his teeth nipping and biting as he thrust again, then paused. She savored every second of the pause, imprinting the feeling of Heath filling her, owning her, into her memory.

Then he thrust a third time and kept going, finding a rhythm, rocking her world. The arms she gripped were taut with tension, his skin so hot she felt as if he were burning into her soul as he bucked his hips into hers.

She trailed her fingernails lightly over his chest—he'd seemed to like that last time and his groaning confirmed it. As he picked up pace, she ran her fingernails over all the smooth skin she could reach—shoulders, arms, back, sides, neck—urging him on, faster, not wanting it to end, slower, needing more, faster, until it peaked and she shuddered against him, against the wall, digging her nails into his back, barely aware of anything, aware of the whole universe, before he shuddered and jerked against her and everything went still, labored breathing the only sound in the bathroom.

Heath rested his forehead against her shoulder, her head leaning back on the wall behind her.

"Holy mother of God," he rasped.

A laugh bubbled up from deep inside her chest—at the shock in his tone, at how ridiculously good every cell in her body felt, at the pure joy of being alive.

Finally his breathing slowed, and he released a long breath before withdrawing himself and gently lowering her to the floor. It was weird that it had only been a short time since they'd stumbled into this room, full of desperate anticipation, and now everything was different. The connection between

Heath and her. The world around them. Her. Still
not steady on her feet, she leaned her head against
his shoulder, and he wrapped his arms around her,
pulling her tight. Wanting nothing more in the world
than to be here and now, with Heath, she sank into
the embrace.

Endless moments later, he carried her into the
bedroom and laid her down with such care and gentleness that she didn't want to let him go as he stood
back. He disappeared back into the bathroom, then
returned, condom gone, and stretched out beside her.
Heath lying in her bed could become her most favorite thing.

Gently, he cupped her face and kissed her nose,
eyelids, then lips. "I don't know if it's because of
the buildup or what, but that was one hell of a roller
coaster."

She wrapped herself around him, still too fuzzy-
headed to think, but warm and content. An earth-
quake could have ripped through Queens and she
wouldn't have cared. "That's us," she murmured.
"Never a dull moment."

Heath nuzzled into her neck and the last thing she
noticed before slipping into to sleep was his breath
becoming deep and even as he drifted off as well,
his arms holding her close as he did.

Freya stood shoulder to shoulder with Heath on
the doorstep of a ground-floor apartment in an un-
fashionable part of Brooklyn.

"You ready?" she asked.

He huffed out a humorless laugh. "I'm not sure what ready would look like in this situation."

She reached for his hand and squeezed. "Have you worked out what you want to say?"

"Not yet," he said. "I'm hoping for inspiration once I meet them."

As Heath knocked on the door, Freya scuffed her sneakers on the concrete step. She wanted Heath to meet his mother's family, of course she did, but she couldn't help but be aware this was one of only two things he had left to do before he returned to Australia. And she wasn't ready to let him go just yet.

In the three days since she'd invited him back to her apartment, and into her bed, they'd spent idyllic hours, taking his bike to as many tourist destinations as they could manage—some places she'd wanted to share with him, others that she'd always wanted to see herself. By unspoken, mutual agreement, they'd continued their mission to help Heath forget he was Joseph Rutherford II for a while and pretend they were outside the Rutherford bubble. They were just plain old Heath and Freya, who could have met at a party, or an ice cream shop. A nice, warm fantasy world. Sometimes they'd laughed and kissed, and other times they'd talked and made love, and it had been the most amazing three days of her life.

But she'd known they were living on borrowed time and today they were back to the real world. One day closer to the day she'd lose him.

The door opened and a woman appeared. She seemed to be in her late sixties or so, with stylish blond hair to her shoulders and the same dark eyes and high cheekbones as Heath. "Can I help you?"

This time when Freya squeezed Heath's hand, he squeezed it back, tight.

"This is going to seem random," Heath said with an attempt at a smile, "and I apologize up front for that. You don't know me, but I think I'm your—"

The woman squinted at him. "Joseph?"

Heath hesitated and Freya held her breath.

"Is it you?" she asked, gaze roaming his features as her jaw slackened. "You're Evelyn's son, aren't you?"

Heath swallowed hard. "Yeah, actually, I am."

"Oh, sweet Jesus." She turned back into the house and yelled, "Thomas, you'd better come out here."

A man with salt-and-pepper hair and a lanky frame ambled out of a doorway and down the hall. "If it's…" he began, then stopped, eyes widening. He looked from Heath, to his wife, then back to Heath. "It can't be." He shook his head. "Of course it can't. Sorry. You look like a couple of my grandsons, so for a moment—"

Heath stuck out his hand. "My birth name was Joseph Rutherford, but I go by Heath Dunstan now. And I think you might be my mother Evelyn's parents."

The man took Heath's hand, his face still confused. "Joey?"

Mrs. O'Donohue leaped forward and wrapped her arms around Heath, repeating, "It's you, it's really you."

Mr. O'Donohue put a hand on his wife's shoulder. "Bring him in out of the cold, Theresa. Come inside and sit down. And bring your friend."

As they crossed the threshold, Heath put a hand on the small of Freya's back and they followed their hosts into a small parlor. "This is Freya Wilson. She's the person who found me and gave me your address."

Mrs. O'Donohue grabbed her and pulled her into a tight hug. "Thank you," was all she said, but Freya could feel the other woman's body trembling, and when she pulled away, she gestured to a worn green sofa with a cheerful knitted rug draped over the back, and said, "Sit, sit."

Heath and Freya sat. Heath shifted his weight and rubbed a hand across his stubbled jaw, so she placed a steady palm on his back.

"Is Evelyn traveling with you?" Mrs. O'Donohue asked. Her face had the look of someone who dared not allow herself to hope.

A tremor ran through Heath's body. Freya wished she could offer more comfort, that she had the right to stand between him and pain. She'd never had the urge to do that for a man before, not even for Milo or Dominic, but maybe that was because Heath had the courage to show more emotion and vulnerability in this room than either of her ex-husbands had in the entirety of her marriages.

All she could do was be here, beside him.

"My mother passed away a bit over four years ago," Heath said, his voice only breaking a little. "I'm so sorry. It was an accident—she was on the side of a street and a driver ran off the road and hit her."

Mrs. O'Donohue bent forward suddenly, as if she'd been struck. "Oh, Evelyn."

"If it helps," Heath said, "it was instant. She didn't suffer. And she'd been having a great day before that—we'd been to the beach...."

Freya spied a tissue box on the other side of the room. She retrieved it and handed a tissue each to Heath's grandparents, then realized this was bigger than a one-tissue conversation and passed them the whole box.

Mr. O'Donohue wiped his eyes. "It does help to know she'd been happy, yes. But still..." His voice, thick with emotion, trailed off.

"Come," his grandmother said, choking back a sob. "I need to light a candle for my baby girl." She took them into the next room, which was dominated by a huge dining table and a row of three china cabinets along one wall. She stopped at the middle cabinet, found a match and lit a candle. The entire cabinet was filled with family memorabilia, from snapshots in mismatched frames, to small trophies and ribbons, and little boxes and trinkets.

The older woman picked up a photo in a dark wood frame and hugged it to her chest, then handed it to Heath. Freya leaned in to see that it was his mother, but younger than the photo in Sarah's house, maybe fifteen or sixteen, on a set of swings with her blond hair flying out behind her, laughing and free.

Then, one at a time, his grandmother passed him photos of other family members, explaining who they were and their relationship to him as she went. A couple of his cousins looked more like his brothers, which explained how the O'Donohues had recognized Heath at the front door.

"This is your family," his grandmother said, a hand on his shoulder. "If we'd known you were coming, they would all have been here. We've missed you."

"I'll come back, I promise," he assured them. "I can't wait to meet them all."

"Good," she said, smiling despite her eyes still being red and watery. "I'm your nan and this is your pop, and no matter what has happened before now, you're a part of this family and we love you."

Heath hugged his nan and Freya felt herself fall in love with his grandparents. She'd never had grandparents of her own, and the O'Donohues seemed like the ones she'd always dreamed of. They'd known exactly what Heath needed to hear and hadn't hesitated to tell him. Then again, they'd had over twenty years to prepare for this day.

"When that vile man…" his nan said, then stopped. "When your father…"

"It's okay," Heath said with a rueful smile, "I know he was a vile man."

She nodded. "When that vile man died, we wondered if Evelyn would come back. The surveillance stopped, and the bullying stopped—"

"Hang on," Freya said, suddenly alert. "We discovered the trails left by the private investigators that Joseph had watching you, but what do you mean by bullying?"

Mr. O'Donohue scowled. "He had people drop in here or at our jobs all the time when Evelyn first went missing, trying to intimidate us into telling them anything we knew. To be honest, we didn't know if she'd escaped and he was hoping we knew where she'd gone, or if he'd killed you both and was making us too scared to tell anyone about our suspicions. Either way, it was a hell of a way to live."

Freya made a mental note to let Sarah know that she should organize some victim support for the family. She knew Sarah would be horrified and would want to do whatever she could to fix things that her brother had broken.

"And then," Mr. O'Donohue continued, "he bought the company we worked for. After that our boss kept an eye on us for Rutherford as well."

"He did what?" Heath said, outraged.

"Something else to hold over our heads," his grandmother said.

Freya wondered if Heath was putting two and two together—this meant that he was the one who now owned that company. Heath appeared to be too caught up in the story, but she knew it wouldn't take him long to work it out.

"But that's all in the past now," Mrs. O'Donohue said. "That man is gone and you've made your way back to us. We've been waiting, and wishing, for this day for a long time."

Heath glanced at Freya and she had the sense he was using her to center himself, so she smiled softly and he turned back to his grandparents. "I have some other news that you'll like."

"I'm not sure my heart can take more," his nan said.

"My mother—Evelyn—she had a second child. Mae. She's sweet and brave and kind and awesome. You're going to love her."

His grandmother gasped loudly and hugged him.

His grandfather swiped the moisture on his cheeks and said, "Another granddaughter. Mae. Do you have a photo?"

Heath scrubbed a hand through his hair. "Ah, no. I had to change my cell when I arrived in the US and lost all my photos, but I promise I'll bring her over to visit you as soon as I can."

Freya began to frown, but stopped herself, instead staying very still and keeping her expression neutral. Heath had kept the same cell, she knew that for a fact because she'd been on the plane with him. Plus, she'd been forwarded the emails where Sarah's lawyers had told him that his would work here. So why would he lie? And why lie about something that was harmless to him but would bring so much joy to people who deserved it? Unless…

Unless it wouldn't be harmless to someone else. And the one person Heath consistently protected was Mae. But her photo? Freya filed that away to think more about later.

"Tell us something about your lives," his nan said.

"Sure. Um, well, the three of us have been living a modest life in Australia. I own a beachside bar, Mae teaches school, and Mom had lots of different jobs, but for the three years before she died she was working in the kitchen of a nursing home, and she loved it."

"I knew it," Mrs. O'Donohue said. "I knew my baby wouldn't have done the things that vile man accused her of."

Freya's ears pricked up. "What things?"

"He yelled about her kidnapping his son and stealing millions of dollars. Said she was probably living the high life on a tropical island. But we knew our daughter. Either she was in hiding or he'd killed her, and we just prayed that she'd gotten away."

Heath took his grandmother's hands. "She didn't do anything bad. She did everything right. You raised a heroic woman who kept us all safe."

His pop pressed a closed fist to his mouth and blinked hard. "Thank you," he said with a muffled voice.

Mrs. O'Donohue leaned over and put her hand on his knee, exchanging a loving look with her husband. Then she straightened and turned to her guests. "Coffee?"

Freya followed Mrs. O'Donohue to the kitchen and helped gather mugs and plates as the other woman chatted away, regaining her composure through familiar tasks.

Ten minutes later, the four of them were seated around the large dining table with coffee and cookies. A few minutes doing something else had worked as a circuit breaker, and the O'Donohues were peppering Heath with questions about his life in Australia.

"There's something I want to bring up," Heath eventually said, laying a hand flat on the table, "and please just hear me out. I've inherited Joseph's money and I want to make some reparations for the trauma he caused you all—"

"No," his pop said firmly.

"That money is yours," his nan said. "You keep it and don't waste it on us."

"All I'm saying is—" Heath began but his grandfather talked over the top of him.

"We're the ones who need to make reparations to you. We suspected Joseph was bad news, but Evelyn wouldn't hear anything against him before they were married. And after—" He looked to his wife, who leaned over and took his hand.

"Well," she said, looking across at Heath, "after, whenever we asked, she lied. She was clearly lying, and she knew that we knew she was lying, but she did it anyway."

Mr. O'Donohue picked up his coffee and gripped the mug fiercely. "If we'd done more, protected her more, protected *you* more, then you all would have been safe and wouldn't have had to run."

Heath shook his head. "Even if you'd known, there was nothing you could have done."

"It's sweet of you to try to let us off the hook," his nan said, "but we've had to live with that guilt since she disappeared. And we should live with it."

His pop looked down into his coffee. "We've often wondered if she was alive somewhere, blaming us for not keeping her safe."

Heath reached over and grabbed one hand of each of his grandparents. "I have a strong sense of what sort of man my father was, and knowing that, I'm confident in saying that there was nothing you could have done. Joseph had all the power. And she knew that, too—my mother didn't blame you, not even close. She raised Mae and me on stories of how great you all were. Of how much you loved her, and how much she loved you."

"Oh, sweet girl." Mr. O'Donohue pressed his closed fist to his mouth again.

Freya reached for a tissue from the box at the center of the dining table and dabbed at her eyes. She wasn't even part of this family, yet she was overcome with wanting them all to be okay.

Heath smiled, his entire face lit with love. "She told us about Sunday lunches with all the family, and that even though there wasn't much money, you always made sure there was enough for her dance lessons because you knew how much she loved it. Oh, and Mae's favorite story was that when you put Mom to bed at night, you'd give her a kiss on each cheek and a last one on the nose to make sure all the dreams were good ones. Mom did that to both of us for years."

They stayed for another hour, swapping stories and growing a bond, and Freya watched, thrilled that this had gone so well for him, but also trying not to worry that another item on his list of things to get done in New York had just been ticked off his list.

Seven

Heath waited until the next morning to call Mae. Telling her about her grandparents should be joyful news, but after leaving the O'Donohues' place, he'd been consumed by anger at his father. The man hadn't just destroyed Heath's, Mae's and their mother's lives but also hurt the entire O'Donohue family, first by making their daughter disappear out of fear of him, and then retraumatizing them with the surveillance and intimidation. Hell, even Sarah's life had been impacted through her ongoing search for him.

His father had left behind a trail of destruction.

The whole situation was so much messier than he'd hoped. He'd wanted to just wrap stuff up, meet some family members that he could stay in occasional contact with and go home. But his mother's family, the company stuff with the Newports, Freya…

Freya.

His head swam as he remembered making love to her in the shower the day his bike had arrived. And the next night when he'd turned up at her apartment with takeout, but the food had grown cold as they made love on her dining table. And the time here in his bedroom while Sarah had been away for the day.

He crossed to the windows of his bedroom and then frowned. When had he started thinking of this room in Sarah's apartment as *his* bedroom? He really needed this call to Mae—beyond sharing the news, he needed her to ground him in the real world—*his* real world—again.

He pulled his cell from his pocket and called his sister, checking his watch as he did. It would be early evening there, so he had a good chance of catching her.

Mae answered immediately.

"Heath," she yelled, but a dull roar behind her almost drowned her voice out.

He recognized the rows of bottles behind her and grinned. "You're at my bar."

"Well, you left Tina short-staffed by vanishing, so I've been doing some shifts here and there after school hours."

"Thank you for that. How have you been?"

Mae squinted, then said, "Hang on." She pulled the

cell away and Heath got a view of a packed room, which was gratifying and made him yearn for home in equal measures.

"Tina," Mae called. "This is Heath. I'm going to take it upstairs."

His sister's face appeared on the screen again, but it was wobbling as she walked up the stairs. After she shut the door to his apartment, it was quiet enough that he could hear more clearly.

"When are you coming back?" she demanded as she flopped down on his sofa.

"Shouldn't be too much longer. Maybe in a few days." He'd done most of the things he wanted already—found his mother's family, visited the Bellavista office and scoped out the situation here. He just needed to have a closer look at the accounts of the inheritance that Sarah had asked him to do, and see if he could find a way to square things with the O'Donohues after the damage his father had done. Everything else could be done from home, with a visit or two back to New York when he needed.

"Have you bought me a big present?" She waggled her eyebrows and he laughed.

"Since you ask, I do have something for you. But it's not something I bought, and it's not something you're expecting."

"Should I guess?" she asked, eyes alight.

"You'll never get it, but you should make sure you're sitting down so you don't fall over."

"Okay, now you're overhyping. You need to learn to manage expectations, Heath."

"I found Mum's parents."

Mae's entire face went slack. "What do you mean you found them? How?"

"It's a long story and I promise I'll explain in depth when I get home."

Her eyes flickered to the door in an unconscious attempt to check for anyone listening, just as their mother had taught them. "Is it safe to be in contact with them?"

It was the same question he would have asked if their positions had been reversed—they'd never known what, exactly, they were hiding from, which meant they'd not known what a safe thing was and what wasn't. Given that their mother had told them they couldn't see her family, Mae was smart to be suspicious now. And it turned out their mother had been right—Joseph had been watching the O'Donohues until he died.

"It is safe, and I'll explain that when I get home, too. It's another long story."

"Really?" Mae bit down on a smile, her caution clearly warring with her excitement. He nodded and she released the smile. "What are they like?"

"They're so much like her, Mae—warm and lovely, and they want us in their lives."

"You told them about me?"

"They had no idea she was pregnant when she

left, so you were a surprise to them, but they couldn't have been happier. They're dying to meet you."

"I can't believe this is real," she said, tears starting to leak from the corners of her eyes. "How soon can we make it happen?"

"What about we start with a video call? I'll go over to their place and call you. They said there are aunts and uncles and cousins who will come, too. And then once I'm home we can start planning a trip over here for both of us so you can meet them all in person."

"Yes, do that," she said, beaming.

The call only lasted a couple of extra minutes since Mae had to get back to the bar, but he promised he'd arrange a time for her to meet their family soon. He'd have to ensure that call happened without Freya in the room, since one look at Mae and Freya would know Mae was a Rutherford—she looked like a younger version of Sarah. Of course, that was why he'd had to lie to his grandparents and say he didn't have any photos of his sister. They'd see her soon enough, both on a video call and, once he could arrange it, in person, so he didn't feel too guilty about them. The problem was that he'd lied in front of Freya—he should have been expecting the question so he could have handled it better instead of the line about his cell.

He thought back to Freya's reaction and realized something he hadn't been consciously paying attention to back then—when he'd told his grandparents that he had a new cell, Freya had stilled. She'd noticed something wasn't right. His stomach turned as it clicked into place. Freya was smart, and she may have put two and two together already, but either way, he needed to find out what she knew, or thought she knew. Once Mae's parentage was out, she'd have reporters at her door and disrupting her school. A secret billionaire teaching little kids at a public school? The press would eat that up, and the Australian press wouldn't be part of the deal Sarah's PR consultant had made over here. Mae had to be allowed to hear the news from him in person, have time to adjust, and then make her own choices about how she handled everything else.

Kicking himself for risking Mae's identity, he grabbed his things, jumped on his bike and headed for Freya's apartment. He just hoped she'd be home.

Freya answered a knock on her door to find Heath on the other side, looking flushed, disheveled and altogether too appealing. But the look in his eyes told her this wasn't a normal social call.

"Was I expecting you?" she asked as she stood back to let him in.

"No, er... I..." He speared his fingers through his hair. "I wanted to..."

Intrigued, she closed the door and leaned back against it. She hadn't seen Heath flustered before and couldn't wait to find out what had caused it, so, somewhat amused, she waited.

"The thing is..." He unzipped his bike jacket and

threw it over the back of a dining chair. "Freya... Oh, hell." He dropped onto the sofa and put his head in his hands.

"Heath?" Any trace of amusement fled as she saw his distress, and she crossed the room to sit next to him. "Is something wrong?"

He lifted his head, took a deep breath and said, "I'm going to tell you something, but I need you to promise that it stays between us."

"Promise," she said without hesitation. This was clearly important to him, and she trusted that whatever it was, he wouldn't ask for secrecy unless it was necessary.

"Mae isn't my half sister, she's a full sister." His gaze roamed her face, and she could feel him looking for clues to her reaction, assessing the risk, ready to withdraw at the slightest provocation, so she stayed carefully still and neutral.

"Your mother was pregnant when she ran," she said gently. That confirmed her suspicions—it was why he'd been reluctant to show the O'Donohues a photo of her. "Mae is Joseph's child, too."

He relaxed a fraction, but only a fraction, clearly reassured by whatever he'd read in her expression.

"I couldn't say anything earlier," he said with a half-apologetic shrug. "It wasn't my story to tell. Mae doesn't even know about all of this yet, and once she does it will be up to her whether she claims her Rutherford heritage or stays as a Dunstan. She might want to permanently pretend we have different fathers."

"I understand that totally, but feel I still need to point out that if you'd told us from the start, Sarah would have understood and would have been happy to leave Mae out of everything. Then we could have had a team protecting Mae's position, instead of just you doing it."

"Though, at the start," he said with a half smile, "I had no idea if I could trust any of you."

She smiled in acknowledgment of his point—they could go round in circles for hours, so instead she tried to think the issue through from their current position. "Someone will work it out eventually."

"They absolutely will, because...this is Mae." He pulled out his cell and found a photo of brother and sister together.

Mae was the image of Sarah—the same dark hair, a face narrower than Heath's, the same almond-shaped eyes. But Freya couldn't keep her eyes on his sister; instead she was transfixed by Heath's expression in the photo. There was a lightness in his eyes she'd never seen before. A relaxed, easy smile that she didn't recognize.

"Mae's hair is longer now, but you can see the similarity in that picture."

She could, but she was still hooked by Heath's expression. "Can I flick?" she asked, holding the cell up.

His jaw clenched tight, then released as he nodded. "Sure."

The next photo had obviously been taken at the

same time, but in this one, Heath was throwing his head back, laughing. In all their time together, riding to tourist spots, exploring Manhattan, making love in her bed, she'd never once seen him with his guard down like this. She flicked again and the next photo had caught Heath and Mae in the middle of something playful—it looked as though he was pushing a yellow hat down on her head and she was fighting him with one hand, squeezing his nose with the other, her face red with laughter. His eyes were so wide, the white around his irises was showing, probably from what Mae was doing, and he was clearly having the time of his life. A pang of envy hit her square in the chest—for a sibling she could be silly with, for Heath to be that relaxed around her...

He glanced over and saw the photo she'd paused on and frowned. "That's just us mucking around, here's a better one." He flicked through a few and stopped on one of Mae, standing on the beach with the golden glow of sunset dusting her skin, looking at the camera with all the affection she clearly felt for her brother who'd been holding it.

She suddenly realized what she was holding in her hand and looked up at him. "You don't normally let people flick through your photos, do you?"

"Never."

"Thank you." She handed the cell back. "Thank you for trusting me."

As he shoved the cell back in his trouser pocket, his brows drew together. "You know, when I knocked on your door I wasn't going to tell you about Mae. I wanted to find out if you'd pieced it together."

That explained why he'd stumbled over his words so much when he'd first arrived. "And what were you going to do if I had?"

"The three of us had a system." He stretched his legs out in front of him. "If people became suspicious, we'd start by trying to distract them, and if that didn't work, we'd escalate to changing the narrative."

"Making up a story?" she asked. Her work at the FBI was very firmly behind the scenes—she had a desk with three computer screens and lots of powerful software. One of her favorite things was chasing a lead across spreadsheets, ledgers, bank statements, and whatever other list of numbers she could access. She hadn't had to think as much about the rest of the situation, the sorts of things he and his family had been doing to survive. Because this was Heath, though, she was equal parts fascinated and appalled that he'd lived that way.

"Essentially, yes," he said, his mouth twisting wryly. "Thinking on our feet, finding another explanation for what they thought they'd worked out, or had seen."

She tucked her legs underneath her on the sofa. "And if that didn't work?"

"Move," he said simply.

"Move towns?" She'd lived in the same city her entire life, and couldn't imagine having to drop everything and move on short notice.

"Sure," he said as if it wasn't a big deal. "We moved states a couple of times, too."

She leaned back and regarded him. His family had a system to deal with people who were suspicious and he'd turned up today just to snoop a little and work out what she knew. And then hadn't carried through. "You didn't try to change the narrative with me."

"I've surprised myself, to be honest." The tension around his eyes showed how much the act had cost him.

"Why?"

"With you," he said, taking her hand and running his thumb across her palm, "it's…the first time, besides with my mother and sister, that I've been able to trust someone."

"I won't betray that trust. I promise." What he was doing to her palm sent a shiver down her spine.

"I know you won't."

She scanned his face, wondering what he was thinking, trying to imagine living a life where trust and truth were scarce, but all thought utterly stopped as he leaned closer and his lips brushed over hers.

It was soft, feather-like, yet it sent tingles down to her toes. Her eyes drifted closed and she felt the sweep of his lips again. The light touch drew the hunger that was always just below the surface when he was near, and she couldn't have pulled away if she'd tried.

"Heath," she said against his mouth, "I want…"

"What?" His fingers gently stroked the side of her face. "What do you want?"

But she didn't know how to put it into words, or if there even were words for the yearning that threatened to consume her whole. Heart fluttering against her ribs, she wound her arms around his neck and pulled his mouth back to hers. She could kiss him for days and still not have enough—she'd never wanted someone as much as she wanted Heath.

Breaking the kiss, he slid hands beneath her thighs and smoothly lifted her into his lap, and the feel of his solid chest pressed against her breasts sent an insistent throb through her body. His mouth trailed a path to her ear before circling her lobe. As his teeth gently nipped, a shiver raced across her skin. The sound of his warm breath, its tickle against her ear, was too much. She grabbed his face with both hands and turned it back to her, meeting his lips with hers, rising up on knees that were either side of his hips, wanting everything all at once, yet not wanting to rush and miss a moment.

He cupped her breasts, stroking, gently squeezing through the fabric of her T-shirt and soft bra, lightly pinching the hardened peaks the way she liked. Desire built low in her belly, and then his hands were gone and he was pulling her shirt over her head and unhooking her bra, until finally his hot mouth was there at her breasts where his hands had been, tongue and teeth working, hands encircling. She wrapped her arms around his head, holding him there, not willing to risk this slice of heaven slipping away. One hand left her breast and tracked lower, lower, and brushed over the front of her yoga pants.

She glanced down at him, and his eyes were filled with the trust he had in her, and she wanted that more than anything. Didn't just want his body this time, she wanted a deeper connection with him.

Holding his gaze, she eased back. "I want more."

"How much more?" His voice was gravel-rough.

"Everything," she said, since it was the only word in her mind. "Everything you have."

His eyebrows rose but she wasn't sure he understood, wasn't sure that she understood herself, so all she could do was show him. She unbuttoned his shirt and pushed the sides open, placing kisses on the skin as it was revealed. They'd made love many times in the days since she'd first brought him back to her apartment, but there had always been a tinge of urgency, of desperation. Knowing their time together was counting down, and not wanting to waste a moment. But now, as she kissed his bare shoulder, allowing her fingers to drift down his arms, now it felt more real. *This* was the more that she wanted.

She lightly scraped her fingernails over the delicate skin in the crook of his elbow, seeing how it made him shiver, and then kissed the same spot. They'd been living in an idyllic bubble, pretending they were just two people with no baggage, but when he'd told her the truth about his sister and showed her the photo, that bubble burst. No, before that. It was the moment he put his head in his hands, allowed her to see that raw emotional response—it was as if it was a crack in the mask he showed the world. The fantasy was gone. And she couldn't be sad about it. She'd seen glimpses of the real Heath, glimmers of the person he kept hidden, and she wanted more of that.

Trailing kisses down his forearm, she reached his hand and turned it over and pressed her lips to his palm. His breath caught and she glanced up to find him watching her with blazing intensity.

"Freya," he said, his voice rasping. "God, the way you look at me. It undoes me."

Gently he pushed her onto her back, then leaned over her, his eyes dazed, but one side of his mouth hitched up. "You're more than I deserve," he whispered, then captured her mouth again.

His body heat seeped into her, adding to the heat her own body was generating, so between them there was a chance of combustion, which seemed a small sacrifice for the bliss humming through her veins.

His hand snaked down to her yoga pants again, this time pushing them down over her hips, and as his fingers slid home, she squirmed with the rush of feeling, digging her fingers into his shoulders.

Exquisite tension built inside, little by little, and she said, "Don't stop," though her voice sounded anguished to her own ears.

"What if I stop—"

"No," she pleaded, gripping his shoulders tighter.

"—to do this?"

His fingers stilled and she opened her mouth to protest, but he moved down her body and within seconds his mouth replaced his fingers, and the glide of his tongue made her whimper. As the pleasure grew, his hand found hers, his fingers gripping hers tight, anchoring her, and the tension climbed higher, impossibly high, until it peaked and burst, and she cried out his name.

She lay for minutes, or maybe it was hours, dimly aware that Heath had disappeared, trying to find the energy to open her eyes. When she did, she saw he'd dispensed with his clothes and was rolling a condom along his erection.

Suddenly, she was wide-awake again, her skin too cold without him close, and so she reached for him. The grin he gave her was hungry, and he prowled back over her, holding himself up with hands either side of her head. Then he lowered himself to give her a searing kiss and she lifted her legs, wrapping them around his waist, needing to be touching him.

As he guided himself to her, she stroked the smooth skin of his hips, around to the ridges of his abdomen, and when he finally thrust into her, a groan was torn from his throat. She caught her breath and let her eyes drift closed, just to home in on the feel on him inside her. Revel in it.

He began to move, slowly at first, and she found his rhythm, joined him in the movements, and then faster, more urgently, and she scraped her nails over his back, pleasing him, urging him, matching him.

He dipped his head, met her gaze for a long moment when it felt as if his soul spoke to hers, then his mouth landed on hers in a searing kiss, and his fingers slid down her body, unerringly finding her sensitized flesh and stroking. An explosion of sensation rocked her whole body, and she clung to him, riding it out, never needing anyone more. Even as she was still holding him tight, his body shuddered his own release and then his weight pressed her down into the sofa cushions, where it was just the two of them, cocooned, safe from the world.

As they lay there entwined, she stroked his hair. That had definitely been more—more real, more connected, and she was starting to worry how she'd survive without him in her bed after he left the country.

Eight

Heath carried the round of boulevardiers that he'd just made at the discreet little bar in Sarah's living room and handed one to Sarah in her favorite wing-back chair and another to Freya, who was kneeling on the carpet, staring at columns and columns of numbers on a laptop screen. Then he settled on the divan with the third glass and tried to look at Freya across from him with the interest of someone who was only thinking about money and business. He idly wondered if he was pulling it off.

In theory, he was here to go through the figures and records around his inheritance, but in practice, he was watching, spellbound, as Freya put her accounting skills to use. He knew his way around

profit-and-loss statements and the basic spreadsheets he needed to run the bar, but he was so far
out of his league with the reams of paper Sarah had
handed them, and the documents Freya was scroll-
ing through on the screen, that all he could really do
was sit back, watch and appreciate.

And there was so much to appreciate. The way
she'd pulled her long hair back into a no-nonsense
ponytail as she concentrated, but tiny red wisps had
escaped and floated around the sides of her face.
The way she bit down on her lip as she concentrated,
and the way he felt the pressure from her teeth all
the way on the other side of the table. Flashbacks of
Freya in his arms last night filled his head and he
had to focus on dragging in enough air for his lungs.
They'd agreed the night was to say goodbye, but it
sure as hell hadn't felt like the end of something.
He couldn't imagine not touching her again. He was
leaving as soon as they sorted out these accounts—
perhaps even tomorrow—and he needed to stay focused on that. In fact, leaving was what he should
be thinking about now, instead of the feel of Freya's
leg around his waist…

He cleared his throat. "Sarah, this paperwork is
the last thing I need to do here, so I'll probably be
heading home in the next day or two."

"So soon?" his aunt said, a note of dismay in her
voice. "Surely you could stay longer? I've been planning a party to introduce you."

He winced. He'd completely forgotten about her

party. "I've left things on hold—my assistant manager has stepped up to run the bar while I'm gone, but I can't impose on her indefinitely. And I have my sister, and friends. My whole life has been in a state of suspended animation while I've been here."

"I was hoping," she began, then clearly thought better of it, shook her head and smiled. "I will miss you desperately. And I'll keep your room upstairs permanently made up, in case you ever decide to drop in. It's your room now."

Heath reached over and grasped his aunt's hand. She was one of the good guys, and he was going to miss her, too. Strange how his opinion had done a complete backflip from when he'd arrived and wasn't even sure if he could trust her. "I appreciate that. And how about we compromise about the party? I need to get home, but I could come back at some stage for the party?"

"Deal," she said, and smiled at him, her eyes suspiciously damp.

He released her hand and took a sip of his amber drink, glancing up again as Freya huffed out a breath.

Across the low coffee table from him, Freya sat back on her haunches and gave the laptop screen the side-eye. "Sarah, you didn't just keep this ticking over—you've increased his money. So far, I can see you've more than doubled it and I'm nowhere near done.

Startled, Heath sat up. "What do you mean?"

"Bellavista is now only one portion of your money,"

Freya said, waving at the assorted papers and screens. "You have investments all over the place and you own several companies outright."

Sarah grinned. "Well, I do have a degree in business." She raised her glass. "Just because our father left the company to Joseph doesn't mean he was the best choice."

Freya's eyebrows lifted higher as she turned another page. "I think you've proven that beyond doubt."

"I chose for return on investment and tried to balance risk through diversification." Sarah's eyes sparked as she spoke, her entire face glowing.

"You should keep the money that you made while you were managing it," Heath said. That should be a fairly simple calculation for Freya to work out. "There's more there than I need anyway." More than he and Mae could use in their lifetimes.

"Don't even try that," Sarah said with mock severity. "I did it for you. Besides, I have my own portfolio, it's not as if I'm destitute."

Freya gasped, her gaze flying to his. "You own Leyland Energy."

"Oh. Yes," Sarah said, a little sheepish. "Okay, I'll admit that everything but *that* one was a sound business decision. I apologize, Heath, but that decision was made for personal reasons, and hasn't actually increased your net worth."

"You did it out of spite," Freya said with approval and wonder.

Sarah gave a pure sorry-not-sorry look and Heath laughed.

"Maybe just a little thought of revenge went into that," Sarah said. "Over a few years I bought more and more stock under different company names, and then bought his debts, too, so now the estate pretty much owns it all."

It was such poetic justice that Heath shook his head. "Does he know?"

"Not a clue," Sarah said. "I didn't want to say anything that would make him suspicious and make him interfere until I had most of it, and by then we had a strong lead on you, so I waited, since it's actually your decision."

Freya gave up all pretense of reading the spreadsheets and scooted back on the carpet to lean against the wall. "Holy crap."

"Prairie and Constance are executives at the company," Sarah said, one eyebrow arched, "and as far as I know, they're expecting to inherit, so that piece of paper in your hand is pretty much the fortunes of the entire Leyland family."

Heath looked over at his aunt. "Even if that strategy had lost me money, I'd still approve of it. Good work, Sarah."

But it did raise the question of what he was going to do about the company. He couldn't leave it in limbo—regardless of who owned it, the company needed stability and certainty for the sake of the staff and customers, so he was going to have to address it somehow. He might approve of Sarah's strategy, but it did add another obligation to his plate, and one more thing he should address before he left for home. And that wasn't even starting to think about how this would impact Freya, who still looked shell-shocked.

He scrubbed a hand over his jaw. "I might stay a few extra days after all, if that's okay."

Sarah tried to smother her smile but was wholly unsuccessful. "I think that can be arranged."

He glanced at Freya, who nodded at him, and then went back to her spreadsheets on the screens and leafing through the pages. "Sarah, this is amazing. I can't believe you achieved all this."

Heath slid down onto the floor so he was at the same level as the accounts. And Freya. And if his leg struggled to have enough room under the coffee table, and ended up resting against Freya's, then that couldn't be helped.

"Okay," he said, "time for me to get familiar with these numbers. Let's start going through it all one at a time."

Sarah stood. "I'll make coffee."

Two days later, Freya looked around the elevator she and Heath were riding up to the Leyland Energy offices and couldn't ignore that she was getting more and more unsettled the closer they were to the fourteenth floor. It had been a faint sensation earlier in the day, growing stronger in the car, and by the time they made it to the pavement in front of the building, it had reached an intensity she could no longer ignore.

The elevator bell dinged, but before the doors could open, she jabbed the button to keep them closed.

Heath looked over at her and raised an eyebrow. "Freya?"

"I don't think I should be here."

"Sure you should," he said with certainty. "I own the company and I asked you to come with me to look at the books, so it makes complete sense for you to be here."

"You could get one of Sarah's people that we left waiting in the lobby. They're all good people. You don't need me specifically." They'd brought some of the staff Sarah had employed to manage his inheritance portfolio, and asked them to hang back so they didn't look like they were storming the office en masse.

He turned to face her in the confined space. "This whole 'taking control of a company that I didn't know existed a week ago' thing is new to me, so I'd say that I do need you."

She bit down on her lip as she considered his point. He wasn't used to a corporate environment, so of course a little moral support would be helpful. She could do this. She drew in a deep breath and let go of the button. "Okay."

His hand was up like a flash, pressing the button in again, keeping the doors closed. "There's more to this. Are you scared of them?" With his free hand, he cupped the side of her face. "Don't you want to see the looks on the Leyland family's faces when they find out?"

"Yes," she admitted. "The thing is, I want to see that too much."

His brows drew together. "Okay, I'm lost."

"For most of my life, I've defined myself against these people." Who she really was deep down. "I wanted to be like my mom and like Sarah, but I also desperately wanted to not turn into the miserable, spiteful type of person that the Leylands are."

He nodded slowly. "You're not scared of them. You're scared you'll gloat, and then become like them."

"I'd *like* to say that it's not even a possibility, that I'm emotionally mature enough to walk in there and take the moral high ground, and not revel in the misfortunes of others..."

"Freya Wilson, if you forget everything else about our time together, I want you to remember this." His eyes softened and he gave her his lopsided smile. "You are the most emotionally mature person I know. You make decisions based on whatever you think is the right thing to do—you're only involved in this whole debacle in the first place because you were helping Sarah, someone you loved. You are a good person. If I had a kid here right now, I'd point to you and say, 'Try to be like her when you grow up, and you won't go wrong.'"

"Heath," she began, but couldn't get more words out past the lump in her throat.

"I'm not going to push you to come in with me now, because I trust that whatever decision you make will be the right one. It always is. You're extraordinary, Freya."

As she looked into his dark brown eyes, her whole heart melted into a pile of goo in her chest, only just able to keep beating through sheer luck. She could easily promise to remember his words as he'd asked—this moment would be etched in her memory until the day she died.

"Thank you," she whispered. "You don't know what a gift you just gave me."

Still smiling, he dipped his head and placed a chaste kiss gently on her lips, and, if it wasn't for the elevator starting to ding its protest about being kept in limbo for so long, she would have deepened that kiss and lost herself in him. But the noise was getting more annoying and they needed to leave the elevator.

"Okay," she said, and squared her shoulders. "Let's do this."

"Let's do this," he repeated, and released the button.

The doors slid open and a young woman with red cat's-eye glasses was waiting. "Are you here for the meeting in the boardroom?"

Sarah's people had asked for a meeting with Leyland and his two senior executives—Prairie and Constance—without giving away the identity of the new owner, so this poor woman had likely been waiting for the stalled elevator without knowing who, exactly, she was waiting for.

"We are," Heath said. "Sorry we're a few minutes late."

She led them down a hall and into a boardroom dominated by an oval table, with three people sitting at the far end, and then slipped outside, closing the door behind her.

Prairie's eyes narrowed. "What the hell are you two doing here?"

"Good morning," Freya said, and passed a folder to Prairie. "This is Heath Dunstan. He owns several companies that, combined, own ninety-two percent of Leyland Energy."

Ignoring the folder, Prairie swung to face her father. "Is this true?"

Freya watched her biological father pale and then stammer. "I… It can't…" He reached for a folder that Freya handed him. "I don't know."

Freya's chest clenched at the sight of him looking so lost. Her eyes flickered to Heath's steady gaze— she had her answer. If she'd thought this moment would be satisfying, she'd been wrong. It was… hollow. And awful.

The two women hadn't taken the folders she'd offered so she put them on the table in front of them.

"Good morning," Heath said, his voice strong and sure. "Thank you for meeting with me at short notice. As Ms. Wilson said, I have a ninety-two percent stake in this business, and as such, there are some things I'd like to discuss."

Constance hadn't taken her focus from Freya since they'd entered. "You did this," she said. "You've always wanted to be part of this company. To have what was ours."

Heath took a small step forward, positioning himself to shield her from her half sister, but Freya lifted her hand an inch or so, hoping he'd read her, and he did. He waited, giving her the floor.

"Why would you think I wanted anything of yours?" She might have wished at times for a father, or for sisters, but she'd been a very young child when she'd realized their family was not anything to be jealous of—so these were not the sisters and this was not the father she'd have chosen.

Constance unfurled herself from the chair and stretched to her full height. "Don't think he hasn't told us," she said, tipping her head to her father.

"Told you what?" Freya asked, confused. "That he paid for my school fees and gave my mom a small allowance toward my food and health care?"

"Small," Prairie spat. "No need to deny it just because your *boyfriend* is listening. We know about the constant demands for money. Constance couldn't have a Corvette when she turned sixteen because Father had to buy you one, and I couldn't take my friends to Europe for my twenty-first because your clothing allowance had to be increased."

Freya hesitated. The claims were so outrageous

that at first they didn't compute in her brain, and she couldn't think of anything to say. A glance at Leyland changed that—his face had reddened, and he was casting furtive glances around the room, as if looking for an escape route.

The thumping beat of her heart seemed to reverberate through her entire body as it all slotted into place in her mind. Her hands trembled, and she wasn't sure she could speak. A warm hand settled on the small of her back and she felt Heath's presence, his support, and her head was clear again.

"You told them what, exactly?" she said, her voice sounding calmer than she'd expected.

Leyland lifted his chin, clearly having given up on escaping and deciding to brazen it out. "The details might be different, but the principle is the same. I had to support you as well as my girls, and something had to give. They bore the brunt of it."

Heath tensed when Leyland said "my girls," but instead of being hurt, Freya felt an eerie sense of detachment wash over her. She wasn't at risk of gloating any more than she was jealous. These people were nothing to her. Strangers. However, she did owe them what she'd owe anyone she was negotiating or interacting with—the truth.

"He's been lying to you," she said simply. "There was no car, no clothing allowance, and he regularly missed payments to cover school fees." She saw her half sisters in a different light—living with someone who'd been gaslighting them their whole lives.

Not that she was sympathetic—they'd made their choices, too. "You might have been jealous of what you thought I was getting, but rest assured, I'm not jealous of your family. Not even a little bit."

Constance shimmied her shoulders, as if shaking those truths off. "Even if all that is true, what are you doing here now? Circling like a vulture because your boyfriend suddenly—*and bizarrely*—has our company land in his lap?"

This time Heath did step forward. "Freya is a forensic accountant. I've asked her here in the capacity of consultant. And since we don't seem to be getting anywhere here, Mr. Leyland, please escort Ms. Wilson to the CFO's office, and give her access to all of Leyland Energy's accounts." He turned back to the two women at the table and raised an eyebrow. "If you think there's a chance that she'll find discrepancies in the accounts once she starts going through them, you might want to start looking for another job now."

Prairie gathered her things from the table and held them close to her chest. "I will not stay here and be spoken to like this by some Australian bartender. You'll have my resignation on your desk by the end of the day."

Constance was right behind her. "Mine too. You think you can run the company without us?"

"I'll take my chances," Heath said, smiling mildly. "Just so you know, there are already security officers stationed at each exit who will check your bags for company property, and a few of my people are in the corridor now to accompany you to your desks."

Prairie gasped indignantly. "You were planning on firing us if we didn't resign?"

"I was prepared for any eventuality." As the two women swept through the meeting room door, Heath dug his hands into his pockets. "Mr. Leyland? Will you take Ms. Wilson to the CFO's office, or shall I?"

Freya's chest swelled with pride. Heath might be out of his element here in this New York boardroom, but she'd never seen anyone more magnificent. He stood tall and calm, seemingly patient, yet unquestionably in control of the situation. It was all she could do to not reach out and touch him, to feel all that leashed power under her fingertips.

The older man pushed to his feet and angrily snatched up his pen and notepad from the table, leaving the unopened folders, and stalked out and down the hallway.

Heath put a hand on her arm. "Let me know when you're ready to go," he said softly.

Freya nodded and followed her father down the hall.

It was three hours before they were ready to leave. Constance, Prairie and their father had all been escorted off the premises after tending their resignations, and Heath had spoken to the staff about the changes, both as a group, and then quick meetings with those in key senior positions. Freya had all the passwords changed, then copied the accounts onto a portable hard drive so she could continue looking at home, and also to ensure that there was a record in case anyone still loyal to the Leylands did anything underhanded. Having spoken to many of the workers, though, she was pretty confident that no one liked or respected the Leylands enough to sabotage anything.

Her mom pulled up in the black Suburban and Freya and Heath climbed in the back.

"Well," he said as he fastened his seat belt, "that morning seemed to take approximately three years."

She chuckled and slid her hand across the seat to hold his, just out of the view of her mom's mirror. "What did you say to the senior staff you met with?"

"That even though I won't be keeping the company, their jobs were safe for now."

She turned in her seat. "Are you serious?"

"I'm a bartender. I'm always serious," he said, mimicking her joke from a couple of weeks ago at the fundraiser.

The streets and buildings of Manhattan whizzed past the window behind him as she regarded his expression, trying to read him. "You seemed like you belonged in there."

"Freya," he said, "I don't belong in a boardroom. Besides, I can't run a business like that from Australia, so it wouldn't be fair to anyone if I tried."

Her stomach dropped hard. Australia. For a few hours, as they worked together on the shared mission of taking over Leyland Energy, she'd managed to forget. Had felt like they were something of a team.

That had been a mistake—Heath hadn't forgotten. He'd been thinking ahead to when he was gone.

"What will you do with it?" she asked, hoping her voice gave nothing away.

"I thought I'd give it to Lauren."

The car jerked to a sudden stop and they both lurched forward, caught by their seat belts, and then a cacophony of horns blared around them, and the car took off again.

Freya glanced up at the rearview mirror to find that her mother looked as shocked as Freya felt.

"Is this some kind of bribe?" her mother asked, voice hard and uncompromising.

Heath frowned. "Why would I need to bribe you?"

In the driver's seat, black-clad shoulders shrugged. "So I'll back off about you two being involved."

"We're not involved," Freya said. After all, Heath had just mentioned leaving the country, without seeming to be torn up about it in the slightest. People who were *involved* weren't that casual; they had some form of attachment.

Her mother gave her the same look in the rearview mirror that she had when Freya used to claim she'd finished her homework, then, looking back at the road, said, "Who does that? Gives a company away on a whim?"

Freya almost laughed. She knew the answer to that one. "Heath does," she said, squeezing his hand. If other people in his position were giving away a company, they'd be doing it publicly after working out all the angles. Or for brownie points, complete with a photo op. *Some* advantage. Heath wasn't like any of them. She almost laughed.

"I'm righting a wrong," Heath said, voice deep and grave. "Think of it as a lump sum compensation for the child support you should have been paid. No need to tell me that Leyland did the bare minimum, and less whenever he could get away with it."

Her mother blinked rapidly, and Freya had to swallow past a lump in her throat. So many people simply didn't see her mother. Being a chauffeur meant she was invisible to most, and to Leyland's family she was a trivial annoyance. But Heath saw her, and what the situation had cost her, and thought she was important enough to do something for. "Thank you," she said softly.

"What's the point of inheriting all this money if I can't do something with it?"

In the front, her mom clicked the traffic signal and smoothly took a corner. "I don't know how to run a company."

"Sarah does," Freya said, sensing her mother softening. "You could ask her for help. I'm sure she'd love the chance to outperform Leyland, just on principle alone."

Heath waved a hand dismissively. "Or sell it. Or shut it down and liquidate the assets."

Lauren shot them an outraged glance in the mirror. "All the staff!"

Heath grinned. "See, you're already a better boss than Leyland."

Freya laughed because he was right. Her mother and Sarah would be a formidable combination. Heath tugged gently on their joined hands and she looked at him, and in that moment of perfect happiness, she had a horrible realization.

She was in love with him.

She probably had been for a while but now she couldn't deny it anymore. The problem was, he didn't play fair—in just a few hours, he'd made her mother happy, had served up karma to the Leylands in a controlled yet thorough way, and had supported her in the elevator in a way that she'd never forget. She could guard against him in bed, but not against this. And there was no question he was leaving. Her lungs cramped tight, making it hard to draw in air. She'd been so close to making it through till he left with her armor intact, this meeting today had been the last thing on his list. Now her armor was shattered.

The car glided to a stop outside Sarah's apartment building, and with a quick goodbye to her mother, who was uncharacteristically distracted, they climbed out.

Standing on the pavement, Freya looked up at the towering building, not quite ready to meet his eyes and see what they held. "I guess that's your list done now."

Heath dug his hands into his pockets. "As soon

as I can get organized with flights and things, I'll head home."

"What you just did for Mom. That was everything," she said, finally looking at him. "I don't know how to thank you."

A smile danced around the corners of his mouth, not quite blooming. "I can think of something."

"Anything." She had no idea what he was going to say, but it didn't matter. She'd never be able to repay him for handing Leyland's business to her mother.

Heath dipped his chin. "The first thing I need to do when I get home is tell Mae about all of this. And she's going to have questions. I'll need an accountant by my side. You happen to be an accountant. One who is across this whole messy situation. And you can answer any question Mae might have about Sarah and the Rutherfords from personal experience."

Freya rocked back on her heels. Go with him to Australia? That was the country where she'd felt free enough to act out of character and have a one-night stand with a hot bartender...with him. How would she cope there now that she knew she loved him?

"Come on," he said, his voice deep and rich, "remember it's summer there. So warm. And I'll make you a mango daiquiri as soon as we reach Noosa."

He was the devil himself, tempting her, luring her with things. Besides, how could she say no to the man who just gave her mother a company and righted years of wrongs, when all he was asking for was help with his sister?

"I can give you three days, maybe four, including travel time. My leave is almost up and, strangely, my boss will expect me back at work."

"That's enough." He stepped up in her space and dropped a kiss on her cheek, lingering just a few seconds too long for a normal peck. "Thank you."

And Freya said, "You're welcome," pretending that she was simply helping a friend, even though she suspected that she'd agreed because she wasn't quite ready to say goodbye to him yet. The price for this weakness was probably going to be steep—falling deeper in love with him—but she was going to do it anyway. How bad could it be?

Nine

It took a couple of days for the arrangements to be made for the trip back to Australia. Heath had been pleased, if a little surprised, that Freya had agreed to accompany him, and since that moment he had been busy making plans. Her first trip to Noosa had ended badly when he'd thrown her out, but this time...

Recently, she'd spent every spare hour they had showing him around New York, so on his visit to his hometown, he intended to repay the favor. He'd use the days to show her the best Queensland had to offer. And their nights? He'd show her the best *he* had to offer.

He'd been thinking about what would happen to them after he returned home for good, and realized he wasn't ready to give her up. Couldn't imagine not holding her in his arms again, not seeing her smile light up her face, and his heart.

One option was convincing her to move to Australia. She had deep ties to her mother and Sarah, but he could easily pay for her to go home and visit as often as she wanted, though leaving her job might be a challenge. Another option was a long-distance relationship—he planned on visiting America semi-regularly, to see both sides of his family and check in on his businesses and investments. And if Freya sometimes visited him in Australia as well, they might be able to make it work. If she enjoyed this trip, if he could sell his town and what a relationship could offer, maybe he could ask her soon.

When they finally made it to his Noosa bar just at dusk, luggage in hand, Freya looked around the bustling scene and smiled.

"A lot of memories here," she said. "Especially considering my visit was short."

"Good ones?" he murmured near her ear. Her long red hair was down, a little messy as it brushed across her shoulders and down her back, and her long, mint-green dress was somewhat rumpled after their flights. But she'd never looked better to him.

"Some good ones." She looked up at him, the overhead lights dancing on her tawny eyes. "I met this hot bartender and flirted my heart out."

He grinned. "Anything happen?"

"Bar-top karaoke, a one-night stand, a private

jet to New York, a motorbike ride to a New Jersey beach…" She pulled her bottom lip into her mouth and then released it and his pulse spiked. "So, yeah, you could say something happened."

"Maybe you'll bump into him again. I've heard he might be in tonight."

A group of people came in the door and jostled them on the way past. Heath instinctively pulled Freya close. "Come on, we should head upstairs before any of the staff notice me and I get sucked into working. Mae should be waiting upstairs."

When they reached his apartment up the metal staircase, he opened the door, ushered Freya in ahead of him and dropped his bags. Mae was asleep on his sofa but woke when the bags hit the floor.

"Heath!" she shrieked, launching herself at him, and he pulled her into a bear hug.

"Hey, Mae," he said into her hair. And then he laughed for the joy of seeing his sister, for the relief of being in his own home again, even if he was slightly punch-drunk from the flights and the shuttle.

After he released her, he put a hand on the small of Freya's back. "This is Freya Wilson. She's been helping me with some stuff."

"Stuff?" Mae raised an eyebrow, looking back and forth between them suggestively.

Mae had never been slow on the uptake, or scared of speaking her mind—two of the things he loved about his sister, but right now, when he had to tell her much more than she was expecting, he needed them all to stay focused.

"There are some things I have to tell you." He sank his hands into his pockets, trying to look calm, in control of the situation, but aware that Mae was likely seeing right through him. "How about we go for a walk along the beach? I've just come from winter and the night feels warm and—"

Mae crossed her arms. "This sounds serious, so I'd rather know whatever it is now."

"It's..." He scrubbed a hand through his hair, trying to get his brain to work after all the travel. "It's a lot. I don't want to just blurt it out. We don't even—"

Mae plonked herself on a dining chair. "No secrets, that's our rule. If there's something, then tell me now."

Sighing, he pulled a dining chair out for Freya, then dropped down on the remaining one, resting his forearms on the small round table. "I'm not really sure where to start," he admitted.

"Tell me the crux of it first, and details after."

"Right, okay." Ideally, he'd have smoothed the way a bit, led up to it, but then this was Mae and she wouldn't be happy if he didn't come completely clean now she knew there was something to tell. He'd kept this from her for long enough. "I didn't just meet Mom's family when I was in the States. I also met our father's."

Mae leaned back as if she'd been struck. "What the hell, Heath?" She threw her hands out in front of her. "Should I start with Mom telling us that our father was bad news and never be tempted to look for him? Or maybe with the *we don't keep secrets from each other* thing?"

"It seems like Mom had good reason to hide us from our father, but here's more of the news—he's dead, so it's safe." He held her gaze steady, so she got the full meaning. "We're safe."

She blinked. "We're safe?" He nodded and waited a beat while she processed that. Then her eyes narrowed. "But you're telling me this after your trip. Our whole lives we've had no secrets, and this is a huge one. Did you mean to cut me out like that, or did you just forget about me?"

Heath flinched, but it was a fair question. In her position, he would have been just as annoyed. "When I left, it was because Freya had found me and wanted me to go back with her. I wanted to scout the situation out first—make sure it was safe before involving you."

"We're a team, Heath," she said, and the hurt in her eyes slayed him. "You and me. With Mom gone, there's *only* you and me."

He felt Freya adjust her weight on the chair beside him, but Mae needed all his attention now. After keeping her in the dark during his trip, she deserved that.

"We're still a team," he said, "but Mom also always told me to look after you. To keep you safe. You know she did. And you also know she'd have found a way to haunt me and make my life miserable if I'd done this wrong."

"She would." Mae bit down on a reluctant smile, then blew out a breath. "So, he's dead? Really gone?"

"Really gone. But he left something behind."

"A puppy?" Mae said, her lips twitching. "Debts? A rambling house we need to flip?"

He pushed his chair back and crossed the small room to the kitchen. After grabbing a bottle of water from the fridge and three glasses, he plonked them all in the middle of the round table, then sat again and said, "Money."

"Great," she said, her eyes widening the way they did when she was joking. "Because I have my eye on a sweet yellow convertible—"

"He was rich. Really rich. That's why Mom had to go to such lengths to keep us safe. He really did have private investigators looking for us like she expected."

"How rich?" Mae asked, the humor falling from her expression. "Tens of thousands? Hundreds of thousands?"

Heath looked to Freya, who said, "Billions."

"What?" Mae screeched, her face paling.

He poured water into the three glasses and shoved one at Mae, saying, "Drink," then handed one to Freya.

Mae downed most of the glass and then peeked over the rim and said, "Billions?"

"I know, right?" Heath wrapped a hand around

the back of his neck, still not believing it even after everything that had happened in New York. "And now it's ours. His name was Joseph Rutherford, and he still had his will made out to me, even though he hadn't seen me since I was a toddler."

Mae laced her hands together on the tabletop. "Did he know about me?"

"No one did. Mom covered her tracks well. So no one suspects that you're a Rutherford and I can keep it that way if you want. Or you can do a DNA test and claim your spot in the family tree. I'll split the inheritance with you fifty-fifty whatever you decide, and just say that I'm splitting it with my half sister."

Freya lifted one shoulder. "No one would think twice about that—everyone there has half siblings and complex family structures."

Mae flickered a glance to Freya, then back to Heath. "No one suspects, but this woman knows about my bloodline? You told her?"

"She guessed," he said simply, and—given the way he and Mae were raised—wholly inadequately.

A line appeared between Freya's brows as she said, "Heath didn't betray you, I promise. I worked it out."

Mae was silent for a beat, then another. "Who *are* you?"

"I'm an accountant," Freya said, straightening, "who's been working closely with the estate, and—"

"No, but who are you?" Mae had the look of a spaniel who'd caught a scent. She would have made a good FBI agent herself. "There's more to this."

Heath gave Freya's shoulder a reassuring squeeze. He and Freya had deliberately not put a label on this thing between them, so he didn't have a ready word to offer. But he hoped that after he had a chance to talk to her, to tell her that he wanted more, that perhaps they'd have some sort of official status. He glanced over at her, the redhead who sparkled like a precious jewel in his life, and said, "She's a friend."

"Your aunt Sarah," Freya said, her voice calm, despite the fine lines of stress appearing around her eyes, "your father's sister, is my godmother. I grew up in her household, so this is all personal to me. Not as much as it is for you, obviously, but I want it all to work out well for you, Heath and Sarah."

"Do you." Mae's eyes, wide and knowing, landed back on him. "She seems nice, but you realize that's probably what our mother thought about our father when they started dating? We might have the genes, Heath, but we're not from that world."

Freya's hand trembled as she tucked a wisp of hair behind her ear, but she didn't turn away. "I'm not from that world, either."

"It's true," Heath said, sliding a hand on Freya's knee under the table. Seeing her flinch had felt like a punch to his own stomach. "She's like us—she has the genes but isn't one of them. She and her mom don't have money. She's skirted around the edges of that society."

Mae rested her chin on her hand, and tapped a finger against her mouth. "Doesn't have money? And out of interest, do she and her mom have any money now? Have they profited from your—our—money in any way?"

Freya blushed, and Heath slid an arm around her waist, letting her know that whatever Mae was getting at, he wasn't buying it. "It's not like that," he said. "The estate ended up owning her biological father's company and it was the right thing to do."

"Look," Mae said, waving his explanation away and focusing on Freya again, "you seem great, really you do. And I hate to be suspicious, but to be honest, our mother raised me—*us*—this way, so I don't have much choice about the way my brain works. She also raised us to understand that the only people we could truly trust were each other. And for that reason, you don't need to cover for me anymore. I'll go to America and do the DNA tests and face the music myself."

Heath smiled, proud of his little sister. "There's a party next week. Sarah's throwing it to introduce me as the lost heir to our father's fortune. It would be great if you were there, too, and she could introduce us together."

Mae shrank back, suddenly looking less sure of herself. "I don't think that will work. I need to give my school more notice than that to find a replacement for the class."

"Whenever it suits you," Freya said, "Sarah's people will organize your paperwork and tickets. I'll tell them you'll be in touch, and you can let them know through Heath or contact them directly. I'll send you the contact details."

He watched Mae swallow and shrink a little more and reached for her hand. "When you go, I'll be there. We're a team."

"Thanks," she said. "You were right. It is a lot now that I'm thinking it through."

"I've got your back," he said softly. "Do you want me to tell Sarah when I go back, or wait until you're there?

Mae blew out a breath. "I'm happy for you to play it by ear. But just so we're clear—I'm still mad at you."

"I wouldn't expect otherwise." He knew she'd forgive him—as she'd said, they were a team—but it still hurt to have Mae mad at him. "How about you forgive me tomorrow, and I can tell you more then about the money and Sarah—I think you'll like her."

His sister was overwhelmed, as well as being hurt that he'd kept this secret, and she needed him, but so did Freya—she had to feel bruised after that conversation and he wanted some time alone with her now to check that she was okay.

"Tomorrow works." She lifted her glass and finished the water. "I need a few moments to let it all sink in anyway. Plus, I have to teach in the morning. Give me twenty-four hours to absorb this and we can have dinner tomorrow night and you can tell me the rest."

"Deal." They both stood and he pulled her into

another bear hug. "Don't stay mad too long, though. You know I can stand anything but that."

"You'll probably have to make me waffles to make up for it." Her voice was muffled against his shoulder.

"Absolutely," he said without hesitation. "With strawberries."

She arched her neck back so she could hit him with a narrowed gaze. "For a week."

He tried to suppress his smile but wasn't altogether successful. "I can do that."

"Then I'll think about it," she said, then scooped up her bag and left.

As she watched Heath's sister leave the room and close the door behind her, Freya felt the walls of the apartment closing in, until she could barely draw a breath. In less than twenty minutes, her entire world had changed. She'd long suspected that Heath hadn't let her see his real self, and watching him talk to his sister now, along with Mae's own words, confirmed it. For the third time in her life, she'd fallen for a man who wore masks and kept parts of himself hidden, but of the three, this was by far the worst—unlike the fleeting feelings she'd had for her ex-husbands, her love for Heath was so deep it filled every fiber of her being.

"Can I interest you in that beach walk?" Heath said, taking her hand and interlocking their fingers. "I need to see the water."

"Sure," she said, and conjured a semblance of a smile. She needed air, and space to think, and the beach outside his door was a thousand times better than staying between these walls.

They wound their way down the metal stairs and through the throng of patrons at the bar, then kicked off their shoes at the wooden boardwalk, and left them there as they headed for the water's edge. The sand was still warm underfoot from the day's sun, and the moon's reflection on the ocean was like a ribbon of liquid silver over the undulating water. The whole scene seemed unreal, more of a dreamlike painting—maybe because she'd just come from a New York winter, but mostly because her head was spinning. And she still couldn't get her lungs to work properly.

"I've been thinking about us," Heath said once they'd walked away from tourists and locals enjoying the summer evening.

"Me too." The light breeze lifted her hair and wisps blew across her face. She foraged in a pocket until she found a band, and then drew her hair back into a bunch at the nape of her neck.

"Glad to hear it," he said, his voice deep and smooth. "Freya, I don't want us to end. I don't think I can let you walk out of my life."

Earlier in the day, she would have been thrilled to hear him say those exact words. But now everything was different, and her skin felt too hot, her pulse too fast, and she couldn't go back to how she'd felt that morning. "I can't stop thinking about that conversation with Mae."

He stopped, turning to face her, expression serious. "You have to know that I don't suspect you were playing me for Leyland Energy."

"I had a moment of mortification that Mae thinks that," she admitted, "but you know me, and you know how it all happened."

One corner of his mouth kicked up in a lopsided smile. "Then what do you mean?"

Freya arched her neck back to look up at the stars, pinpricks in the dark, velvet sky, hoping their timelessness, their sheer magnitude, would help her keep her situation in perspective. Or at least help her find the right words to explain it to Heath. It didn't help. If anything, it made her dizzy.

Taking a deep breath, she looked back to him. "Seeing you with Mae, it struck me that you were different with her than I've seen you."

"Mae is my sister," he said, brows drawing together as he tried to work out what she was saying. "She's the only person I've known for any real length of time. Plus our small family was close, so Mae and I are pretty comfortable with each other."

She was glad he was close to his sister. With the sort of life Heath, Mae and their mother had lived through, it was good they'd at least been able to rely on one another. But what worried her, what affected her, wasn't about their sibling bond. "You had your guard down with Mae—it was written on your face. You were almost a different person with her."

And it reminded her of the expressions she'd seen in the photos he'd shown her the day he'd admitted Mae was a Rutherford—joyful, playful, real. Expressions she hadn't seen on him in person.

He tilted his head. "I'm not sure what you're getting at."

"What this means is that while I've had my heart on my sleeve, you've been playing a role. Keeping yourself hidden. Wearing a mask. You've never had your guard down with me. Maybe I've known a Heath-Joseph hybrid, not the real you."

"I think I have been myself." He rubbed a finger across his forehead. "But I've changed my identity a few times in my life. I might have been Heath for a while now, but I still remember being Brad Lacey, and I started school as Will Morgan, so—" he shrugged "—maybe I did pick up a little of Joseph Rutherford II."

"And when Mae said that you'd both been taught not to trust anyone, that it was only you two against the world…" She let the thought trail off, watching his face for his reaction.

He shook his head slowly. "She didn't mean that neither of us can ever have a relationship."

It was definitely part of what Mae had been saying, but it was more than that, and she wasn't sure Heath even realized. "I feel like I've been running around after you, making a fool of myself, following you back to Australia, hoping there might be a future for us, and all the while you've been keeping the essence of who you are under lock and key."

No strangers allowed, and no admittance for her.

"We haven't known each other that long," he said, dark eyes intense on her. "So there are going to be things we don't know about each other yet. Parts of ourselves we haven't shown."

"It might have been a short time, but you're the only person besides my mother and Sarah who I've been my authentic self with." Her stomach turned over, making her feel nauseas. "From the start, the karaoke in your bar—I let my hair down with you. But you haven't done the same back."

His eyes widened, as if her point had hit home, and he finally understood what she was saying. "It's not easy for me," he said. "You know that all this is new to me—I've never had a long-term relationship before. What I *have* had is a lifetime of training and practice at being suspicious and never trusting."

"Needing space to grow is one thing," she said as gently as she could, "but you don't really want to move past that, do you?"

He turned, looking out over the crashing waves, watching for so long she wasn't sure he was going to answer at all, until he finally said, "I don't know. That way of living has kept me safe, and I don't know what the alternative looks like."

It was understandable that he'd taken those lessons from his childhood and made them central to how he lived his life, but her heart was too bruised to live that way alongside him. A few wisps of hair had broken free of the ponytail and were feathering the edges of her face, so she pulled them back tightly behind her ears, then started walking again. Heath fell into step beside her.

"Here's the situation from my perspective," she said, not looking at him, not daring in case she faltered in what she needed to say, instead keeping her gaze steadfastly to the front. "You might have shared your body, and we've been allies in a range of situations, but you've kept me at an emotional distance, not letting me near your heart or your true self. Fair to say?"

He made a noise as if about to reply, then hesitated and dug his hands into his pockets. "That's probably a fair assessment."

"Well, take out the specifics and that pretty much describes both of my marriages."

"Hey, that's harsh," he said, speeding up to stand in front of her, making her stop walking and look at him. "I'm nothing like them."

She grabbed his hands, linking them at their sides, and squeezed. "I know that, Heath. Of course you're nothing like them. But I've had two husbands who both kept me at an emotional distance. In both marriages, I had hoped that we'd grow closer, but it never happened."

"That's because they're assholes," he said, scowling.

She coughed out a laugh. "True, but the thing is, I

just don't think I can take that much on faith again."
She released his hands and crossed her arms tightly
under her breasts, as if she could physically hold herself together even as her heart felt like it was bleeding
in her chest. "I can't start a relationship with someone when I don't know if I'll ever get through all
the barricades and have access to your heart. When
I was younger, before Milo and Dominic, maybe I
could have. But I honestly don't have the strength
anymore. If it happened again, I'd be crushed, and I
can't do that to myself."

He reached out to cup the side of her face, and
she leaned into his hand, all that warmth, all that
strength, all that Heath...

"What I know," he said, his voice strained, "is I
want you in my life now. I don't know what I'll be
able to promise in the future."

"I do." She shrugged a shoulder, in a gesture that
was too tense to be nonchalant. "I know what I'd be
able to promise in the future."

He dropped his hand from her cheek and shoved
it back in his pocket. "What?"

"I love you, Heath." Her throat was rough, but she
forced the words out anyway. "I'll love you in the future, too, so I'd want you in my life, now and then."

He hesitated, as if waiting for a punchline, so she
waited, and they stood together for a long moment
with only the sound from the waves smashing into
the sand.

"Your mouth is saying one thing," he said, brushing a thumb over her lips, "but your eyes are telling a completely different story."

"I've realized tonight that I can't have that future." A voice in her head screamed at her not to do this, that this couldn't be right, and she had to try hard to ignore the voice and just get through this conversation. "If I stay now, I'll always be wondering if there are some other parts of yourself that you don't trust me enough to show. Or if there's something you're still guarding and hiding. That's not a relationship I can be in."

His Adam's apple bobbed down then up in his throat. "I don't know how else to be."

"No judgment," she said quickly. "Honestly, no judgment at all. I know why you had to be this way, I understand that more than most people—I knew your father." Her eyes were beginning to sting and she squeezed them shut for a long moment to relieve them. "But I also know my limits and I know what I need. You'll find someone else who doesn't have a scarred heart like mine, who will be able to meet you halfway."

His chest rose and fell faster, deeper. "I don't like this. Seriously, how am I supposed to watch you walk away?"

"I guess the same way that I'll do the walking away—by gathering up my last shred of dignity and pretending I remember how to put one foot in front of the other." Easier said than done, obviously, because a tear slid down her face and she wiped at it with her wrist. "And I should get started on that process."

He jerked back. "You mean now? We only landed a few hours ago—surely you can stay the night?"

"It will be even harder to leave in the morning." That voice in her head was back, screaming at her again, telling her she couldn't walk away from *Heath*, that it couldn't possibly be over. She tensed every muscle she could to try to retain some control over herself. "I need to go now."

A tiny wince flashed across his face and was gone again, so fast she would have missed it if she hadn't been watching. "So we head back to my apartment now and grab your bags, then I just see you at Sarah's party like we mean nothing to each other?"

Another piece of her heart broke, leaving a deep ache in her chest. "We'll never mean nothing to each other, Heath, but other than that…yes, I guess so."

He scrubbed his hands over his face, then nodded. "We'd better head back then."

It was over. The rest of her heart shattered and she had to focus as she walked back beside him in case she doubled over and fell down on the sand. There would be time enough for grieving when she got back to the States.

Ten

Heath walked out from the bedroom Sarah had allocated him at her house in the Hamptons, adjusting the sweater he'd just pulled on. Despite the bite in the air, winter was on the way out, and with today's sunshine he could see the glimmers of spring. The new warmth suited the optimism of his mood—he was here to make things right, first with Sarah, and then with Freya.

After Freya had returned home from Australia, Heath had spent a lot of time with Mae—telling her about everything that had happened on his trip, about the new family members they had and about Freya. He'd realized in those conversations how badly he'd ruined things. Freya was his future. He was here to convince her she could trust him, that who he was when they were together was the real him and that they made sense together.

Sarah's house was full of party planners and their staff—people up ladders, carrying in trays of food and cartons of drinks, moving furniture around, looking busy and calling out to each other—everyone rushing to have things perfect for the party Sarah was throwing him tonight.

He found his aunt in the kitchen, talking to various people about faucets and facilities. When she caught sight of him, she smiled and excused herself from the assorted people, threaded her elbow through his and said, "Can we go somewhere quiet?"

"If you can think of somewhere," he said. The party staff seemed to be everywhere.

They looked in the doors of several rooms before finding one empty, and sneaked in. It was decorated in wood paneling with floor-to-ceiling bookshelves and dominated by a heavy desk.

"This was my father's study," Sarah said, smiling wistfully. "I haven't changed much. You would have liked your grandfather—he was nothing like your father. He and Joseph clashed terribly. Couldn't stand each other."

"I'm already on your father's side." Anyone liked by Sarah and disliked by Joseph was more likely to be a good person than not.

She smiled and sank into one end of a divan, pointing to the other end for him.

"I owe you an apology for being awful when I first arrived," he said as he settled himself onto the divan.

Her brows drew together. "You weren't awful. To be honest, I expected much worse, given how my family had treated you and your mother."

That was generous of her. He liked her more every time they talked. "Still, I see now that you had my best interests at heart."

"Thank you for the apology, and I offer one in return. Sorry for dumping that announcement on you at the hospital fundraiser. Freya pulled me up on that just a few days ago, and in retrospect, I see that I could have handled that better."

An uncomfortable flashback of that moment filled his mind, but they'd come a long way since then. "It was all uncharted territory. None of us knew what we were doing."

"Speaking of uncharted territory," Sarah said with a twinkle in her eye, "what are you going to do about Freya?"

His pulse quickened at the sound of her name, his need to be with her growing with every second he was back here. He had no idea if Freya had mentioned their relationship to Sarah or how it ended, but her mother Lauren knew and had probably told her friend, so he didn't pretend to be unaware of what she was talking about. And he had to remember that Freya was Sarah's goddaughter. "I know how important she is to you…"

"Heath, you're both important to me."

He felt those words deep in his solar plexus. Growing up with just a family of three, he was still getting used to hearing that someone else cared enough to prioritize him. "I'm going to fix things. I want her in my life."

Sarah smiled warmly. "Should I be on the lookout for some groveling? A grand gesture that will overtake my party?"

Heath had a moment of panic—he hadn't planned anything so grand. "I thought a conversation might work."

"An honest heart-to-heart is perfect." Sarah laced her hands together over her middle, looking pretty damn content for a woman whose house was full of people setting up for a monster party.

"Since we're having our own heart-to-heart here, there's something I haven't told you that I want to share." He'd been thinking about Mae's instruction, to play it by ear about telling Sarah of her identity, and it felt right.

"Now would be a good time," Sarah said. "It would let me justify hiding out a little longer from the chaos outside that door."

"My sister." His best friend, his only family for several years. "Mae. She's a Rutherford."

Sarah's eyes widened in slow motion, and her mouth opened for a few moments before any sound came out. "Mae? She's mine, too?"

Heath pulled his cell from his pocket and brought up a photo of his sister—just a snap he'd taken while they were out hiking, but he'd always liked it because she looked so happy.

"Oh," Sarah said, her voice thick with tears. "She looks like…"

"You," Heath said gently. "I know."

Sarah looked up sharply. "Does she know?"

"I told her when I went back to Australia. I mean, she always knew we had the same father, just not that you'd found me. And I told her that I'll split the inheritance fifty-fifty. I'm sorry I didn't tell you earlier, but I had no idea what I was walking into—"

"You had to make sure it was safe for her first." She put her hand over his forearm. "Of course you did."

Heath's chest expanded at her understanding. "She's getting leave from her teaching job and organizing to come over so she can meet you and the O'Donohues."

Sarah pulled him into a hug. "Two of you. I can't believe there's two of you. I mean, I would have welcomed her as your sister, anyway, but all these years when I started to doubt I'd ever find you, and now you're here and I have a niece as well."

"She'll love you," he said, his voice muffled by her hair. "She's already excited to meet you."

Sarah released him and wiped her cheeks with the back of her hand. "I'm excited to meet her, too." Then she visibly pulled herself together and adjusted her vest. "In the meantime, and before we lose the room, a quick word about tonight. You know the press will be here. It's part of the deal my team made—they held off on breaking the news of your return, suppressed it even, in return for this exclusive."

Heath grimaced. He'd forgotten about that. "What do I need to do?"

"They're sending a photographer, so we'll do some family shots of the two of us, some of you casually talking to people, that sort of thing."

"And the reporter?" he asked, suspicious because she'd led with the photographer.

"The reporter will talk to a few people, but don't worry—" she waved a hand "—we've been careful with who we invited. And they'll ask you a couple of questions."

There it was. Against all his instincts, he was talking to someone in the media. "I'm not great at this—I've had a lifetime of trying not to be noticed. The local paper took my photo when I was four, coming down the playground slide in a park near our house. My mother freaked out and we had to move towns and change our names again."

"Oh, Heath." Sarah pressed a hand to her mouth.

"I'm fine," he said to reassure her, "and Mae's fine. I'm just not...a natural with the press."

"Okay, noted." She patted his knee, and he suspected it was partly to comfort herself that he was really fine. "Which means you might like this." She pulled a folded slip of paper from the top of a wooden desk behind her and handed it to him. "I have a PR consultant on staff—Barbara. She came up with a bunch of possible questions, ranked by how likely they are to be asked, and she's given some possible replies."

He ran a finger down the list, scanning. "'Where have you been?' A reasonable question, and my reply is, 'Australia, mainly. A beautiful seaside town called Noosa.' Easy enough." He went further down the list. "'How do we know you're really Joseph Rutherford II?' And I say, 'That was my first question, too, but we did several DNA tests, just to be sure.'"

"You can improvise on the spot if you want, of course. These are to give you a starting point."

"They're useful. I appreciate it." He glanced to the bottom of the list and read the last question. "'You have several fake passports and your family illegally entered Australia. Does that make you a criminal?' Ouch."

"We don't think they'll take that tack, but better to be prepared than not. What do you think of the reply?"

"'My mother ran from domestic violence,'" he read. "'She found herself in a difficult situation, with no good options. In the process of running, she lost her family, but it was the only way she felt she could protect me. I believe, though, that we shouldn't be picking over what she did to survive, we should be questioning a system that didn't protect her and forced her hand.'" He glanced up at her. "That's good."

"I don't want your mother's sacrifice, her heroism, lost in this," she said, her gaze steady and full of love. "Joseph was violent and unpredictable and thought he was above the law. Her fears weren't unfounded, and her solution was brave."

He had to swallow hard to get his voice to work. "I appreciate that more than I can say."

"Barbara will be on hand, so if you get into difficulties, she'll step in, but we're both expecting it to be a light piece."

"Okay, good," he said, relieved.

There was a knock on the door, then it swung open and several party planners came in, carrying a table. "So sorry," one of them called, "but we need this room."

"We were leaving," Heath said, standing. "I'll see you a bit later, Sarah. I'm going to check in with Mae."

It wasn't a great time to call Mae in Australia, so he'd check she was awake first, but he really wanted to tell her about Sarah's reaction to learning Mae was her niece. And to get her advice on what he could say to Freya.

It was almost four hours later, with the party in full swing, when Heath stood with Sarah, each with a champagne flute angled to touch the other's but held in suspended animation.

"Sarah, could you raise your chin a fraction? Perfect." The photographer clicked away as he spoke. "Joseph, can you smile?"

Heath's face ached from all the smiling he'd already done. There had been formal shots of Sarah sitting on a wingback chair, the skirt of her black dress artfully arranged, and Heath standing behind her with a hand on her shoulder. And then Heath sitting on the wingback and Sarah standing behind him with a hand on his shoulder. Heath in the middle of a group of strangers—who Sarah said were all friends—arms around them, fake-laughing. Heath looking pensively at a portrait of his grandfather. If he never posed for another photograph again in his life, he'd be a very happy man. But he summoned a smile, held his glass against Sarah's and waited for the clicks to stop.

From the corner of his eye, he saw a flash of bright red hair and his heart seized. Part of his attention had been scanning the rooms for a glimpse of that hair, of her, since the first guests had arrived. Now that he'd seen her, there was a tremor in his hands, and a light in his soul.

"Excuse me," he said, putting his glass on a nearby table. "There's someone I need to greet." Without waiting for permission, he wove a path through the gathered people, searching. Then her hair flashed at him again through gaps in the crowd. She had it wound in an updo, a style that wouldn't have looked out of place on a sixties movie star, and his fingers begged to be allowed to touch it. He didn't have the right yet, but his goal tonight was simple: woo this woman back.

Finally, there was a break and he emerged from the crush to stand in front of her, lost in her ethereal beauty, under the spell of the aura that surrounded her. She wore a long silky dress in the same tawny brown as her eyes that moved with her and flirted around her calves when she turned.

"Heath," she said, her face lighting up for an instant before the mask of professional acquaintances fell back into place. That one instant of real reaction to him gave him hope.

"Freya," he said through a dry throat. Then leaned close to kiss her on the cheek, taking the opportunity to inhale the light, floral scent on her skin.

"I've brought some people to see you." She stepped back to reveal the O'Donohues dressed to the nines and beaming at him.

"Heath," his grandmother said, and pulled him into a tight embrace as his grandfather clapped him on the back.

"I'm so glad you came," he said, meaning it even more than he'd thought he would. Having people here he knew, and who he knew were on his side, was priceless. "When I called, you didn't seem keen."

His pop patted Freya's shoulder. "Freya explained when she visited that Sarah was nothing like her brother, and that she was the one who'd been looking for you, to bring you back to us."

He glanced at Freya. "Thank you." He'd had no idea that she'd been working behind the scenes on his behalf. Then again, that was what she always did— she got on with the job—from the job she'd chosen at the FBI, to doing things for her mother and Sarah, to helping him. No grandstanding, no empty promises, she just made things happen.

"And," his grandmother said, "she arrived this afternoon with a fleet of cars. Told all of us to be ready in our best party clothes and she'd let us know. A line of limousines was on the curb when she knocked on our door."

"Freya," he began but couldn't finish the thought. Thank you hardly seemed enough. And then his grandmother's words sank in. "All of you?"

Freya swept an arm in front of the people standing around them. "This is your family, Heath. Aunts, uncles, cousins. We've brought twenty-two of your relatives from your mother's side tonight."

As his grandparents began introducing everyone, Heath reached for Freya's hand and squeezed. To thank her, and to anchor him in a moment where he was meeting his extended family for the first time. A moment she made possible on so many levels.

If he hadn't already decided to win her back, now would be the moment he'd commit body and soul to that plan. She was amazing.

When the introductions were over and most of his family had drifted away—after he'd promised to come visit them—Heath pulled Freya close and whispered in her ear. "Can we talk? Somewhere quieter?"

"Heath," she said, her voice cracking on his name. "I didn't do this to win you back."

"Honestly, that hadn't occurred to me." Doing something for an ulterior motive simply wasn't the way she was wired. Freya did what she thought was the right thing to do. "Though I am here to win *you* back."

She sucked her bottom lip into her mouth and bit down as she scanned his face. "We've been through this already, Heath."

"But you're judging our relationship based on fears created by your ex-husbands," he said quietly. "Those things you're worried about, that I'm not showing you my true self, aren't actually a problem for us."

"I think it's better if—"

"Please, give me fifteen minutes after all this is over, and I'll prove it to you." The only way to prove it was to bare his soul, put his heart on his sleeve and hope she saw through to the real him beneath. He could do that, even if the idea scared him to death.

"Okay," she said on a sigh. "Fifteen minutes, but I'm not promising anything."

"Deal," he said, already counting down the hours and minutes until the party was over.

Freya turned from Heath, holding herself together by a thread. The man she loved was clearly going to ask her to take him back as soon as they were alone. The question was, would she have the strength of character to walk away from him a second time?

She took a glass of white wine from a passing waiter's tray and downed half of it in one gulp. The days since she'd returned to the States had been desolate. She'd been fine, *her life had been fine*, before she met Heath Dunstan, so why did it feel like it had a giant black hole in its center now that he was out of it?

She downed the rest of the wine.

Someone slid their arm through her elbow, and she glanced to the side to see Sarah.

"Come with me. The reporter is about to ask Heath some questions and it'd be good for him to have a few friendly faces in front of him."

"Am I a friendly face, though? We're in a delicate—"

"Freya," Sarah said with mock severity.

"Okay, all right." There was really no other option when Sarah asked for something.

The reporter was young and blonde with very white teeth, and she seemed completely in her element as she tapped her cell and smiled at the people around her. "Thank you so much," she said to Heath, holding her cell toward him. "I'm Kristin and I'm thrilled to meet the lost heir to the Bellavista fortune! I just have a few questions for you for the piece that will go with the photos."

Heath smiled, all easy charm. "Great to meet you, Kristin. Go right ahead."

"How are you liking New York? Is it much different from your life in Australia?"

Freya felt Sarah exhale at the easy question. "Were you worried?" she whispered.

Sarah gave a tiny shrug. "You never know."

"The weather is certainly different," Heath said into the cell's microphone. "I came from a subtropical summer right into a New York winter, so that was quite a shock. And what's with all the cars driving on the wrong side of the road?" His comic timing earned him a chuckle from the onlookers who'd gathered. "But people have been welcoming and kind in both places, which is the important thing."

Freya didn't let herself react to the blatant lie— many people in her world had been horrible to him— but she felt Sarah relax a little more.

"And what do you say to the whispers that you're not really Joseph Rutherford's son? I mean, you look a lot like photos of your mother, but the Rutherfords? Not so much."

"You prepped him, right?" Freya said in Sarah's ear.

Sarah nodded. "He'll be fine."

"That was my first question, too," Heath said smoothly, "but we did several DNA tests, just to be certain.'"

"Sure, good." Kristin glanced around at her growing audience, clearly getting into the swing of performing for them. "I understand you love surfing. Are you missing the Australian beaches?"

"I haven't had enough free time to miss surfing or the beaches yet, but some of the best surfing beaches in the world are right here in the USA."

"Excellent," Kristin said, and tossed her hair. "Your life up until a few months ago was based on lies and illegally obtained identities. In fact, you were in Australia illegally. Do you have anything to say about that?"

Murmuring broke out among the group of onlookers.

Freya blinked. "Did she really just ask that?"

"Don't worry," Sarah whispered back, but Freya could feel the tension radiating from her godmother's entire being.

"When we left, my mother was running from domestic violence. She found herself in a difficult situation, with no good options. And because she had to run, she lost her family—good people, many of whom are here tonight. All to protect me. I believe, though, that we shouldn't be picking over what she did to survive, we should be questioning a system that didn't protect her and forced her to make those choices."

The crowd's murmuring changed to a positive tone, accompanied by nods.

"Well done on the prep work," Freya whispered to Sarah.

The reporter smiled more broadly, flashing those very white teeth. "But you recently had another one made, didn't you? Another illegally obtained passport, mere weeks ago."

Freya's stomach went into free fall, and Sarah's grip on her arm tightened painfully.

Heath's eyes flew to hers, his face pale. "Er…"

All the air was sucked out of the room and Freya waited for Heath to deny it. To deny that even as he'd stood on that beach and told her she was seeing the real him with no secrets, he had an escape plan. Another identity in his back pocket. And neglected to even mention it to her.

"Your mother is gone," Kristin continued, "and your father is dead. Yet only a few weeks ago, you—"

Sarah's PR consultant, Barbara, smoothly inserted herself between Heath and the reporter, a dreamboat of a Hollywood actor on her arm. "Kristin, do you know Zane? He was just asking to meet you."

Zane Andrews, one of the hottest—and famously reclusive—movie stars, held out a hand, his expression the perfect mix of sheepish and seductive. "It's true. I begged Barbara to introduce us. I don't suppose you have a moment to get a drink?"

Kristin's eyes widened and she darted glances between Heath and Zane, clearly paralyzed by indecision about which option was a better coup.

"I'm so sorry," Zane said. "Is this a bad time? I saw you across the room and didn't stop to think. I just knew I had to meet you."

Kristin turned to face him, giving him a smile that was a little too wide, flashing those fluorescent white teeth, and took his hand. "Zane, you total snack." Kristin didn't release his hand, and Barbara sidled toward Heath. "This is going to sound like I'm making it up, but I'm low-key not surprised that you and I are meeting up. You have been living rent-free in my head ever since that iconic performance…" Her voice faded away as Zane led her across the room.

Freya blinked. "What the actual hell?"

"Zane's mother is an old friend. He was our backup plan," Sarah said as if that explained everything, then rushed to Heath's side. Sarah and Barbara, one on each side of Heath, edged him away from the crowd while chatting and laughing, without it looking like there was any damage control happening at all.

The rest of the crowd dispersed now that the show was over and Freya was left standing on her own, trying to make sense of what she'd just heard. And what it meant...

One of Heath's cousins said her name—a teen from the group she'd shared a limo with on the way up— pointing to a tiny tomato tart in his other hand. "These are so good. You want me to bring you some?"

Freya almost laughed at the absurdity of the offer in the moment her life was crumbling, but her lungs were cramped too tight. "I'm good. Hey, I'm going to make my own way back. I forgot I have something early tomorrow. Can you say goodbye to your family for me?"

He stuffed the tart in his mouth and wiped his hands on the sides of his shirt as he reached for her arm, but she'd seen the move coming and politely ducked before he could try to convince her to stay.

"I'll see you later," she said as she turned and rushed for the front door, grabbing her coat from the hooks on the way out. Once she made it out into the dark, she pulled out her cell to order a ride, and just as she completed the screen, footsteps sounded on the pavement behind her.

"Freya." Heath's low, rumbling voice moved through her, pulled at her.

She squeezed her eyes shut against its power.

"Freya, wait." He overtook her, turning to stand in front of her, tall and broad and everything she wanted but couldn't let herself have.

"I need to go," she said, knowing it didn't sound convincing.

"I got those passports before I left Australia." He splayed his hands, sounding as reasonable as anyone who didn't realize the implications of what they'd done. "I didn't know what I was walking into and needed a backup plan in case things went pear-shaped."

She shivered, only partly from the cold, but remembered she had a coat over her arm. "It's fine," she said as she pushed her hands through her coat sleeves and belted it at her waist. "I get it. Look, I'm just heading home, so I'll see you—"

"Hang on, you said we could talk."

She couldn't help a humorless smile at the irony. The man who kept secrets, who refused to discuss the important things, wanted to talk. "You know, I think it would be better if we just leave it here."

"That's not how we should leave it." He reached for her hand but when she didn't take it, he let it drop. "You know there's something strong, something precious between us. Something we can't ignore."

"I'm not ignoring it, Heath. I'm simply walking away from it."

"I love you, Freya," he said and the words hit like a sledgehammer to rock, cracking open her inside to the raw, vulnerable core of her. He took a small step closer, closing the distance. "I realized after you left Australia. I love you."

"Heath, no. I can't do this."

"Why?" His voice was steady but his eyes pleaded. "Tell me that at least."

She crossed her arms tightly under her breasts. "Do you remember what I said to you on the beach back in Noosa?"

"You accused me of not trusting you and keeping my guard up, but that's not true."

"I said that you've kept me at an emotional distance, not letting me near your heart or your true self. And that I'd always be wondering if there were other parts that you didn't trust me enough to show me. Or something you're still guarding and hiding." That entire conversation was etched in her memory. "From my job where I literally spend my days uncovering hidden truths, to my relationships with people like my father and sisters where I was an embarrassing secret, to my marriages where my ex-husbands both kept their true intentions and true feelings hidden from me, my whole life has been about needing the truth. Just wanting openness and clarity. Learning to be true to myself. I worked so hard to become someone with integrity, with honor."

"And you've done an amazing job at it."

Even as she was separating herself and her life from him, compliments from this man had power over her, had real meaning, but she couldn't let that sway her. "Thank you. But this is my line in the sand. I can't compromise on truth. I love you, Heath, but I can't build a future with you."

He wrapped a hand around the back of his neck. "You know, that picture you've drawn of me, it's not entirely accurate."

"The evidence all points that way." Her heart could lie to her; she'd learned that young. Evidence, though, that never lied. The solidness, the reliability of evidence and data was what had pulled her toward mathematics in school, and then a degree in accounting. It was what she had to rely on when everything else was unstable. "And having a fake passport stuffed away is consistent with that picture. You're still living like you're on the run—having an escape route, not trusting someone you claim to love enough to share that information. It makes me wonder if that was even the last thing you were keeping hidden. Tell me honestly, if we were together, could you promise to be an open book?"

Heath looked thunderstruck for a long moment, then he took an unsteady step back. She waited a beat, then two, but he didn't say anything.

She drew in a long, painful breath. "Heath, you're a wonderful person, and I wish you all the love and all the good things in the world because you deserve it. And you deserve someone who can accept you the way you are. That's not me. It breaks my heart to admit it, because I want it to be me, but it's just not."

"You're right." He scrubbed both hands over his face. "You're right. Thank you for being honest. You're right, and that hits hard." He arched his neck to look at the night sky, then back to her, his dark eyes tormented. "I can't give all of myself to a relationship. If I could, I'd want it to be with you, too."

He drew in a shuddering breath, the world of pain in his eyes calling to her very being. She reached for him and he met her halfway, their bodies bumping together as their mouths met, the kiss chaotic, earnest, desperate. His hands were in her hair, ruining the style, but she couldn't bring herself to care while she had these stolen moments of Heath kissing her again. Her hands held the sides of his face, his beautiful, beloved face.

As they eventually eased back, Freya tried to catch her breath, and it seemed Heath was having the same problem as he leaned his forehead against hers. It would be all too easy to forget everything else, to risk heartbreak and just lose herself in this man. She couldn't do it, couldn't betray herself that way, so she straightened and took a deep breath.

"What will you do now?" she asked, her breathing still not quite regular.

He shrugged. "Go back to Australia. That is, if they'll have me—there's some legal paperwork I'm going to have to sort out."

Her rideshare car arrived and she waved to the driver.

"Your ride?" Heath asked, stuffing his hands in his pockets.

"Yes." She looked at him, scanning his features, committing everything to memory. They'd see each other again when their paths around Sarah crossed, but this was the last time she'd see him in this personal, intimate way. Something inside her splintered, but she held it together through sheer force of will. "I guess I'll see you around."

He dug his hands in his pockets, resigned. Broken. "See you around."

She climbed into the back seat of the car and closed her eyes as it drove her away from the man she loved.

Freya dropped the bakery bags on her mother's kitchen counter and slid the cardboard tray with two take-out coffees beside them.

"That looks like a lot of food," her mother said.

"I'm comfort eating, and I need you to support me by having half of these." She'd pretty much just walked into her favorite bakery and ordered one of everything that looked good. Maybe carbs and sugar would work when nothing else had.

Her mother peeked in the bags one by one. "Well, it's a lot, but I do like a challenge."

Freya moved around the kitchen of the suite below Sarah's apartment. Years ago, Sarah had the apartment below hers converted into two suites, one each for her housekeeper and her chauffeur, so this place was Freya's childhood home—as comforting as the raspberry muffin in the second bakery bag.

"Are we comfort eating about the state of the world in general," her mother asked as she took two plates from the cupboard, "or something specific?"

Freya paused as she was lifting the paper coffee cups from the tray. "Let's say whichever of those options means I don't have to talk about it?"

"Ah. Something specific then."

"I'll have you know," Freya said, one hand on a hip, "the plight of the North Atlantic right whale is deeply disturbing. Whaling, shipping traffic, getting tangled in fishing gear—we really should be doing more to protect them."

"No argument here. But you've been concerned about whales since you were a teenager and never once has it led to you turning up unannounced with a large assortment of baked goods."

Freya held up a brownie and wiggled it. "You're complaining about a random cake delivery?"

"How was the party last night?" her mother asked innocently and grabbed the brownie. She took a huge bite and grinned as she was chewing.

Freya narrowed her eyes. "Sarah said something to you."

"Just that you left early, and I'm going to go out on a limb here and ask if it had something to do with

Heath Dunstan." She took another bite and snagged one of the coffees.

"Why would you assume my mood has anything to do with him?"

"Because I know you fairly well. And because I've seen the two of you together. *And* because—"

"Okay, okay," Freya said and walked over to the sofa with her coffee and a muffin. She put the coffee on a side table and rested the plate with the muffin on her lap. "Yes, it's about Heath."

"Are you ready to admit that you love him yet?" The teasing tone was both sweet and irritating.

"Not that it matters," Freya said, "but yes, I love him." It was pathetic how happy it made her to admit that aloud to someone. Even if she wasn't going to ride off into the sunset with Heath, to be able to acknowledge this huge feeling inside her was affirming. Or maybe she was punishing herself, picking at a scab.

"Love always matters."

She picked up her coffee, sipped, then picked at the rolled cardboard rim as she got her thoughts together. She needed to end this line of questioning and the only effective way of doing that would be to explain the disaster that unfolded at Sarah's party.

"Last night," she said, still picking at the cup, "I found out that after I met him in Australia and told him about the inheritance, he had new passports and identities made for him and his sister." Her fingers trembled faintly, so she put the cup down on the side table in case she spilled it. "I'd been thinking there might be a future for us, but at the same time, he had a foot out the door."

"Wasn't that a sensible thing, though?" her mother said gently. "Given that his mother was hiding from Joseph, he would have been taught to have an exit plan."

"Absolutely true. But it's the secrecy—he's been saying that he wants to be with me, even while he has all these other layers that he won't share." Her mother opened her mouth but before she could say anything, Freya held up a hand. "I get why, of course I do, but after Milo and Dominic both keeping huge parts of themselves hidden, having agendas I didn't know about and secrets everywhere, I just can't do that again."

"So what's the plan then? Never get close to anyone for the rest of your life?"

"Well, before I met Heath, I did think I'd just never marry again. I'd come to terms with that. Now I think it's a possibility that I *could* be with someone, but it would have to be a person I could one hundred percent trust. Someone totally transparent."

Her mother scoffed. "Nobody is totally transparent. Besides, you're standing in a glass house while you make these declarations."

"Wait, what do you mean by that?" A glass house? Maybe coming here this morning had been a mistake…

"Remind me—when you first met, and you were searching for Joseph's heir, did you tell Heath up front who you were?"

Freya shifted her weight on the sofa cushions. "That would have been counterproductive since I was gathering information. But I didn't know him then, so it's different." In this moment, she was extra glad she hadn't told anyone about the one-night stand that had been done without real names. She had a feeling that would make her mother's argument stronger.

"And have you been dating Heath while he's been in New York?"

Freya reached for the coffee, her mouth suddenly dry. Memories of being with Heath assaulted her— her arms wrapped around him on the back of his bike, kissing him at the bar on the Hudson, meeting his mother's family, loving him in her shower, toasting to a life free from self-important assholes with blue cocktails at the hospital fundraiser. All that she'd lost… Everything inside her was suddenly so heavy, so barren, so aching, that she pressed a fist to her chest to try and relieve it.

"I wouldn't say dating, exactly," she said, trying for a casual tone, then took another sip of coffee as cover.

"Involved, then. Yet you kept that a secret from everyone else. Doing things like holding hands on the back seat where you thought they were out of range from the rearview mirror?"

Freya's cheeks were suddenly warm. "Okay, yes. Sure. We've been…involved."

"So answer me this—why did *you* lie or keep secrets from people you love?"

"Hey," she said, wincing, "that's a low blow."

The arched eyebrow indicated no regret. "Allow me to suggest that your reason was always to protect or help someone. You wanted to help Sarah find her nephew, so you kept quiet until you were sure. And you worried about the fallout for Sarah if you dated and it ended badly—she might feel pressure to choose sides, or whatever the reason you had in your head."

Damn it, she hadn't even thought of that problem for Sarah. She'd been more worried that if things turned awkward, Heath might stay away and Sarah would lose out on having as many visits from him. Now she had an extra thing to worry about. She stuffed a piece of muffin into her mouth and chewed.

"Isn't Heath always trying to protect his sister?"

Freya stopped with another piece of muffin halfway to her mouth. "How do you *know* so much?"

"No one notices the chauffeur." She grinned. "Maybe at first, but people tend to forget we have ears and eyes."

"Not a mistake I'll make again," Freya said, thinking back over every conversation she'd ever had when her mother had been driving.

"Sweetheart, is it such a bad thing if you're with someone who's willing to protect you? To have your back? That's what you'd be to each other."

"I thought we were talking about Heath?" She glared at the muffin, which wasn't helping at all, put it down on the plate and went back to the kitchen. In the third bag, under a Cronut, she found a slice of cherry pie. Perfect. She grabbed a fork and took it back to the sofa.

Her mother waited until she was settled before saying, "One of the things I admire about you is that after some bad experiences, instead of seeking revenge or throwing people under the bus on your social climb, you devoted yourself to an organization that protects people."

"Mom, I'm an accountant, not a special agent."

"But you could be an accountant in a private firm. With your contacts, you'd be doing well, and amassing your own wealth. Instead, you're working for a salary in an organization that aims to help. *And*," she said with emphasis, "that organization often uses secrecy as a tool when it's helping people."

She put the rest of the pie down beside the muffin and frowned. "You want me to start keeping more secrets now, Mom?"

Her mother didn't rise to the bait. "What I see when I look at you and Heath is two peas in a pod. Two people doing the best they can to protect their people. To help people. You make a good pair."

"Hang on," Freya said, bringing her legs up underneath her. "You were against him from the moment he arrived. You stopped just short of taking out billboards against us being in a relationship. What happened?"

"I noticed the changes in you." She reached out and took Freya's hand. "Since you met him, you have more self-belief. You're more like yourself than you've ever been. And if we're still comparing Heath to Milo and Dominic—you grew smaller in each marriage, as if you had to make room for them by sacrificing parts of yourself. With Heath, it's the opposite. Since you met him, you've stared down Leyland, Constance and Prairie. You told Sarah she'd done the wrong thing in announcing Heath's return at the gala. Even in walking away from Heath because you thought it wasn't right for you—you knew, deep down, that Milo and Dominic weren't right, but you married them anyway."

"You know, this comfort eating session has been very light on the comfort." Freya looked at the bags over on the counter, still with most of the baked goods in them, and frowned. "And the eating."

"You didn't need comfort, sweetie. And that's why you're here."

She closed her eyes and pressed lightly to stop them from stinging. It was true. She'd wanted comfort, but more than that she'd needed to feel connected to someone who loved her, and to try to sort out the mess in her head. "It's too late now, anyway. I've told him no twice, and last night"—she grimaced—"I convinced him he's not ready for a relationship either."

"That's a thorough job you've done there."

"Even if I hadn't, I still think I made the right decision." Muscles all twitchy, Freya pushed to her feet and put the empty coffee cup on the counter, then went to the window. "I think I need to go away for a few days. I still have some of the extended leave and I don't want to be in New York while Heath is still here. Bumping into him would be just too painful."

"The cabin is empty."

Freya whipped back around. "Really?" The cabin would be perfect—no memories of Heath, and far enough away to ensure they didn't cross paths.

"Sure." Her mother smiled, but it didn't reach her eyes. "Key's on the hook in the pantry."

"Thank you." She took the key and then hugged her mom. "I'm taking the bakery bag with the Cronut, though." She snagged the third bag. "I'll call you when I get there."

Eleven

Heath stood outside Sarah's apartment building, tapping his foot, waiting for the car to arrive. The midmorning crush of pedestrians along the pavement was busy enough that he had to duck out of the way of groups of people as they passed, which only served to make him more restless. He checked his watch. Fifteen minutes since he'd sent the text to Lauren.

In the four days since the party in the Hamptons, he'd tried to rid himself of this bone-deep restlessness. He'd hiked until he was exhausted, taken his bike out to clear his mind, explored the streets and stores of Manhattan to keep himself occupied. None of it had made a dent.

The familiar black Suburban pulled up to the curb and he jumped in the back seat.

"Does Sarah know you ordered the car?" Lauren said, clearly unimpressed.

He pulled the seat belt across himself and clicked it into the holder. "I thought it was better not to bother her."

"If you're going to run away, best not to bother with goodbyes to people who matter," she muttered sourly, but before he could reply, she added, "The text said the airport. Where are your bags?"

"No bags," he said, and realized he hadn't thought this plan through.

"Suit yourself." She pulled away from the curb.

Once they were a block away, Heath cleared his throat. "I don't want to go to the airport."

Lauren blew out a breath. "Make up your mind."

"Take me to where Freya's staying." It was a pulse deep inside him, the desperate need for her, the insistent *wanting* just to see her face, to talk to her, to hold her, to erase the pain he'd caused and make her smile again.

His life was more chaotic than ever. From the Australian government now questioning his right to return, to the red tape Mae's emergence as a new Rutherford would create once she arrived in New York, his head was spinning. Add in the challenges of trying to manage his Bellavista holdings while Sebastian Newport was hostile, and it was a lot. Yet

all he could think about, all he wanted, was Freya.
He wanted to hear her voice as they strategized and
planned. He wanted her in his arms and in his bed. He
wanted to pass the time in her company. Just… Freya.

In the front seat, Lauren straightened. "You want
to see Freya?"

"I've been to her apartment every day and she's
never home." He gave Freya's mother a charming
smile in case she looked back at him, one that said
you can trust me. "She's not answering her cell or
any other way I've tried to reach her. She hasn't visited Sarah. I'm guessing she's away, somewhere out
of range."

Through the rearview mirror, she gave him a flat
stare. "She's away, but not out of range. If she's not
replying to you, she doesn't want to chat."

Part of him wasn't surprised—the way she'd said
goodbye after the party four days ago had seemed
pretty final. The part of him that had hoped, that had
clung to the slim chance they could fix this, *that* part
withered inside him. She really didn't want to hear
from him. And if she was ghosting him, then they
really were over. A numbing darkness descended
over him.

"Right," he said as evenly as he could.

"Out of interest, why do you want to see her? I
thought you two ended things on the night of Sarah's party."

He considered giving her a half-truth or brushing
off the question, but he didn't have the energy to put

up another damn wall, or to work out what he should say, or what was best to say. So he closed his eyes and laid his head back on the headrest. "I've known since I was a child that the world is not a fair place," he said slowly. "That people aren't always who they pretend to be, and to be careful who you trust. We moved a lot, and were always ready to move again, meaning I didn't have old friends, the sort you've known for years, and certainly not long-term girl-friends. And living in that environment meant the only people I'd known long enough to be honest with me were my mother and sister, and they were in the same situation. Freya is the first person to hold a mir-ror up to me, to challenge me and to give me the bru-tal truth. I needed it. I know I have flaws, and I make mistakes. Hell, there's a ridiculous amount of stuff I don't know, especially since my world changed so much with the inheritance."

"Go on," Lauren said, her tone giving nothing away.

He turned his head and opened his eyes to watch the cars zipping past, honking at each other, getting on with their lives. "There are only two things I'm sure of. The first is my sister Mae. She's a nonnego-tiable in my life, and I'd die for her if I had to. The second…" He stopped, swallowed hard. "The sec-ond is Freya. She's amazing. Her heart is huge, she's kind and loving and gives of herself constantly. But she's also strong—she's not afraid of anyone, despite what she thinks. She'd stand in the path of danger to protect someone if she had to."

He speared his fingers through his hair. "I know I don't deserve her. I'm not in her league at all—my heart isn't nearly as big or as strong as hers. But whatever there is of this heart, whatever state it's in, it belongs to her. I love her with everything inside me."

The car came to a stop and he looked out to see Sarah's apartment building. They'd done a loop and come full circle, which seemed fitting.

"Thanks for listening," he said, and meant it. Maybe instead of hiking and riding, he should have talked it out with someone sooner.

As he opened the door his cell pinged.

"She's at a cabin in Greenwich," Lauren said, her voice thick. "I just sent you the address. Take your bike."

Freya was curled up on a window seat, reading. The spring sunshine was on her back and she had nowhere she needed to be, nothing she needed to do besides read her book. She idly wondered where Heath was and what he was doing—the same thing she'd wondered every few minutes since the last time she'd seen him.

Annoyed at herself, she snapped the book shut. The decision to break things off with him had been her only option, and she stood by it, regardless of what her mother had said. She glanced around the room. A cat would be nice. A little warm body on her lap while she read or watched TV. Maybe a tabby cat—

The thought was interrupted by a knock at the front door. Uncurling herself, she crossed the room and opened the door. Heath stood on the stoop, zipped into his black riding gear, his dark blond hair mussed from the helmet, expression uncertain. She gripped the door tightly to stop herself instinctively swaying toward him. Or grabbing his lapel and dragging him inside and kissing him senseless.

"Freya." His voice, deep and rough, sent shivers along her spine.

"Mom told you where I was." Her mother was the only person who knew she was here, and she was normally the safest person to hold a secret. "How did you convince her?"

He ran a hand through his hair. "To be honest, I'm not entirely sure."

For a long moment, she drank him in, knowing that was all she could allow herself. It hurt too much to keep seeing him and having to turn him away. She'd found her line in the sand, and it was about truth and integrity, and she was strong enough now to stand by it. Even if it meant the man she loved was on the other side.

"I'm sorry you've wasted a trip, but I'm really not up for going over this again." She started to close the door.

"Really?" He lifted an upturned palm. "After all we've been through, you're not letting me in?"

"For crying out loud, Heath, I've missed you so much that if I invite you in, I'd have you in my bed faster than you could explain why you're here, and then it will be even harder to let you go again. I only have a certain amount of strength. It's just better if you don't come inside."

He nodded, considering. "Is there somewhere outside we can talk then?"

Her shoulders slumped. "We can't keep doing this. Why are you here, Heath?"

"Because you won't answer my calls or texts." He held up a hand before she could state the obvious. "There's just one more thing I need to tell you and then I'll let you go. I give you my word. I won't pursue you—I'm not my father. If you really want to cut ties after today, I'm gone."

"Heath—" she began.

"Remember when you first told me who you were, and who you thought I was, you asked for ten minutes. You said, 'Give me ten minutes to explain, and then I'll leave. I promise.' I'm asking for the same deal."

It was hard to argue with that. She sighed. At least he hadn't stuck his shoe in the door the way she had. "You only gave me five."

"I'm counting on you being a nicer person than I was that day." He gave her his lopsided smile and her heart damn near combusted in her chest.

She had a feeling she was going to regret this, but she grabbed a coat from the hook near the door, stepped out and closed it behind her. "You can have the whole ten. There are a couple of Adirondack chairs down the back of the yard," she said, and set off, not waiting to see if he followed.

He fell into step fairly quickly, hands in the pockets of his jacket. "Sarah has holiday homes all over the place."

"This place is Mom's." Her mother had been buying and selling stocks and real estate on Sarah's advice for years, and built up her own small portfolio. She called this cabin her retirement home and normally had it rented out to help pay the mortgage. Being free right now had been a stroke of luck.

He looked back at the cabin—a plain name for such a beautiful colonial-style home—and whistled.

They reached the chairs, positioned in the midafternoon sun, overlooking the rocky waterfront. The light breeze whipped her hair around her face, so Freya tucked it behind her ears and sat down.

"Okay, your ten minutes starts now, so I'd use it wisely." She pulled the collar of her coat together at her throat as if it was armor that would protect her from the allure of this man.

"Whether or not you send me away today," he said, leaning forearms on his thighs, hands linked, "I want you to know that you've had a profound impact on me. You've changed me. I keep thinking back to that day at your apartment, when you'd worked out Mae's identity and I changed my mind and came clean with the information. That was the beginning—a moment in time where I changed course because of you. From then, I started questioning everything I was doing, and seeing myself through your eyes, right up until you served up some brutal home truths at Sarah's party. Or maybe it was before that." He leaned back in his chair and wrapped a hand around the back of his neck. "It probably was. The timing is irrelevant, the important thing is that I'm not the same person I was before we met. I might still be suspicious and have a hard time trusting, and I'm difficult to get to know. But I'm a better person than before, and I wanted you to know how grateful I am for that gift."

A great big ball of emotion had formed in her throat as he'd started talking, and now it had grown too large, making it difficult to say anything. Heath had just casually laid out his flaws before her, as if it was nothing. But it wasn't nothing. That had taken a huge amount of strength. She looked out at the water, wrestling control back from her emotions.

Finally, she turned to him. "I'm sorry I ever said you had anything in common with my ex-husbands."

"Yeah, that was harsh," he said, but his smile took the edge off it.

"I'm serious. Neither of them would have been able to casually admit a bunch of flaws like that, much less acknowledge any personal growth. Dominic would deny he has any flaws at all, and Milo is proud of most of his. The sorts of things we see as moral failings, he sees as assets." Everything with her husbands had been about face value and how they presented themselves to the world. "In the ways that count, you're their polar opposite."

"Well, that's something at least," he said, trying to suppress a smile and not succeeding very well. "Thank you."

Admitting all of that had taken courage, and she owed him the same in return. She wound a few strands of her hair around a finger. "Mom thinks you've had a good effect on me, too."

His jaw dropped. "Seriously? What did she say?"

"She thinks that when I was with both Milo and Dominic, I grew smaller." The more she'd thought about that, the more her mother's words perfectly summed up her marriages. "With you, though, she thought I'd grown, and had been standing up more. She said that since I met you, I'd been more myself than I've ever been."

"What do you think?" he asked, dark gaze steady on her.

This was something she'd thought a lot about since arriving at the cabin, so it was an easy question to answer. "Besides my mother and godmother, who are both biased, I don't think I've ever had anyone believe in me the way you do, and that's pretty powerful."

"Then the rest of the world has no sense, but I'm glad to have been of service." He ran a hand over his stubbled chin. "Speaking of your godmother, when I was staying with Sarah in the Hamptons, she asked if I was going to make a grand gesture to win you at the party."

Her stomach dropped. "Thank God you didn't."

"Not a fan?" he asked, one eyebrow raised.

"Let me put it this way—Milo had me follow a trail of rose petals to a giant sign that lit up with the words *marry me* and a string quartet playing." Milo had been smugly confident and she'd been naive.

Heath grimaced. "Did you like that?"

"At the time I thought I did." She'd been nineteen, looking for a place in the world, and had fallen for his lines. "And his social media friends definitely liked him filming it."

"Ah."

It should have been a red flag when she'd realized he was talking more to the camera than he was to her on the day he was proposing. She was still embarrassed that she'd missed that neon warning signal. "And Dominic had a huge diamond ring engraved with our initials that he presented at a surprise party with all our friends and family. He even had fireworks." The surprise had been flawless—not only hadn't she suspected he was throwing a party, she hadn't thought they were serious enough for a proposal, but she'd been swept up in his certainty and joyfully accepted.

Heath drew in a sharp breath. "Kinda hard to say no in those circumstances."

She coughed out a laugh at the truth in that. "I've often wondered if part of the reason I agreed to marry both of them was their proposals didn't give me much of a way out."

"Well, I have the smallest gesture you've ever seen." He reached into his pocket, pulled something crumpled out and handed it to her. "This is for you."

It was a small piece of thin paper, scrunched and creased. She smoothed it out on the leg of her jeans to reveal it was a receipt. She looked closer. "You bought me a bottle of water?"

"Uh, no. I drank the water already."

"Your grand gesture is a single bottle of water that you already drank?" She couldn't hold back a laugh. "You're right. I've never seen a gesture so small."

"It's not the water," he said firmly, but his eyes were dancing. "I pulled in at a truck stop on the way up for water. The receipt was the only paper I had on me. Your gesture is on the other side."

She turned it over and saw a string of numbers. "You got me numbers. That's sweet, since you know I like numbers, but my job gives me pages and pages every day, so six single digits might not be as special as you think. Though, again, top marks for being the smallest gesture I've ever seen."

He looked heavenward, trying to hide his grin as he did. From his other pocket, he withdrew his cell and handed it to her. "It's the pass code."

She looked sharply over at him. "This is the pass code to your *cell*?"

"Try it," he said.

Incredulous, she tapped in the numbers and, sure enough, the lock screen disappeared, revealing his email program, texts, social media apps, photos, call register, everything. The day he'd shown her the photo of Mae on here, he'd said he never let people even flick through on his cell. And now he was giving her complete access with the pass code?

"You're so private." She tucked her hair back behind her ears as the breeze picked up. "Why would you do this?"

"This is me laying myself bare to you, Freya." His voice cracked slightly, his expression earnest. "There's nothing more hidden from you. I'm completely stripped down."

"You said it was small. *This is huge.*" She smoothed the creased receipt with her fingers, the most precious gift she'd ever been given—the gift of complete trust. "I can't think of any more significant gesture than this."

She turned his cell over in her hands, not needing to open it again, not needing to do anything with it. The gesture had been his trust in her, and that was all she needed. She handed it back to him, but pocketed the receipt. She'd always treasure this slip of paper as something beyond precious. Especially since he'd given it at a time when he must not be feeling a whole lot of good will toward the human race.

"I saw that reporter, Kristin's, piece in the *New York Daily*. I'm sorry, Heath." The paper had printed the details about Heath's past fake identities, though Sarah's people had managed to keep the most recent passport out of the article.

"Thanks." He tapped a finger on the chair's armrest. "The Australian government saw it, too, and is reviewing whether I'm allowed to go home."

"Ouch," she said. "What are you doing about it?"

"I've retained an immigration lawyer who's confident we can work it out, but it will take some time. And in the meantime, I'm fine here since Joseph Rutherford II is still a US citizen. Maybe I'll even decide to settle here after all."

She couldn't tell if he was serious or not, but either way, she'd played a part in this, which needed acknowledging. "I'm sorry, Heath. I'm the one who dragged you into all of this when I turned up on your doorstep. I set it all in motion."

"I'm not sorry." He shrugged his broad shoulders. "For the first time in my life I'm free. Everything's out in the open. My actions don't have to be guided by what would keep me safe, or what would keep my mother or Mae safe. I can make choices based purely on what I want."

The world seemed to slow down; the sounds around them quieted. "And what do you want?" She was frozen, unable to look away, desperately needing to know, yet fearing what he'd say.

"You," he said, his heart in his eyes. "Just you, in whatever capacity you're willing to offer. I'm still prepared to walk out of your life if your answer is no. I gave my word on that." His Adam's apple bobbed. "But if it was just up to me, then my answer is you."

Slowly, she reached her hand out, just intending to touch him, to feel the warmth of his skin against hers, and then he said it again.

"Just. You."

And the way he looked at her changed everything. Without stopping to think, she switched chairs to sit on his lap. "I don't think it's going to be no this time."

He wrapped his arms around her, pulling her tight against him, and buried his face against her throat. She could feel his heart hammering against his ribs through their coats, and thought he could probably feel hers, too. Slowly, he lifted his face and she leaned down to meet his lips with hers, in a kiss that had all the messy mix of emotions she was feeling, and was as much of a promise as anything they'd said.

"I know you don't want to get married again," he said, his mouth against her cheek, "and that's totally fine. I'll take whatever I can have with you. I can be your long-term boyfriend, your partner, your significant other."

She stroked the side of his face, thinking it through. He'd said that he was free to make choices based on just what he wanted. If she were to do the same, what would she choose? "What if I wanted you to be my husband?"

He leaned back to look in her eyes. "You said never again."

"This wouldn't be like it was with them." Marriage to Heath wouldn't even be in the same universe as her previous experiences. "I've never been married to someone I love, or to someone who loves me."

"I do," he said with certainty.

"There's no one here who can perform the ceremony yet, Heath," she teased.

"I meant," he said, grinning, "that I do love you."

"And I love you, too." She felt the wetness on her cheeks without even realizing she was crying. Heath wiped them away with the side of his thumb, and then kissed her again, slowly, his lips moving over hers, gently, the kiss so sweet it almost broke her heart.

After long seconds, or minutes, he ended the kiss and rested his forehead against hers. "You'd really be willing to marry me?"

"As long as we can have a cat," she said, only half joking. "Maybe a tabby cat."

"I'm in," he said, then his eyes widened as if something had occurred to him, just before throwing his head back and laughing.

For the sheer pleasure of it, she threaded her hands into his hair. "What?"

"You mother told you I'd been good for you." He paused while she nodded. "She also gave me the address of where you were staying. Never in a million years would I have predicted your mother playing fairy godmother."

Freya burst out laughing. "You know what? I'm going to relish living my life with you."

He pulled her down for a kiss, and just before their lips met, he whispered, "Ditto."

* * * * *

HARLEQUIN
PLUS

Try the best multimedia subscription service for romance readers like you!

Read, Watch and Play.

Experience the easiest way to get the romance content you crave.

Start your **FREE TRIAL** at
<u>www.harlequinplus.com/freetrial</u>.